Mary Higgins Clark is the author of twenty-two bestselling novels of suspense, a memoir, three collections of short stories, and with her daughter, Carol Higgins Clark, is co-author of two Christmas novellas. She lives with her husband in Saddle River, New Jersey.

Also by Mary Higgins Clark, from Pocket Books

Second Time Around
Daddy's Little Girl
On the Street Where You Live
Before I Say Goodbye
All Through the Night
We'll Meet Again
Pretend You Don't See Her
My Gal Sunday
Moonlight Becomes You
Silent Night
Let Me Call You Sweetheart
Remember Me
Weep No More, My Lady
Stillwatch
A Cry in the Night
The Cradle Will Fall
A Stranger is Watching
Where are the Children?

Non-fiction
Kitchen Privileges

With Carol Higgins Clark
He Sees You When You're Sleeping
Deck the Halls

MARY HIGGINS CLARK

YOU BELONG TO ME

POCKET
BOOKS

LONDON • SYDNEY • NEW YORK • TOKYO • TORONTO

First published in Great Britain by Simon & Schuster UK Ltd, 1998
This edition published by Pocket Books, 2004
An imprint of Simon & Schuster UK Ltd
A Viacom company

Copyright © Mary Higgins Clark, 1998

This book is copyright under the Berne Convention.
No reproduction without permission.
® and © 1997 Simon & Schuster Inc. All rights reserved.
Pocket Books & Design is a registered trademark of
Simon & Schuster Inc.

The right of Mary Higgins Clark to be identified as author of this
work had been asserted in accordance with sections 77 and 78 of
the Copyright, Designs and Patents Act, 1988.

1 3 5 7 9 10 8 6 4 2

Simon & Schuster UK Ltd
Africa House
64–78 Kingsway
London WC2B 6AH

Simon & Schuster Australia
Sydney

www.simonsays.co.uk

A CIP catalogue record for this book is available from
the British Library

'You Belong to Me', words and music by Pee Wee King, Redd
Stewart and Chilton Price. Copyright © 1952 (Renewed 1980)
Ridgeway Music Company, Inc. All rights reserved.
Reprinted by permission of the Publisher and Warner Bros.
Publications U.S. Inc, Miami, FL 33014

ISBN 0 7434 8432 0

This book is a work of fiction. Names, characters, places and
incidents are either a product of the author's imagination or are
used fictitiously. Any resemblance to actual people living or
dead, events or locales is entirely coincidental.

Printed and bound in Great Britain by
Cox & Wyman Ltd, Reading, Berkshire

Acknowledgments

A thousand thanks always and forever to my editor Michael V. Korda, and his associate, senior editor Chuck Adams. They have been and always are marvelous friends and magnificent advisors as the tale I tell unfolds.

Blessings to Rebecca Head, Carol Bowie, and copy supervisor Gypsy da Silva, who have burned the midnight oil with me once again.

I am so grateful to my publicist and friend Lisl Cade, whose advice and friendship I cherish. Gratitude to my agent, Eugene Winick, who is always a staunch supporter.

Kudos to my daughter Carol Higgins Clark for her always on target insight as the story progresses.

Finally, thanks to "Himself," my husband John Conheeney, and my entire family for their encouragement and understanding.

Love you all.

For my husband, John Conheeney,
and for our grandchildren
Elizabeth and David Clark,
Andrew, Courtney, and Justin Clark,
Jerry Derenzo,
Robert and Ashley Lanzara,
Lauren, Megan, Kelly, and John Conheeney,
David, Courtney, and Thomas Tarleton
With love

Prologue

He had played this same game before and had anticipated this time out it would be something of a letdown. It came as a pleasant surprise then to find that it gave him even more of a thrill.

He had boarded the ship in Perth, Australia, only yesterday, planning to sail as far as Kobe, but he had found her immediately, so the extra ports would not be necessary. She had been seated at a window table in the liner's paneled dining room, a discreetly elegant space typical of the *Gabrielle*. The luxury cruise ship was the perfect size for his purposes, and in fact he always traveled on smaller ships, always chose a segment of a deluxe world tour.

He was cautious by nature, although in truth there was little likelihood of his being recognized by previous shipmates. He had become a master at altering his appearance, a talent he had discovered during his college drama club fling at acting.

As he studied Regina Clausen, he decided that she could use a makeover. She was one of those fortyish women who could have been quite attractive if she only knew how to dress, how to present herself. She was wearing an expensive-looking ice-blue dinner suit that would have been stunning on a blonde, but it did nothing for her very pale complexion, making her look washed out and wan. And her light brown hair, her natural and not unflattering color, was so stiffly set that even from across the wide room it seemed to age her, and even to date her, as though she were a suburban matron from the fifties.

Of course he knew who she was. He had seen Clausen in action at a stockholders' meeting only a few months ago, and he had also watched her on CNBC in her capacity as a stock research analyst. Certainly in those venues she had come across as forceful and very sure of herself.

That was why, when he had spotted her sitting wistfully and alone at the table, and later had witnessed her tremulous, almost girlish pleasure when one of the male hosts asked her to dance, he knew right away how easy it was going to be.

He raised his glass, and with the faintest movement in her direction, offered a silent toast.

Your prayers have been answered, Regina, he promised. *From now on, you belong to me.*

Three years later

1

Barring a blizzard or something bordering on a hurricane, Dr. Susan Chandler walked to work from her brownstone apartment in Greenwich Village to her office in the turn-of-the-century building in SoHo. A clinical psychologist, she had a thriving private practice and at the same time had established something of a public persona as host of a popular radio program, *Ask Dr. Susan*, that aired each weekday.

The early morning air on this October day was crisp and breezy, and she was glad she had opted for a long-sleeved, turtleneck sweater under her suit jacket.

Her shoulder-length dark blond hair, still damp from the shower, was windblown, causing her to regret not wearing a scarf. She remembered her grandmother's long-ago admonishment, "Don't ever go out with a wet head; you'll catch your death of cold," then realized that she seemed to think about Gran Susie a lot these days. But then, her grandmother had been raised in Greenwich Village, and Susan sometimes wondered if her spirit wasn't hovering nearby.

She stopped for a light at the corner of Mercer and Houston. It was only seven-thirty, and the streets weren't crowded yet. In another hour they would be teeming with Monday morning, back-to-work New Yorkers.

Thank God the weekend's over, Susan said to herself fervently. She had spent most of Saturday and Sunday in Rye with her mother, who had been in low spirits—understandably so, Susan thought, since Sunday would have been her fortieth wedding anniversary. Then, not helping the general situation, Susan had had an unfortunate encounter with her older sister, Dee, who was visiting from California.

Sunday afternoon, before coming back to the city, she had made a courtesy call to her father's palatial home in nearby Bedford Hills, where he and his second wife, Binky, were throwing a cocktail party. Susan suspected that the timing of the party was Binky's doing. "We had our first date four years ago today," she had gushed.

I dearly love both my parents, Susan thought as she reached her office building, but there are times when I want to tell them to please, grow up.

Susan was usually the first to arrive on the top floor, but as she passed the law offices of her old friend and mentor, Nedda Harding, she was startled to see that the lights in the reception area and hallway were already on. She knew Nedda had to be the early bird.

She shook her head ruefully as she opened the outer door—which should have been locked—walked down the hallway past the still-dark offices of Nedda's junior partners and clerks, then stopped at the open door leading to Nedda's office, and smiled. As usual,

Nedda was concentrating so intensely that she was not even aware that Susan was standing there.

Nedda was frozen in her usual work pose, her left elbow on the desk, forehead resting on her palm, and her right hand poised to turn the pages of the thick file that was spread out before her. Nedda's short-clipped silver hair was already rumpled, her half glasses were slipping down her nose, and her solid body gave the impression of being ready to leap up and run. One of the most respected defense attorneys in New York, her somewhat grandmotherly appearance offered little indication of the cleverness and aggressive energy she brought to her work, never more apparent than when she cross-examined a witness in court.

The two women had met and become friends ten years ago at NYU, when Susan was a twenty-two-year-old second-year law student and Nedda was a guest lecturer. In her third year, Susan had scheduled her classes so that she could work two days a week clerking for Nedda.

All her friends, Nedda being the only exception, had been shocked when, after two years in the Westchester County District Attorney's office, Susan quit her job as assistant D.A. to go back to school and earn her doctorate in psychology. "It's something I have to do," was her only explanation at the time.

Sensing Susan's presence in her doorway, Nedda looked up. Her smile was brief but warm. "Well, look who's here. Good weekend, Susan, or should I ask?"

Nedda knew about both Binky's party and Susan's mother's anniversary.

"It was predictable," Susan said wryly. "Dee got to Mom's house on Saturday, and the two of them ended up sobbing their hearts out. I told Dee her depression was only making it harder for Mother to cope, and she blasted me. Said that if two years ago I had watched *my* husband swept to his death in an avalanche the way *she* had watched Jack die, I'd understand what she was going through. She also suggested that if I lent Mom a shoulder to cry on instead of always telling her to get on with her life, I'd be a lot more help to her. When I said that my shoulder is getting arthritic from all the tears, Dee got even angrier. But at least Mom laughed.

"Then there was Dad and Binky's party," she continued. "Incidentally, Dad now requests that I call him 'Charles,' which says it all on *that* subject." She sighed deeply. "And that was my weekend. Another one like that and I'll be the one who needs counseling. But then I'm too cheap to hire a therapist, so I'll just end up talking to myself."

Nedda eyed her sympathetically. She was the only one of Susan's friends who knew the full story about Jack and Dee, and about Susan's parents and the messy divorce. "Sounds to me as though you need a survival plan," she said.

Susan laughed. "Maybe you'll come up with one for me. Just put it on my tab, good friend, along with all I owe you already for getting me the radio job. Now I'd better get going. I've got stuff to prepare before the show. And by the way—have I said thanks recently?"

A year earlier, Marge Mackin, a popular radio host and a close friend of Nedda's, had invited Susan to sit in on her program during a highly publicized trial to comment, both as a legal expert and a psychologist. The success of that first on-air visit led to regular appearances on the program, and when Marge moved on to host a television program, Susan was invited to replace her on the daily radio talk show.

"You're being silly. You wouldn't have gotten the job unless you could handle it. You're darn good and you know it," Nedda said briskly. "Who's your guest today?"

"This week I'll be concentrating on why women should be safety conscious in social situations. Donald Richards, a psychiatrist specializing in criminology, has written a book called *Vanishing Women*. It deals with some of the disappearances he's been involved with. Many of the cases he solved, but a number of interesting ones are still open. I read the book and it's good. He covers the background of each woman and the circumstances under which she vanished. Then he discusses the possible reasons why such an intelligent woman might get involved with a killer, followed by the step-by-step process of attempting to find out what happened to her. So we'll talk about the book and some of the more interesting cases, and then we'll generally discuss how our listeners might avoid potentially dangerous situations."

"Good subject."

"I think so. I've decided to bring up the Regina Clausen disappearance. That one always intrigued me. Remember her? I used to watch her on CNBC and thought she was great. About six years ago I used my birthday check from Dad to buy a stock she recommended. It turned into a bonanza, so I guess I feel oddly like I owe her something."

Nedda looked up, frowning. "Regina Clausen disappeared about three years ago, after disembarking from a world cruise in Hong Kong. I remember it very well. It got a lot of publicity at the time."

"That was after I left the district attorney's office," Susan said, "but I was visiting a friend when Regina Clausen's mother, Jane—she lived in Scarsdale at that time—came in to talk to the D.A. to see if he could help, but there was no indication that Regina had ever left Hong Kong, so of course the Westchester County District Attorney had no jurisdiction. The poor woman had pictures of Regina and kept saying how much her daughter had looked forward to that trip. Anyhow, I've never forgotten the case, so I'll talk about it on air today."

Nedda's expression softened. "I know Jane Clausen slightly. She and I graduated from Smith the same year. She lives on Beekman Place now. She was always very quiet, and I gather Regina was also very shy socially."

Susan raised her eyebrows. "I wish I had realized you know Mrs. Clausen. You might have been able to arrange for me to speak with her. According to my notes, Regina's mother had no inkling that her daughter might be involved with someone, but if I could get her to talk about it, something that didn't seem important at the time might come out and provide some clues."

Nedda frowned in concentration. "Maybe it's not too late. Doug Layton is the Clausen family lawyer. I've met him several times. I'll call him at nine and see if he'll put us in touch with her."

At ten after nine, the intercom on Susan's desk buzzed. It was Janet, her secretary. "Douglas Layton, an attorney, is on line one. Brace yourself, Doctor. He doesn't sound happy."

Every day, Susan wished that Janet, an otherwise excellent secretary, did not feel the need to do a commentary on the people who called. Although the real problem, Susan thought, is that her reaction usually was right on target.

As soon as she began to speak to the Clausen family lawyer it became very clear that he was indeed not happy. "Dr. Chandler, we absolutely resent any exploitation of Mrs. Clausen's grief," he said brusquely. "Regina was her only child. It would be bad enough if her body had been found, but because it has not, Mrs. Clausen agonizes constantly, in a kind of limbo, wondering under what circumstances her daughter may be living, if indeed she is alive. I would have thought a friend of Nedda Harding would be above this kind of sensationalism, exploiting grief with pop psychology."

Susan clamped her lips together for an instant to cut off the heated response she was tempted to make. When she spoke, her tone was chilly, but calm. "Mr. Layton, you've already given the reason the case *should* be discussed. Surely it is infinitely worse for Mrs. Clausen to be wondering every day of her life whether her daughter is alive and suffering somewhere than to have definite knowledge of what really happened to her. I understand that neither the police in Hong Kong nor the private investigators Mrs. Clausen hired were able to uncover a single clue as to what Regina did or where she might have gone after she disembarked. My program is heard in five states. It's a very long shot, I know, but *maybe* someone who is listening today was on that ship, or was visiting Hong Kong at the same time, and will call in to tell us something helpful, hopefully about seeing Regina after she left the *Gabrielle*. After all, she was on CNBC regularly, and some people have an excellent memory for faces."

Without waiting for a response, Susan hung up, leaned over and turned on the radio. She had made promos for today's program, referring to her guest author and to the Clausen case. They had run briefly last Friday, and Jed Geany, her producer, had promised that the station would air them again this morning. She uttered a fervent plea that he had not forgotten.

Twenty minutes later, as she studied the school reports of a seventeen-year-old patient, she heard the first of the promos. Now let's keep our fingers crossed that someone who knows something about the case is listening too, she thought.

2

It was definitely a lucky stroke that his car radio had been tuned to the talk radio station on Friday; otherwise he'd never have heard the announcement. As it was, traffic had slowed to a crawl, and he was barely listening. But at the mention of the name Regina Clausen, he had turned up the volume and concentrated intently.

Not that there was anything to worry about, of course. He reassured himself of that. After all, Regina had been the easiest, the most eager to comply and fall in with his plans, the most anxious to agree that no hint of their shipboard romance be apparent to others.

As always, he had taken every precaution. Hadn't he?

Now, hearing the promo again Monday morning, he became less sure. Next time he'd be especially careful. But then, the next one would be the last. There had been four so far. One more to go. He'd select her next week, and once she was his, his mission would be complete and he would finally be at peace.

Of course he had made no mistakes. It was his mission, and no one was going to stop him. Angrily he listened again to the promo, and to the warm, encouraging voice of Dr. Susan Chandler: "Regina Clausen was a renowned investment advisor. Beyond that, she was a daughter, a friend, and an extremely generous benefactor of numerous charities. We'll be talking about her disappearance on my show today. We'd like to solve the mystery. Maybe one of you has a piece of the puzzle. Listen in, please."

He snapped off the radio. "Dr. Susan," he said aloud, "get off it and fast. All this is none of your business, and I warn you, if I have to make you my business, your days are numbered."

3

Dr. Donald Richards, the author of *Vanishing Women* and her guest for the day, was already in the studio when Susan arrived. He was tall and lean, with dark brown hair, and appeared to be in his late thirties. He pulled off his reading glasses as he stood up to greet her. His blue eyes were warm and his smile brief as he took the hand she extended to him. "Dr. Chandler, I warn you. This is my first book. I'm new at this publicity business and I'm nervous. If I get tongue-tied, promise you'll rescue me."

Susan laughed. "Dr. Richards, the name is Susan, and just don't think about the microphone. Pretend we're hanging over the back fence and gossiping."

Who's he kidding? she wondered fifteen minutes later, as Richards discussed with calm and easy authority the true-life cases in his book. She nodded in agreement as he said, "When someone vanishes—I'm talking now, of course, of an adult, not a child—the question the authorities first ask is if the disappearance was voluntary. As you know, Susan, it's surprising just how many people suddenly decide to do a U-turn on their way home and start a whole new life, take on a whole new existence. Usually it's because of marital or financial problems, and it's a pretty cowardly way out—but it *does* happen. Whatever the circumstances, however, the first step to tracing someone who has disappeared is to see if charges start to show up on their credit cards."

"Either charged by them or by someone who stole those cards," Susan interjected.

"That's right," Richards agreed. "And usually when we encounter a voluntary disappearance we find the person just couldn't face whatever it is that's troubling him or her for another day. This kind of disappearance is really a cry for help. Of course, *some* disappearances are not voluntary; some involve foul play. That, how-

ever, is not always easy to determine. It's very difficult,
for example, to prove someone guilty of murder if the
body is never found. The murderers who don't get
convicted are often the ones who dispose of their victims so thoroughly that proof of death cannot be
established. For example . . ."

They discussed several of the open cases he'd covered in his book, instances in which the victim had
never been found. Then Susan said, "To remind my
audience, we're talking with Dr. Donald Richards,
criminologist, psychiatrist, and author of *Vanishing
Women*, a fascinating and totally accessible book of
case histories of women who have disappeared, all of
them in the last ten years. Now I'd like your opinion,
Dr. Richards, on a case that is not covered in your
book, that of Regina Clausen. Let me fill our listeners
in on the circumstances of her disappearance."

Susan did not need to consult her notes. "Regina
Clausen was a highly respected investment advisor
with Lang Taylor Securities. At the time of her disappearance, she was forty-three years old, and, according
to those who knew her, very shy in her personal life.
She lived alone and usually took vacations with her
mother. Three years ago, her mother was recovering
from a broken ankle, so Regina Clausen went alone on
a segment of the world cruise of the luxury liner
Gabrielle. She embarked in Perth, planning to sail to
Bali, Hong Kong, Taiwan, and Japan, and disembark
in Honolulu. However, in Hong Kong she got off the
ship, saying that she was going to spend extra time
there and rejoin the *Gabrielle* when it docked in Japan.
That kind of alteration of itinerary is the sort of thing
seasoned travelers regularly do, so her announced plan

aroused no suspicions. Regina took only one suitcase and a carry-on with her when she disembarked, and she was reported to have been in good spirits, and appeared very happy. She took a cab to the Peninsula Hotel, checked in, dropped her bags in her room, and left the hotel immediately. She was never seen again.

"Dr. Richards, if you were just starting to investigate this case, what would you do?"

"I'd want to see that passenger list and find out if anyone else arranged to stay in Hong Kong," Richards said promptly. "I'd want to know if she received phone calls or faxes on the ship. The communications office would have records. I'd want to question her fellow passengers to see if anyone noticed that she had been getting particularly friendly with someone, most likely a man, also traveling alone."

Richards paused. "That's for openers."

"All of that was done," Susan told him. "A thorough investigation was undertaken, working through the steamship company and private investigators, and through the authorities in Hong Kong. Three years ago, the British were still in charge there. All that could be determined for certain was that Regina Clausen vanished the moment she left that hotel."

"I'd say she was meeting someone and went to great pains to keep it a secret," Richards said. "It could have been a shipboard romance. I assume that angle was investigated."

"Yes, but none of the other passengers noticed her spending time with anyone in particular," Susan told him.

"Then she may have planned to meet someone in Hong Kong and for her own reasons wanted her decision to leave the ship there and catch up with it later to appear spontaneous," Richards suggested.

In her headphones, Susan heard a signal from the producer that calls were waiting. "Now, after these messages, let's go to the phones," she said.

She pulled off her earphones. "A couple of messages otherwise known as commercials. They pay the bills."

Richards nodded. "Nothing wrong with that. I was out of the country when the Clausen case was in the news, but it *is* an interesting one. From the little I know of it, however, I'd guess it's a guy who's to blame. A shy, lonely woman is particularly vulnerable when she's out of a familiar environment in which she has the reassurance and security of her job and family."

You must know my mother and sister, Susan thought wryly.

"Get ready. We're about to go back on air. We take fifteen minutes of questions," she said, "then that's it. I'll answer, then we'll both field."

"Whatever you say."

They put on their headphones, through which they heard the ten-second countdown. Then she began. "Dr. Susan Chandler with you again. My guest is Dr. Donald Richards, criminologist, psychiatrist, author of *Vanishing Women*. Before the break we were discussing the case of socialite stockbroker Regina Clausen, who disappeared in Hong Kong three years ago while on a segment of a world cruise of the luxury liner *Gabrielle*. Now why don't we go to our phones?" She looked at the monitor. "We have a call from Louise, in Fort Lee. You're on, Louise."

The calls were run of the mill: *"How can such smart women make the mistake of being taken in by a killer?"*

"What does Dr. Richards think of the Jimmy Hoffa case?"

"Isn't it a fact that even years later, because of DNA, the identity of a skeleton can be established?"

And then there was time for a final commercial and one more call.

During the break, the producer spoke to Susan from the control room. "There's one final call I want to put through. I warn you though, whoever it is, she's blocked off our Caller ID from her end. At first we weren't going to put her on, but she says she may know something about Regina Clausen's disappearance, so it's worth paying attention. She said to call her Karen. It's not her name."

"Put her on," Susan said. As the on-air light flashed, she spoke into the microphone: "Karen is our last caller, and my producer tells me she may have something important to tell us. Hello, Karen."

The caller spoke with a husky voice, almost too low to hear. "Dr. Susan, I took a segment of a round-the-world cruise two years ago. I was feeling pretty rotten because I was in the middle of a divorce. My husband's jealousy had become intolerable. There was a man on the trip. He made a big play for me, but he did it in a quiet, even discreet, way. At the places we docked, he'd have me meet him at some designated spot away from the ship, and we'd explore that port together. Then later we'd split up and return to the ship separately. He said the reason for such secrecy was that he hated exposing us to gossip. He was quite charming and very attentive, something I needed very badly at the time. Then he suggested that I leave the ship in Athens and spend more time there. Then we were going to fly to Algiers, and I could pick up the ship in Tangier."

Susan was reminded of the feeling she had gotten when she was in the prosecutor's office and was on the verge of learning something meaningful from a witness. She realized that Donald Richards was leaning forward as well, straining to catch every word. "Did you do what this man suggested?" she asked.

"I was going to, but my husband phoned just then and begged me to give our marriage another chance. The man I was planning to meet had already disembarked. I tried to phone to say I was staying on the ship, but he wasn't registered at the hotel where he said he'd be staying, so I never saw him again. But I *do* have a photo with him in the background, and he gave me a ring that was inscribed 'You belong to me,' which, of course, I never got to return."

Susan chose her words carefully. "Karen, what you're telling us may be very important in the investigation of Regina Clausen's disappearance. Will you meet me and show me that ring and photograph?"

"I . . . I can't get involved. My husband would be furious if he knew I'd even considered changing my plans because I'd met someone."

There's something she isn't telling us, Susan thought. Her name isn't Karen, and she's been trying to disguise her voice. And soon she's going to hang up.

"Karen, please come to my office," Susan said quickly. "Here's the address." She rattled it off, then added, her voice pleading, "Regina Clausen's mother needs to find out what happened to her daughter. I promise, I'll protect your privacy."

"I'll be there at three o'clock." The connection was broken.

4

Carolyn Wells turned off the radio and walked nervously to the window. Across the street, the Metropolitan Museum of Art was blanketed in the quiet typical of Monday, its closing day.

Since making that phone call to the *Ask Dr. Susan* radio show, she'd been unable to shake off a terrible sense of foreboding.

If only we hadn't teased Pamela to do one of her readings for us, she thought, remembering the unsettling events of the previous Friday evening. She had cooked a fortieth birthday dinner for her former roommate Pamela, and had invited as well the other two women with whom they used to share an apartment on East Eightieth Street. The group included Pamela, now a college professor; Lynn, partner in a public relations firm; Vickie, a cable TV anchorwoman; and herself, an interior designer.

They had decreed it to be a girls' night in, which meant no husbands or boyfriends, and the four of them had gossiped with the easy comfort of old friends.

They hadn't asked Pamela to do a reading for years. When they were younger and new to the city, they had almost made a ritual of somewhat jokingly asking her to assess their future with the new boyfriend, or the new job offer. Later, though, her powers had been treated more seriously. A fact that Pamela no longer even liked to acknowledge was that her gift of second sight caused her to be called upon, however discreetly, by the police in cases of kidnappings and missing persons. But her friends knew that while sometimes she could not help with the investigation, at other times she was able to "see" with stunning accuracy details that had helped to solve disappearances.

Then after dinner last Friday, when they'd all been relaxing with a glass of port, Pamela had relented and agreed to do a quick reading for each of them. As usual, she asked each woman to choose a personal object for her to hold while she did their individual readings.

I was the last, Carolyn thought, remembering the emotions aroused by that night, and something told me not to have a reading. And why did I pick out that damn ring for her to hold? I never actually wore it, and it's certainly not valuable. I don't even know why I've kept it.

The fact was she had plucked the ring out of her costume-jewelry box that night because, earlier in the day, she had had Owen Adams, the man who had given it to her, on her mind. She knew why she had been thinking about him. It was just two years ago that she had met him.

When Pamela held the ring, she had noticed the almost illegible inscription inside the band and had examined it closely.

" 'You belong to me,' " she had read, her tone half amused, half horrified. "A little strong in this day and age, isn't it, Carolyn? I hope Justin meant it as a joke?"

Carolyn remembered her discomfort. "Justin doesn't know a thing about it. Back when we were separated, some guy gave it to me on a cruise. I'd just met him, so I didn't really know him; but I've always been curious about what happened to him. He's been on my mind lately."

Pamela had closed her hand over the ring, and in an instant a perceptible change came over her. Her whole body became tense, and the expression on her face was suddenly grave. "Carolyn, this ring could have been the cause of your death," she said. "It may *still* be. Whoever gave it to you meant to harm you." Then, as though it were burning her hand, she dropped the ring on the coffee table.

It was at that moment that the key had turned in the door, and they had all jumped like guilty schoolgirls caught being naughty. By unspoken consent, they immediately changed the subject. They all knew that the separation was a taboo subject for Justin, and they knew as well that he had no use for Pamela's readings.

Carolyn remembered how she had quickly scooped up the ring and put it in her pocket. It was still there.

Justin's excessive jealousy had been the cause of the breakup two years ago. Carolyn finally had had enough. "I can't live with someone who is always suspicious if I'm a few minutes late," she had told him. "I have a job—make that a *career*—and if I'm stuck in the office because of a problem, then that's the way it is."

The day he called her on the ship, he had promised to change. And God knows he's *tried*, Carolyn thought. He's been in therapy, but if I get involved in this Dr. Susan thing, he'll think there really *was* something between Owen Adams and me, and we'll be back to square one.

She made a sudden decision. She wouldn't keep the appointment with Susan Chandler. Instead, she would send her the shipboard picture taken at the captain's cocktail party, the picture that showed Owen Adams in the background. She'd crop it so that she wasn't in the picture, and she'd send it, along with the ring and Owen's name, to Chandler. I'll print a note on plain paper, she thought, so they'll never be able to trace it to me. And I'll keep it short and simple.

If there was any tie between Owen Adams and Regina Clausen, it would be up to Chandler to find it. It would only look ridiculous for Carolyn to write that a psychic friend had claimed the ring was a symbol of death! Nobody would take *that* seriously.

5

"This is Dr. Susan Chandler, thanking our guest, Dr. Donald Richards, and all of you for being with me today."

The red on-air signal went dark. Susan pulled off her headphones. "Well, that's it," she said.

Her producer, Jed Geany, came into the studio. "Do you think that woman was on the level, Susan?"

"Yes, I do. I can only hope she doesn't change her mind about meeting me."

Donald Richards left the studio with Susan and

waited while she hailed a cab. As she got in, he said hesitantly, "I think it's less than fifty-fifty that Karen will come to see you. If she does, though, I'd like to talk with you about what she has to say. Maybe I can help."

Susan didn't understand why she felt an immediate flash of resentment.

"Let's see what happens," she said, her tone noncommittal.

"Meaning 'don't butt in,' " Richards said quietly. "I hope she shows up. Here's your cab."

6

In her Beekman Place apartment, seventy-four-year-old Jane Clausen turned off the radio, then sat for a long time staring through her window at the swiftly flowing current of the East River. With a characteristic gesture, she smoothed back a wisp of soft, gray hair that had settled on her forehead. In the last three years, ever since her daughter Regina's disappearance, she had felt as if she were frozen inside, always listening for the sound of a key in the latch, or a phone ringing, expecting to hear Regina's thoughtful greeting, "Mother, am I catching you at a busy time?"

She knew Regina was dead. In her heart it was a certainty. It was a knowledge that was primal, instinctive. She had known it from the start, from the moment she received the call from the ship to say that Regina had not reboarded as she had planned.

This morning her lawyer, Douglas Layton, had phoned angrily to warn her that Dr. Susan Chandler was planning to discuss Regina's disappearance on the radio. "I tried to dissuade her, but she insisted that it would be a favor to you if the full truth came out, and then she hung up," he had said, his voice tense.

Well, Dr. Chandler was wrong. Regina—so intelligent, so highly respected in the financial world—had been one of the most private individuals ever born.

Even more private than I am, Jane Clausen thought matter-of-factly. Two years ago that television program about missing persons had wanted to do a segment about her daughter. She had refused to cooperate then for the same reason that just now, listening to Dr. Chandler's program, she had been anguished when that author, Donald Richards, suggested that Regina might have been foolish enough to go off with some man she scarcely knew.

I know my daughter, Jane Clausen thought. That wasn't her style. But even if she *had* made that kind of mistake, she deserved better than to be exposed on television or radio for the world to pity or gloat over. Jane could imagine the tabloids blaring the fact that with her background and all her financial success, Regina Clausen had not been wise or sophisticated enough to see through a rogue.

Only Douglas Layton, the lawyer in the investment firm that handled the family assets, knew how desperately she had sought an answer to her daughter's disappearance. Only he knew that the top-flight private investigators had searched thoroughly, trying to solve the disappearance even long after the police had given up.

But I've been wrong, Jane Clausen thought. I've convinced myself that Regina's death was in some way an accident. That's made losing her more bearable. The scenario that she had created in her mind, and that had comforted her, was that Regina, who had a history of heart murmurs, had suffered the kind of sudden heart attack that took her father at such a young age, and that someone—perhaps a cabdriver—had been afraid of getting in trouble and had disposed of her body. In this fantasy, Regina would have neither known what was happening, nor would she have suffered.

But then how to explain the phone call, the one from Karen, who phoned in to report a man who had urged her to leave her cruise? She had talked about a ring—a ring with "You belong to me" inscribed on the inside of the band.

Jane Clausen had instantly recognized the phrase, and hearing the familiar words this morning had chilled her to the bone. Regina had been scheduled to disembark from the *Gabrielle* in Honolulu. When she did not return to the ship, her clothes and effects that had been left on board were packed and shipped home from that port. At the request of the authorities, Jane had gone through them thoroughly to see if anything was missing. She had noticed the ring because it was so frivolous, so obviously inexpensive—a pretty little turquoise thing, the kind that tourists purchase on a whim. She had been sure that Regina either hadn't noticed the sentiment engraved inside the band, or had ignored it. Turquoise was her birthstone.

But if this woman who called herself Karen had been given a similar ring only two years ago, did it mean that the person responsible for Regina's death might still be preying on other women? Regina had disappeared in Hong Kong. Karen said she was supposed to get off her ship to go to Algiers.

Jane Clausen stood, waited for the pain in her back to ease, then walked slowly from the study to the room that she and her housekeeper carefully referred to as the guest room.

A year after the disappearance, she had given up Regina's apartment, then had sold her own too big house in Scarsdale. She had bought this five-room apartment on Beekman Place and furnished the second bedroom with Regina's own furniture, filled the drawers and closets with her clothing, put her pictures and knickknacks around.

Sometimes, when she was alone, Jane brought a cup of tea into the room, sat on the brocade love seat Regina had purchased at an auction, and let her mind remember and relive a happier time.

Now she went to the dresser, opened the top drawer, and removed the leather box in which Regina had kept her jewelry.

The turquoise ring was in a velvet-lined compartment. She picked it up and slipped it on her finger.

She went to the telephone and phoned Douglas Layton. "Douglas," she said quietly, "today at quarter of three you and I are going to be in Dr. Susan Chandler's office. I assume you listened to the program?"

"Yes, I did, Mrs. Clausen."

"I have got to talk to the woman who phoned in."

"I'd better call and tell Dr. Chandler we're coming."

"That's exactly what I *don't* want you to do. I intend to be there and speak to that young woman myself."

Jane Clausen replaced the receiver. Ever since she had heard how little time she had left, she had contented herself with the knowledge that this terrible sense of loss soon would be over. But now she felt a blazing new need—she had to make sure that no other mother experienced the pain *she* had felt these past three years.

7

In the cab on the way back to her office, Susan Chandler mentally reviewed the appointments she had scheduled for the day. In less than an hour, at one, she was supposed to conduct a psychological evaluation of a seventh grader who was showing signs of moderate depression. She suspected that it went deeper than the typical preadolescent self-image problem. An hour later she was seeing a sixty-five-year-old woman who was about to retire and as a result was spending sleepless nights gripped with anxiety.

And at three o'clock she hoped she would be meeting the woman who called herself Karen. She had sounded so frightened when she phoned, though, that Susan worried she might change her mind. What did she have to be afraid of? she wondered.

Five minutes later, as Susan opened the door to her office, her secretary, Janet, greeted her with an approving smile. "Good program, Doctor. We've gotten a lot of calls about it. I can't wait to see what this Karen is like."

"Nor can I," Susan said, a pessimistic tone creeping into her voice. "Any important messages?"

"Yes. Your sister, Dee, phoned from the airport. She said she was sorry she missed you yesterday. She wanted to apologize for exploding at you Saturday. She also wanted to know what you thought of Alexander Wright. She met him at the party after you left. She says he's terribly attractive." Janet handed her a slip of paper. "I wrote it down."

Susan thought of the man who had overheard her father asking her to call him Charles. Fortyish, about six feet, sandy hair, an engaging smile, she remembered. He had come over to her when her father turned away to greet a new arrival. "Don't let it get you down. It was probably Binky's idea," he had said encouragingly. "Let's get some champagne and go outside."

It had been one of those glorious early fall afternoons, and they had stood on the terrace, languidly sipping from fluted glasses. The manicured lawn and formal gardens provided an exquisite setting for the turreted mansion her father had built for Binky.

Susan had asked Alex Wright how he knew her father.

"I didn't until today," he had explained. "But I've known Binky for years." Then he had asked her what she did and raised his eyebrows when she said she was a clinical psychologist.

"I'm really not so completely out of touch," he had explained hurriedly, "it's just that I hear the title 'clinical psychologist' and think of a rather serious older person, not a young and extremely attractive woman, such as you, and the two things don't go together."

She had been dressed in a dark green, wool crepe sheath accented with an apple green scarf, one of the outfits she had purchased recently to wear to her father's must-attend events.

"Most of my Sunday afternoons are spent in a bulky sweater and jeans," she told him. "Is that a more comfortable picture?"

Anxious to be away from the sight of her father gushing over Binky, and not anxious to run into her sister, Susan had left soon afterwards—though not before one of her friends whispered that Alex Wright was the son of the late Alexander Wright, the legendary philanthropist. "Wright Library; Wright Museum of Art; Wright Center for the Performing Arts. Big, *big* bucks!" she had whispered.

Susan studied the message left by her sister. He *is* very attractive, she thought. Hmmm.

Corey Marcus, her twelve-year-old patient, tested well. But as they talked, Susan was reminded that psychology involves the emotions more than the intellect. The boy's parents had been divorced when he was two, but they had continued to live near each other, had stayed friendly, and for ten years he had gone comfortably from home to home. But now his mother had been offered a job in San Francisco, and the comfortable arrangement was suddenly threatened.

Corey struggled to blink back tears as he said, "I know she wants to take the job, but if she does, it means I won't see much of my dad."

Intellectually, he appreciated what this job opportunity meant to his mother's career. Emotionally, he hoped she would turn down the job rather than separate him from his father.

"What do you think she should do?" Susan asked.

He thought for a moment. "I guess Mom really should take the job. It's not fair for her to have to pass it up."

What a good kid, Susan thought. Now *her* job was to help him put a positive spin on the change the move would make in his life.

Esther Foster, the sixty-five-year-old soon-to-be retiree who came in at two o'clock, looked drawn and pale. "Two weeks till the big party, translated as 'clean out your desk, Essy.'" Her face crumbled. "I've given my life to this job, Dr. Chandler," she said. "I recently ran into a man I could have married who now is very successful. He and his wife have a wonderful life together."

"Are you saying you're sorry you didn't marry him?" Susan asked quietly.

"Yes, I am!"

Susan looked steadily into Esther Foster's eyes. After a moment a hint of a smile pulled at the corners of the woman's mouth. "He was dull as dishwater then, and he hasn't improved that much since, Dr. Chandler," she admitted. "But at least I wouldn't be alone."

"Let's define the meaning of 'alone,'" Susan suggested.

When Esther Foster left at quarter of three, Janet appeared with a container of chicken soup and a package of crackers.

Less than a minute later, Janet informed her that Regina Clausen's mother and her attorney, Douglas Layton, were in the reception area.

"Put them in the conference room," Susan directed. "I'll see them there."

Jane Clausen looked very much the same as she had when Susan had glimpsed her in the office of the Westchester County District Attorney. Impeccably dressed in a black suit that must have cost the moon, gray hair perfectly coiffed, she had about her an air of reserve that, like her slender hands and ankles, suggested breeding.

The lawyer, who had been so sharp on the telephone this morning, seemed almost apologetic. "Dr. Chandler, I hope we're not intruding. Mrs. Clausen has something important to show you, and she'd very much like having the opportunity to meet the woman who called in on your program this morning."

Susan suppressed a smile as she detected a telltale tinge of red beneath his deep tan. Layton's dark blond hair was sun streaked, she noticed, and though he was soberly dressed in a dark business suit and tie, he still somehow managed to give the impression of an outdoor man.

Sailing, Susan decided for no particular reason.

She glanced at her watch. It was ten minutes of three, time to get directly to the point. Ignoring Layton, she looked straight at Regina Clausen's mother. "Mrs. Clausen, I'm not at all sure that the woman who called the program earlier is going to show up. I am afraid that if she realizes you are here she may make a beeline for the door. I'm going to ask you to stay in this room with the door closed; let me see her in my office, and after I've had a chance to find out what she may know, I'll ask her to consider speaking with you. But you understand that if she does not agree, I can't allow you to infringe on her privacy."

Jane Clausen opened her purse, reached inside, and pulled out a turquoise band. "My daughter had this ring in her stateroom on the *Gabrielle*. I found it when her possessions were returned to me. Please show it to Karen. If it's like the one she has, she simply *must* talk to me, although please emphasize that I have no wish to know her true identity, only every detail of the man she began to become involved with."

She handed the ring to Susan.

"Look at the inscription," Layton said.

Susan peered at the tiny lettering, squinting. Then she walked over to the window and held the ring up to the light, turning it until she could read the words. She gasped and turned back to the woman who stood waiting. "Please sit down, Mrs. Clausen. My secretary will bring you tea or coffee. And just pray that Karen shows up."

"I'm afraid I can't stay," Layton said hurriedly. "Mrs. Clausen, I'm so sorry, but I was unable to cancel my appointment."

"I do understand, Douglas." There was a slight but distinct edge in the woman's voice. "The car is waiting for me downstairs. I'll be fine."

His face brightened. "In that case, I'll take my leave." He nodded to Susan. "Dr. Chandler."

Susan watched with increasing frustration as the hands of the clock crawled to five after three, then ten after three. Quarter past became three-thirty, then quarter of four. She went back to the conference room. Jane Clausen's face was ashen. She's in physical pain, Susan realized.

"I could use that tea now, if the offer is still open, Dr. Chandler," Mrs. Clausen said. Only a faint tremor in her voice revealed her acute disappointment.

8

At four o'clock, Carolyn Wells was walking down Eighty-first Street toward the post office, a manila envelope addressed to Susan Chandler under her arm. Irresolution and doubt had been replaced with the sense of an absolute need to get rid of the ring and the picture of the man who had called himself Owen Adams. Any temptation to keep the appointment with Susan Chandler, however, had disappeared when her husband, Justin, phoned at one-thirty.

"Honey, the craziest thing," he had said, a joking tone in his voice. "Barbara, the receptionist, had the radio on this morning, listening to some call-in advice program; she said it was called *Ask Dr. Susan*, or something like that. Anyway, she said some woman named Karen was one of the callers and she sounded a lot like you and talked about meeting a guy on a cruise two years ago. Anything you haven't told me?"

The joking tone disappeared. "Carolyn, I want an answer. Anything I should know about that cruise?"

Carolyn had felt her palms become clammy. She could hear a question in his voice, a suspicion, the sound that was the sign of mounting anger. She laughed it off, assuring him that she didn't have time to listen to the radio in the middle of the day. But given Justin's past history of almost obsessive jealousy, she worried that she hadn't heard the last of this. Now all she wanted to do was to get this ring and this photo out of her life for good.

The traffic was unusually heavy, even for that time of day. The hour between four and five is the most miserable time to try to get a cab, she thought, as she observed frustrated would-be passengers trying to flag down taxis, all of which seemed to be displaying off-duty signs.

At Park Avenue, even though the light turned green, she was forced to wait at the front of an impatient throng of pedestrians as cars and vans continued to spin around the corner. Pedestrians have the right-of-way, she thought. Sure.

A delivery van was turning, its brakes screeching. Instinctively she tried to step back, away from the curb. She could not retreat. Someone was standing directly behind her, blocking her way. Suddenly she felt a hand grab the envelope from under her arm, just as another hand shoved against the small of her back.

Carolyn teetered on the edge of the sidewalk. Half turning, she glimpsed a familiar face and managed to whisper no as she tumbled forward and under the wheels of the van.

9

He had waited for her outside the building in which Susan Chandler had her office. As the minutes ticked by and she still failed to appear, his emotions ran the gamut from relief to irritation—relief that she wasn't going to show up, and anger that he had wasted so much time and now would have to track her down.

Fortunately, he had remembered her name and knew where she lived, so when Carolyn Wells didn't show up at Susan Chandler's office, he had phoned her home and then hung up when she answered. The instinct that had preserved him all these years had warned that even though she failed to keep the appointment today, she was still dangerous.

He had gone to the Metropolitan Museum of Art and sat on the steps with the small crowd of students and tourists who were hanging around even though it was closed. From there, he had a clear view of her apartment building.

At four o'clock his patience had been rewarded. The doorman had held open the ornate door, and she had emerged, carrying a small manila envelope under her arm.

It was a bonus that the weather was so pleasant and that the streets were so filled with pedestrians. He had been able to walk closely behind her and even make out a few letters of the block printing on the envelope: DR. SU . . .

He had guessed that the envelope contained the

ring and picture she had talked about when she called in to the program. He knew he had to stop her before she reached the post office. His opportunity came at the corner of Park and Eighty-first, when frustrated motorists declined to yield the right-of-way to the pedestrians.

Carolyn had half turned when he shoved her, and their eyes had met. She had known him as Owen Adams, a British businessman. On that trip he had sported a mustache and an auburn wig, and worn glasses and colored contact lenses. Even so, he was sure he saw a flicker of recognition in her eyes just before she fell.

With satisfaction he remembered the screams and shrieks as observers watched her body disappear under the wheels of the van. It had been easy then just to slip away through the crowd, the envelope she had been carrying now hidden under his jacket.

Even though he was anxious to see what she had put in it, he had waited until he was in the safety of his office with the doors locked before he ripped the envelope open.

The ring and picture were enclosed in a plastic bag. There was no letter or note with them. He studied the picture carefully, remembering exactly where it had been taken—aboard ship, in the Grand Salon, at the captain's cocktail party for the newcomers who had joined the cruise in Haifa. Of course he had avoided the ritual of having his picture taken with the captain, but clearly he had been careless. In circling his prey, he had made the mistake of getting too close to Carolyn and ended up within camera range. He remembered that he had sensed immediately that aura of sadness about her, something he always required. Hers was so strong that he knew from the outset she was to be the next one.

He looked carefully at the photograph. Even though he was in profile, the mustache obvious, his hair russet, someone studying that picture with a trained eye might recognize him.

His posture was rigidly straight; his habit of hooking the thumb of his right hand in his pocket was also a potential giveaway; his stance, right foot a half step ahead of the left and bearing most of his weight because of an old injury, likewise would be noticeable to anyone looking for it.

He tossed the picture into the shredder and with grim satisfaction watched it transformed into unrecognizable strips. The ring, he slipped on his pinkie finger. He admired it, looked at it closer, then frowned and reached for a handkerchief with which to polish it.

Another woman would very soon have the privilege of wearing this same ring, he told himself.

He smiled briefly as he thought of his next, his *final* victim.

10

It was four-fifty when Justin Wells returned to his office and tried to get back to work. In a characteristic gesture, he ran his hand through his dark hair, then he dropped his pen, shoved back his chair, and stood up.

A big man, he nonetheless moved from the drafting table with easy, swift grace, a quality that twenty-five years ago had made him an outstanding college football player.

He couldn't do it. He'd been commissioned to design the renovation of a skyscraper lobby, and he could think of nothing. Of course, today he was having trouble concentrating on anything at all.

The cowardly lion. That was the way he characterized himself. Afraid. Always afraid. Every new job began with the agonizing certainty that *this* was the one he would flub. Twenty-five years ago he had felt that way before every football game. Now here he was, a partner in the architectural firm of Benner, Pierce and Wells, and he was still plagued by the same self-doubts.

Carolyn. He was sure that someday she would go for good. She'll be furious if she ever finds out what I'm doing, he told himself as his fingers restlessly moved toward the phone on his desk. He had the number of the station. She'll never know, he assured himself. All I'll do is ask for a tape of today's *Ask Dr. Susan* program. I'll say it's my mother's favorite show, and she missed it today because she had a dentist appointment.

If Barbara the receptionist was right, and it *was* Carolyn who had called in to that show, she had talked about being involved with some man while she was on a cruise.

He flashed back to two years ago, when after that terrible incident Carolyn had impulsively booked passage on a Mumbai to Portugal segment of a world cruise. She had told him at the time that when she returned she intended to file for divorce. She said that she still cared about him but that she couldn't stand his jealousy and constant questions about where she had been all day and who she had seen.

I called just before the ship docked in Athens, Justin remembered. I told her I was willing to go into therapy, to do anything I could, if she would just come home and work with me in keeping the marriage together. And I was right to worry, he thought. Clearly, the minute she was away from me she met somebody.

But maybe Barbara was wrong, he thought. Maybe it wasn't Carolyn who called in. After all, she had met Carolyn only a few times. Then again, Carolyn's voice was distinctive—well modulated, with a hint of an English accent, thanks to childhood summers spent in England.

He shook his head. "*I have to know,*" he whispered.

He dialed the radio station, and after several minutes of listening to seemingly endless instructions— "press one for schedules; press two for information; press three for directory; press four . . . press five . . . hold for operator"—he was finally put through to the office of Jed Geany, the producer of *Ask Dr. Susan.*

He knew he sounded less than genuine when he gave the flimsy excuse that his mother had missed the program and that he wanted a tape for her. Then, when asked if he wanted a tape for the whole program, he botched his story by blurting out, "Oh, just the listener call-ins," and then tried to correct himself by hurriedly adding, "I mean that's Mother's favorite part, but please make a tape of the whole program."

To make matters worse, Jed Geany himself got on

the phone to say they were glad to oblige, because it was good to hear that a listener was that involved. Then he asked for the name and address.

Feeling guilty and wretched, Justin Wells gave his name and the office address.

He had barely hung up when he received a call from Lenox Hill Hospital, informing him that his wife had been gravely injured in an automobile accident.

11

When Susan stopped by Nedda's office at six o'clock, she found her about to lock up her desk for the night. "Sufficient unto the day is the evil thereof," she announced dryly. "How about a glass of vino?"

"Sounds like a great idea. I'll get it." Susan went down the corridor to the closet-sized kitchen and opened the refrigerator. A bottle of pinot grigio was cooling there. As she examined the label, a memory flashed through her mind.

She had been five years old, trailing behind her parents in the liquor store. Her father selected a bottle of wine from the shelf. "Is this one okay, honey?" he had asked as he handed it to her mother.

Her mother had read the label and laughed indulgently. "Charley, you're getting there. Excellent choice."

Mom is right, Susan thought, remembering her mother's outburst on Saturday. She taught Dad all the basic social graces, from how to dress to which fork to use at a dinner party. She encouraged him to leave Grandpa's deli and strike out on his own. She gave him the self-confidence to succeed, then he took hers away.

Sighing, she opened the bottle, poured wine into two glasses, shook a few pretzels onto a plate, and returned to Nedda's office. "Cocktail hour," she announced. "Close your eyes and pretend you're at Le Cirque."

Nedda looked at her steadily. "You're the psychologist, but if I can offer a nonprofessional opinion, you look pretty down."

Susan nodded. "I guess I am. The visits with my parents this weekend still bother me, and then today was pretty bumpy." She filled Nedda in on the angry phone call from Douglas Layton, as well as on the call on the program from the woman who identified herself as Karen. And then she told her of Jane Clausen's surprise visit. "She left the ring with me. She said I should keep it just in case 'Karen' ever does show up. I also get the feeling Jane Clausen isn't well."

"Do you think there's a chance you'll hear from Karen again?"

Susan shook her head. "I simply don't know."

"I'm surprised that Doug Layton phoned you this morning. When I spoke to him, he didn't seem at all upset about the program."

"Well, he changed his mind," Susan said. "He came to my office with Mrs. Clausen, but he didn't stay. He said he had an appointment he couldn't break."

"If I were he, I'd have broken the appointment," Nedda said dryly. "I happen to know that last year Jane made him a trustee of the Clausen Family Trust.

Wonder what was so important that he would leave her alone here, especially knowing that Jane might have been about to meet someone who could possibly have described the man responsible for her daughter's disappearance, perhaps even her murder?"

12

Donald Richards's sprawling apartment on Central Park West was both his home and office. The rooms he used to see patients were accessible by a separate entrance from the corridor. The five rooms he reserved for himself had the distinctly masculine flavor of a home that had not known a woman's touch for a very long time. It had been four years since his wife, Kathy, a top model, died while on a photo shoot in the Catskills.

He had not been there when it happened, and he certainly could not have done anything about it, still he had never stopped blaming himself. Most certainly he had never gotten over it.

The canoe in which Kathy had been posing overturned. The boat with the photographer and his assistants was twenty feet away. The heavy turn-of-the-century gown she had been wearing pulled her under before anyone could reach her.

Divers never recovered her body. "Even in summer, that lake is so deep that it's icy on the bottom," he was told.

Two years ago, hoping that it would bring some sense of closure, he had packed away the last few pictures of her he still had in the bedroom.

But of course it made no difference, and finally he acknowledged to himself that there was still a sense of unfinished business. Both he and Kathy's parents needed to have her remains buried in the cemetery with her family—her grandparents, and the brother she had never known.

He dreamed of her frequently. Sometimes he saw her lying trapped under one of the rocky ledges in the frigid water, forever the Sleeping Beauty. At other times the dream changed. Her face dissolved and others replaced it. And they all whispered, "It was your fault."

There was no reference to Kathy or what had happened to her on the book jacket for *Vanishing Women*. Under his picture, the brief bio reported that Dr. Donald Richards was a lifelong resident of Manhattan, had received his bachelor's degree from Yale, his M.D. and doctorate in clinical psychology from Harvard, and a master's degree in criminology from NYU.

Following the *Ask Dr. Susan* program, he went directly home. Rena, his Jamaican-born housekeeper, had lunch waiting when he got in. She had worked for him since shortly after Kathy's death, having come to him through her sister, who was his mother's live-in housekeeper in Tuxedo Park.

Don was sure that whenever Rena visited Tuxedo Park, his mother pumped her for information about his personal life. She had made it very clear to him that she thought he should be getting out more.

As he ate his lunch, Don thought about Karen, the woman who had phoned during the broadcast. Susan Chandler had obviously resented his suggestion that he would like to discuss with her anything the woman might disclose, assuming, of course, she kept the appointment. He smiled, remembering how Susan's hazel eyes had darkened, the resistance in them unmistakable.

Susan Chandler was an interesting and very attractive woman. I'll call and invite her to dinner, he decided. Chances are she will be more open to talking about the case in an intimate atmosphere.

It was an intriguing situation. Regina Clausen had disappeared three years ago. The woman who called herself Karen had talked about being involved in a shipboard romance only two years ago. Clearly Susan Chandler would make the inevitable connection that if only one man was involved with both those women, he might still be targeting victims.

Susan is stirring up a hornet's nest for herself, Donald Richards mused. He wondered what to do about it.

13

In the plane on her way back to California, Dee Chandler Harriman sipped a Perrier, slipped off her sandals, and leaned back, causing her honey blond hair to spill around her shoulders. Long used to admiring glances, she deliberately avoided meeting the gaze of the man across the aisle who had twice attempted to start a conversation.

Her plain gold wedding band and a narrow gold choker were the only jewelry she wore. Her pin-striped designer suit was stark in its simplicity. There was no one seated next to her in the second row, for which she was grateful.

She had reached New York Friday afternoon, stayed at the apartment her Belle Aire Modeling Agency maintained in the Essex House, and quietly met with two young models she was hoping to sign up. The meetings had gone well, and the day had been a success.

Too bad she couldn't say the same about Saturday, when she had gone to visit her mother. The sight of her mother's continuing pain over her father's defection had reduced her to sympathetic tears.

I shouldn't have been so nasty to Susan, she reflected. She's the one who was there with Mother, and who took the brunt of the separation and divorce.

But at least she's educated, Dee thought. Here I am at thirty-seven, thankful to have a high school diploma. But then, from the time I was seventeen, the only thing I knew was modeling—there was no time for anything else. They should have insisted I go to college. The two smart moves I made in my life were to marry Jack and to invest my savings in the agency.

Uncomfortably she remembered how she had railed at Susan, telling her that she didn't understand what it was like to lose a husband.

I'm sorry I missed her at Dad's party yesterday, Dee thought, but I'm glad I called her this morning.

I meant it when I said that Alex Wright is terrific.

A smile played on Dee's lips as she thought of the good-looking man with the warm, intelligent eyes— attractive, appealing, a sense of humor, an air of breeding. He had asked if Susan was involved with anyone.

At his request she had given him Susan's office number. She couldn't refuse that, but she decided against offering her home phone.

Dee shook her head at the flight attendant's offer to refill her Perrier. The empty feeling that had begun with the visit to her mother, and that had grown with the sight of her father and his second wife toasting each other, threatened to deepen.

She missed being married. She wanted to live in New York again. It was there that Susan had introduced her to Jack; he had been a commercial photographer. Shortly after they were married, they moved to Los Angeles.

They had five years together; then, two years ago, he'd insisted on skiing that weekend.

Dee felt tears sting her eyes. *I'm sick of being lonely,* she thought angrily. Hastily she reached for her voluminous shoulder bag, fished inside it and found what she was looking for: a brochure describing a two-week cruise through the Panama Canal. *Why not?* she asked herself. *I haven't taken a real vacation in two years.* Her travel agent had told her that a good cabin was still available for the next slated cruise. Yesterday her father had urged her to go. "First class. On me, honey," he had promised.

The ship was sailing from Costa Rica in a week. *I'm going to be on it,* Dee decided.

14

Pamela Hastings did not mind an occasional evening alone. Her husband, George, was on a business trip to California; her daughter, Amanda, was away at college, a freshman this year at Wellesley. It had been less than a month since Amanda's classes had begun, and as much as Pamela missed her, she acknowledged a guilty pleasure in the soothing silence of the apartment, the quiet of the telephone, the unnatural state of neatness in Amanda's room.

Last week had been a busy one at Columbia, what with staff meetings and student conferences, in addition to her normal teaching schedule. She always looked forward to Friday evening, a much anticipated and appreciated oasis, and the get-together at Carolyn's with the "gang of four," as they used to call themselves in the old days, had been fun but had left her with an emotional hangover.

The urgent sense of evil that she had experienced when she held that turquoise ring still frightened her. She hadn't spoken to Carolyn since that evening, but as Pamela turned the key in the lock of her apartment on Madison and Sixty-seventh Street, she made a mental note to call her friend and tell her to get rid of the ring.

She glanced at her watch. It was ten of five. She went straight to the bedroom, exchanged her conservative dark blue suit for comfortable slacks and one of her husband's shirts, fixed a scotch, and settled down to watch the news. This was going to be a peaceful evening, just hers alone.

At five after five, she stared at the image of the cordoned-off section of Park Avenue and Eighty-first Street where there was a massive traffic jam, and crowds of spectators were observing a blood-spattered van with a smashed-in grill.

In stunned disbelief she listened as the off-camera commentator said, "This was the scene at Park and Eighty-first, where a short time ago, apparently due to the pedestrian crush, forty-year-old Carolyn Wells fell into the path of a speeding van.

"She has been rushed to Lenox Hill Hospital, with multiple head and internal injuries. Our reporter at the scene spoke with several of the eyewitnesses to the accident."

As Pamela jumped to her feet, she heard the smattering of comments: "that poor woman . . ."; "terrible that people are allowed to drive like that . . ."; "they've got to do something about the traffic in the city." Then an elderly woman shouted, "You're all blind. She was pushed!"

Pamela stared as the reporter rushed a microphone to that woman. "Would you give us your name, ma'am?"

"Hilda Johnson. I was standing near her. She had an envelope under her arm. Some guy grabbed it. Then he pushed her."

"That's crazy; she fell," another bystander yelled.

The announcer came on again. "You have just heard the testimony of one eyewitness, Hilda Johnson, who claimed she saw a man push Carolyn Wells in front of the van just as he yanked what appeared to be an envelope from under her arm. While Ms. Johnson's report varies from the observations of all others at the scene, the police say they will take her statement into consideration. If her story holds up, it would mean that what seems to be a tragic accident is in fact a potential homicide."

Pamela ran for her coat. Fifteen minutes later, she was sitting beside Justin Wells in the waiting room outside the intensive care unit of Lenox Hill Hospital.

"She's in surgery," Justin said, his tone flat and emotionless.

Pamela slipped her hand into his.

Three hours later a doctor came in to speak to them. "Your wife is in a coma," he told Justin. "It's simply too soon to tell if she's going to make it. But when she was in the emergency room, she seemed to be calling for someone. It sounded like 'Win.' Who would that be?"

Pamela felt Justin's hand grip hers violently as in an anguished voice he haltingly whispered, "I don't know, I don't know."

15

Eighty-year-old Hilda Johnson liked to tell people that she had lived on East Eightieth Street all her life and could remember when the smell of Jacob Ruppert's brewery on Seventy-ninth Street had permeated the air with the pungent aroma of yeast and malts.

"Our neighbors there thought they were moving up in the world when they left Manhattan and relocated their families in the South Bronx," she would reminisce with a rumbling laugh. "Oh well, everything changes. The South Bronx was country then, and this place all tenements. Now this area is toney and the South Bronx is a disaster. But that's life."

It was a story her friends and the people she met in the park heard time and again, but that never deterred Hilda. Small, bony, with thinning white hair and alert blue eyes, she liked to talk.

On brisk days, Hilda enjoyed walking to Central Park and sitting on a sunlit bench. A people-watcher, she was remarkably observant and did not hesitate to comment on anything she felt needed correction.

She had been known to sharply reprimand a gossiping nanny whose charge was wandering from the playground. She regularly lectured children who dropped candy wrappers on the grass. And on frequent occasions she stopped a policeman to point out men who she thought were up to no good, as they hung around the playground, or wandered aimlessly along the paths.

With weary patience the police always listened politely, noting Hilda's warnings and accusations and promising to keep an eye on her suspects.

Her keen powers of observation certainly had served her well that Monday. A little after four o'clock, on her way home from the park, while standing in the crush of pedestrians waiting for the light to change, she happened to be to the right of and just slightly behind a smartly dressed woman with a manila envelope under her arm. Hilda's attention was attracted by the sudden movement of a man who reached for the envelope with one hand, and with the other, shoved the woman forward into the path of a van. Hilda had started to shout a warning, but there was no time. At least she had gotten a good look at the man's face before he had disappeared through the crowd.

In the wild confusion that followed, Hilda was jostled and propelled backwards as an off-duty cop took charge, shouting, "Police. Get back."

The sight of the crumpled, bleeding body on the pavement, the elegant suit marked with tire tracks, made Hilda feel faint, but she recovered enough to speak to the reporter. Then she turned and with great difficulty made her way home to her apartment. Once inside she made tea and, hands shaking, sipped it slowly.

"That poor girl," she kept murmuring, as she relived the incident over and over again.

Finally she felt she had the strength to call the police station. The desk sergeant who answered was one she had spoken to several times in the past, usually when she reported panhandlers approaching pedestrians on Third Avenue. He listened to her story patiently.

"Hilda, we know what you think, but you're mistaken," he said soothingly. "We already talked to a lot of the people who were on that corner when the accident happened. The press of the crowd when the light turned green caused Mrs. Wells to lose her balance, that's all."

"The pressure of a hand on her back deliberately pushing her forward caused her to fall," Hilda snapped. "He grabbed the manila envelope she was carrying. I'm exhausted and going to bed now, but leave word for Captain Shea. I'll be in to see him the minute he gets in tomorrow morning. Eight o'clock sharp."

She hung up indignantly. It was only five o'clock, but she needed to go to bed. She felt a tightness in her chest that only a nitroglycerin tablet under her tongue and some bed rest would ease.

A few minutes later she was dressed in her warm nightgown, her head propped up on the thick pillow that aided her breathing. The darting headache that for a few minutes always accompanied the pill began to subside. The chest pain was fading.

Hilda sighed with relief. A good night's rest and she would go to the police station to give Captain Shea an earful and register a complaint about that boneheaded sergeant. Then she would insist on sitting down with the police artist and describing the man who had pushed that woman. Vile thing, she thought, remembering his face. The worst kind—well dressed; classy-looking; the type of person you would think you could trust. How was that poor girl doing? she wondered. Maybe it would be on the news.

She reached for the remote control and turned on the television just in time to see and hear herself on camera as the witness who claimed to have seen a man push Carolyn Wells in front of the van.

Hilda's emotions were decidedly mixed. She felt an undeniable thrill at being a celebrity, but there was also a sense of annoyance at the comment the broadcaster had made, which clearly suggested she was wrong. Then that lunkhead sergeant had treated her like she was a child. Her final thought as she began to doze off was that in the morning she'd stir them all up. Wait and see. Sleep overcame her just as she began to say a Hail Mary for the gravely injured Carolyn Wells.

16

When Susan left Nedda, she walked home through the twilight to her apartment on Downing Street. The penetrating chill of the early morning, relieved temporarily by the warmth of the afternoon sun, had returned.

She thrust her hands into the generous pockets of her sack-style jacket and picked up her pace. The weather brought to mind a long-forgotten line from *Little Women*. One of the sisters—she couldn't remember whether it was Beth or Amy—said that November was a disagreeable month, and Jo agreed, commenting that that was why she was born in it.

Me too, Susan thought. My birthday is November twenty-fourth. The Thanksgiving baby, they used to call me. Sure. And this year I'm a thirty-three-year-old baby. Thanksgiving and birthdays used to be fun, she mused. At least this year I won't have to jog between two dinners, like someone stealing from one enemy camp to another. Thank God this year Dad and Binky are going to St. Martin.

Of course, my domestic problem is small potatoes when compared with the way Jane Clausen is living, she thought, as she reached her street and turned west.

After they had acknowledged that "Karen" was not going to keep the appointment, Mrs. Clausen had stayed at the office for another twenty minutes.

Over a cup of tea, she had insisted that Susan keep the turquoise ring. "If something were to happen to me, it's important that you have it just in case the woman who phoned you contacts you again," she had said.

She doesn't mean *if* something happens to her; she means *when*, Susan thought, as she turned in to her own building, a three-story brownstone, and began the climb to her apartment on the top floor. It was a roomy place, with a large living room, generous kitchen, oversized bedroom, and small den. Handsomely and comfortably furnished with the items her mother had offered when she moved from the house the family had lived in to a luxury condo, it always felt warm and welcoming to Susan—almost like a physical embrace.

Tonight was no exception. In fact, this evening the place felt particularly soothing, Susan reflected, flipping the switch that turned on the gas-burning log fire in the fireplace.

An at-home night, she decided emphatically as she proceeded to change, slipping into an aging velour caftan. She would make herself a salad and pasta, and pour a glass of Chianti.

A short time later, as she was rinsing watercress, the phone rang. "Susan, how's my girl?"

It was her father. "I'm fine, Dad," Susan said, then grimaced. "I mean, I'm fine, Charles."

"Binky and I were sorry you had to leave so soon yesterday. Party was a blast, wasn't it?"

Susan raised an eyebrow. "A real blast."

"Right."

Oh Dad, Susan thought. If you only knew how phony you sound.

"Susan, you certainly caught Alex Wright's eye. He kept talking to us about you. Guess he was praising you to Dee as well. Told us Dee wouldn't give him your home phone."

"My office number is in the book. If he wants to, he'll call me there. I thought he seemed like a nice guy."

"He's a lot more than that. The Wright family is up there with the best of them. Very impressive."

Dad's still in awe of important people, Susan thought. At least he hasn't managed to convince himself that he was born with a silver spoon. I just wish he didn't need to pretend that he was.

"Let me put Binky on. She wants to tell you something."

Why *me*, Lord? Susan thought as she listened to the phone being handed over.

Her stepmother's trilling "Hello" grated on her ear.

Before she could respond, Binky began to sing the praises of Alexander Wright. "I've known him for years, darling," she chirped. "Never married. Just the kind of man Charles and I envision you or Dee with. You've met him, so you know he's attractive. He's on the board of the Wright Family Foundation. They give away tons of money every year. The most generous, most philanthropic person you'd ever want to meet. Not like these selfish people who only care for themselves."

I can't *believe* you said that, Susan thought.

"Darling, I did something that I hope you won't mind. Alex just phoned and practically demanded I give him your home number. And I'm pretty sure he's going to call you this evening. He said he didn't want to bother you at your office." Binky paused, then coaxed, "Please tell me I did the right thing."

"I'd rather you didn't give out my home number, Binky," Susan said stiffly, then softened. "But in this case, I suppose it's all right. Just please don't do it again."

She managed to cut short Binky's gushing reassurances and hung up feeling as though her evening had suddenly turned sour. Less than ten minutes later, Alexander Wright phoned. "I put the hit on Binky for your home number. I hope that was okay."

"I know," Susan said, her tone remote. "Charles and Binky just called."

"Why don't you refer to your father as 'Dad' when we talk? It's okay with me."

Susan laughed. "You're very perceptive. Yes, I will do that."

"I made a point of catching your program today and thoroughly enjoyed it."

Susan was surprised to realize that she was pleased.

"I was seated at the same table as Regina Clausen at a Futures Industry dinner six or seven years ago. She struck me as a lovely person, a very intelligent lady."

Wright hesitated, then said apologetically, "I know this is last minute, but I just finished a board of directors meeting at St. Clare's Hospital and I'm hungry. If you haven't had dinner and don't have plans, could I possibly interest you in going out? I know you're on Downing Street. Il Mulino is minutes away."

Susan eyed the watercress she had been washing. Somewhat to her surprise she heard herself agreeing to be picked up in about twenty minutes.

As she walked to the bedroom to change to a cashmere sweater and slacks, she convinced herself that the real reason she was going on this impromptu date was to hear any impressions Alex Wright might be able to offer about Regina Clausen.

17

Upon reflection, Douglas Layton acknowledged that Jane Clausen would not take kindly to his failure to stay with her at Dr. Susan Chandler's office.

As a lawyer/investment broker, for the past four years he had been working for the firm that handled the Clausen interests. He had begun his career there as assistant to Hubert March, the senior partner who had known and tended to the Clausens for some fifty years. As March approached retirement, Layton had become the on-the-spot person whom Jane Clausen clearly favored to replace her failing old friend.

To have been named a director of the Clausen Family Trust after so short a time with the firm was an awesome coup, one which Douglas Layton fully appreciated, and with it came significant obligations.

But I had no choice this afternoon, he reminded himself as he entered the elevator at 10 Park Avenue and smiled pleasantly at the young couple who had just bought an apartment on the ninth floor of his building.

He still rented, although with his income he easily could have afforded to buy his own place. As he explained to his friends, "Look, I'm thirty-six. At some point, believe it or not, I'm going to find the right girl and settle down. When I do, we'll shop together.

"And anyhow," he would point out, "while I don't know the guy who owns this place, I sure do like his taste. And even though I could buy my own co-op, I couldn't afford one quite like this."

His friends could not deny the truth of that observation. Without the headaches of ownership, Layton lived in an apartment with a mahogany paneled library, a living room with a dazzling New York view that included both the Empire State Building and the East River, a state-of-the-art kitchen, a large bedroom, and two full baths. It was comfortably furnished with deep couches, inviting club chairs, sufficient drawer and closet space, tasteful wall hangings, and excellent reproductions of fine Persian carpets.

Tonight, as he closed and locked the apartment door, Douglas Layton wondered how long his luck would hold out.

He checked the time; it was quarter past five. He made a beeline for the phone and called Jane Clausen. She did not answer, which was not unusual. If she was going out to dinner, she often would nap around this time, in which case the phone was always turned off. The gossip around the office was that she used to leave the phone on the empty pillow next to her, just in case a call from her daughter Regina came in the middle of the night.

He would try Mrs. Clausen again in an hour or so. In the meantime there was someone else he hadn't spoken to in at least a week. His face suddenly softening, he picked up the phone again and dialed.

His mother had moved to Lancaster, Pennsylvania, ten years ago. Long separated from his father, who had disappeared from their lives, she was much happier to be back among her own numerous cousins.

She answered on the third ring. "Oh, Doug, I'm glad you caught me. In another minute I'd have been gone."

"The hospital? The homeless shelter? The Emergency Hotline?" he asked, his tone affectionate.

"None of those, smarty. I'm going to the movies with Bill."

Bill was her longtime friend, an amiable bachelor whom Doug found very likable and completely boring.

"Don't let him get fresh."

"Doug, you know very well he wouldn't," his mother sputtered.

"You're right—I do know very well. Good old predictable Bill. Okay, Mom, I'll let you go. I just wanted to check in."

"Doug, is everything okay? You sound worried."

He chided himself. He should know better than to call his mother when he was upset. She could always see through him.

"I'm fine," he said.

"Doug, I worry about you. And I'm here if you need me. You know that, don't you?"

"I know, Mom. I'm fine. Love you."

He hung up quickly, then went to the bar in the library and poured himself a stiff scotch. As he gulped it down, he could feel his heart pounding. This was not the time to have an anxiety attack. Why was it that he, who usually was so absolutely in charge of his actions and emotions, got hit like this every so often?

He knew why.

Nervously he flipped on the television and watched the evening news.

At seven o'clock he once again dialed Jane Clausen's number. This time he reached her, but by her reserved tone knew he was in trouble.

At eight o'clock he went out.

18

Alexander Wright spotted his car double-parked outside St. Clare's Hospital on West Fifty-second Street and was in the backseat before his driver was able to get out and open the door for him.

"A long meeting, sir," Jim Curley volunteered as he started the engine. "Where are we heading now?" He spoke with the familiarity of a longtime employee, having been with the Wright family for thirty years.

"Jim, I'm happy to say that as of five minutes ago, we're picking up a very attractive lady on Downing Street and going on to dinner at Il Mulino," Wright answered.

Downing, Curley thought. Must be a new one. Never been there before. Curley took pleasure in the fact that as a good-looking and wealthy bachelor in his late thirties, his employer was on everyone's A list. Within the confines of his extreme care for Alexander

Wright's privacy, Curley enjoyed mentioning to his friends that musical comedy star Sandra Cooper was just as nice as she was beautiful, or how funny Lily Lockin, the comedienne, had been when she chatted with him in the car.

But these discreet tidbits were mentioned only after items appeared in the newspaper columns indicating that this or that woman had been at dinner or a party with sportsman and philanthropist Alex Wright.

As the car made its way through the slow Ninth Avenue traffic, Curley glanced several times in the rearview mirror, observing with some concern that his boss had closed his eyes and leaned his head back against the soft leather of the headrest.

Whoever said that it can be as hard to give away money as it is to earn it was right, Curley thought compassionately. He knew that as chairman of the Alexander and Virginia Wright Family Foundation, Mr. Alex was constantly besieged by individuals and organizations pleading for grants. And he was so nice to everyone. Probably much too generous as well.

Nothing like his father, Curley mused. The old guy was a tough one. So was Alex's mother. She'd bite your head off for nothing. Always on Alex when he was a kid. A miracle he turned out so fine. I hope this lady on Downing Street is fun, he thought. Alex Wright deserved to have some fun. He worked too hard.

As usual, Il Mulino was busy. The scent of good food mingled with the cheerful voices of the diners. The bar was filled with people waiting for tables. The overflowing harvest basket of vegetables at the entrance to the dining room gave a countrylike coziness to the restaurant's simple decor.

The maître d' escorted them to a table immediately. As they wended their way through the crowded room, Alex Wright was stopped several times to greet friends.

Without consulting the wine list, he ordered a bottle of Chianti and one of chardonnay. At her look of consternation, he laughed. "You don't have to have more than a glass or two, but I promise you, you'll enjoy sipping both. I'm going to be honest. I skipped lunch and I'm starving. Do you mind if we look at the menu right away?"

Susan decided on a salad and salmon. He chose oysters, pasta, and veal. "The pasta is what I would have had for lunch," he explained.

As the captain poured wine, Susan raised her eyebrows and shook her head. "I cannot believe that only an hour ago I was in my favorite, somewhat ragged caftan, planning a quiet evening at home," she told him.

"You could have worn the caftan," he suggested.

"Only if I was trying to impress you," she said, eliciting a laugh from Wright.

She studied him briefly as he waved at someone across the room. He was dressed in a conservative dark gray suit with a faint pinstripe, a crisp white shirt, and a small-patterned gray-and-red tie. He was attractive and impressive.

Finally she realized what it was that was puzzling her about him. Certainly Alex Wright had the authority and poise that were the product of generations of breeding, but there was something else about him that intrigued her. I think he's a little shy, she decided. *That's* what it is. She liked that about him.

"I'm glad I went to the cocktail party yesterday," he told her quietly. "I'd decided to stay home and do the *Times* puzzle, but I'd accepted the invitation and didn't want to be rude." His smile was fleeting. "I want you to know I'm grateful to you for coming out to dine with me on such short notice."

"You said you've known Binky quite a long time?"

"Yes, but only the way you know people who go to the same parties. Small ones. I can't stand the biggies. I hope I'm not stepping on your toes when I say she's an airhead."

"A very *persuasive* airhead," Susan said ruefully. "What do you think of that Disney castle my father built for her?"

They laughed.

"But you're still pretty hurt and uncomfortable about the situation?" he suggested. "Sorry; you're the psychologist, not me."

When you don't want to give an answer, ask a question, Susan reminded herself. "You've met my father and sister," she countered. "What about you? Any siblings?"

He told her that he was an only child, the product of a late marriage. "My father was too busy making money to court anyone until he was in his forties," he explained. "Then he was too busy amassing wealth to pay much attention to me or my mother. But I must assure you that with the human misery I read and hear about every day at the foundation, I count myself very lucky."

"In the grand scheme of things, you probably are," Susan agreed. "Me, too."

It wasn't until they were sipping espresso that Regina Clausen's name came up. Alex Wright couldn't tell her very much more than what he had said on the phone. He'd sat at the same table as Regina at a Futures Industry dinner. He found her to be a quiet, intelligent lady. It seemed impossible to think that someone with her background could just disappear.

"Do you put any stock in that call you got on the program?" he asked. "The one from the woman who sounded so nervous?"

She had already decided that she would not discuss with anyone the ring Regina Clausen's mother had given her. That ring, with the same "You belong to me" inscription "Karen" had mentioned, was the only tangible object that might link Regina's disappearance and Karen's experience with an aborted shipboard friendship. The fewer people who knew about it, the better.

"I just don't know," she told him. "It's too early to be sure."

"How did you ever happen to do a radio program in the first place?" he asked.

She found herself telling him how Nedda had introduced her to the former host. She also told him about having worked for Nedda while in law school, about quitting her job in the Westchester County District Attorney's office, and going back to school.

Finally, over brandy, Susan said, "I'm the one who's usually the listener. Enough about me. *Much* too much about me, in fact." Wright signaled for the check. "Not nearly enough," he said briskly.

All in all, it had been a very nice evening, Susan decided as she slipped into bed.

She saw that it was ten of eleven. She had been home twenty minutes. When she had tried to say good-bye at the front door of her brownstone, Alex said, "My father told me to always see a lady safely home. And then I assure you I'll be on my way." He had insisted on going upstairs with her and waiting while she opened her apartment door.

Nothing like a little old-fashioned courtesy, Susan thought as she turned off the light.

She was tired but found she could not stop reviewing the events of the day, going over what had happened and what had not happened. She thought about Donald Richards, author of *Vanishing Women*. He had been an interesting guest. Clearly he would have liked to be invited to the hoped-for meeting with "Karen."

Somewhat uncomfortably, Susan remembered her swift rejection of his hint that he would like to have input into anything Karen might disclose if she kept the appointment.

Would she ever hear from Karen again? she wondered. Would it be wise to make a plea on tomorrow's show for the woman to contact her, if only by phone?

As she started to fall asleep, Susan sensed a warning bell in her subconscious. She stared into the darkness, trying to pinpoint what it was that had set off her internal alarm. Clearly there was something that had happened or that she had heard earlier that day, something that she should have paid attention to. But what was it?

Realizing that she was too tired to focus now, she turned over and settled in for the night. She would think of it tomorrow; surely that would be plenty of time.

19

Hilda Johnson slept for five hours before she awoke at ten-thirty, feeling both refreshed and somewhat hungry. A cup of tea and a piece of toast would go down well, she decided, as she sat up and reached for her robe. She also wanted to see if they would show her again on the eleven o'clock news.

After she watched the news, she would get back into bed and say a rosary for Carolyn Wells, that poor woman who had been hit by the van.

She knew that Captain Tom Shea would be at the precinct station by 8 A.M. sharp. She would be there, waiting for him. As she knotted the belt of her chenille robe, Hilda mentally reviewed the face of the man whom she had seen push Mrs. Wells into the van's path. Now that the shock had worn off, she could remember his face even more clearly than she had seemed to at the time. She knew that in the morning she would have to give the police sketch artist a complete description of the man.

Nearly seventy years ago, she had been a good art student herself. Her grammar school teacher, Miss Dunn, had been very encouraging, saying Hilda had a real talent, especially for sketching faces, but then at age thirteen she had had to go to work, and that left no time for that sort of thing, she thought regretfully.

Not that she had given up sketching entirely, of course. Over the years she often had taken a pad and pen with her to the park and made pen-and-ink drawings that she would frame and give to her friends for their birthdays. She hadn't done it lately, though. There were only a few friends left, and besides, her fingers were too swollen with arthritis to hold a pen easily.

Still, if she could get that man's face down on paper now, while it was still fresh in her mind, it would be that much easier when she went to the police in the morning.

Hilda crossed to the secretary that had been her mother's, and which occupied a place of honor in her tiny living room. She opened the desk section below the mahogany-and-glass cabinet and pulled up a chair. In a drawer was a box of stationery her friend Edna had given her last Christmas. The sheets were large and sunny yellow, and there was lettering across the top that read, "A *bon mot* for you from Hilda Johnson."

Edna had explained that a *bon mot* was a clever saying, and the executive-size paper was something she knew Hilda would enjoy. "Not like those little cards that just about give you the space to write two lines."

It was also the perfect size for making a quick sketch to help Hilda anchor her memory of the thug who had grabbed that poor woman's manila envelope and then pushed her. With painfully stiff fingers, Hilda slowly began to draw. A face started to emerge—not a profile, but more like he was facing three-quarters of the way toward her. Yes, his hair had grown like this, she reminded herself. She drew his ear, well-shaped, close to his head. His eyes had been far apart, and they narrowed as he focused on Wells, his lashes, long, his chin, determined.

When Hilda put the pen down, she was satisfied. Not bad, she thought, not bad at all. She glanced at the clock; it was five of eleven. She turned on the television, then went into the kitchen to fill the kettle.

She had just lit the gas beneath it when the buzzer sounded from downstairs. Who in the name of God at this hour? she wondered as she went into the tiny foyer and picked up the receiver of the intercom.

"Who is it?" She did not attempt to conceal her irritation.

"Miss Johnson, I'm so sorry to disturb you." The man's voice was low and pleasant. "I'm Detective Anders. We have a suspect in custody who may be the person you saw push Mrs. Wells today. I need to show you his picture. If you recognize him, we can hold him. Otherwise we'll have to let him go."

"I thought no one believed me when I said someone pushed her," Hilda snapped.

"We didn't want it to leak that we were on the tail of a suspect. May I come up for just a minute?"

"I guess so."

Hilda pushed the buzzer that unlocked the lobby door. Then with a feeling of self-satisfaction, she went back to the desk and looked at her sketch. Wait till Detective Anders sees *this*, she thought.

She heard the old elevator when it lumbered to a stop on her floor; after that she made out the faint sound of footsteps.

She waited until Detective Anders rang the bell before she opened the door. Must be getting cold, she thought—his coat collar was turned up, and he wore a slouch hat pulled down low on his forehead. Plus he was wearing gloves.

"This will only take a minute, Miss Johnson," he said. "I'm sorry to disturb you."

Hilda cut short his apology. "Come in," she said

briskly. "I've got something to show you too." As she led the way to the desk, she did not hear the soft click of the closing door.

"I did a sketch of the guy I saw," she said triumphantly. "Let's compare it with the picture you have."

"Of course." But instead of a sketch, the visitor laid down a driver's license with a photo ID.

Hilda gasped. "Look! It's the same face! That's the man I saw push that woman and grab the envelope."

For the first time, she looked directly up at Detective Anders. He had removed his hat, and his coat collar was no longer turned up around his neck.

Hilda's eyes widened in shock. Her mouth opened, but the only sound that came from it was a faint murmur: "Oh, no!" She tried to step back, but she bumped into the desk behind her. Her face went ghastly pale as she realized that she was trapped.

Beseechingly she raised her hands. Then in futile protest she turned her palms outward to shield herself from the knife her visitor was about to plunge into her chest.

He jumped back to avoid the spurting blood, then watched as her body sagged and crumbled to the threadbare carpet. A fixed, staring look began to settle in Hilda's eyes, but she managed to murmur, "God . . . won't . . . let you . . . get . . . away . . ."

As he reached over her to take his driver's license and her sketch, her body shuddered violently, and her hand fell on his shoe.

Shaking the hand off, he walked calmly to the door, opened it, checked the hallway, and in four paces was at the fire exit staircase. When he reached the lobby, he opened that door a crack, saw no one coming, and an instant later was on the street, heading home.

The realization of how narrow had been his escape washed over him. If the cops had believed that old bag and gone to talk to her that afternoon, she might have drawn the sketch for them. It would have been in all the papers tomorrow.

As he walked, his right foot began to feel heavier and heavier. It felt almost as if Hilda Johnson's thick-fingered hand were still lying on it.

Had her dying words put a curse on him? he wondered. They had reminded him of the mistake he had made earlier today—the mistake that Susan Chandler, with her trained prosecutor's mind, might just possibly uncover.

He knew he couldn't let that happen.

20

Susan's sleep was restless, filled with troubling dreams. When she awoke she remembered fragments of scenes in which Jane Clausen and Dee and Jack and she were all present. She remembered that at one point Jane Clausen had been pleading, "Susan, I want Regina," while Dee stretched out her hand and said, "Susan, I want Jack."

Well, you *had* him, Susan thought. She got out of bed and stretched, hoping to relieve the familiar clutch at her heart. It bothered her deeply that after all these years, a dream like that could bring all the memories flooding back. Memories of herself at twenty-three, a second-year law student working part-time for

Nedda. Jack, a twenty-eight-year-old commercial photographer, just beginning to make a name for himself. The two of them in love.

Enter Dee. Big sister. Darling of fashion photographers. Sophisticated. Amusing. Charming. Three men in line, wanting to marry her, but she had wanted Jack.

Susan went into the bathroom and reached for the toothpaste. She brushed her teeth briskly, as if by that action she could obliterate the bitter aftertaste she always experienced when she remembered Dee's tearful explanation: "Susan, forgive me. But what is between Jack and me is inevitable . . . maybe even necessary."

Jack's agonized nonexcuse: "Susan, I'm sorry."

And the crazy part, Susan thought, is that they *were* right for each other. They *did* love each other. Maybe even too much. Dee hated the cold. If she hadn't been so in love, and such a good sport, she would have insisted Jack quit dragging her to ski slopes. If she had succeeded in keeping him at home, he wouldn't have been caught in the avalanche. And maybe he would be alive today.

On the other hand, Susan thought as she turned on the hot water in the shower, if Jack and I had ended up together, I might be dead too, because I surely would have been on that slope with him.

Her mother had understood. "I realize that if it had been the other way 'round, Susan, if you'd been attracted to someone Dee cared about, you would have removed yourself from the picture. But something you have to accept, even if you find it hard to understand, is that Dee always has been somewhat jealous of you."

Yes, I would have removed myself from the picture, Susan thought as she slipped off her robe and stepped under the steaming water.

By seven-thirty she was dressed and was having her usual breakfast of juice, coffee, and half an English muffin. She turned on *Good Day, New York* to catch the news. Before she could see more than the opening montage, however, the phone rang.

It was her mother. "Just wanted to catch you before you got too busy, dear."

Pleased to hear that her mother sounded upbeat, Susan pressed the mute button of the TV remote control. "Hi, Mom." And thank God she still expects to be called Mom, she thought, and not Emily.

"Your program yesterday was fascinating. Did that woman who phoned show up at your office?"

"No, she didn't."

"Not surprising. She sounded pretty worried. But I thought you'd be interested to know that I once met Regina Clausen. I was with your father at a stockholders' meeting; that was in the B.B. days, so it would be about four years ago."

B.B. Before Binky.

"Needless to say Charley—Charles was trying to impress Regina Clausen with the terrific investments he'd made, a fact I reminded him of during our financial settlement, but which, of course, he then tried to deny."

Susan laughed. "Mom, be charitable."

"Sorry, Susan, I didn't mean to make a crack about the divorce," her mother said.

"Sure you did. You do it all the time."

"That's true," her mother agreed cheerfully. "But I really did call to tell you about Regina Clausen. She got quite chatty with us—you know what a schmoozer your father can be—and she told us that on her next long vacation, she was planning to go on a cruise. She clearly was excited about it. I told her I hoped the people on board wouldn't keep bothering her for investment advice. I remember she laughed and said something about looking forward to having some fun and excitement, and that did not include discussing the Dow Jones average. She said her father had had a heart attack in his forties, and that before he died he talked with regret about the vacations he'd never made time for."

"What you're telling me just serves to reinforce the theory that she *did* have some kind of shipboard romance," Susan said. "Certainly it sounds like she was open to the idea and probably would have been receptive." She thought of the turquoise ring Jane Clausen had given her. "Yes, I think that's what happened to her, a well-concealed shipboard romance."

"Well, what she said clearly helped put a bug in your father's ear. We separated shortly after that. He had his plastic surgery, got rid of his gray hair, and started running around with Binky. Incidentally he's encouraging Dee to take a cruise now. Did she tell you about that?"

Susan looked at the clock. She didn't want to cut her mother off, but she needed to be on her way. "No, I didn't know Dee was thinking about a cruise herself. But then I missed her call yesterday," she said.

Her mother's voice became troubled. "I'm worried about Dee, Susan. She's down. She's lonely. She's not springing back. She's not strong like you."

"You're pretty strong yourself, Mom."

Her mother laughed. "Not consistently, but I'm getting there. Susan, don't work too hard."

"Meaning find a nice guy, get married, be happy."

"Something like that. Anybody interesting you

haven't told me about? When Dee phoned she mentioned someone she met at the Binky-Charley party who seemed very smitten with you. She said he was terribly attractive."

Susan thought of Alex Wright. "He's not bad."

"According to Dee he's much more than 'not bad.'"

"Bye, Mom," Susan said firmly. After she hung up, she put her coffee cup in the microwave and turned up the TV sound again. A reporter was talking about an elderly woman who had been stabbed to death in her Upper East Side apartment. Susan was just about to turn off the TV when the anchorman replayed the segment from the previous evening's news that included the report that Hilda Johnson, the murder victim, had called the police, claiming that the woman who had been run over on Park Avenue had been deliberately pushed during a mugging.

Susan stared at the television, realizing that the prosecutor in her was refusing to believe that these two events were coincidental, while the psychologist in her was wondering what kind of out-of-control mind could commit *two* such brutal crimes.

21

Even though he had found her terribly irritating, Captain Tom Shea of the 19th Precinct had been fond of Hilda Johnson. As he pointed out to his men, the bottom line was that usually there was some validity to

Hilda's complaints. For example, a derelict she accused of hanging around the playground in the park turned out to have a record of minor sex offenses against young children. And the kid she complained about who kept riding his bike around her neighborhood got caught red-handed mugging an elderly pedestrian.

Standing now in Hilda Johnson's apartment, Captain Shea felt both anger and tenderness at the sight of the limp, chenille-covered remains of the old woman. The crime photographers had taken their pictures. The coroner had done his job. It was okay to touch her.

Shea knelt beside Hilda. Her eyes were staring, her face frozen into an expression of panic. Gently he turned her palm toward him, observing the cuts where she had tried to shield herself from the fatal thrust that had entered her heart.

Then he looked closely. There were smudges on several fingers of her right hand. Ink stains.

Shea stood and turned his attention to the desk, observing that it was open. His grandmother had a desk like this, and she always kept the lid in that position, proud to reveal the little pigeonholes and drawers and the matching blotter and desk set that no one ever used.

He thought back to the previous year, when Hilda had sprained her ankle on some broken pavement, and he had stopped by to see her. The desk was closed then. I bet she always left it closed, he thought.

In the desk there was a box of stationery that obviously had just been opened—the cellophane that had sealed it was still there. He half smiled when he read the lettering: "A *bon mot* for you from Hilda Johnson."

An old-fashioned pen was lying next to the inkwell, the sort of pen people used for sketching. He touched it and then studied the smudge the pen left on his fingers. Next he counted the sheets of paper remaining in the box. There were eleven. Then he counted the envelopes—twelve.

Had Hilda Johnson been writing or sketching on the missing sheet shortly before her death? he wondered. Why would she do that? According to Tony Hubbard, who had been on the desk when Hilda called yesterday, she told him she was going right to bed and would come by the station in the morning.

Ignoring the cameramen, who were packing up their gear, and the fingerprint experts, who were reducing Hilda's painfully neat apartment to a sooty mess, Tom went into the bedroom.

Hilda had gone to bed—that was obvious. The pillow still bore the imprint of her head. It was now eight o'clock. The medical examiner estimated she had been dead between eight and ten hours. So sometime between 10 P.M. and midnight, Hilda got out of bed, put on her robe, went to her desk and wrote or sketched something, then put the kettle on.

When Hilda, notoriously prompt, failed to show up, Captain Shea had tried to call her. Getting no answer, and alarmed, he asked the superintendent to check on her. If he hadn't, it might have been days before her body was discovered. They had found no evidence of a break-in, so that meant that in all likelihood she had opened the door voluntarily. Had she been expecting someone? Or was a suspicious and sharp old bird like Hilda tricked into believing that her visitor was someone she could trust?

The captain went back into the living room. How did she happen to be standing at the desk when she was murdered? he wondered. If she suspected that she was in danger, wouldn't she at least have tried to run?

Had she been showing something to her visitor when she died?—something her visitor took after he killed her?

The two detectives who had accompanied him straightened up as he approached them. "I want everyone in this building interrogated," Captain Shea snapped. "I want to know where each person was last night and what time they got home. I'm particularly interested in anyone who came or went between ten o'clock and midnight. I want to know if anyone is aware of Hilda Johnson writing notes to people. I'm on my way to the station."

There, the unfortunate Sergeant Hubbard, who had joked about Hilda's phone call swearing that Carolyn Wells was pushed and a manila envelope stolen from her, endured the worst dressing-down of his life.

"You ignored a call that could have been significant. If you had treated Hilda Johnson with the respect she deserved and sent someone to talk to her, it's very possible that she'd be alive today, or at least that we'd be on a direct line to a mugger who may now be a murderer. Jerk."

He pointed an angry finger at Hubbard. "I want you to interview every person whose name was taken at the accident scene and find out if anyone noticed whether Carolyn Wells had a manila envelope under her arm before she fell into the street. Got it?"

"Yes, sir."

"Now I hope I don't have to tell you not to specifically *mention* a manila envelope. Just ask if she had anything under her arm and what it was. Got that?"

22

He slept only fitfully, awaking several times during the night. Each time, he turned on the TV, which remained tuned to the local news station—New York 1—and each time he heard the same thing: Carolyn Wells, the woman who had been run over at Park Avenue and Eighty-first Street, was in a coma; her condition was critical.

He knew that if by some unlucky circumstance she recovered, she would tell people that she had been pushed by Owen Adams, a man she had met while on a cruise.

They couldn't trace Owen Adams to him; of that he was certain. The British passport, like all the ones he had used on his special journeys, was a fake. No, the real danger lay in the fact that even without glasses, a mustache, and a wig, at close range he had been recognized by Carolyn Wells yesterday. Which meant that if she recovered, it wasn't impossible that they might run into each other in New York again someday. In a face-to-face situation, she would recognize him again.

That must never happen. So, clearly she could not be allowed to recover.

There was no news about Hilda Johnson on any of the newscasts during the early hours, so her body hadn't yet been discovered. On the news at nine, it was announced that an elderly woman had been found stabbed to death in her Upper East Side apartment. He braced himself for the anchorman's next words.

"As was reported yesterday, the murder victim, Hilda Johnson, had called the police claiming she had seen someone deliberately push the woman who was hit by a van at Park and Eighty-first yesterday afternoon."

Frowning, he pointed the remote control and turned off the television. Unless the police were extremely stupid, they would investigate the possibility that Hilda Johnson was not the victim of a random crime.

If they tied Hilda Johnson's death to Carolyn Wells's supposed accident, there would be a media stampede. It might even come out that Carolyn Wells had been the one who phoned Susan Chandler's program and talked about a souvenir ring with the inscription "You belong to me."

People would read about it, would discuss it, he mused. It was even possible that the little gnome who ran that rattrap of a cut-rate souvenir store in Greenwich Village might remember that on several occasions a particular gentleman whose name he knew had come in to purchase one of the turquoise rings with that inscription.

When he was young he had heard the story of the woman who confessed to spreading scandal and was told that as her penance she was to cut open a feather pillow on a wind-swept day, then retrieve all of the feathers that were scattered. When she said that it was impossible, she was told that it was just as impossible to find and correct all the people who had heard her lies.

It was a story that had amused him at the time. He

had had a mental image of a particular woman he detested, bobbing and running hither and yon to recapture the elusive feathers.

But now he thought of the feather pillow story in a different context. Pieces were escaping from the scenario he had planned so carefully.

Carolyn Wells. Hilda Johnson. Susan Chandler. The gnome.

He was safe from Hilda Johnson. But the other three were still like feathers in the wind.

23

It was one of those golden October mornings that sometimes follow a particularly chilly day. The air felt fresh, and everything seemed to glow. Donald Richards decided to enjoy the morning by walking the distance between Central Park West and Eighty-eighth Street, and the WOR studio at Forty-first and Broadway.

He had already seen one client this morning, fifteen-year-old Greg Crane, who had been caught breaking into a neighbor's home. When the police interrogated Crane, he had admitted trashing three other houses in the swank Westchester community of Scarsdale where he lived.

He's a kid who has everything, but steals and wrecks other people's belongings apparently just for the thrill of it, Richards mused, as he walked at a brisk pace down the sidewalk adjacent to the park. He frowned at the thought that Crane was starting to fit the profile of one of those felons born without a conscience.

The fault certainly didn't appear to lie with the parents, he thought, as he nodded absently at a neighbor who was jogging in his direction. At least everything he had observed and learned about them indicated that they had been good and attentive parents.

He thought again of his session this morning. Some kids who start to display antisocial behavior in their teens can be straightened out, he thought. Others can't. I just hope we've gotten to him in time.

Then his thoughts shifted to Susan Chandler. She had been a prosecutor in juvenile court; it would be interesting to get her reading on a kid like Crane. Actually it would be interesting to get her reading on a *lot* of things, Richards decided, as he circumnavigated Columbus Circle.

He was twenty minutes early for the program and was told by the receptionist that Dr. Chandler was on her way and that he could wait in the green room. In the corridor he ran into the producer, Jed Geany.

Geany gave him a quick greeting and was ready to rush past when Richards stopped him. "I didn't think to ask for a tape of yesterday's program for my files," he said. "I'll be glad to pay for it, of course. Oh, and could you run one today as well?"

Geany shrugged. "Sure. Actually, I'm just about to make a tape of yesterday's program for some guy who phoned in. Says he wants it for his mother. Come on and I'll run one for you as well."

Richards followed him into the engineer's booth.

"You could tell this guy felt like a jerk for asking," Geany continued, "but he claims his mother never misses listening to Susan." He held up the envelope he already had addressed. "Why does that name sound familiar? I've been wracking my brain trying to remember where I've heard it."

Donald Richards opted not to reply, but had to force himself not to show how startled he was. "You can run off both tapes at once?"

"Sure."

As he watched the reels spin, Donald Richards thought back to the one visit he had had from Justin Wells. It had been the usual exploratory session, and Wells never came back.

Richards remembered that he had phoned Wells, urging him to get into treatment—with someone else—saying that he needed help, a lot of help.

Then having made the appropriate gestures, he had been vastly relieved. The truth was that for a very personal reason he was better off avoiding contact with Justin Wells.

24

When she rushed into the studio at ten of ten, Susan saw the disapproving look on her producer's face. "I know, Jed," she said hurriedly, "but I had kind of a crisis. Someone phoned who seemed to have a genuine problem. I couldn't just hang up on her."

She did not add that the "someone" was in fact her sister, Dee, who was back in California and sounded seriously depressed. *I feel so alone here,* she had said. *I'm going to take a cruise next week. Daddy is treating me to it. Don't you think that's a good idea? Who knows? I might even meet someone interesting.*

Then finally Dee had asked, *By the way, have you heard from Alex Wright?*

That was when Susan had realized the real reason for the call and had ended the conversation as quickly as possible.

"You're the one who's going to have the problem if you're not on time, Susan," Geany said matter-of-factly. "Don't blame me. I only work here."

Susan noticed the sympathetic glance Don Richards gave her. "You could have started the show with Dr. Richards," she said. "I told him yesterday he was a natural."

For the first part of the program they discussed how women could protect themselves and avoid getting into potentially dangerous situations.

"Look," Richards said. "Most women realize that if they park their cars in a dark, unattended lot, six blocks from nowhere, they're risking big trouble. On the other hand, those same women can be careless when at home. The way life is today, if you leave your doors unlocked, no matter how seemingly safe the neighborhood is, you're increasing your chances that you'll be the victim of a burglary, or perhaps worse.

"Times have changed," he continued. "I remember how my grandmother never used to lock her door. And if she did, she'd tape up a big sign, 'key in window box.' Those days, unfortunately, are over."

He has a nice manner, Susan thought as she listened to his friendly tone. He's not preachy.

At the next commercial she told him, "I wasn't kidding. I think I'd better look over my shoulder if I want to keep my job. You're darn good on air."

"Well, I'm finding I enjoy it," he acknowledged. "It's the ham in me, I guess. Although I have to admit that when I finish the publicity tour for this book, I'll be glad to go back to my mundane world."

"Not too mundane, I bet. Don't you do a lot of traveling?"

"A fair amount. I testify as an expert witness internationally."

"Ten seconds, Susan," the producer warned from the booth.

It was time to take calls from the listeners.

The first one was an inquiry about yesterday's show: "Did Karen keep her appointment at your office, Dr. Susan?"

"No, she did not," Susan said, "but if she's listening, I'm going to ask her please to get in touch with me, even if only by phone."

Several calls were directed to Donald Richards. One man had heard him testify in court and was impressed: "Doctor, you sounded like you really knew what you were talking about."

Richards raised his eyebrows to Susan. "I certainly hope I did." The next call shocked Susan.

"Dr. Richards, is the reason you wrote the book about vanishing women because your own wife disappeared?"

"Doctor, you don't have to answer . . ." Susan looked at Richards, waiting for a sign that she should cut off the call.

Instead, Richards shook his head. "My wife didn't actually 'disappear,' at least not in the sense we've been discussing. She died in an accident in front of witnesses. We have never been able to retrieve her body, but there is no connection between her death and my book."

His tone was controlled, but Susan could see raw emotion in the expression on his face. She could sense that he did not want her to comment on either the question or his answer, but her instant reaction was that whether he admitted it to himself or not, there had to be a connection between his wife's death and the subject of his book.

She looked at the monitor. "Our next call is from Tiffany in Yonkers. You're on, Tiffany."

"Dr. Susan, I love your program," the caller began. She had a young, animated voice.

"Thank you, Tiffany," Susan said briskly. "How can we help you?"

"Well, I was listening to your program yesterday, and you remember how that woman, Karen, talked about getting a souvenir turquoise ring from some guy, and said that the inside of the band was inscribed 'You belong to me'?"

"Yes, I do," Susan said quickly. "Do you know something about that man?"

Tiffany began to giggle. "Dr. Susan, if Karen is listening, I just want her to know that she was lucky not to bother with that guy. He must have been some cheapskate. My boyfriend bought a ring just like that for me as a joke one day last year when we were in Greenwich Village. It looked good, but it cost all of ten dollars."

"Where in the Village did you buy it?" Susan asked.

"Gee, I don't remember exactly. One of those dumpy little souvenir stores, the kind that sell plastic Statue of Libertys and brass elephants. You know the kind of place."

"Tiffany, if you do remember where it was, or if any of our other listeners know about that shop, please call me," Susan urged. "Or let me know about any other places that might carry that ring," she added.

"The little guy who runs the shop told us he made the rings himself," Tiffany said. "Listen, I broke up with my boyfriend, so you can have the ring. I'll mail it to you."

"Commercial," Jed warned into Susan's earphone.

"Many thanks, Tiffany," Susan said hurriedly, "and now for a message from our sponsors."

The moment the program was over, Donald Richards stood up. "Again, thanks, Susan, and forgive me if I rush off. I have a client waiting." Then he hesitated. "I'd really like to have dinner with you sometime," he said quietly. "You don't have to answer now. I'll call you at your office."

He was gone. Susan sat for a moment, gathering her notes and thinking about the last call. Was it possible that the souvenir ring Jane Clausen had found among Regina's possessions had been purchased in the city? If so, did that mean that the man responsible for her disappearance was from New York?

Still deep in concentration, she got up and went into the control room. Geany was putting a cassette into an envelope. "Richards got out fast," he said. "I guess he forgot he had asked me to make tapes of the programs." He shrugged. "So I'll mail them with this one." He pointed to the envelope addressed to Justin Wells. "That guy phoned yesterday to get a tape of the program. Said his mother missed it."

"Flattering," Susan observed. "See you tomorrow."

In the cab on the way back to the office, she opened the newspaper. On page three of the *Post* there was a picture of Carolyn Wells, an interior designer who had been injured in the accident yesterday afternoon, on Park Avenue. Susan read the story with keen interest. This was the case she had heard about on the news this morning—the one where the elderly woman claimed she had seen someone push Carolyn Wells.

Further down the column, she read, "husband, well-known architect Justin Wells . . ."

A moment later she was on the cell phone to the station. She caught Jed Geany just as he was leaving for lunch.

By the time the cab reached her office, Susan knew that Jed was sending the package addressed to Justin Wells to her by messenger.

Susan mentally reviewed her day. She had back-to-back appointments all afternoon. But after that she would take the tape to Lenox Hill Hospital, where, according to the chatty receptionist, Justin Wells was keeping vigil at his wife's bedside.

He may not want to talk to me, Susan thought as she paid the cabbie, but there's no question—whatever reason he has for wanting a tape of yesterday's program, it isn't because his mother missed it.

25

Jane Clausen had not been sure if she would be well enough to attend the meeting of the Clausen Family Trust. It had been a difficult, pain-filled night, and she longed to spend the day resting quietly at home.

Only the haunting knowledge that her time was running out gave her the drive necessary to get up at precisely the usual time, 7 A.M., to bathe, dress, and eat the light breakfast that Vera, her housekeeper of many years, had prepared for her.

As she sipped coffee, she picked up *The New York Times* and began to read the front page, then set the paper down. She simply could not concentrate on the events that apparently commanded the attention of the rest of the world. Her own world was narrowing to the point of vanishing, and she knew it.

She thought back to the previous afternoon. Her disappointment that "Karen" had not kept the appointment at Dr. Chandler's office continued to grow. Jane realized she had many questions for the woman: *What did the man you met look like? Did you have a sense of danger?*

The thought had come to her in the middle of the night. Regina had a keen intuition. Clearly if she had met a man and been attracted by him enough to change her itinerary, he must have appeared to be aboveboard.

"Aboveboard." And now that word was bothering her because it raised questions about Douglas.

Douglas Layton, a member of the Layton family, bore a name of distinction, one that guaranteed his background. He had spoken with affection of his cousins in Philadelphia, the children of her now-deceased contemporaries. Jane Clausen had known those Philadelphia Laytons when they were quite young, but had lost touch over the years. Still, she remembered them well, and several times lately when he mentioned them Doug had mixed up their names. She had to wonder how close he really was to them.

Doug's scholastic background was excellent. There was no question he was very intelligent. Hubert March, who was grooming Doug to be his successor, had suggested electing him to the board of trustees of the foundation.

So what *is* bothering me? Jane Clausen asked herself as she nodded her acceptance of the coffee refill that Vera was offering.

It was what happened yesterday, she decided. It was the fact that Douglas Layton was too busy with someone else to wait with her at Dr. Chandler's office.

When he called last evening, I let him know I wasn't pleased, Jane Clausen thought. She knew that should be the end of it, but it wasn't.

She considered what was beneath the surface. Douglas Layton knew he had a lot to lose by walking out of Dr. Chandler's office with that trumped-up excuse.

And clearly it was *trumped up*. She was sure he had been lying about his so-called appointment. But *why?*

This morning at the trustees' meeting they were going to decide on a number of substantial grants. It's very hard to accept the recommendations of someone you are beginning to have doubts about, Jane Clausen thought. If Regina were here, we'd talk this over together. *Two heads are better than one, Mother. We prove that, don't we?* Regina used to say. We were good problem-solvers together.

Susan Chandler. Jane thought of how strong a liking she had taken to the young psychologist. She's both wise and kind, she thought, remembering the compassion in Susan's eyes. She knew how disappointed I was yesterday, and she could see that I was in pain. Having that cup of tea with her was so comforting. I've never had much use for the business of rushing to therapists, but she came across immediately as a friend.

Jane Clausen stood up. It was time to go to the meeting. She wanted to take the time to study all the requests for grants thoroughly. This afternoon I'll phone Dr. Chandler and make an appointment to see her, she decided.

She smiled unconsciously as she thought, *I know Regina would approve.*

26

I must go down to the seas again . . .

The cadence of the words was a drumbeat in his head. He could see himself on the pier, showing his identification to a courteous member of the crew, hearing his greeting—*"Welcome aboard, sir!"*—walking up the metal gangway, being shown to his cabin.

He always took only the best accommodations, first class, with a private verandah. A penthouse suite would not be suitable—that would be too noticeable. He sought only to give the impression of impeccable taste, of substance, of the kind of reserve that comes with generations of breeding.

Of course it was easy to accomplish. And after gently rebuffing the first attempts at probing, he found that fellow passengers respected his privacy, perhaps even admired him for being so reserved, and turned their curiosity to more interesting subjects.

Once his presence had been established, he was free to prowl and select his prey.

The first voyage of that kind had been four years ago. Now the journey was almost over. Just one more to go. And now it was time to find her. There were a number of appropriate ships going to the place that had been ordained for the death of this last lonely lady. He had decided on the identity he would assume, that of an investor who had been raised in Belgium, the son of an American mother and British diplomat father. He had a new salt-and-pepper wig, part of so excellent a disguise that it somehow managed to give the visual effect of altering the contours of his face.

He couldn't wait to live the new role, to find the one, to let her fate be joined to Regina's, whose body, weighted with stones, rested beneath the busy waterway that was Kowloon Bay; to meld her story with that of Veronica, whose bones were rotting in the Valley of the Kings; with Constance, who had replaced Carolyn in Algiers; with Monica in London; with all these sisters in death.

I must go down to the seas again. But first there was

unfinished business to be attended to. This morning, listening once more to Dr. Susan's program, he had decided that one of the feathers in the wind needed to be removed immediately.

27

It had been fifty years since Abdul Parki had first arrived in America, a shy, slender sixteen-year-old from New Delhi. Immediately he had begun working for his uncle; his job was sweeping the floors and polishing the brass knickknacks that filled the cluttered shelves of his uncle's tiny souvenir shop on MacDougal Street in Greenwich Village. Now Abdul was the owner, but little else had changed. The store might have been frozen in time. Even the sign reading KHYEM SPECIALTY SHOP was an exact duplicate of the one that his uncle had hung.

Abdul was still slender, and though he had of necessity overcome his shyness, he had a natural reserve that kept him distant from his customers.

The only ones he ever talked to were those who appreciated the skill and effort he put into the small collection of inexpensive rings and bracelets he made himself. And though he, of course, had never inquired as to the reason, Abdul often wondered about the man who had come back on three different occasions to purchase turquoise rings with the inscription "You belong to me."

It amused Abdul, who himself had been married to his late wife for forty-five years, to think that this customer regularly changed girlfriends. The last time the man had been in, his business card had fallen from his wallet. Abdul had picked it up and glanced at it, then apologizing for being forward, he returned it. Seeing the look of displeasure on his customer's face, he had apologized again, calling the customer by name. Immediately he knew he had made a second mistake.

He doesn't want me to know who he is, and now he won't come back—that had been Abdul's immediate and regretful thought. And given the fact that a year had passed without a reappearance, he suspected that to be the case.

As his uncle had before him, Abdul closed the shop every day promptly at one o'clock, then went out for lunch. On this Tuesday afternoon he had the sign in his hand—CLOSED—RETURN AT 2 P.M.—and was just about to put it on the door, when his mysterious customer suddenly appeared, came inside, and greeted him warmly.

Abdul broke into a rare smile. "It's been a long time, sir. It's good to see you again."

"Good to see *you*, Abdul. I thought surely you'd have forgotten me by now."

"Oh, no, sir." He did not use the man's name, careful not to remind the customer of his mistake the last time they had been together.

"Bet you can't remember my name," his customer said, his tone genial.

I must have been wrong, Abdul thought. He wasn't angry at me after all. "Of course, I remember it, sir," he said. Smiling, he proved that indeed he did.

"Good for you," his customer said warmly. "Abdul, guess what? I need another ring. You know the one I mean. Hope you have one in stock."

"I think I have three, sir."

"Well, maybe I'll take them all. Here I'm keeping you from your lunch. Before any other customers show up, why don't we put the sign out and lock the door? Otherwise you'll never get out of here, and I know you're a creature of habit."

Abdul smiled again, pleased at the thoughtfulness of this remarkably friendly old customer. Willingly, he handed him the sign and watched him turn the lock. It was then that he noted with surprise that, even though it was a mild and sunny day, his customer was wearing gloves.

The handmade items were inside the glass-topped counter, near the cash register. Abdul went to the counter and removed a small tray. "Two of them are here, sir. There's one more in the back, on my work-bench. I'll get it."

With quick steps he walked through the curtained area that led to the small stockroom, one corner of which he had made into a combination office and workplace. The third turquoise ring was in a box. He had finished the engraving on it only the day before.

Three girls at once, he thought, smiling to himself. This guy does get around.

Abdul turned, the ring in his hand, then gasped in surprise. His customer had followed him into the stockroom.

"Did you find the ring?"

"Right here, sir." Abdul held it out, not understanding why he suddenly felt nervous and cornered.

When he saw the sudden flash of the knife, he understood. I was right to be afraid, he thought, as he felt a sharp pain and then slipped into darkness.

28

At ten minutes of three, just as her two o'clock patient was leaving, Susan Chandler received a call from Jane Clausen. She immediately sensed the tension lurking beneath the quiet, well-bred voice and the request for an appointment.

"I mean a *professional* visit," Mrs. Clausen said. "I need to discuss some problems I'm having, and I feel that I'd be very comfortable talking them over with you."

Before Susan could respond, Jane Clausen continued: "I'm afraid it's very important that I see you as soon as possible, even today, if that can be arranged."

Susan did not need to consult her calendar to answer. She had clients coming in for appointments at three and four o'clock. After that she had intended to go immediately to Lenox Hill Hospital. Obviously that would have to wait.

"I'll be free at five o'clock, Mrs. Clausen."

As soon as she broke the connection, Susan dialed Lenox Hill Hospital, having already looked up the number. When she finally got through to an operator, she explained she was trying to reach the husband of a woman in intensive care.

"I'll put you through to the ICU waiting room," the operator told her.

A woman answered. Susan asked if Justin Wells was there.

"Who's calling?"

Susan understood the reason for the hesitation in the other woman's voice. The media must be hounding him, she thought. "Dr. Susan Chandler," she said. "Mr. Wells requested a tape of a radio program I did yesterday, and I wanted to bring it to him myself if he's still going to be at the hospital at six-thirty."

From the muffled sound in her ear, she could tell that the woman had covered the receiver with her hand. Even so, she could make out the question being asked: "Justin, did you request a tape of Dr. Susan Chandler's program yesterday?"

She could hear the answer distinctly: "That's ridiculous, Pamela. Someone's playing a sick joke."

"Dr. Chandler, I'm afraid there's been a mistake."

Before she could be disconnected, Susan said hurriedly, "I apologize. That was the message I received from my producer. I'm terribly sorry to have bothered Mr. Wells at a time like this. May I ask how Mrs. Wells is?"

There was a brief pause. "Pray for her, Dr. Chandler."

The connection was broken, and an instant later a computer voice was saying, "If you'd like to make a call, please hang up and try again."

Susan sat for a long minute, staring at the phone. Had the request for the tape been intended as a practical joke, and if so, why? Or had Justin Wells made the call and now needed to deny it to the person he addressed as Pamela? And again, if so, why?

Susan realized these were questions that would have to wait. Janet was already announcing the arrival of her three o'clock client.

29

Doug Layton stood outside the partly opened door of the small office Jane Clausen kept for herself in the Clausen Family Trust suite in the Chrysler Building. He didn't even have to strain to hear what she was saying on the phone to Dr. Susan Chandler.

As he listened, he began to perspire. He was fairly certain that *he* was the problem she wanted to discuss with Chandler.

He knew he had bungled their meeting this morning. Mrs. Clausen had arrived early, and he had brought coffee to her, planning to smooth over any irritation she might still feel. He frequently had coffee with her before the trust meeting, using the time to discuss the various requests for grants.

When he had arrived this morning, she had the agenda spread out before her and looked up at him, her eyes cool and dismissive. "I don't care for any coffee," she had told him. "You go ahead. I'll see you in the boardroom."

Not even a cursory "Thank you, Doug."

There was one file that had drawn her attention in particular, because she brought it up at the meeting, asking a lot of tough questions. The file contained information on moneys marked for use at a facility for orphaned children in Guatemala.

I had everything under control, Doug thought angrily, and then I blundered. Hoping to head off any discussion, like an imbecile, he had said, "That orphanage was particularly important to Regina, Mrs. Clausen. She once told me that."

Doug shivered remembering the icy gaze Jane Clausen had directed at him. He had tried to cover himself by adding hastily, "I mean, you quoted her as saying that yourself at one of our first meetings, Mrs. Clausen."

As usual, Hubert March, the chairman, was half asleep, but Doug could see the faces of the other trustees, who stared at him appraisingly as Jane Clausen said coldly, "No, I never said any such thing."

And now she was making a date to see Dr. Chandler. Hearing the click of the telephone receiver on the cradle, Doug Layton tapped on the door and waited for Mrs. Clausen's response. For a long moment, she did not respond. Then as he was about to knock again, he heard a faint groan, and rushed in.

Jane Clausen was leaning back in the chair, her face contorted in pain. She looked up at him, shook her head, and pointed past him. He knew what she meant. Get out and close the door behind you.

Silently he obeyed. There was no question that her condition was worsening. She was dying.

He went directly to the receptionist. "Mrs. Clausen has a touch of a headache," he told the woman. "I think you should hold any calls until she's had a chance to rest."

Back in his own office, he sat at his desk. Realizing

that his palms were soaked, he pulled a handkerchief out of his pocket, dried them, then got up and went out to the men's room.

There he dashed cold water on his face, combed his hair, straightened his tie, and looked in the mirror. He always had been grateful that his appearance—dark blond hair, steel-gray eyes, and aristocratic nose—had been the product of the Layton genetic code. His mother was still vaguely pretty, but he winced at the memory of his maternal grandparents, with their plump, nondescript features.

Now he was sure that in his Paul Stuart jacket and slacks and maroon-and-blue tie, he looked the part of the trusted advisor who would handle the affairs of *the late* Jane Clausen in the manner she would have wanted. There was no question that on her death Hubert March would turn the running of the trust over to him.

Everything had gone so well until now. In her final days Jane Clausen could not be allowed to interfere with his master plan.

30

In Yonkers, twenty-five-year-old Tiffany Smith was still stunned that she actually had gotten through to Dr. Susan Chandler herself, and had talked to her, live, on air. A waitress on the evening shift at The Grotto, a neighborhood trattoria, she was famous for never forgetting a customer's face or what they had ordered at previous dinners.

Names, though, didn't matter, so she never bothered to remember them. It was easier to call everyone "doll" or "honey."

Since her roommate's marriage, Tiffany lived alone in a small apartment on the second floor of a two-family house. Her routine was to sleep till nearly ten each morning, then to listen to Dr. Susan in bed while she enjoyed her first cup of coffee.

As she put it, "Being between boyfriends, it's comforting to know that a lot of women are having problems with their fellows too." A wiry-thin, teased blonde, with narrow, shrewd eyes, Tiffany displayed a sardonic outlook on life that was appealing to some and off-putting to others.

Yesterday, when she heard the woman who called herself Karen talk with Dr. Susan about the turquoise ring some guy had given her on a cruise, she thought immediately about Matt Bauer, who had given her a similar ring. After they broke up she tried to pretend that the sentiment engraved on it, "You belong to me," was stupid and gooey, but she didn't really mean it.

The phone call to Dr. Susan this morning had been an impulse, and almost immediately she regretted telling her that Matt was a cheapskate, just because the ring had only cost ten dollars. It actually was pretty, and she admitted to herself that she made that remark only because Matt had dropped her.

As the day wore on, Tiffany thought more and more about that afternoon last year she had spent with Matt in Greenwich Village. By four o'clock, as she got ready for work, fluffing her hair and applying her makeup, she realized that the name of the shop where they bought the ring was not going to come to her.

"Let's see," she said aloud. "We went to the Village for lunch at a sushi bar first, then went to see that dumb movie Matt thought was so great, and that I pretended to like. Not a word of English, just a lot of jabbering. Then we were walking around and passed that souvenir shop, and I said, 'Let's stop in.'

"Then Matt bought me a souvenir." That was back when Matt really acted as though he liked me, Tiffany thought. We were trying to decide between a brass monkey and a miniature Taj Mahal, and the owner was giving us all the time we needed. He was behind the glass counter where the cash register was when that classy guy came in.

She had noticed him right away, because she had just turned away from Matt, who had picked up something else and was reading the tag that said why it was special. The guy didn't seem to realize they were there, because they'd been standing behind a screen with camels and pyramids painted on it. She hadn't been able to hear what the man said, but the owner took something from the glass counter by the cash register.

The customer was a doll, Tiffany reflected, remembering still the attractive man she had seen in the shop that day. She figured he was the kind who went out with the people she only read about in the columns. Not like the jerks who stuff themselves at The Grotto, she thought. She remembered the look of surprise on his face when he turned around and saw her standing there. After the man left, the store owner said, "That gentleman has purchased several of these rings for his ladyfriends. Maybe you'd like to see one."

It was pretty, Tiffany thought, and she knew Matt could see by the amount rung up on the cash register that it cost only ten dollars, so she didn't mind telling him she'd like to have it.

Then the owner showed us the inscription, Tiffany remembered, and Matt blushed and said that was fine, and I thought maybe it was a sign that this time I'd met a guy who would last.

Tiffany penciled her eyebrows and reached for her mascara. But then we broke up, she thought ruefully.

Wistfully she looked at the turquoise ring that she kept in the little ivory box that her grandfather bought for her grandmother on their honeymoon trip to Niagara Falls. She took it out and held it up and admired it. I'm not going to send it to Dr. Susan, she thought. Who knows? Maybe Matt will call me up sometime. Maybe he still doesn't have a steady girlfriend.

But I promised Dr. Susan I'd send it, she reminded herself. So what shall I do? Wait a minute! Tiffany thought. What Dr. Susan really seemed interested in was the *location* of the shop. So instead of sending the ring, maybe I can just narrow down the location enough to help her. I remember that there was a porno shop across the street, and I'm pretty sure it was only a couple of blocks away from a subway station. She's smart. She should be able to find it with that information.

Relieved that she had made the proper decision, Tiffany put on her blue dangle earrings. Then she sat down and wrote Dr. Susan a note describing the location of the shop as she remembered it, and explaining why she was hanging on to the ring. She signed the note, "Your sincere admirer, Tiffany."

By then, she was running late, as usual, and didn't take the time to drop the letter in the mailbox.

She thought of that omission later, as she was plopping four orders of reheated lasagna in front of pain-in-the-neck customers at The Grotto. I hope they burn their mouths, she thought—they only use their tongues to complain.

Thinking about the customers' tongues gave her an idea. She would call Dr. Susan tomorrow instead of writing. Once she was on the air, she could explain that she wanted to apologize for making that crack about the ring being cheap, that she only said it because she missed Matt so much. He was such a nice guy, and could Dr. Susan suggest some way they might get together again? He hadn't answered her calls last year, but she was pretty sure he wasn't going around with anyone else yet.

Tiffany watched with satisfaction as one of her customers took a bite of lasagna and grabbed for the water glass. That way, maybe I'll get some free advice, she thought, or maybe Matt's mother or one of her friends will be listening and hear his name and tell him, and he'll be flattered and give me a call.

What's to lose? Tiffany asked herself as she turned to a table of newly seated diners, people whose names she didn't know but whom she recognized as always leaving a lousy tip.

31

Alex Wright lived in the four-story brownstone on East Seventy-eighth Street that had been his home since childhood. It was still furnished as his mother had left it, with dark, heavy Victorian tables, buffets, and bookcases; overstuffed couches and chairs upholstered in rich brocades, antique Persian carpets, and graceful objets d'art. Visitors exclaimed about the traditional beauty of the turn-of-the-century mansion.

Even the fourth floor, most of which had been designed as a play area for Alex, remained the same. Some of the built-ins, commissioned from F.A.O. Schwarz, were so distinctive that they had been part of a feature in *Architectural Digest*.

Alex said he had not redecorated the brownstone for one reason only: At some point he intended to get married, and when that happened he would leave any changes to his wife. On one occasion when he made that statement, a friend had teased, "Suppose she's into supermodern designs, or even wants something retro and psychedelic?"

Alex had smiled and replied, "Wouldn't happen; she never would have gotten to fiancée status."

He lived relatively simply, never having been comfortable with a staff of servants in the house, perhaps because both his mother and father were known as difficult employers. The constant turnover of help, as well as the muttered comments he overheard about his parents, had distressed him as a child. Now he employed only Jim, as chauffeur, and Marguerite, a marvelously efficient and blessedly quiet housekeeper. She arrived at the Seventy-eighth Street house promptly at eight-thirty each morning, in time to prepare breakfast for Alex, and she stayed to cook dinner on those occasions when he planned to be home, which wasn't more than twice a week.

Single, attractive, and with the allure of the Wright fortune behind him, Alex had always been firmly entrenched on the social A list. Nonetheless he had maintained a relatively low public profile, because while he enjoyed interesting dinner parties, he abhorred personal publicity and always avoided the big society events that some people found exhilarating.

On Tuesday he spent the better part of the day at his desk in the foundation headquarters, then in the late afternoon played squash with friends at the club. He hadn't been sure of his evening plans and had instructed Marguerite to prepare what he called a "contingency dinner."

So, when he arrived home at six-thirty, his first stop was to check the refrigerator. A bowl of Marguerite's excellent chicken soup was ready for the microwave oven, and lettuce and sliced chicken were prepared for a sandwich.

Nodding his approval, Alex went to the drinks table in the library, selected a bottle of Bordeaux, and poured himself a glass. He had just begun to sip when the phone rang.

The answering machine was on, so he decided to let it screen his calls. He raised his eyebrows when Dee Chandler Harriman announced herself. Her voice, low and pleasing, was hesitant.

"Alex, I hope you don't mind. I asked Dad for your home number. I just wanted to thank you for being so nice to me the other day at Binky and Dad's cocktail party. I've been down a lot lately, and although you don't know it, you really helped, just by being a nice guy. I'm going to try to kill the blues by going on a cruise next week. Anyhow, thank you. I just had to let you know. Oh, by the way, just for the record, my phone number is 310-555-6347."

I guess she doesn't know I asked her sister out to dinner, Alex thought. Dee is gorgeous, but Susan is much more interesting. He took another sip of his wine and closed his eyes.

Yes, Susan Chandler *was* interesting. In fact, she had been on his mind all day.

32

Jane Clausen phoned Susan shortly before four o'clock to tell her that she could not keep their appointment. "I'm afraid I have to rest," she apologized.

"You don't sound very well, Mrs. Clausen," Susan had said. "Should you see your doctor?"

"No. An hour's nap does wonders. I'm just sorry to miss the chance to talk with you today."

Susan had told her that if she wanted to come later, it would be fine. "I'll be here for quite a while, I have a great deal of paperwork to catch up on," she assured her.

Thus, at six o'clock she was still in her office when Jane Clausen arrived for their meeting. The ashen complexion of her visitor reinforced Susan's realization of how seriously ill the woman was. The kindest thing that could happen to her would be to know the truth about Regina's disappearance, she thought.

"Dr. Chandler," Mrs. Clausen began, a touch of hesitation in her voice.

"Please call me Susan. Dr. Chandler sounds so formal," Susan said with a smile.

Jane Clausen nodded. "It's hard to break old habits. All her life, my mother called our neighbor, who was her closest friend, Mrs. Crabtree. Too much of that reserve rubbed off on me, I suppose. Maybe too much on Regina as well. She was quite reticent socially." She glanced down for a moment and then looked directly at Susan. "You met my lawyer yesterday. Douglas Layton. What did you think of him?"

The question surprised Susan. I'm the one who's supposed to gently prod, she thought wryly. "He seemed nervous," she said, deciding to be direct in her response.

"And you were surprised that he didn't wait with me?"

"Yes, I was."

"Why were you surprised?"

Susan did not have to consider her answer. "Because it was entirely possible that you were going to meet a woman who might have shed light on your daughter's disappearance—perhaps even a woman who could have described a man who might have been involved in that disappearance. It was potentially a very significant moment for you. I would have expected him to stay with you for support."

Jane Clausen nodded. "Exactly. Susan, Douglas Layton told me all along that he did not know my daughter. Now from something he said this morning, I think that he *did* know her."

"Why would he lie about that?" Susan asked.

"I don't know. I did some checking today. The Laytons of Philadelphia are indeed his second cousins, but they say they scarcely remember him. He, on the other hand, has spoken at length of his familiarity with them. It turns out that his father, Ambrose Layton, was a ne'er-do-well who went through his inheritance in a few years, then disappeared."

Jane Clausen spoke slowly, frowning in concentration. Her words were measured. "It is to Douglas's credit that he received scholarships to Stanford University, then to Columbia Law School. Clearly he is very intelligent. His first job, with Kane and Ross, involved a great deal of traveling, and he's a gifted linguist, which is one of the reasons he moved so quickly into a position of power when he went with Hubert March's firm. He is now on the board of our foundation."

She is trying to be fair, Susan thought, but she's not just worried—I think she's afraid.

"The point is, Susan, Douglas definitely gave me the impression that he knew his cousins intimately. Thinking back, I realize that he told me that after I said I'd lost touch with them. Today, I realized he was eavesdropping when I spoke with you. The door was partially open, and I could see him reflected in the glass of the cabinet. I was terribly startled. Why would he do that? What reason has he to skulk around me?"

"Did you ask him?"

"No. I had a weak spell and wasn't up to confronting him. I don't want to put him on guard. I am going to have one particular grant audited. It was one we were reviewing at today's meeting, an orphanage in Guatemala. Doug is scheduled to go there next week and present a report at the next trustees' meeting. I questioned the amounts we've been giving, and Douglas blurted out that Regina had told him it was one of her favorite charities. He said it as though it had been thoroughly discussed between them."

"Yet he's denied knowing her."

"Yes. Susan, I needed to share this with you because I have suddenly realized one possible reason why Douglas Layton rushed out of this office yesterday."

Susan knew what Jane Clausen was about to tell her—that Douglas Layton had been afraid to come face to face with "Karen."

Jane Clausen left a few minutes later. "I think that tomorrow morning my doctor will want me to go into the hospital for some further treatment," she said as she was departing. "I wanted to share this with you first. I know that at one time you were an assistant district attorney. In truth, I don't know whether I brought my suspicions to you to receive insight from a psychologist, or to ask a former officer of the court how to go about opening an inquiry."

33

Dr. Donald Richards had left the studio right after the broadcast and belatedly he realized that Rena would have prepared lunch.

He found a pay phone and dialed his home number. "I forgot to tell you; I have to run an errand," he told Rena apologetically.

"Doctor, why do you always do this to me when I'm fixing something hot for you?"

"That's the kind of question my wife always asked me. Can you put it on a back burner or something? I'll be an hour or so." He smiled to himself. Then, realizing why his eyes felt strained, he took off his reading glasses and slipped them into his pocket.

When he reached his office an hour and a half later, Rena had his lunch ready for him. "I'll put the tray on your desk, Doctor," she said.

His two o'clock appointment was a severely anorexic thirty-year-old businesswoman. It was her fourth visit, and Richards listened and jotted notes on a pad.

The patient was opening up to him at last, talking about the painful experience of growing up overweight and never being able to stay on a diet. "I loved to eat, but then I'd look in the mirror and see what I was doing to myself. I began to hate my body, then I hated food for *doing* that to me."

"Do you still hate food?"

"I loathe it, but sometimes I think how great it would be to enjoy the act of dining. I'm dating someone now, someone really important to me, and I know I'm going to lose him if I don't change. He said he's tired of watching me push food around the plate."

Motivation, Don thought. It's always the first major step to any change. Susan Chandler's face flashed through his mind.

At ten of three, after he had seen the patient out, he phoned Susan Chandler, reasoning that she undoubtedly spaced appointments as he did—see a patient for fifty minutes, then take a ten-minute break before the next appointment.

Her secretary told him that Susan was on the phone. "I'll wait," he said.

"I'm afraid she has another call already waiting."

"I'll take my chances."

At four minutes of three he was about to give up; his own three o'clock patient was already in the reception area. Then Susan's voice, a bit breathless, came on. "Dr. Richards?" she said.

"Just because you're in your office doesn't mean you can't call me Don."

Susan laughed. "I'm sorry. I'm glad you called. It's been a bit hectic here, and I wanted to thank you for being a great guest."

"And I want to thank you for all the great exposure. My publisher was very happy to hear me talking about the book on your program for two days." He glanced at his watch. "I've got a patient coming in and you probably do too, so let's cut to the chase. Can you have dinner with me tonight?"

"Not tonight. I have to work late."

"Tomorrow night?"

"Yes, that would be nice."

"Let's say sevenish, and I'll call you at the office tomorrow when I figure out a place."

A really planned date, he thought. Too late now.

"I'll be here all afternoon," Susan told him.

Richards jotted down the time—sevenish—muttered a hasty good-bye, and put down the receiver. Even though he knew he had to hurry to see his patient, he took a moment to reflect on tomorrow night, wondering just how much he should disclose to Susan Chandler.

34

Dee Chandler Harriman had timed her call to Alex Wright with the hope of catching him at home. She had phoned from the modeling agency office in Beverly Hills at quarter of four. That meant it was quarter of seven in New York, a time that she thought Alex might be home. When he didn't pick up, she decided that if he were out to dinner, he might try to reach her later in the evening.

With that hope, Dee went directly from work to her condo in Palos Verdes, and at seven o'clock was listlessly preparing herself a meal of a scrambled egg, toast, and coffee. In the past two years, I've hardly ever stayed home in the evening, she thought. I *couldn't* without Jack. I had to be with people. But tonight, she realized, she was feeling more bored and restless than she was lonely.

I'm tired of working, Dee admitted to herself. I'm ready to move back to New York. But not to get another job. "I can't even fix a decent scrambled egg," she complained aloud, as she realized that the flame under the pan was too high and the egg was turning brown. She remembered how Jack had loved to fool around in the kitchen. That's another thing Susan is better at than I am, she thought. She's a good cook.

But that wasn't always a necessary talent. Anyone who married Alex Wright wouldn't have to worry about recipes and shopping lists, she told herself.

She decided to eat in the living room and was setting her tray on the coffee table when the phone rang. It was Alex Wright.

When she replaced the receiver ten minutes later, Dee was smiling. He had called because he was concerned. He said she sounded so down, and he thought she might want to chat. He explained that he had enjoyed his evening with Susan, and was about to invite her to a dinner Saturday night, celebrating a recent grant from the Wright Foundation to the New York Public Library.

Dee congratulated herself on her quick thinking. She had told him that, on the way to Costa Rica to board the cruise, she was going to stop in New York and would be there over the weekend. Alex had taken the hint and invited her to the dinner too.

After all, Dee told herself as she picked up the tray with the now-cold food, it isn't as if Susan is really involved with him yet.

35

After Jane Clausen left her office on Tuesday evening, Susan went over paperwork until nearly seven, then phoned Jed Geany at home. "Problem," she announced briskly. "I called Justin Wells to see about getting the tape to yesterday's program to him, and he absolutely denies having requested it."

"Then why would he have wanted it marked to his personal attention?" Geany asked, his tone reasonable. "Susan, I can tell you this. Whoever the guy was who called was nervous. Maybe Wells doesn't want anyone to know about his interest in the tape. Or maybe the reason he wanted it doesn't exist. That's possible. He's probably afraid now that we'll send him a bill for it. In fact, at first he asked for just the call-in section of the program. I think that's actually the only thing he was interested in."

"The woman who was hit by a van on Park Avenue yesterday is his wife," Susan said.

"See what I mean? He has other things on his mind, poor guy."

"You're probably right. See you tomorrow." She hung up the phone and sat pondering the situation. One way or another, I'm going to meet Justin Wells, she decided, and right now I'm going to listen to the call-in section of yesterday's program.

She took the cassette out of her shoulder bag, snapped it into the tape recorder with the second side up, and pushed the FAST-FORWARD button. At the call-in section, she stopped the tape, pushed PLAY, and began to listen intently.

All the calls were run-of-the-mill, except for the one from the woman with the low, strained voice who identified herself only as "Karen," and who talked about the turquoise ring.

That *has* to be the call Justin Wells—or whoever it was—is interested in, she thought, but it's been a long day, and I can't figure out why now. She collected her coat, turned off the lights, locked the office door, and started down the corridor to the elevator.

They need to put in better lighting here, she decided. Nedda's office was completely dark, and the long hallway was deeply shadowed. Unconsciously, she quickened her steps.

The day had been tiring, and she was tempted to hail a cab. She resisted, however, and feeling somewhat virtuous, she began to walk home. On the way she found herself thinking through Jane Clausen's visit and the concern she had voiced about Douglas Layton. Mrs. Clausen was clearly very ill. Was that affecting her perception of Layton? Susan wondered.

It *is* possible that Layton had a meeting he couldn't change yesterday, she thought, and he may simply have been waiting for Mrs. Clausen to get off the phone before going into her office this morning.

But what about Mrs. Clausen's belief that he had known Regina and lied about it? Chris Ryan's name jumped into Susan's mind. A retired FBI agent she had worked with when she was in the Westchester County D.A.'s office, Chris now had his own security firm. He could do a little discreet digging about Layton. She decided that she would contact Mrs. Clausen in the morning and suggest that.

Susan looked about her as she walked. The narrow streets of Greenwich Village never failed to fascinate her. She loved the mix of turn-of-the-century townhouses on quiet streets, and the traffic-filled main arteries that suddenly twisted or changed direction like streams wandering through mountains.

As she walked, she found herself glancing around to see if she could catch a glimpse of a souvenir shop like the one today's caller—Tiffany—had talked about. She hadn't really thought much about her. Tiffany claimed she too had a turquoise ring similar to the one "Karen" had discussed, and she said that her boyfriend had bought it in Greenwich Village. Let her send it, please, Susan prayed. If I could just get to compare it with the one Mrs. Clausen gave me. Then, if it turned out that they were identical, and were made right around here, it might be a first step toward solving Regina's disappearance.

A mazing how much a cold walk clears the brain, Susan thought as she finally reached her front door. Inside the apartment, she followed the at-home ritual she had planned for the night before. It was eight o'clock. She changed into a caftan, went to the refrigerator, and got out the salad makings she had begun to prepare before Alex Wright's unexpected call.

Tonight is definitely stay-at-home time, she decided as she reached in the cupboard for a package of linguine. While the water for the pasta was heating, and the basil-and-tomato sauce was defrosting in the microwave, she turned on her home computer and checked her e-mail.

It was run-of-the-mill stuff except for a few comments on how interesting Dr. Richards was, and suggestions that Susan should have him back as a guest. On impulse, she checked to see if Richards had a website.

He did. With increasing interest, Susan zeroed in on the personal information: Dr. Donald J. Richards, born in Darien, Connecticut; raised in Manhattan; attended Collegiate Prep; B.A. Yale; M.D. and Ph.D. clinical psychology Harvard; M.A. criminology NYU. Father, late Dr. Donald R. Richards; mother, Elizabeth Wallace Richards, of Tuxedo Park, N.Y. No siblings. Married to Kathryn Carver (deceased).

A long list of published articles followed, as well as reviews of his book *Vanishing Women.* Then Susan found information that raised her eyebrows. A brief biography stated that Dr. Richards had spent a year between his junior and senior years in college, working on a round-the-world ocean liner as assistant cruise director, and under the heading of "recreation," that he frequently took short cruises. As his favorite ship, he had named the *Gabrielle.* Noting that that was the one on which he had met his wife.

Susan stared at the screen. "But that's the same ship Regina Clausen was on when she disappeared," she said aloud.

36

Pamela stayed with Justin Wells in the waiting room of the ICU at Lenox Hill Hospital until nearly midnight. At that time a doctor came out and urged them both to go home. "Your wife has stabilized somewhat," he told Justin. "Her condition may not change for weeks. You won't do her any favor if you get sick yourself."

"Has she tried to talk anymore?" Justin asked.

"No. Nor will she anytime soon. Not as long as she remains in this deep coma."

Justin sounds almost *afraid* that she'll talk—what's that about? Pamela wondered, then decided that she was so tired her brain was playing tricks. She took Justin's hand. "We're going," she said matter-of-factly. "We'll get a cab, and I'll drop you off."

He nodded, and like an obedient child, let her lead him out. He did not talk on the short ride to Fifth and Eighty-first Street, but sat hunched forward, his hands clasped together, his neck drooping as though all the force of his powerful body had drained away.

"We're here, Justin," Pamela said when the taxi stopped and the doorman opened the door to let him out.

He turned and looked at her, his eyes dull. "All of this is my fault," he said. "I called Carolyn a little while before the accident. I know I upset her. She probably wasn't paying attention to the traffic. If she dies, I'll feel like I killed her."

Before Pamela could answer, he was out of the cab. But what could I tell him? she wondered. If Justin had reverted to one of his jealous or suspicious moods when he called, then indeed Carolyn would have been distracted and upset.

But she wouldn't have been so foolish as to show him that turquoise ring and talk about the man who gave it to her, would she? And why in the name of God would he have wanted a tape of the *Ask Dr. Susan* program, she wondered. *That* made no sense at all.

As the cab waited behind a car trying to park, another scenario came to Pamela's mind. Was it possible that the old woman on the television had been right, that Carolyn had been pushed? And if so, was Justin, for his own reasons, trying to set up the belief that she had been distracted and unwittingly stepped into the path of the van?

Then Pamela remembered something—something she had dismissed at the time. Two years ago, before she went on the cruise, Carolyn had said, "Justin's insecurity about our relationship is so deep that sometimes I'm afraid of him."

37

Sometimes at night he took long walks. He did it when everything built up to the point that it became necessary to ease the tensions. This afternoon had gone easily enough. The old man in the souvenir shop had died quietly. There's been nothing about his death on the evening news programs, he thought, so the odds were that when the store didn't reopen, nobody had cared enough to see if anything was wrong.

His goal tonight had been just to walk, however aimlessly, through the city streets, so he was almost surprised to find himself near Downing Street. Susan Chandler lived on Downing. Was she in now? he wondered. He realized that his walking here tonight, especially in a relatively unconscious state, was an indication that he could not allow her to keep making trouble. Since yesterday morning, he'd had to eliminate two people—Hilda Johnson and Abdul Parki, neither of whom he had ever intended to kill. A third, Carolyn Wells, was either going to die or would have to be eliminated should she ever recover. Even though she didn't know his real name, if she were able to talk, he had no doubt she would tell the doctors and the police that the man she knew as Owen Adams on the cruise was the one who had pushed her.

Even though the potential risk was slight, since all the credentials for Owen Adams were untraceable to him, he couldn't afford to let it go that far. The real danger was that Carolyn had recognized him, and if she recovered then there was no telling what could happen. They could conceivably meet at a cocktail party or in a restaurant. New York was a big city, but circles overlapped and paths crossed. Anything was possible.

Of course, as long as she was in a coma she posed no immediate danger. The real danger might be Tiffany, the girl who had called in to Dr. Susan Chandler's program today. As he walked along

Downing Street, he cursed himself. He remembered his visit last year to Parki's shop—he had thought it was empty. From the sidewalk he hadn't been able to see that young couple standing behind the screen.

The minute he had noticed them, he knew he had made a mistake. The girl, one of those boldly attractive young women, had been eyeing him, sending signals that she found him attractive. It wouldn't matter, except he was sure she could recognize him if she saw him again. If Tiffany was the one who phoned in to *Ask Dr. Susan* today about the ring, and Tiffany and that girl from the shop were the same person, she had to be silenced. Tomorrow he would find a way to learn from Susan Chandler if this Tiffany person had sent the ring, and if so, what she had written to accompany it.

Another feather in the wind, he thought. When would it end? One thing for certain. By next week, Susan Chandler must be stopped.

38

On Wednesday morning, Oliver Baker was both nervous about being in the police station and thrilled by his role as witness. He had spent Monday night enthralling his wife and teenage daughters with his story of how if he had been a few feet nearer to the curb, he might have been the one to start across the street first and been hit by that van. Together they had watched the five, the six, and the eleven o'clock news on Monday night, on which Oliver had been one of the bystanders interviewed. "There but for the grace of God, go I, that was my feeling when I saw the van hit her," he had told the reporter. "I mean, I could *see* the look on her face. She was lying on her back, and in that split second she knew she was going to get hit."

A mild, eager-to-please man in his mid-fifties, Oliver was the produce manager at a D'Agostino's supermarket, a position he thoroughly enjoyed. He delighted in knowing the store's more upscale customers by name, and in being able to ask personal questions like, "Gordon enjoying his first year at prep school, Mrs. Lawrence?"

Seeing himself on television was one of the most exciting experiences Oliver had ever known, and now, to be asked to come into the police station to discuss the incident further, just added more drama.

He waited on a bench in the 19th Precinct station, the soft tweed hat his brother had brought him from Ireland in his hand. Looking around with downcast eyes, it occurred to him that someone might think he was in trouble himself, or perhaps had a relative in jail. That thought made his lips twitch, and he told himself to remember to tell that to Betty and the girls tonight.

"Captain Shea will see you now, sir." The desk sergeant pointed to a closed door past his desk.

Oliver quickly stood, straightened the collar of his jacket, and walked with swift but timid steps to the captain's office.

At Shea's brisk command to "Come in," he turned the handle and pushed the door slowly as though afraid of inadvertently hitting someone behind it. But a moment later, seated across the desk from the captain, Oliver lost his hesitancy in the exhilaration of telling his now-familiar story.

"You were not directly behind Mrs. Wells?" Shea interrupted.

"No, sir. I was somewhat to the left."

"Had you noticed her at all prior to the incident?"

"Not really. There were a lot of people at the corner. The light had just changed to red when I got there, so by the time it was about to change again, there was a pretty good crowd at the corner."

This is going nowhere, Tom Shea thought. Oliver Baker was the tenth witness they had interviewed, and like most of the accounts, his story differed somewhat from the others. Hilda Johnson had been the only one who definitely had insisted that Carolyn Wells had been pushed; now Hilda was dead. There was complete disagreement among the bystanders as to whether or not Mrs. Wells was carrying anything. Two were fairly certain they had noticed a manila envelope; three couldn't be sure; the remainder were certain it had not existed. Only Hilda had been adamant, claiming someone had yanked a manila envelope from under the victim's arm as she was pushed.

Oliver was eager to continue his story. "And let me tell you, Captain, I had bad dreams last night, thinking of that poor woman sprawled on the road."

Captain Shea smiled sympathetically at Oliver, encouraging him to continue.

"I mean," Oliver added, "as I was telling Betty—" He paused. "Betty's my wife. As I was telling her, that poor woman was probably just doing an errand, maybe going to the post office, and never knew when she left her home that she might not see it again."

"What makes you think she was going to the post office?" Shea snapped.

"Because she had a stamped manila envelope under her arm."

"You're *sure* of that?"

"Yes, I'm sure. I think it started to slip, because just as the light changed, she began to turn, then lost her balance. The man behind her tried to steady her, I think, and that's how he happened to take the envelope. The old woman was all wrong about the way it happened. I wonder if that man mailed it for her? That's what I would have done."

"Did you get a look at him, at this man who took the envelope?" Shea asked.

"No. I couldn't take my eyes off Mrs. Wells."

"That man who took the envelope—did he try to help her?"

"No, I don't think so. A lot of people turned away— one woman almost fainted. A couple of men did rush to help, but they seemed to know what they were doing and yelled at everyone else to stay back."

"You have no impression of what this man looked like, the one who took the envelope as he was perhaps trying to steady Mrs. Wells?"

"Well, he had on a topcoat, a Burberry or one that *looked* like a Burberry." Oliver was proud that he had said "Burberry" instead of just raincoat.

When Oliver Baker had left, Captain Shea leaned back in his chair and folded his hands across his chest. His gut instinct was still telling him that there was a connection between Hilda Johnson's insistence that Carolyn Wells had been pushed and Hilda's own death only hours later. But nobody else on the scene corroborated Hilda's version. And there was always the possibility that Hilda's television appearance had attracted some nut to her.

In that case, he told himself, like many victims of circumstance, both Hilda Johnson and Carolyn Wells had simply been in the wrong place at the wrong time.

39

On Wednesday morning, Doug Layton set his strategy into place. He knew he had a long way to go to placate Jane Clausen before he left on the trip, but during the sleepless early morning hours he had worked out a plan.

How often over the years had his mother talked to him—worried, troubled and anxious, tearful in her pleas that he stay out of any more trouble. "Look at the way your dad threw his life away, Doug. Don't be like him," she would say. "Be like your cousins."

Sure, Doug thought impatiently as he threw back the covers and got out of bed. Be like the cousins, who had generations of money behind the Layton name, who didn't have to worry about scholarships, who had virtually automatic entry into the best schools.

Scholarships—he smiled at the memory. It had taken a lot of doing to keep ahead of the game. Fortunately he had been smart enough to maintain his grades at an adequate level, even if it meant occasionally having to make unauthorized visits to the offices of the professors to get an advance glimpse at crucial tests.

He remembered the mathematics professor in prep school who found him in her office. He had been able to talk his way out of that situation by turning the tables and asking if anything was wrong. He told her that he had gotten an urgent message, ordering him to see her immediately. The teacher ended up apologizing to him, saying that one would think students with SATs looming before them might have better things to do with their time than to leave silly messages.

He always had been able to talk himself out of trouble. More than a test grade was in question now, however; this time the stakes were enormous.

He knew that Mrs. Clausen always had an early breakfast, and if she didn't have a meeting or doctor's appointment, she could be counted on to linger over a second cup of coffee at the small table at the window of the dining room. She once had told him that watching the strong tide of the East River gave her a certain comfort. "All life is governed by a tide, Douglas," she said. "When I become saddened, seeing the river reminds me that I cannot always control the events of my own life."

She had welcomed his occasional calls requesting a chance to drop by for a cup of coffee so they could go over a particular grant request before it came up at the board meeting. On all but one grant his advice to her had been sound, and she had learned to trust and depend upon him. On only one matter had he deliberately given her misinformation, and he had done it so carefully that she had no reason to suspect anything was amiss.

Jane Clausen hasn't got anyone left who is close to her, he reminded himself as he showered and dressed, careful to choose a conservative dark blue suit. That was something else—he had worn a jacket and slacks to the meeting yesterday. It had been a mistake; Mrs. Clausen did not approve of what she considered to be casual dress at board meetings.

I've had too much on my mind, Doug told himself with irritation. Jane Clausen is lonely and she's sick; it shouldn't be too difficult to calm her down.

In the taxi on the way to Beekman Place, he carefully rehearsed the story he would give her.

The concierge insisted on announcing him even though he said not to bother, that he was expected. When he stepped out of the elevator, the housekeeper was waiting at the apartment door, holding it open only a little. Her voice slightly nervous, she told him that Mrs. Clausen was not feeling well, and suggested he leave a message.

"Vera, I *must* see Mrs. Clausen for just a minute," Doug said firmly, his voice low. "I know she's at breakfast. She had a weak spell in the office yesterday and was upset when I begged her to call the doctor. You know how it is with her when she's in pain."

Seeing Vera's uncertain look, he whispered, "We both love her and want to take care of her." Then he put his hands under her elbows, forcing her to step aside. In four long strides he was across the foyer and through the French doors that led to the dining room.

Jane Clausen was reading the *Times*. At the sound of his footsteps, she looked up. Doug had two immediate impressions: her initial expression of surprise at seeing him was replaced by a look akin to fear. The situation is worse than I realized, he thought. His second impression was that Jane Clausen could not be more than hours away from another hospital stay. Her skin tone was ashen.

He did not give her a chance to speak. "Mrs. Clausen, I've been terribly troubled that you misunderstood me yesterday," he said, his voice soothing. "I was mistaken when I said Regina had told me the orphanage in Guatemala was a favorite charity of hers, and, of course, I was mistaken when I suggested that you had told me that. The truth is that when he invited me to be on the board, Mr. March himself was the one who explained a great deal about that orphanage, and about how Regina happened to visit it and was so touched by the plight of the children there."

It was a safe enough story. March wouldn't remember having said it, of course, but he also would be afraid to deny it because of his growing awareness of his own forgetfulness.

"Hubert was the one who told you?" Jane Clausen said quietly. "He was like an uncle to Regina. It was just the sort of thing she would confide to him."

Doug knew instantly he was on the right track. "As you know, I'm going down there next week so the board can have a firsthand report on the progress of the work being done at the orphanage. I know how precarious your health has been of late, but would you consider joining me so you could see for yourself the wonderful work the orphanage is doing for those poor kids? I'm sure if you did, any doubts you might have about the wisdom of continuing the grant would be resolved. And I promise I'd be at your side every waking moment."

Layton knew, of course, that there wasn't a chance in the world Jane Clausen could make the trip, yet he waited expectantly for her reply.

She shook her head. "I only wish I could go."

It was as though he was watching ice melt. She wants to believe me, Doug thought, mentally congratulating himself. There was just one more area he had to cover: "I have an apology to make about leaving you unescorted at Dr. Chandler's office on Monday," he said. "I did have an appointment of long standing, but I should have broken it. The problem was, I could not reach the client, and she was coming in from Connecticut to meet me."

"I gave you very short notice," Jane Clausen said. "I'm afraid that's getting to be a habit of mine. Yesterday I insisted another professional person see me almost instantly."

He knew that she meant Susan Chandler. How much had she told that woman? he wondered. Had she brought him up? He was sure she had.

When he left a few minutes later, she insisted on walking him out. As they neared the door, she casually asked, "Do you see your Layton cousins much?"

She's been checking, Doug thought. "Not in recent years," he said quickly. "When I was little we saw them regularly. Gregg and Corey were my heroes. But when my father and mother separated, the contact was broken. I still think of them as my big brothers even though I'm afraid there was no love lost between their mother and mine. I don't think Cousin Elizabeth thought my mother was quite her social equal."

"Robert Layton was a wonderful man. I'm afraid Elizabeth, though, was always difficult."

Doug smiled to himself as he rode down on the elevator. The visit had been successful. He was back in the good graces of Jane Clausen, and once again on the road to the chairmanship of the Clausen Family Trust. One thing was certain: From now on, and most certainly during the time left to Jane Clausen, he wouldn't make any more mistakes.

Leaving the building, he took care to exchange a few words with the concierge, and to tip the doorman generously when he hailed a cab for him. Little courtesies such as those paid off. There was always the chance that either or both would remark on how pleasant Mr. Layton was.

Once in the cab, however, the look of benign good humor vanished from Doug Layton's face. What had Clausen talked about to Dr. Chandler? he wondered. Besides being a psychologist, Chandler had a trained legal mind. He couldn't help but be concerned, because she would be the first one to seize on something that didn't ring true.

He glanced at his watch. It was eight-twenty. He should be at the office before nine. That would give him a good hour to get some paperwork out of the way before it was time to listen to today's installment of *Ask Dr. Susan.*

40

On Wednesday morning, Susan woke at six, showered, and washed her hair, quickly blowing it dry with practiced ease. Muddy blond, she thought as she looked in the mirror and rearranged a few stray strands. Well, at least it has a natural wave, and it's low maintenance.

For a moment she studied her reflection, appraising herself dispassionately. Eyebrows, too heavy. If so, then they would just stay that way. She didn't like the idea of tweezing them. Skin, good. She could at least be proud of that. Even the faint scar on her forehead, the result of connecting with the blade of Dee's ice skate when they had both fallen at once while skating years ago, was almost gone. Mouth, like her eyebrows, too generous; nose, straight—that was okay—eyes, hazel like Mom's; chin, stubborn.

She thought about what Sister Beatrice had told her mother when she was a junior in Sacred Heart Academy: "Susan has a stubborn streak and, in her, it's a virtue. That chin comes jutting out, and I know there's something going on that she thinks needs fixing."

Right now I think a lot of things need fixing, or at least looking into, Susan thought, and I've got the list ready.

She took the time to squeeze a grapefruit for juice, then made coffee. She brought cup and glass into the bedroom while she dressed. A camel's hair jacket and slacks and a maroon cashmere turtleneck sweater— both purchased at a great sale—were her choice of outfit. Last night's weather report had indicated that it would be another one of those in-between days when a topcoat felt heavy and a suit wasn't enough. This outfit should do the trick, she decided. Besides, if for any reason she got so busy today that she couldn't get home to change, it would do comfortably for dinner with Dr. Donald Richards. Yes, Dr. Richards, whose favorite cruise ship was the *Gabrielle*.

* * *

In the interest of saving time, she decided against her usual walk and took a cab to the office, arriving at seven-fifteen. Entering her building, she was surprised to find that even though the lobby door was unlocked, the security desk was unmanned. The security in this place is nonexistent, she thought as she went up in the elevator. The building had been sold recently, and she wondered if this failure in service was the beginning of a subtle campaign by the new owners to get rid of existing tenants so they could raise the rents. Time to read the fine print on the lease, she decided as she got off the elevator to find the top floor completely dark. "This is ridiculous," she murmured under her breath as she searched for the corridor light switches.

But even the lights did not brighten the hallway adequately. No wonder, Susan thought, noting that two of the bulbs were missing. Who's managing this building now anyhow? she wondered ruefully. Moe, Larry, and Curly? She made a mental note to speak to the superintendent later, but once she was in her office the annoyance faded from her mind. She got to work immediately, and for the next hour she caught up on correspondence, then prepared to put in motion the plan she had made the night before.

She had decided to go to Justin Wells's office and confront him about the tape and about her belief that his wife was the mysterious caller. And if he was not there, she was going to play that segment of Monday's program for his secretary or receptionist. Certainly the most interesting thing on the tape was the call from "Karen," in which she talked about meeting a man on a cruise ship who had given her a ring that sounded identical to the one found to have been in

Regina Clausen's possession. If, as she suspected, Wells in fact had requested the tape, then the woman who called herself Karen just might be someone his staff knew, Susan thought. And could it be a mere coincidence that Justin Wells's wife was in an accident so soon after the phone call?

Susan scanned the rest of her notes, cataloguing points that still concerned her. "Elderly witness to Carolyn Wells's accident." Had Hilda Johnson been right when she declared that someone had pushed Carolyn? Equally significant, was Johnson's murder a few hours later another coincidence? "Tiffany." She had called to say that she had a turquoise ring with an inscription identical to the ones Regina and Karen had. Would she send it in?

I'll have to talk about her on the program today, Susan thought. That way, maybe she'll at least call in again, although actually I need to see her. If the ring is the same as the others, I've got to get her to come in and meet me. She just has to remember where it was bought. Or maybe she would be willing to ask her ex-boyfriend if he can remember.

The next notation on her list was about Douglas Layton. Jane Clausen had shown very real fear yesterday when she visited Susan and talked about him. Layton *had* acted suspiciously, Susan thought, the way he bolted minutes before Karen was due to arrive at the office. Was he afraid to meet her? And if so, why?

The last item concerned Donald Richards. Was it just a coincidence that his favorite cruise ship was the *Gabrielle*, and that his book was about vanished women? Was there more to this seemingly pleasant man than met the eye? Susan wondered.

She got up from her desk. Nedda surely would be in her office by now, and she would have coffee brewing. Susan locked the outer door and, slipping her office key in her pocket, went down the hall.

Again today, Nedda's office door was unlocked. Susan went through the reception area, down the hall, and headed for the kitchen, following the inviting aroma of perking coffee. There she found Nedda, her notorious fondness for sweets in evidence, slicing an almond coffee cake she had just warmed in the oven.

The older woman turned when she heard Susan's footsteps, then smiled brightly. "I saw your light and knew you'd be in at some point. You have a homing pigeon's instinct when I stop at the bakery."

Susan reached into the cabinet for a cup and went over to the coffeepot. "Why don't you lock your door when you're in here alone?"

"I wasn't worried—I knew you'd be in. How's the home front?"

"Quiet, thankfully. Mom seems to have recovered from her bout of anniversary blues. Charles phoned to ask me if I didn't think the party was a real blast. Actually I did have a rather interesting date as a result of it. With Binky's friend Alex Wright. Sophisticated; eminently presentable. He runs his family's foundation. Very nice guy."

Nedda raised her eyebrows. "My goodness gracious, as my mother would have said. I'm impressed. The Wright Family Foundation gives away a fortune every year. I've met Alex several times. A bit reticent perhaps, and he apparently hates the limelight, but from what I've heard he is very much a hands-on guy, and not someone who's content to just get perks from being on the board. Supposedly, he personally checks out every major request for a grant. His grandfather started accumulating wealth; his father turned millions into billions, and the word is they both still had their first communion money when they died. I hear Alex is pragmatic, but I gather he isn't cut from the same cloth. Is he fun?"

"He's nice, very nice," Susan said, surprised at the warmth in her voice. She glanced at her watch. "Okay, I'm off. Got a couple of calls to make." She wrapped a generous slice of the almond coffee cake in a paper napkin and picked up her cup. "Thanks for the CARE package."

"Any time. Stop by for a glass of vino tonight."

"Thanks, but not tonight. I've got a dinner date. I'll fill you in on *him* tomorrow."

When Susan got back to her own office, Janet was there and on the phone. "Oh, wait a minute, here she is," Janet said. She covered the receiver with her hand: "Alex Wright. He said it's personal. And he sounded so disappointed when I told him you weren't here. I bet he's cute."

Stifle it, Susan thought. "Tell him I'll be right there." She closed the door with unnecessary force, placed the cup and coffee cake on her desk, and picked up the phone. "Hello, Alex."

There was amusement in his voice. "Your secretary is right. I *was* disappointed, but I have to say no one has ever referred to me as 'cute' before. I'm flattered."

"Janet has a truly irritating habit of covering the receiver with her hand, and then raising her voice to give her off-the-cuff remarks."

"I'm still flattered." His tone changed. "I tried you at

home half an hour ago. I thought that was a respectable hour, assuming you got to your office around nine."

"I was here at seven-thirty today. I like to get an early start. The early bird and all that sort of thing."

"We're compatible. I'm an early riser too. My father's home training. He thought that anyone who slept past 6 A.M. was missing a chance to pile up more money."

Susan thought of what Nedda had just told her about Alex Wright's father. "Do you share his sentiments?"

"Heavens no. In fact, some days, when I don't have a meeting, I deliberately pound the pillow or read the papers in bed, just because I know how much that would have irritated him."

Susan laughed. "Be careful. You're talking to a psychologist."

"Oh my gosh, I forgot. Actually, I really feel sorry for my father. He missed so much in life. I wish he'd learned to smell the flowers. In many ways he was a magnificent human being. . . . Anyway, I didn't call to discuss him, or to explain my sleeping habits. I just wanted to tell you that I had a very enjoyable time with you Monday evening, and I'm hoping you're free again on Saturday night. Our foundation has made a grant to the New York Public Library, earmarked for the rare-books division, and there's going to be a black-tie dinner in the McGraw Rotunda at the main library on Fifth Avenue. It's not a big affair—only about forty people. Originally I was going to beg off, but I really shouldn't, and if you come with me, I might actually enjoy it."

Susan listened, flattered to realize that Alex Wright's voice had taken on a coaxing tone.

"That's very kind of you. Yes, I am free, and I'd love to go," she said sincerely.

"That's great. I'll pick you up around six-thirty, if that's okay."

"Fine."

His voice changed, suddenly hesitant. "Oh, Susan, by the way, I was talking to your sister."

"Dee?" Susan realized she sounded astonished.

"Yes. I met her at Binky's party after you left. She phoned my apartment last night and left a message for me, and I returned the call. She's going to be in New York this weekend. I told her I was inviting you to the dinner and asked her to join us. She sounded pretty down about life."

"That was kind of you," she replied. When she got off the phone a moment later, she sipped the cooling coffee and stared at the coffee cake that she no longer had any appetite to eat. She remembered how, seven years ago, Dee had phoned Jack, telling him how upset she was with her new publicity photos and asking him to take a look at them and advise her.

And that, Susan thought with a pang of bitterness, was the beginning of the end for Jack and me. Could history be repeating itself? she wondered.

41

Tiffany had not slept well. She had been too excited about the prospect of sending a message to her ex-boyfriend through the *Ask Dr. Susan* program. At eight o'clock on Wednesday morning, she finally sat up in bed and plumped the pillows behind her.

"Dr. Susan," she said aloud, rehearsing the call she would make, "I've really missed my boyfriend, Matt. That's why I was so mean when I talked about the ring yesterday. But I've been thinking about it, and, I'm sorry, I can't send the ring to you after all. The truth is, I really love it, because it reminds me of him."

She hoped Dr. Susan wouldn't be mad at her for changing her mind.

Tiffany held up her left hand and looked wistfully at the turquoise band that was now on her ring finger. She sighed. When you think about it, she decided, the ring actually hadn't brought her any luck at all. Matt had started worrying immediately about how much she had made of the inscription, "You belong to me." That had led to the fight that broke them up only a couple of days later.

I *did* tease him about it a lot, Tiffany recalled, with a rare flash of insight, but we did have fun together. Maybe he'll remember that and want to get back together if he hears about my mentioning him on the program.

She began to rethink what she would say to Dr. Susan, revising her comments to put more about Matt in them. "Dr. Susan, I want to apologize for what I said yesterday and explain why I can't send the ring to you like I said I would. My ex-boyfriend, Matt, gave it to me as a souvenir of the nice day we had together in Manhattan. We'd just had a wonderful lunch in a sushi bar."

Tiffany shuddered at the memory of the slimy fish that he had eaten; she had insisted that hers be cooked.

"Then we went to a wonderful foreign movie . . ."

Boring, Tiffany thought, remembering the way she had tried not to squirm too much during the endless scenes where people did nothing, and then, when they finally said something, she couldn't watch them because she was so busy trying to read the stupid subtitles. Dumb movie.

But it had been in the theater when Matt had linked his fingers in hers, and his lips had brushed her ear, and he had whispered, "Isn't this *great?*"

"Anyhow, Dr. Susan, the ring may be just a little souvenir, but it reminds me of all the fun Matt and I had together. And not just that day, but all the others too."

Tiffany got out of bed and reluctantly began to do some sit-ups. That was something else she had to do something about. She had put on a few pounds in the last year. Now she wanted to get rid of them, just in case Matt phoned and asked her out.

By the time she had completed what seemed to her like her hundredth sit-up, Tiffany had mentally polished her speech to Dr. Susan and was very pleased with it. She had decided to add one more thing. She was going to say that she worked as a waitress at The Grotto in Yonkers. Tony Sepeddi, her boss, would love it.

And if Matt gets word that I'm holding on to the ring because I see it as a cute souvenir of our relationship, and if he thinks about the good times we had together, then he's bound to decide to give us another try, Tiffany thought happily. It was just as her mother always had told her: "Tiffany, follow and they flee. Flee and they follow."

42

The tension at the architectural firm of Benner, Pierce and Wells, located on East Fifty-eighth Street, was the kind that you could actually feel, Susan thought as she stood in the paneled entrance area and waited while a nervous young receptionist, whose nameplate read BARBARA GINGRAS, hesitantly informed Justin Wells of her presence.

She was not surprised when the young woman said, "Dr. Susan, I mean Dr. Chandler, Mr. Wells wasn't expecting you and can't see you now, I'm afraid."

Realizing the girl had recognized her name from the radio program, Susan decided to take a chance: "Mr. Wells phoned my producer and asked for a copy of Monday's *Ask Dr. Susan* program. I really just wanted to give it to him personally, Barbara."

"So he *did* believe me?" Barbara Gingras said, beaming. "I told him that Carolyn—that's his wife—had phoned you Monday. I always try to catch your program and was listening when she called in. I know her voice, for heaven's sake. But Mr. Wells acted real annoyed when I told him about it, so I didn't say another word. Then his wife was in an awful accident, so the poor guy's been too upset for me to even have a chance to talk to him."

"I understand that," Susan said. She already had the tape ready to play Monday's call from "Karen." Turning the cassette player on, she placed it on the receptionist's desk. "Barbara, could you please listen for just a moment."

She kept the volume low as the troubled voice of the woman who had called herself Karen began to play.

As Susan watched, the receptionist bobbed her head excitedly. "Sure, that's Carolyn Wells," she confirmed. "And even what she's talking about makes sense. I started work here just about the time she and Mr. Wells were separated. I remember, because he was a basket case. Then, when he made up with her, it was like day and night. You never saw a guy so happy. Clearly he's crazy about her. Now, since the accident, he's been a basket case again. I heard him tell one of his partners that the doctor told him that her condition wasn't likely to change for a while, and they didn't want him getting sick too."

The outer door opened, and two men entered. They looked at Susan curiously as they passed the reception area. Barbara Gingras seemed suddenly nervous. "Dr. Susan, I'd better not talk to you anymore. Those are my other two bosses, and I don't want to get into trouble. And if Mr. Wells comes out and catches us talking, he might get mad at me."

"I understand." Susan put away the tape recorder. Her suspicions had been confirmed; now she needed to figure out what to do next. "Just one more thing, Barbara. The Wellses have a friend named Pamela. Have you ever met her?"

Barbara frowned in concentration; then her face cleared. "Oh, you mean Dr. Pamela Hastings. She teaches at Columbia. She and Mrs. Wells are great buddies. I know she's been at the hospital a lot with Mr. Wells."

Now Susan had learned everything she needed to know. "Thank you, Barbara."

"I really enjoy your program, Dr. Susan."

Susan smiled. "That's very nice of you." She waved and opened the door to the corridor. There she immediately pulled out her cellular phone and dialed information. "Columbia University, general directory, please," she said.

43

At precisely nine o'clock on Wednesday morning, Dr. Donald Richards had appeared at the reception desk on the fifteenth floor of 1440 Broadway. "I was a guest on the *Ask Dr. Susan* program yesterday and Monday," he explained to the sleepy-looking woman seated at the desk. "I asked to have tapes made of the programs, but then I left without getting them. I wonder if Mr. Geany is in yet?"

"I think I saw him," the receptionist replied. She picked up the phone and dialed a number. "Jed, Susan's guest from yesterday is here." She looked up at Dr. Richards. "What did you say your name was?"

I didn't, Don thought. "Donald Richards."

The receptionist muttered the name into the phone, then added that he said he had forgotten some tapes he asked for yesterday. After listening a moment, she snapped the receiver back on the hook. "He'll be right out. Take a seat."

I wonder which charm school *she* went to, Richards thought as he selected a chair near a coffee table on which lay copies of the morning newspapers.

Jed came out a moment later, a package in his hand. "Sorry I forgot to remind you yesterday, Doc. I was just about to send these down to the mailroom. At least you still want them and didn't change your mind like what's his name."

"Justin Wells?" Richards responded.

"Exactly. But he's going to get a surprise; he's getting what he asked for anyway. Susan is dropping the tape from Monday's show at his office this morning."

Interesting, Richards thought, *very* interesting. It can't be too often that the host of a popular radio show plays errand girl, he mused. After thanking Jed Geany, he put the small package in his briefcase, and fifteen minutes later was getting out of a cab at the garage around the corner from his apartment.

Donald Richards was driving north on the Palisades Parkway, toward Bear Mountain. He turned on the radio and tuned in *Ask Dr. Susan*. It was a program he had no intention of missing.

When he reached his destination, he remained in his car until the program was over. Then he sat quietly for several minutes longer before getting out of the car and opening the trunk. He took a narrow box from inside and walked to the water's edge.

The mountain air was cold and still. The lake surface shimmered under the autumn sun, but even so, there were dark areas that hinted at the water's depth. The trees surrounding the lake had begun to change color and were far more vivid in their yellow and orange and cardinal red shades than the ones he had seen in the city and suburbs closer in.

For a long time he sat on the ground at the lakeside, his hands clasped over his knees. Tears glistened in his eyes, but he ignored them. Finally he opened the box and removed the dewy fresh, long-stemmed roses that were nestled inside. One by one, he tossed them on the water, until all two dozen were floating there, undulating and separating as the slight breeze touched them.

"Good-bye, Kathryn." He spoke aloud, his tone somber; then he turned and went back to the car.

An hour later he was at the gatehouse at Tuxedo Park, the luxurious mountain hamlet that had at one time been the summer vacation retreat of New York City's very rich and very social. Now many, like his mother, Elizabeth Richards, were year-round residents. The security guard waved him by. "Good to see you, Dr. Richards," he shouted.

He found his mother in her studio. At age sixty she had taken up painting, and in twelve years of serious application, her natural talent had developed into a genuine gift. She was seated at the easel, her back to him, every inch of her slight, slender body totally absorbed in her work. A shimmering evening gown was hanging next to the canvas.

"Mother."

He could see her begin to smile even before she had turned fully to face him. "Donald, I was beginning to give up on you," she said.

A momentary flashback hit him, the memory of a game they had played in his childhood. Coming home from school to his family's penthouse apartment on Fifth Avenue, knowing that his mother probably would be in her study on the northeast corner, rushing to it, deliberately making noise as he clattered on the wooden floor that bordered the carpet, calling out to her—"Mother, Mother"—because even as a child he loved the sound of the word, wanted to hear her voice as she replied, "Is that Donald Wallace Richards, the nicest little boy in Manhattan?"

Today she rose and came to him, her arms extended, but instead of an embrace, she grazed his shoulders with her fingertips and then brushed his cheek with her lips. "I don't want to get paint on you," she said, stepping back and looking her son full in the face. "I was just beginning to worry that you might not be able to make it."

"You know I would have called." He realized he sounded curt, but his mother didn't seem to notice. He had no intention of telling her where he had spent the last few hours.

"So what do you think of the latest effort?" Her arm linked in his, she brought him over to the canvas. "Do you approve?"

He recognized the subject—the wife of the current governor. "The First Lady of New York! I'm impressed. The name Elizabeth Wallace Richards on a portrait is getting to be hot stuff."

His mother touched the sleeve of the dress that hung next to the canvas. "That's her inaugural ball gown. It's lovely, but dear God, I'm going blind painting all that intricate beading."

Still arm in arm, they walked down the wide staircase and through the foyer to the family dining room, which overlooked the patio and gardens.

"I really think the old-timers knew what they were doing when they closed these places on Labor Day," Elizabeth Richards observed. "Do you know we had a flurry of snow the other night, and here it is only October?"

"There's an obvious solution to that," Don said dryly as he held the chair for her.

She shrugged. "Don't try being a psychiatrist with me. Sure I miss the apartment—and the city—sometimes, but staying here is the reason I'm getting so much work done. I hope you're hungry."

"Not really," he said with some hesitation.

"Well, you'd better pick up that knife and fork. As usual, Carmen has been fussing for you."

Whenever he visited Tuxedo Park, his mother's housekeeper always outdid herself to prepare one of his favorite meals. Today it was her special chili, made hot and spicy. While his mother nibbled on chicken salad, Don ate enthusiastically. When Carmen refilled his water glass, he sensed that she was observing him, anticipating a reaction.

"It's great," he pronounced. "Rena is a terrific cook, but your chili is unique."

Carmen, a thinner version of her sister, his own housekeeper, beamed. "Dr. Donald, I know my sister takes good care of you in the city, but I tell you, I taught her to cook, and she's not up to me yet."

"Well, she's getting close," Don warned, remembering that Carmen and Rena were in constant touch. The last thing he needed was for Rena's feelings to be hurt because Carmen repeated some compliment he had given her. He decided to get off that subject fast. "All right, Carmen, now what kind of report has Rena been giving you about me?"

"I'll answer that," his mother said. "She says you're working too hard, which is the usual. That you looked dead tired when you came back from doing publicity for your book last week, and that you seem worried about something."

Don had not expected the last comment. "Worried? Not really. Sure, I have things on my mind. I've got some very troubled patients. But I don't know any living person who doesn't have *some* concerns."

Elizabeth Richards shrugged. "Let's not fret over semantics. Where were you this morning?"

"I had to go by a radio studio," Don hedged.

"You also rearranged your calendar so that your first appointment is not until four o'clock."

Don realized that his mother was now keeping track of him through his secretary as well as his housekeeper.

"You went to the lake again, didn't you?" she asked.

"Yes."

His mother's face softened. She put her hand over his. "Don, I didn't forget that today is Kathy's anniversary, but it *has* been four years. You're going to be forty next month. You've got to move on, get on with your life. I want to see you meet a woman whose eyes will light up when you walk in the door at the end of the day."

"Maybe she'll have a job too," Don said. "There're not too many women who are just homemakers these days."

"Oh, stop it. You know what I mean. I want you to be happy again. And allow me to be selfish: I want a grandchild. I'm jealous when my friends whip out pictures of their little darlings. Each time all I can think is 'Please God, me too.' Don, even psychiatrists may need help recovering from a tragedy. Did you ever consider that?"

He did not answer, but sat with his head down.

Then she sighed. "All right, enough. I'll let you off the hot seat. I know I shouldn't pull this on you, but I do worry about you. When was the last time you took a vacation?"

"Bingo!" Don said, his face brightening. "You've given me a chance to defend myself. Next week, when I finish a book signing in Miami, I'm going to take six or seven days off."

"Don, you used to *love* going on cruises." His mother hesitated. "Remember how you and Kathy called yourselves 'the sailaways,' and you'd take those spur-of-the-moment trips, having your travel agent book you on a segment of a long cruise? I want to see you do that sort of thing again. It was fun for you then; it can be fun again. You haven't set foot on a cruise ship since Kathy died."

Dr. Donald Richards looked across the table into the blue-gray eyes that reflected such genuine concern. Oh yes I have, Mother, he thought. Oh yes I have.

44

Susan could not reach Pamela Hastings immediately. She got through to her office at Columbia, but was told that Dr. Hastings was not expected there until shortly before eleven. Her first class was eleven-fifteen.

Chances are she stopped at Lenox Hill to visit Carolyn Wells, Susan thought. It was already nine-fifteen, so it was unlikely that she would have enough time to reach Pamela there. Instead she left a message asking that Dr. Hastings call her at her office anytime after two o'clock, and emphasizing that she needed to speak to her on a confidential and urgent matter.

Once again she saw disapproval in Jed Geany's eyes when she arrived at the studio only ten minutes prior to broadcast time.

"You know, Susan, one of these days . . ." he began.

"I know. One of these days you'll be starting without me, and that won't go over well. It's a character flaw, Jed. I cut things too close timewise. I even talk to myself about it."

He gave her a reluctant half smile. "Your guest from yesterday, Dr. Richards, stopped by. He wanted to pick up the tapes of the programs he was on. Guess he couldn't wait to play them again and hear how good he sounded."

I'm seeing him tonight, Susan thought. I could have brought them. What was the big rush? she wondered. Then, realizing it was nothing she had time to be concerned about now, she went into the studio. Picking up her notes for the show, she put on her headphones.

When the engineer announced the thirty seconds warning, she said quickly, "Jed, remember that call from Tiffany yesterday? I don't expect to hear from her, but if she does call in, be sure to record her phone number when it comes up on the ID."

"Okay."

"Ten seconds," the engineer warned.

In her earphones Susan heard, "And now stay tuned for *Ask Dr. Susan,*" followed by a brief musical bridge. She took a deep breath and began, "Hello and welcome. I'm Dr. Susan Chandler. Today we're going right to the phones to answer any questions you have in mind, so let's hear from you. Maybe between us we can put whatever is bothering you in perspective."

As usual, the time went quickly. Some of the calls were mundane: "Dr. Susan, there's someone in my office who's driving me crazy. If I wear a new outfit, she asks me where I bought it, then shows up wearing the exact same thing a few days later. This has happened at least four times."

"Clearly this woman has some self-realization problems, but they don't have to be yours. There's a simple, immediate solution to your problem, however," Susan said. "Don't tell her where you buy your clothes."

Other calls were complex: "I had to put my ninety-year-old mother in a nursing home," a woman said, her voice weary. "It killed me to do it, but physically she's helpless. And now she won't talk to me. I feel so guilty I can't function."

"Give her a little time to adjust," Susan suggested. "Visit her regularly. Remember that she wants to see you even if she ignores you. Tell her how much you love her. We all need to know that we're loved, especially when we're frightened, as she is now. Finally, and most important, stop beating up on yourself."

The problem is that some of us live too long, Susan thought sadly, while others, like Regina Clausen and maybe Carolyn Wells, have had their lives cut short.

The show's time was almost up when she heard Jed announce, "Our next call is from Tiffany in Yonkers, Dr. Susan."

Susan looked up at the control box. Jed was nodding—he would copy Tiffany's phone number from the Caller ID.

"Tiffany, I'm glad you called back today—" Susan began, but she was interrupted before she could continue.

"Dr. Susan," Tiffany said hurriedly, "I almost didn't have the courage to phone, because I may disappoint you. You see . . ."

Susan listened with dismay to the obviously rehearsed speech about why Tiffany couldn't send her the turquoise ring. It sounded almost as though she were reading it.

"So like I said, Dr. Susan, I hope I'm not disappointing you, but it was such a cute souvenir, and Matt, my former boyfriend, gave it to me, and it kind of reminds me of all the fun times we had when we went out together."

"Tiffany, I wish you'd call me at my office," Susan said hurriedly, then had a sense of déjà vu. Hadn't she spoken those same words to Carolyn Wells forty-eight hours earlier?

"Dr. Susan, I won't change my mind about giving

you the souvenir ring," Tiffany said. "And if you don't mind, I want to tell you that I work at—"

"Please do not give your employer's name," Susan said firmly.

"I work at The Grotto, the best Italian restaurant in Yonkers," Tiffany said defiantly, almost shouting.

"Cut to commercials, Susan," Jed barked into her headphone.

At least now I know where to find her, Susan thought wryly as she automatically began to say, "And now a message from our sponsors."

When the program was over, she went into the control room. Jed had written Tiffany's phone number on the back of an envelope. "She sounds dumb, but she was smart enough to get in a free plug for her boss," he observed acidly. Self-promotion on the show was strictly forbidden.

Susan folded the envelope and put it in her jacket pocket. "What worries me is that Tiffany is obviously lonely and trying to get back with her old boyfriend, and she sounds very vulnerable. Suppose some nut was listening to the program and heard her and got ideas about her?"

"Are you going to contact her about that ring?"

"Yes, I think so. I just need to compare it with the one Regina Clausen had. I know it's a long shot that they came from the same place, but I won't be sure unless I can check it out."

"Susan, those kinds of souvenir rings are a dime a dozen, as are the shops that sell them. Those guys who run the shops all claim their stuff is handmade, but who are they kidding? For ten bucks? No way. You're too smart to believe that."

"You're probably right," Susan said in agreement. "Besides . . ." she began, then stopped herself. She'd been about to tell Jed her suspicion that Justin Wells's critically injured wife was the mysterious Karen. No, she thought, it's better to wait until I see where that information leads me before I spread the word.

45

When Nat Small noted that Abdul Parki's souvenir shop still hadn't opened at noon on Wednesday, he became concerned. Small's shop, Dark Delights, a porn emporium, was directly across the street from the Khyem Specialty Shop, and the two men had been friends for years.

Nat, a wiry fifty-year-old with a narrow face, hooded eyes, and a troubled past, could smell trouble just as distinctly as anyone who got near him could smell the combination of stale cigars and liquor that was his personal scent.

It was common knowledge on MacDougal Street that his sign announcing that he did not sell to minors had nothing to do with reality. That he never had been caught at it was due to the fact that he knew by instinct when an undercover cop opened the door of his well-equipped store. If there happened to be a young customer already there, attempting to make a purchase, Nat would immediately start demanding proof of age—as loudly as he could.

Nat had one abiding credo, and it had served him well: stay away from the cops. That was why he tried every other avenue available to him when he first became concerned about his friend's failure to open for business that Wednesday morning. First he tried peering in at the door of Abdul's shop; seeing nothing, he then phoned Abdul at home; not reaching him there, he tried phoning Abdul's landlord. Of course, he got the usual answering machine runaround: "Leave a message," it said. "We'll get back to you." Yeah, right, Nat thought. Everyone knew the landlord didn't give a damn about the place and would jump at any opportunity to get out of the long-term lease Abdul had gotten during one of the city's periodic real estate downturns.

Finally, Nat did the one thing that showed the depth of his friendship: He called the local precinct and reported his concern that something might have happened to Abdul. "I mean, you could set your clock by that little guy," he said. "Maybe he didn't feel well yesterday, 'cause I noticed he didn't reopen after lunch. Maybe he went home and had a heart attack or something."

The police checked Abdul's small, exquisitely neat apartment on Jane Street. A bouquet of now-drooping flowers lay next to the smiling photo of his late wife. Otherwise there was no sign of recent habitation, and no indication that he had been there. At that point, they decided to go into the shop and investigate.

It was there they found the blood-soaked body of Abdul Parki.

Nat Small was not a suspect. The police knew Nat, and they all knew he was too smart to get involved in a murder; besides, he didn't have a motive. In fact, the very absence of motive was the most troubling aspect of the case. There was nearly one hundred dollars in the cash register, and it didn't look as though the killer even had made an effort to open it.

Still, it probably was robbery, the police decided. And the killer, probably a druggie, got scared off by something, maybe even by a customer coming in the shop. As the police scenario played out, the killer hid in the back until the customer left, then bolted. He'd been smart enough to put up the "closed" sign and snap the lock. And he gave himself plenty of time to get away.

What the police wanted from Nat and from other shopkeepers on the block was information. They did learn that Abdul had opened the shop as usual on Tuesday morning at nine o'clock and had been seen sweeping his sidewalk around eleven, after some kid scattered a bag of popcorn there.

"Nat," the detective said. "Use that brain for something besides the gutter. You're right across the street from Parki. You're always putting the latest filth in your front window. Did you notice anyone going in or out of Abdul's shop sometime after eleven?"

By the time he was being questioned at three o'clock, Nat had had plenty of time to think, and to remember. Yesterday had been slow, but then Tuesdays always were. Around one he had been putting some display boxes for newly arrived X-rated films in the front window. Although he hadn't actually stared at him, he had noticed a well-dressed guy standing on the sidewalk outside his shop. He seemed to be looking over the stuff already on display. But then, instead of coming inside, he had crossed the street and gone directly into Abdul's shop, without even pausing to look in the window.

Nat had a pretty good impression of what the guy had looked like, even though he had seen him only in profile, and the man had been wearing sunglasses. But even if that well-dressed guy had gone into Ab's place around one, he certainly wasn't the one who killed the poor little guy, Nat told himself. No, there was no use even mentioning him to the cops. If he did, he would end up wasting the whole afternoon in the precinct station with a cop-artist. No way.

Besides, Nat thought, that guy looks just like all my customers. The Wall Street guys and the lawyers and doctors who buy my stuff would go ballistic if they thought that I was talking to the cops about one of their kind.

"I seen nobody," Nat informed the cops. "But let me warn you guys," he added virtuously. "You gotta do something about the druggies 'round here. They'd kill their grandmothers for a fix. And you can tell the mayor I said so!"

46

Pamela Hastings feared that the students in her Comparative Lit course had wasted their time by coming to class today. The combination of two sleepless nights and the continuing acute worry about her friend Carolyn Wells had left her physically and emotionally spent. And now her suspicion that Carolyn's injuries might not have been accidental, and that in fact Justin might have been angry or jealous enough to have deliberately tried to kill her, had proven to be almost totally distracting. She was painfully aware that today's lecture on *The Divine Comedy* was both disjointed and uneven, and she was relieved when it was over.

Making matters even worse was the message she received to call Dr. Susan Chandler. What could she say to Dr. Chandler? Certainly she had no right to discuss Justin with a perfect stranger. Still she knew she could not avoid at least returning the call.

The Columbia campus was bright with sunshine, colorful with the turning leaves. It's a good day to be alive, Pamela thought ironically as she walked through it. She hailed a cab and gave the now all-too-familiar destination: "Lenox Hill Hospital."

After less than two days the nurses in the station outside the intensive care unit almost seemed like old friends. The one on desk duty answered Pamela's unasked question: "She's holding her own, but still very critical. There is a chance that she's coming out of the coma. We felt she was trying to say something earlier this morning, but then she lapsed back. It's a good sign, though."

"Is Justin here?"

"He's on his way."

"Is it okay if I go in to see her?"

"Yes, but only stay for a minute. And talk to her. No matter what most of the doctors say, I swear some supposedly comatose people know exactly what's going on. They just can't reach us."

Pam tiptoed past three units that housed other desperately ill patients before she reached the one in which Carolyn was lying. She looked down at her friend, heartsick at what she saw. Emergency surgery had been performed to reduce brain swelling, and Carolyn's head was covered in bandages. Tubes and drains invaded her body from all angles. Her nose was covered with an oxygen mask, and purple bruises on her neck and arms were testimony to the violent impact of the van.

Pamela still found it almost impossible to believe that something so terrible as this could have followed the happy evening she had shared with Carolyn only a few nights ago.

Happy until I started doing readings, she thought—and Carolyn brought out that turquoise ring . . .

Careful not to exert any pressure, she placed her hand over Carolyn's. "Hi, babe," she whispered.

Did she sense a faint stirring, or was she just wishing for response?

"Carolyn, you're doing great. They tell me you're on the verge of waking up. That's wonderful." Pamela stopped. She had been about to say that Justin was frantic with worry, but realized that now she was afraid to bring up his name. Suppose he *had* pushed Carolyn? Suppose Carolyn had realized that it was him behind her on that corner?

"Win."

Carolyn's lips had barely moved, and what came from them was more a sigh than a word. Still, Pamela knew she had heard it accurately.

She bent over the bed, putting her lips to Carolyn's ear. "Babe, listen to me. I think you said 'Win.' Is that a name? If that's what you mean, squeeze my hand."

She was sure she felt a hint of pressure.

"Pam, is she waking up?"

Justin was there, looking somewhat disheveled, his face flushed and strained, as though he had been running. Pamela did not want to tell him what she thought Carolyn had said. "Get the nurse, Justin. I think she's trying to talk."

"*Win!*"

This time the word was clear, unequivocal, and the tone was imploring.

Justin Wells bent over his wife's bed. "Carolyn, I'm not going to let anyone else have you. I'll make it up to you. Please, I'll get help. I promised last time that I would, and I didn't, but this time I will. I promise. I promise. Just please, please come back to me."

47

Although Emily Chandler had maintained her membership in the Westchester Country Club after the divorce, she did not go there very often for fear of running into her successor, Binky. But since she loved golf, and Binky wasn't a golfer, the only real area of concern was a chance encounter in the clubhouse. And because she did enjoy meeting her friends for lunch there occasionally, Emily had figured a way to avoid any unpleasant meetings.

She would call the maître d', ask if the Trophy Wife was expected, and if he said she wasn't, then Emily would make a reservation.

That was how it worked out on Wednesday, and as a result, she and Nan Lake, a longtime pal—whose husband, Dan, regularly played golf with Charles—were meeting for lunch.

Emily had dressed with special care for the meeting. Always in the back of her mind there lurked the possibility that Charley might just happen to be there as well. Today she had chosen a Féraud pant suit in a tiny blue-and-white check that she knew suited her ash blond hair. Earlier, while looking in the mirror for a final check, she had thought of the many times people expressed surprise that she was Dee's mother.

"You look like *sisters!*" they would exclaim, which made her very proud, though she knew they were exaggerating.

Emily also knew it was time to put the divorce behind her, time to get on with her life. In many ways she had succeeded in overcoming the initial outrage and bitterness she had felt over what she still considered to be Charley's betrayal. But even after four years, some nights she still woke up and lay sleepless for hours, not angry but infinitely sad, remembering that for a very long time she and Charley had been happy together—*genuinely* happy.

We had *fun*, she thought, as she prepared to leave for the club. She turned on the alarm system of the town house she had bought after the breakup. Every step of the way, we had fun. Charley and I were in love. We did things together. It wasn't as though I let myself fall apart; I've kept my body in good shape. Emily got into her car. For God's sake, she asked herself, what made him change overnight; what made him just throw away our life together?

The sense of desertion was so great that she knew, even though she found it almost impossible to admit to herself, that it would have been easier if Charley-Charles had died instead of just leaving her. But hard to admit or not, it was a fact, and she knew Susan suspected and probably understood.

She didn't know what she would have done without Susan. She had been there for her from the first day, when Emily had really doubted that she could go on. It had been a long process, but now she felt she was almost able to make it on her own.

She had followed Susan's advice to make a list of the activities in which she always had intended to become involved—and then to do something about it. As a result she was now an active volunteer with the hospital auxiliary, and this year was chairing its annual fundraiser. Last year she had been an active campaigner for the governor's reelection.

One other activity she had undertaken she had kept to herself, not even telling Susan, perhaps because it was the most important thing she ever had done. She had started volunteering at a hospital for chronically ill children.

She found it a truly rewarding experience, and it helped her to put things into perspective. It reminded her of the old saying, which was so very true: You feel sorry for the man who has no shoes until you meet one who has no feet. After those mornings at the hospital, she returned home and reminded herself to count her blessings each and every day.

She arrived at the club before Nan and went directly to the table. She had been feeling guilty ever since Sunday, the fortieth anniversary of her marriage to Charley. She had been so down and depressed—and also so self-indulgent. She knew she had upset Susan with her tearful outburst on Saturday, and then Dee had made it worse by lacing into Susan, saying *she* didn't understand what it was to lose someone.

Susan understands a lot more than Dee likes to believe, Emily told herself. At the time of Charley's and my breakup, Dee was in California with Jack, busy and happy. First, Susan had had to get over Jack's betrayal, and then she was there, giving support to me. Plus, Charley didn't have time for her once Binky came into the picture, which must have hurt, since she always had been a Daddy's girl.

"Are we off in a dream world?" a teasing voice asked.

"Nan!" Emily jumped up and hugged her friend, as they exchanged brief air kisses. "Yes, I guess I am." She looked with fondness at Nan. "You look great."

It was true. At sixty, Nan, a slender brunette with a fine-boned face and body, was still a beautiful woman.

"And so do *you*," Nan said emphatically. "Let's face it, Em. We're hanging in there."

"Fighting the good fight," Emily agreed. "A tuck here, a nip there. Age gracefully, but not too fast."

"So, have you missed me?" Nan asked. She had been in Florida with her ailing mother for over a month, having returned only the week before.

"You know I have. There were a few bumpy days there," Emily confided.

They decided to forget the calorie counting today. A glass of chardonnay and a club sandwich sounded just the thing to both of them.

The wine arrived, and serious gossip began.

Emily told her friend how blue she had been on Sunday. "What really got me was that the Trophy threw that party on *our* fortieth anniversary—and Charley let her do it."

"You know it was deliberate," Nan said. "It's so typically Binky. I have to confess to you that even *I* was at the party for a little while. I didn't see Susan, though. Apparently she had already left. I guess she just made a token appearance."

There was something in Nan's voice that reflected concern. Emily did not have to wait to find out what it was.

"Em, in the long run, it probably won't matter, but Binky can't stand Susan. She knows that it was Susan who talked Charles into taking a vacation alone so he could think things through quietly right after he told you he wanted to break up. That Binky got her man anyway doesn't seem to matter. She'll still never forgive her."

Emily nodded.

"She does, however, seem to like Dee. So, Binky invited Alex Wright to the party so the two of them could meet. Only Dee wasn't there when he arrived, so he ended up having a long chat with Susan, and from what I hear, he was pretty much taken with her. That certainly wasn't part of Binky's master plan."

"Meaning what?"

"Meaning that if by any chance Susan *does* hear from Alex, and a relationship does begin to develop between them, she should be aware that Binky will do her best to sabotage it. Binky loves to pit people against each other. She's a manipulator par excellence."

"By pitting people against each other, you mean Susan and Dee?"

"Yes, I do. For Binky to be so furious, Alex Wright must have been pretty emphatic about how attractive he found Susan. Because, believe me, she *was* furious. Of course, I don't know Alex well at all. I gather he's not a party kind of guy, but I do know that the Wright Family Foundation—which he runs—has done immeasurable good, and while some guys with vast amounts of family money turn into playboys, he's apparently serious about what's important. In fact, he's just the kind of guy I wish Susan would get involved with—since I couldn't foster a match between her and Bobby."

Bobby was Nan's oldest son. He and Susan had been friends since childhood but never had been romantic about each other. Bobby was married now, but Nan still joked about the fact that she and Em had lost their chance to have joint grandchildren.

"I wish both Susan and Dee would meet someone they could be happy with," Emily said, uncomfortable in the knowledge that, even without prodding from Binky, Dee would willingly go after Alex Wright if she became interested in him.

She was aware also that Nan had subtly but quite deliberately made that point. Her message was that Susan should be made aware of Binky's scheming, and that Dee should be told to leave Alex Wright alone.

"And now for a piece of gossip you'll *really* be interested in," Nan said, bending closer to her friend and glancing around to be sure the waiter was not near the table. "Charley and Dan played golf together yesterday. Charley is thinking of retiring! Apparently the board of Bannister Foods wants a younger chairman-CEO and has been making overtures about offering him a golden parachute. Charley told Dan that he'd rather leave gracefully than be forced out. But there's just *one* problem: When he broached the subject to Binky, she had a fit. He told Dan that she said that living with a retired husband was like having a piano in the kitchen. Which to my mind translates to 'useless and in the way.'"

Nan paused and leaned back. Then, arching her eyebrows for effect, she continued: "Do you think there could be trouble in paradise?"

48

Before leaving the studio, Susan phoned her office. She knew there was a strong possibility that her one o'clock appointment might have canceled. The patient, Linda, a forty-year-old copywriter whose pet, a golden retriever, had just been put down, was trying to work her way out of depression and bereavement. They'd had only two sessions, but already Susan was sure that the basic source of Linda's trouble was not the honest grief over the loss of a beloved pet, but the recent, sudden death of the adoptive mother from whom Linda had been estranged.

Her hunch that Linda would cancel proved correct. "She says she's really sorry, but that an important meeting came up at work," Janet explained.

Maybe yes, maybe no, Susan thought, making a mental note to call Linda later. "Any other messages?" she asked.

"Just one. Mrs. Clausen wants you to call her anytime after three. Oh, and you've got a gorgeous bouquet of flowers sitting on your desk."

"Flowers! Who sent them?"

"The card is sealed, so of course I didn't open it," Janet replied smugly. "I'm sure the note must be personal."

"Open it now, please, and read it to me." Susan raised her eyes to heaven. Janet was an excellent secretary in so many ways, but her need to editorialize was a source of constant exasperation.

Janet was back a moment later. "I *knew* it was personal, Doctor." She began to read: "'Thanks for a great evening. Looking forward to Saturday.' It's signed 'Alex.'"

Susan felt a sudden lifting of her spirits. "Nice of him," she said, careful to keep her tone noncommittal. "Janet, since I don't have anything on my schedule until two o'clock, I think I'll run an errand."

Less than a minute later, Susan was outside, hailing a taxi. She had decided that the next thing she had to do was to talk to whoever on the police force was in charge of the investigation of Carolyn Wells's accident. Now that she was certain that it was Carolyn who called the show on Monday and identified herself as Karen, she had to find out if the police had given any credence to the version of the incident that elderly woman had given them—that Carolyn Wells had been pushed in front of the van.

The article she had read in the *Times* this morning

had reported that the investigations into both Carolyn's accident and Hilda Johnson's murder were being handled by the 19th Precinct.

Clearly that was the place to start looking for answers.

Despite Oliver Baker's resolute eyewitness account that Carolyn Wells had lost her balance and fallen, Police Captain Tom Shea was still not satisfied. Given Hilda Johnson's perhaps too-public proclamation that she had seen someone push Wells, he was having trouble accepting the elderly woman's death as a mere coincidence, and the result of a random killing. It all came back to several basic questions: How did the perp get into the building in the first place? Then, how did he get into Hilda's apartment? And finally, *why* her apartment, and why *only* her apartment?

In the hours since her body had been discovered, a team of detectives had spoken to every single tenant in the building. With only four apartments to the floor and only twelve floors, that hadn't been too much of a task.

Most of the tenants were like Hilda—elderly, long-time residents. They were all adamant that they hadn't buzzed in a deliveryman or anyone else late Monday evening. Those who had been in and out of the building during the time in question swore they had neither seen a stranger loitering nearby nor allowed anyone to come in when they used their keys to enter the lobby.

Hilda Johnson must have let someone into the building herself, and then into her apartment, Shea concluded. So it had to be someone she believed she could trust. From what he knew of Hilda—and since he had been at this precinct he had come to know her fairly well—he had trouble imagining who that person might have been. Why wasn't I on duty Monday afternoon? he asked himself again, fuming at fate. It had been his day off, and he and Joan, his wife, had driven to Fairfield College in Connecticut, where their daughter was a freshman. It was only when he watched the eleven o'clock news that night that Tom learned about the accident and saw Hilda interviewed.

If only I had called her then, was the thought that nagged him. If I hadn't gotten an answer I'd have suspected trouble right away, and if I *had* talked to her, I might have gotten a description of the person she thought had shoved Carolyn Wells in front of the van.

It was only a quarter of one now, but Tom could feel weariness in his whole body—the kind caused by angry self-recrimination. He was sure Hilda's death could have been avoided, and now he was back to square one on solving not just her murder, but what could well be another attempted murder. He had been a cop for twenty-seven years, since he was twenty-one; he could think of nothing in all that time that depressed him more than this.

His phone rang, interrupting his mental self-flagellation. It was the desk sergeant, telling him that a Dr. Susan Chandler wanted to talk to him about Carolyn Wells's accident on Park Avenue.

Hoping she might be another eyewitness to the incident, Shea quickly responded, "Send her in." A few moments later, he and Susan were studying each other with cautious interest.

Susan immediately liked the man sitting across the

desk from her—his lean, clean-cut face; the alert, intelligent expression in his dark brown eyes; the long, sensitive fingers that were silently tapping the desk.

Sensing that this was not the kind of police officer who wasted time, she got right to the point. "Captain, I have to be back in my office at two. You know how traffic can be in New York; since it took me forty minutes to get up here from Broadway and Forty-first, I'll make this brief."

She quickly summarized her background and even felt a fleeting amusement that the faint disapproval on Shea's face when she said she was a psychologist was replaced by a look of camaraderie when she told him that for two years she had been an assistant district attorney.

"My interest in Carolyn Wells is that I am certain it was she who called in to my radio program Monday morning with potentially valuable information about Regina Clausen, a woman who has been missing for several years. During the call, Wells made an appointment to come in and see me. She failed to keep the appointment, however; then later, according to one witness, she may have been pushed in front of a van on Park Avenue. I need to find out if there is any connection between her—for now, let's call it an accident—and the call she made to me."

Shea leaned forward as a look of deep interest filled his face. Oliver Baker had said that the block printing on the manila envelope Carolyn Wells had been carrying was large, and that he was pretty sure he had glimpsed the word "Dr." on the first line of the address. Maybe Dr. Susan Chandler was putting him on the track to something, perhaps even a connection between Hilda Johnson's insistence that Carolyn Wells had been pushed and Hilda's own murderer.

"Have you received a manila envelope that could have been from her in the mail?" Shea asked.

"Not as of yesterday. The mail wasn't in when I left my office this morning. Why?"

"Because both Hilda Johnson and one other witness saw Carolyn Wells carrying a manila envelope, and the second witness thought it was addressed to Dr. Something. Did you expect her to send anything to you?"

"No, but then she might have decided to mail in the picture and ring she promised to give me. Let me play the tape of her call for you."

When it was finished, Susan looked across the desk and noted the intensity of Captain Shea's expression.

"You're sure that woman is Carolyn Wells?" he demanded.

"I'm absolutely positive," she replied.

"You're a psychologist, Dr. Chandler. Would you agree that that woman is afraid of her husband?"

"I would say that she is nervous about his reaction to what she told me."

Captain Shea picked up the phone and barked out an order. "See if we have any record of a complaint against a Justin Wells. Probably something domestic. About two years ago."

"Dr. Chandler," he said, "I can't tell you how grateful I am that you came in. If I get the report I expect—"

He was interrupted by the ringing of the phone. He picked up the receiver, listened, and then nodded.

He hung up and looked at Susan. "It's what I thought. I knew that what you told me rang a bell. Dr. Chandler, two years ago Carolyn Wells swore out a complaint against Justin Wells, which she later withdrew. In the complaint she contended that, in a jealous rage, her husband had threatened to kill her. Would you know if Wells had learned of that call she made to your program?"

Susan knew she had no choice but to tell the exact truth. "He not only learned of it, he phoned on Monday afternoon, requesting a copy of the tape; then, when I called him about it last night, he denied any knowledge of the request. I tried to deliver the tape to his office this morning, and he refused to see me."

"Dr. Chandler, I can't thank you enough for this information. I must ask you to leave this tape with me."

Susan stood up. "Of course. I have the master tape at the studio. But Captain Shea, what I really wanted to ask you to follow up was the possibility that there was a connection between the man Carolyn Wells met on the ship and Regina Clausen's disappearance. There was a turquoise ring with the inscription 'You belong to me' in Regina Clausen's belongings." She was about to tell him about the calls from Tiffany, and her report that someone in Greenwich Village sold and perhaps even made rings just like that, when Shea interrupted.

"Dr. Chandler, it's a matter of record that Justin Wells was—and probably is—fiercely jealous of his wife. The tape shows she's afraid of him. My guess is that she didn't tell her husband anything about her relationship with the guy she met on the ship. I think when Wells heard about that program, he went nuts. I want to talk to him. I want to know where he was between four and four-thirty Monday afternoon. I want to know who told him about the call to your program, and how much that person told him."

Susan knew that everything Captain Shea said

made sense. She glanced at her watch; she had to get
back to her office. But something still wasn't right.
Every instinct in her body told her that even if Justin
Wells, in a fit of jealous rage, *did* push his wife in front
of that van, there still might be a connection between
the man Carolyn had met on the trip and Regina
Clausen's disappearance.

As she left the police station, she decided there was
one link she would follow up herself: She would track
down Tiffany, whose phone number she had and who
worked at The Grotto, "the best Italian restaurant in
Yonkers."

49

Jim Curley had been sure something was up when he
picked up his boss at noon at the Wright Family
Foundation and was told to stop by Irene Hayes
Wadley & Smythe, an elegant Rockefeller Center
florist. Once there, instead of sending Jim inside,
Wright had had him wait while he got out of the car
himself and went inside the shop, carrying a box under
his arm. He returned fifteen minutes later, trailed by a
florist who carried a lavish bouquet in a large vase.

The vase was wedged in a carton to give it stability,
and Wright instructed the florist to put it on the floor of
the backseat, where he could be sure it wouldn't tip over.

With a smile, the florist thanked Wright, then closed
the door. Wright, his voice buoyant, had said, "Next

stop SoHo," then gave Jim an unfamiliar address. Noting the perplexed look on the driver's face, he had added, "Before you die of curiosity, we're going to Dr. Susan Chandler's office. Or at least, *you're* going there to deliver these flowers. I'll wait in the car."

Over the years, Jim had delivered flowers to many attractive women for his boss, but he never before had known Alex Wright to personally select them.

With the informality that came with long years of service, Jim had said, "Mr. Alex, if I may say so, I liked Dr. Chandler. She's a nice woman and really attractive. I found there was something warm and natural about her, if you know what I mean."

"I know what you mean, Jim," Alex Wright had responded, "and I agree."

Jim had pulled the car into an illegal parking spot on Houston Street, sprinted around the corner to the office building, caught an elevator just as the door was closing, and on reaching the top floor, hurried down the corridor to the office that displayed the discreet sign, DR. SUSAN CHANDLER. There he had deposited the flowers with the receptionist, refused the proffered tip, and rushed back to the car.

Once again he took advantage of his long-established loyalty to ask a question: "Mr. Alex, isn't that the vase that was on the table in the foyer, the Waterford your mother brought back from Ireland?"

"You've got a good eye, Jim. The other night when I escorted Dr. Chandler to her door, I could see that she had a vase very similar to that one, only smaller. I thought it could use a companion piece. Now you'd better step on it. I'm already late for lunch at the Plaza."

* * *

A t two-thirty, Alex was back at his desk at the offices of the Wright Family Foundation. At quarter of three his secretary announced a call from Dee Chandler Harriman.

"Put it through, Alice," he said, a note of curiosity in his voice.

Dee's voice was both warm and apologetic. "Alex, you're probably busy giving away five or six million dollars, so I won't keep you but a minute."

"I haven't given away that much money since yesterday afternoon," he assured her. "What can I do for you?"

"Nothing too difficult, I hope. Somewhere around dawn I made a momentous decision. It's time to move back to New York. My partners at the modeling agency out here are willing to buy me out. A neighbor who's renting in my building has been salivating for my condo and will take it right off my hands. So here's why I'm calling: Can you recommend a good real estate agent? I'm in the market for a four- or five-room co-op on the East Side, preferably somewhere between Fifth and Park, and definitely in the mid-seventies."

"I'm not going to be a lot of help, Dee. I've been living in the same house since I was born," Alex told her. "But I could inquire about a broker for you."

"Oh, thank you, that would be such a help. I hate to bother you, but I had the feeling you wouldn't mind. I'm arriving there tomorrow afternoon. That way I can start looking on Friday."

"I'll come up with a name for you by then."

"Then give it to me over a drink tomorrow night. My treat."

She hung up before he could respond. Alex Wright leaned back in his chair. This was an unexpected complication. He had heard the change in Susan's voice when he told her he had invited her sister to the dinner at the library. That was why he had sent the flowers today and had taken such pains to make them special.

"Do I need this?" he muttered aloud. Then he remembered that his father had been fond of saying that any negative situation could be turned into a plus. The trick, Alex thought wryly, was to figure out how to make that happen in this case.

50

With weary resignation, Jane Clausen entered the hospital room. As she suspected, her doctor had insisted that she go in for immediate treatment. The cancer that was inevitably winning the battle with her body seemed intent on not giving her the strength or the time to take care of all that needed tending to. Jane wished she could just say "No more treatment," but she wasn't ready to die—not quite yet. She had a sense that some unfinished business might actually be taken care of, if she were only given the time, now when she had a glimmer of hope that she might learn the truth about Regina's fate. If the woman who had phoned in to Dr. Chandler's program would only come forward and show the picture of the man who had given her the turquoise ring, they would have a starting point at last.

She undressed, hung her clothes in the small

wardrobe, and put on the gown and robe Vera had packed for her. Another bout of chemotherapy would begin in the morning.

When dinner was served, she accepted only a cup of tea and a slice of toast, then got into bed, took the painkiller the nurse brought her, and began to drift off.

"Mrs. Clausen."

She opened her eyes and saw the solicitous face of Douglas Layton bending over her.

"Douglas." She wasn't sure if she was pleased that he had come, but she did find some comfort in his obvious concern.

"I called you at home because we needed your signature on a tax form. When Vera told me you were here, I came right over."

"I thought I signed everything at the meeting," she murmured.

"One of the pages was overlooked, I'm afraid. But it can wait. I don't want to bother you with it now."

"That's foolish. Give it to me." *I wasn't feeling well at the meeting,* Jane thought. *I'm surprised I didn't miss more.*

She reached for her glasses and glanced at the form Douglas was offering. "Oh, yes, that one." She took the pen he gave her and wrote her signature, carefully, making an effort to keep it even on the line.

Tonight, in the dim light in the hospital room, Jane Clausen thought how much Douglas looked like the Laytons she had known in Philadelphia. A fine family. Yet how quick she had been to mistrust him yesterday. That was the trouble, she thought. Her illness and all the medication were robbing her of judgment. Tomorrow she would phone Dr. Chandler and tell her she was sure she had been wrong in her suspicions about Douglas—wrong, and terribly unfair to him.

"Mrs. Clausen, can I get you anything?"

"No, nothing at all, but thank you, Douglas."

"May I stop in tomorrow?"

"Call first. I may not be up to visitors."

"I understand."

Jane Clausen felt him lift her hand and graze it gently with his lips.

She was asleep before he tiptoed from the room, but even had she been awake, given the darkness of the room, she probably would have been unaware of the satisfied smirk on his face.

51

After her second phone call to *Ask Dr. Susan*, Tiffany was intensely pleased with herself. She had gotten across exactly the message she wanted, and now she just hoped that someone would report her call to Matt. And she was sure her boss, Tony Sepeddi, would be thrilled when he heard about the plug she had managed to get in for The Grotto.

Later she was struck by a sudden possibility: *Suppose Matt showed up at The Grotto tonight?* Tiffany studied herself in the mirror. She definitely was overdue for a dye job; the dark roots of her hair were popping out. They look like railroad tracks, she told herself. Plus her bangs were getting long. He could almost mistake me for a sheepdog, she thought playfully, as she punched in the number of her hairdresser.

"Tiffany! My gosh, we're all talking about you. One of the customers told us yesterday that you'd been on *Ask Dr. Susan*, so we turned it on today. When I heard you, I yelled at everybody to keep quiet. We even turned off the dryers. You sounded terrific. So natural and cute. And listen, tell your boss at The Grotto you should get a raise."

Tiffany's request for an immediate appointment was enthusiastically granted. "Come right over. You're a celebrity. We gotta make sure you look like one."

Forty-five minutes later, Tiffany was sitting at a sink, the two inches of hair closest to her scalp processing. It was four-twenty when she got back home, her shiny hair caressing her shoulders, her nails freshly tipped and painted in the dark blue shade that Jill had encouraged her to try.

Gotta be out of here in fifteen minutes, she warned herself. Plug or no plug, Tony was a devil about getting in to work late.

Even so, she took the extra time to run the iron over the blouse and skirt that she knew looked really great on her. Maybe if Matt showed up, they could go someplace when she got off at midnight, maybe someplace nice for a nightcap.

She hesitated about wearing the turquoise ring that had inspired this moment of celebrity, then decided to leave it on. But if Matt did show up and happened to mention it, she wouldn't make a fuss about it. She would just let him see it, casually . . .

Tiffany had just opened the door to leave her apartment when the phone rang. I'll let it go, she thought, I don't want to get stuck talking.

On the other hand, she thought, quickly reconsidering, it might be Matt. She ran across the small living room to her even smaller bedroom and managed to pick up the receiver on the third ring.

It was Matt's mother. She didn't bother with greetings but cut straight to the chase: "Tiffany, I must insist that you stop talking about my son on the radio. Matthew took you out only a few times. He told me he had nothing in common with you. Next month he is moving out to Long Island. He has just become engaged to a very attractive young woman he's been seeing for some time. So please forget him, and do not talk about your dates with him, particularly where his friends or his fiancée will hear about it."

A decisive click sounded in Tiffany's ear.

Shocked, she stood perfectly still for a full minute, the receiver in her hand. *Engaged?* I hadn't even heard he was dating anybody, she thought, feeling the despair seep through her body.

"If you'd like to make a call . . ."

The operator's voice sounded as if it were coming from another planet. Tiffany slammed down the receiver. She had to get to work; already she knew she would have to rush to keep from being late. Tears streaming from her eyes, she ran down the stairs, ignoring the greeting from her landlord's six-year-old son, who was playing on the porch.

In the car, the hurt and disappointment washed over her, and she could hardly breathe for the sobs that were racking her body. She wanted to pull over somewhere and cry it out of her system, but she knew she didn't have time.

Instead, when she reached The Grotto, she chose a

remote spot in the parking lot and sat for a moment in the car. Then she pulled out her compact. She had to get ahold of herself. She couldn't walk in there like this; she couldn't let them see her crying over some jerk who ate slimy fish and only took her to lousy movies. "Who needs him anyhow?" she asked out loud.

A new layer of foundation, fresh eye shadow, and lipstick helped repair the damage, even though her lip wouldn't stop quivering. *Well, if you don't want me, then I don't want you,* she thought fiercely. *I hate you, Matt. You jerk!*

It was one minute of five. She might make it on time after all, but she had to get moving. All she needed right now was for Tony to start blasting her.

On the way to the kitchen door, she passed the Dumpster. She paused for a moment and looked at it. In one sweeping gesture, she pulled the turquoise ring from her finger and tossed it inside, where it disappeared into a half-open plastic bag stuffed with lunchtime refuse. "Lousy ring brought me nothing but lousy luck," Tiffany muttered, then ran to the kitchen door, pushed it open, and yelled, "Hi, guys, has Tony heard about the big plug I gave this dump today?"

52

Susan's two o'clock appointment arrived only five minutes after she had reached her office. In the cab, she had managed to clear her head of anything other than the patient's history. Meyer Winter was a sixty-five-year-old retired executive who had overcome the damage caused by a stroke. Now, although he used a walking stick and had a slight limp, there was nothing to suggest the length and severity of his illness.

Nothing, that is, except the profound depression caused by the fear that it could happen again, she reminded herself.

Today's visit was his tenth, and when he left, Susan felt she could see visible improvement, the kind of turnaround in attitude that she found so deeply rewarding. It was her own response to victories like this one that made her really glad of her decision six years ago to make psychology her lifework, instead of the law.

As soon as Mr. Winter left, Janet came in with her messages. "A Dr. Pamela Hastings phoned. She's at home and says she's anxious to talk with you."

"I'll call her right now."

"Aren't those flowers gorgeous?" Janet asked.

Susan had barely noticed the vase of flowers that sat on her office credenza. Now, as she crossed to them, her eyes widened. "There must be a mistake," she said. "That vase is Waterford."

"No mistake," Janet assured her. "I tried to tip the guy who brought the bouquet, but he refused. He said it was from his employer. My guess is he was a chauffeur, or something like that."

Of course. Alex heard something in my voice after he told me he had invited Dee along on Saturday night, Susan thought. That explains a gesture so grand as this. How perceptive of him. And how *stupid* of me, to allow my feelings to be so transparent.

The gift was beautiful, but her pleasure at receiving it was diminished by her understanding of the reason behind it. For a moment she debated whether to call Alex right away to say that she couldn't possibly accept the vase. Then she shook her head—she could deal with all that later. Right now there were more pressing things. She reached for the phone.

The conversation was brief, and it ended with Pamela Hastings promising to be at Susan's office at nine o'clock the next morning.

Susan glanced at her watch: She was only seconds away from her next appointment. Clearly she had no time to speculate about the obvious fact that Pamela Hastings was upset about something other than her friend's grave condition. She had said, "Dr. Chandler, I have a hard decision to make. It concerns what happened to Carolyn Wells. Perhaps you can help me."

Susan had wanted to press her for more information, but she knew it might be an involved discussion, and it would just have to wait.

"Mrs. Mentis is here," Janet announced, sticking her head in the door.

At ten of four, Donald Richards phoned. "Just calling to confirm tonight, Susan. Seven o'clock at Palio, on West Fifty-first—all right?"

After that call, Susan realized she still had a few minutes before her next patient. She looked up Jane Clausen's number and quickly dialed it. There was no response, so she left a message for her on the answering machine.

* * *

It was five after six before she'd seen her last patient out. Janet already had left for the day. Susan would have liked to go home for at least a few minutes, but she knew that she had barely enough time to freshen up here at the office before she would have to take a taxi to the restaurant.

She had wanted to reach Tiffany at home earlier, and to try to persuade her at least to make an appointment so they could compare her turquoise ring with the one Jane Clausen had found among Regina's possessions. But Tiffany was surely at work now, and the restaurant probably was at the height of its dinner hour. I'll call her there later, when I get home, Susan thought. She said she works nights, so she probably stays fairly late. If I miss her, I'll try her at home in the morning.

Susan shuddered. Why did thinking about Tiffany give her such an uneasy feeling? she wondered. It was a sensation akin to what her grandmother used to call "sixth sense."

53

He didn't know Tiffany's last name, but even if he did, and even if she was registered in the Yonkers phone book, it wouldn't be wise to try to track her down at home. Besides, it wasn't necessary. She had already told him where he could find her.

He phoned The Grotto in midafternoon and asked

to speak to her. As anticipated, he was told that she wasn't there—that she came on at five.

He had long ago learned that the best way to get information was to let someone correct an erroneous statement. "She gets off about eleven, right?" he suggested.

"Midnight. That's when the kitchen closes down. You wanna leave a message?"

"No, thanks. I'll try her at home again."

Come tomorrow, if whoever he had just spoken to at The Grotto remembered the call, he probably would dismiss it as being from one of Tiffany's friends. After all, hadn't he indicated that he knew Tiffany's home number?

He hoped the hours leading up to his excursion to Yonkers turned out to be pleasant. Still, he couldn't wait for the time to pass until he could get to her. It was a rendezvous he looked forward to with great anticipation. Tiffany had studied him. And probably, like many people in the restaurant business, she had a good memory for faces. It had been pure luck she hadn't blathered to Susan Chandler that she had seen a man buying one of the special turquoise rings in the shop when she was there.

He could imagine what Chandler would have said: *Tiffany, what you're telling me is very important. I must meet you . . .*

Too late, Susan, he thought. And too bad.

What about Tiffany's boyfriend—Matt?

Carefully he reviewed the scene in Parki's shop. He had phoned ahead to be sure Parki had a ring in stock. When he entered the shop, he already had in his hand the exact change, including tax, and, as instructed,

Parki had the ring waiting at the register. It was only when he turned to leave that he saw the couple. He remembered the moment distinctly. Yes, he had been directly in the girl's line of vision. She had seen him clearly. The fellow she was with was looking over the junk on the shelves, his back to him. He wasn't a problem, thank God.

Parki was out of the way. And after tonight, Tiffany too would no longer be a concern.

A line from "The Highwayman," a poem he had memorized as a child, ran through his mind: "I'll come to thee by moonlight, though hell should bar the way."

He chuckled grimly at the thought.

54

Late Wednesday afternoon, when Justin Wells returned to his office from the hospital, he was appalled to find a message to call Captain Shea of the 19th Precinct to set up a visit to the station house to discuss his wife's accident. The message concluded ominously with the words, "You know where we are located."

The memory of that terrible evening when Carolyn had sworn out a complaint against him was something Justin had never allowed himself to dwell on.

I shouldn't have threatened to kill her, he reminded himself as he crumpled the message in his hand. I never meant to hurt her, I just grabbed her arm when she started walking out of the apartment. I didn't mean to twist it. It happened because she tried to pull away.

Then she had run into the bedroom, locked the door, and called the cops. What followed had been a nightmare for him. The next day she had left him a note saying that she was withdrawing the criminal complaint and filing for divorce. Then she disappeared.

He had begged Pamela Hastings to tell him where Carolyn had gone, but she wouldn't give him any information. It was only when he thought to call Carolyn's travel agent and say that he had mislaid the number where she could be reached that he had gotten the name of the ship she was sailing on and was able to contact her.

That had been exactly two years ago.

One of the promises he had made to Carolyn at the time was to start therapy, and he had—but then he couldn't stand the thought of revealing himself to anyone, even to a sympathetic listener like Dr. Richards, and that was the end of that.

Of course, he never told Carolyn. She thought he was still seeing Richards.

Justin paced his office, remembering how Carolyn had been different over the weekend: she seemed quieter, a little nervous. He had felt himself getting suspicious. And she had been late getting home one night last week—claimed she was going over plans with the client whose house she was decorating in East Hampton.

Then on Monday, Barbara, the receptionist, told him in front of his partners that she was sure it was Carolyn she had heard on the *Ask Dr. Susan* radio program, talking about a guy she met when she and her husband were separated.

He had called Carolyn and asked her about it. He knew he upset her. Then he had left the office. He didn't want to think about the rest of the day.

Now Carolyn was in the hospital, still in a coma, and she kept trying to say someone's name. "Win," it sounded like. Was that the guy she had gotten involved with on the ship? he wondered.

The thought of it made Justin's chest feel as if it were going to explode. He could feel perspiration beading up on his forehead.

He smoothed out the note and looked at it again. He had to call Captain Shea. He didn't want him phoning the office again. As it was, Barbara had given him a funny look when she handed him the message.

The thought of that terrible night two years ago almost sickened him—the cops arresting him, bringing him to the station, handcuffed like a common thief.

Justin picked up the receiver, then depressed the button to cut off the dial tone. Finally he lifted his finger and forced himself to make the call.

An hour later he was giving his name to the desk sergeant at the 19th Precinct, acutely aware that some of the cops might remember his face. Cops were good at that.

Then he was sent into Captain Shea's office, and the questioning began.

"Any trouble with your wife since last time, Mr. Wells?"

"Absolutely not."

"Where were you between four and four-thirty Monday afternoon?"

"I was taking a walk."

"Did you stop at your home?"

"Yes, I did. Why?"

"Did you see your wife?"

"She was out."

"What did you do then?"

"I came back to the office."

"By any chance were you at the corner of Eighty-first and Park around four-fifteen?"

"No, I walked down Fifth Avenue."

"Did you know the late Hilda Johnson?"

"Who's that?" Justin paused. "Wait a minute. She's the woman who said Carolyn didn't fall but was pushed. I saw her on television. I gather, though, that nobody believed her."

"Yes," Shea said quietly. "She's the woman who insisted that your wife was pushed in front of that van. Hilda was a very careful woman, Mr. Wells. She never would have buzzed someone into the lobby of her building, then opened the door of her apartment unless she felt she could trust that person."

Tom Shea leaned across his desk, his manner confidential. "Mr. Wells, I knew Hilda. She was a regular character in this neighborhood. I am sure she would have opened both those doors to the husband of the woman she insisted had been pushed. She would have been anxious to tell him her story personally. You didn't happen to go visit Hilda Johnson later that night, did you, Mr. Wells?"

55

Donald Richards was waiting at the bar at Palio when Susan arrived at ten after seven. He cut short her apology.

"Traffic was terrible, and I just walked in the door myself. And you might be interested to hear that I had lunch with my mother today. She was listening to your program when I was on and was very impressed with you. However, she lectured me on the fact that I had arranged to meet you here. In her day, a gentleman apparently always called for a young lady at home, and escorted her to the restaurant."

Susan laughed. "Given the traffic in Manhattan, by the time you picked me up in the Village, and then came back to midtown, the restaurants would be closed." She looked around. The horseshoe-shaped bar was busy and flanked on both sides by small tables, all of them occupied. A magnificent mural depicting the famous Palio horse race, painted primarily in reds, soared above them, covering the walls on all four sides of the two-story room. The lighting was subdued, the atmosphere was both warm and sophisticated. "I've never been here. It looks very nice," she said.

"Neither have I, but it comes highly recommended. The dining room is on the second floor."

Richards gave his name to the young woman at the desk. "Reservation confirmed. We're free to use the elevator," he told Susan.

She tried not to show how keenly she was studying

Donald Richards. His hair was dark brown, with just a touch of auburn—"leaf brown" was the way Gran Susie would have described it, she thought. He was wearing wide glasses with a steel gray frame. The lenses enhanced his gray-blue eyes—or were his eyes pure blue, and their color subtly altered by the frame?

She was sure he had changed for the evening. Yesterday and Monday when he came to the studio, he had worn a blazer and slacks. The impression she had gotten of him was of someone slightly rumpled, professorial. Tonight he looked markedly different, dressed in an obviously expensive dark blue suit and silver-and-blue tie.

The elevator arrived. They got in, and as the door closed, he observed, "May I say you look very attractive. That's a great suit."

"I'm not sure if I'm fancy enough for you," Susan said candidly. "As my grandmother would put it, 'you're all duded up.' "

"You're fancy enough, I assure you."

That's the second time in five minutes I've thought of Gran, Susan thought. What gives?

They emerged on the second floor, where the maître d' greeted them and took them to their table. He asked for their drink orders, and Susan requested chardonnay; Donald Richards, a martini, straight up.

"I don't usually have a 'see-through,' " he explained, "but it's been a heavy-duty day."

Was that because of lunch with your mother? Susan wondered. She warned herself not to seem curious about him. She couldn't let herself forget that he was a psychiatrist and would see through any effort to probe.

She was burning with questions, however, and wondered if she would ever find a "safe" way to ask them. For example, why had he reacted with such distress when a caller asked about his wife's death? Wouldn't it have been natural to discuss the fact that he was familiar with cruise ships when Susan talked about Regina Clausen disappearing while on a cruise? And according to Richards's bio, the ship Regina was on—the *Gabrielle*—was his favorite. She had to get him to talk about it.

The best way to steer a conversation to where you want it to be is to disarm the other person, she told herself, put him at ease. Susan smiled warmly across the table. "A listener phoned today to say that after hearing you, she went out and bought your book and is thoroughly enjoying it."

Richards returned her smile. "I heard her. Obviously a woman of great discrimination."

You heard her? Susan wondered. Busy psychiatrists don't usually listen to two-hour advice programs.

Their drinks came. Richards raised his glass in a toast to her. "I'm grateful for the pleasure of your company."

She knew it was the sort of remark that people make over a cocktail. Still Susan felt there was something behind the casual compliment—an intensity in the way he said it, a sudden narrowing of his eyes, as though he were studying her under a microscope.

"Dr. Susan," he said, "I'm going to admit something. I looked you up on the Internet."

That makes *two* of us, Susan thought. Turnabout is fair play, I suppose.

"You were raised in Westchester?" he asked.

"Yes. Larchmont, then Rye. But my grandmother

always lived in Greenwich Village, and I spent a lot of weekends with her when I was growing up. I always loved it. My sister is much more the country-club type than I ever was."

"Parents?"

"Divorced three years ago. And unfortunately not one of those agree-to-disagree situations. My father met someone else and fell head over heels in love. My mother was devastated and has gone through the various stages of being heartbroken, angry, bitter, in denial. You name it."

"How did you feel about it?"

"Sad. We were a close-knit, happy family, or so I thought. We had fun together. We really liked each other. After the divorce, though, *everything* changed. I sometimes think that it was like a ship striking a reef and sinking, and while all on board survived, everyone got in a different lifeboat."

She realized suddenly that she had said more than she intended, and was grateful he did not pursue it.

Instead he said, "I'm curious. What made you leave being an assistant district attorney and go back to school for a doctorate in clinical psychology?"

Susan found that an easy question to answer. "I guess I realized I was restless. There are people who are hardened criminals, and I got real satisfaction from getting them off the streets. But then I prosecuted a case where a woman killed her husband because he was about to leave her. She got fifteen years. I'll never forget the stunned, disbelieving look on her face when she heard the sentence. I could only think that if she had been caught in time, had gotten help, released that anger before it destroyed her . . ."

"Terrible grief can trigger terrible anger," he said quietly. "No doubt later you saw your mother in that situation and realized that could have been her being sentenced."

Susan nodded. "For a brief period into the separation, my mother was both suicidal and violent, at least in the way she talked about my father. I did my best to help her. In some ways I miss the courts, but I know it was the right decision for me. How about you? What took you into this field?"

"I always wanted to be a doctor. In medical school I realized to what extent the way the mind works affects physical health, and so I chose that path."

The maître d' arrived with menus, and after a few minutes of discussing the pros and cons of the various food groups, they ordered their dinners.

Susan had hoped to use the break in conversation to steer the discussion more toward him, but he returned immediately to talk of her radio show.

"There was something else my mother brought up today," he said, casually. "Did you ever hear anything more from Karen, the woman who called on Monday?"

"No, I didn't," Susan said.

Donald Richards broke off a piece of roll. "Did your producer send Justin Wells a copy of that program?"

It was not a question Susan had expected. "Do *you* know Justin Wells?" she asked, unable to keep her surprise from showing in her voice.

"I've met him."

"Personally or professionally?"

"Professionally."

"Were you treating him for excessive and dangerous jealousy of his wife?"

"Why do you ask that?"

"Because if the answer is yes, I think you have a moral obligation to tell what you know about him to the police. I didn't mean to be evasive when you asked about Karen, but the truth is, while I didn't hear from her again, I have learned something more about her. It turns out that the woman who called herself Karen is Justin Wells's wife, whose real name is Carolyn, and she fell or was pushed in front of a van a few hours after she called me."

Donald Richards's expression was not so much surprised as grave and reflective. "I'm afraid you're probably right, I *should* speak to the police," he said grimly.

"Captain Shea of the 19th Precinct is handling the investigation," Susan told him.

I was right, she thought. The obvious connection between what happened to Carolyn Wells and the phone call to me is her husband's jealousy.

She thought of the turquoise ring with the sentimental inscription. The fact that Tiffany had gotten one in Greenwich Village probably meant nothing at all. Like plastic Statues of Liberty, or ivory Taj Mahals, or heart-shaped lockets, they were the kind of thing indigenous to souvenir and trinket shops everywhere.

"How's your salad?" Richards asked.

It was obvious he intended to change the subject. And rightly so, Susan thought with relief. Professional ethics. "Absolutely fine. And I've told you about myself. What about you? Any siblings?"

"No, I'm an only. Grew up in Manhattan. My father died ten years ago. That's when my mother decided to live in Tuxedo Park year round. She's a painter, quite good, perhaps even *very* good. My father was a born sailor and used to take me along to crew for him."

Susan mentally crossed her fingers. "I was interested to see that you took a year off from college to work as an assistant cruise director. Your father's influence, I assume?"

He looked amused. "We both get information from the Internet, don't we? Yes, I enjoyed that year. Did the round-the-world cruise, taking in most of the major ports, then I hit the smaller destinations. Pretty much traveled the globe."

"What exactly does an assistant cruise director do?"

"Helps to organize and coordinate the shipboard activities. Everything from scheduling the paid entertainers and making sure they have whatever they need to do their acts, to running bingo and planning costume balls. Smoothe ruffled feathers. Spot lonely or unhappy people and draw them out. You name it."

"According to your bio, you met your wife on the *Gabrielle*; it says also that it was your favorite ship. That was the ship Regina Clausen was traveling on when she disappeared."

"Yes. I never met her, of course, but I can certainly understand why the *Gabrielle* would have been recommended to her. She's a wonderful ship."

"If you had known about Regina Clausen's disappearance, would you have been tempted to include her among those you discuss in your book?" She hoped the question sounded offhand.

"No, I don't think so."

At some point he's going to tell me to stop the

grilling, Susan thought, but so far, so good, so I'll keep going until he does. "I'm curious," she said. "What gave you the idea for writing *Vanishing Women*?"

"I got interested in the subject because six years ago I had a patient whose wife disappeared. She simply didn't come home one day. He envisioned her in all sorts of situations—being held prisoner, wandering with amnesia, murdered."

"Did he ever learn what happened to her?"

"Two years ago, he did. There was a lake at the bend of the road near their home. Somebody went scuba diving there and saw a car—her car, as it turned out—on the bottom. She was in it. She probably missed the turn."

"What happened to him?"

"His life changed. The next year he remarried; now he's a totally different person from the man who came to me for help. What struck me is that perhaps the greatest pain in losing someone you love is in not knowing what happened to her . . . or him. And that made me research other cases of women who seemingly vanished without a trace."

"How did you select the cases you used in the book?"

"I quickly realized that in most cases the cause of the disappearance was foul play. On that basis, I analyzed how women got into a particular situation, and then suggested ways to prevent that kind of thing from happening to anyone else."

During the course of their conversation, salad plates had been cleared and replaced by entrees. They had continued talking through the meal, niceties— comments on the food (highly favorable), comparisons with other favorite restaurants (New York City is a feast for diners)—interspersed among the more obviously probing questions.

Don Richards finished the last bit of his Dover sole, then leaned back in his chair. "It seems to me that this has been a Q-and-A, with me being the answer man," he said good-naturedly. "I've filled you in about myself. Let's talk about you for a while, Susan. As I told you, I'm a sailor. What do you do for recreation?"

"I ski a lot," Susan said. "My father is a terrific skier, and he taught me. Just as you sailed with your dad, mine always took me along with him when he went skiing. My mother hates the cold and my sister does too, and wasn't interested, so he had plenty of time for me."

"Still ski with him?"

"No. I'm afraid he's hung up his skis."

"Since his new marriage?"

"About that time." Susan was grateful that the waiter arrived with the dessert menu. She had wanted to learn about Donald Richards, yet here she was, revealing too much about herself.

They both decided to skip dessert and order espresso. After it had arrived, Richards brought up Tiffany's name. "It was kind of sad to listen to her today. She's terribly vulnerable, don't you think?"

"I think she wants desperately to fall in love, and to be loved," Susan said in agreement. "It sounds like Matt was the nearest thing to a lasting relationship that she's ever had. She's given his name to her need."

Richards nodded. "And I bet that if Matt *does* call her, it won't be because he's happy that she's been making so much of his impulse to buy a souvenir ring. That would scare most guys off."

Is he downplaying the ring? Susan wondered. The words of the song "You Belong to Me" began to drift through her mind: *See the pyramids along the Nile / Watch the sunrise on a tropic isle . . .*

When they left the restaurant, Richards hailed a cab. As they got in, he gave the driver her address. Then he looked at her sheepishly. "I'm not a mind reader. I saw that you're listed in the phone book . . . under S. C. Chandler. What's the *C* stand for?"

"Connelley. My mother's maiden name."

Once they had arrived at her apartment building, he had the cab wait while he escorted her upstairs. "Your mother would be pleased," Susan told him. "A perfect gentleman." She thought of Alex Wright, who had done the same thing two nights ago. Two gentlemen in three days, she reflected. Not bad.

Richards took her hand. "I think I said thank you for the pleasure of your company at the beginning of the evening. I say it again, even more emphatically."

He looked soberly at her and added, "Don't be afraid of a compliment, Susan. You are, you know. Good night."

Then he was gone. Susan double locked the door and leaned against it for a moment, trying to sort out her feelings. Then she crossed to the answering machine. There were two messages. The first was from her mother: "Phone me any time up until midnight."

It was quarter of eleven. Without listening to the second message, and keeping her fingers crossed that nothing was wrong, Susan began to dial.

Her mother's nervousness was obvious in her voice as she barely acknowledged Susan's greeting and began to stammer out the reason for her call. "Susan, this is crazy, and I feel as though I'm being put in the position of choosing between my daughters, but . . ."

Susan listened to her mother's fumbling explanation of how Alex Wright apparently had enjoyed meeting her at the party Sunday, but how Binky had been trying to set him up with Dee. "We know that Dee is lonely and restless, but I'd hate to see her interfere with a friendship that you might be enjoying." Her mother's voice trailed off. This conversation was obviously very difficult for her.

"You'd hate to see Dee move in again on someone who may have expressed interest in me. That's it, isn't it, Mom? Well look, I had a very pleasant dinner with Alex Wright, but that's all. I gather Dee has been calling him. In fact, he's invited her to join us at a dinner party Saturday night. I'm not in competition with my sister. When I meet the right person for me, we'll both know it, and I won't have to worry about him straying when my sister crooks a finger at him. Because if that's the kind of man he is, then I don't want him."

"You're insinuating I'd take your father back," her mother protested.

"No, where do you get that?" Susan said. "I understand exactly how rotten you feel about what Dad pulled on you. I feel rotten about it too. But there's something about breaking a trust that for a lot of people, myself included, would deal a mortal blow to a relationship. So let's see what happens. I have had, after all, exactly one date with Alex. The second time around we might bore each other silly."

"Just understand that poor Dee is so unhappy," her mother pleaded. "She called me this afternoon to say that she's moving back to New York. She misses us, and she's tired of the modeling agency. Your father is treating her to a cruise next week. I hope that will pick up her spirits."

"I hope so too. Okay, Mom, talk to you soon."

Finally she played the second message; this one was from Alex Wright: "A business dinner was canceled, and I worked up the nerve to try you on short notice again. Not very good manners, I know, but I *did* want to see you. I'll give you a call tomorrow."

Smiling, Susan replayed the message. Now that's one compliment Dr. Richards wouldn't find me resisting, she thought. And I'm *mighty* glad Dee is signed up for a cruise next week.

It was only sometime later, when she was in bed and drifting off to sleep, that Susan remembered she had wanted to phone Tiffany at The Grotto. She just had to persuade her to come in and at least compare her turquoise ring with the one found among Regina Clausen's possessions. Turning on the light, she looked at the clock. It was quarter of twelve.

I could catch her, she thought. Maybe if I invite her to come to the studio tomorrow, and offer to take her out for a quick lunch, she'll accept.

She got the phone number of The Grotto from information and dialed. The phone rang for a long time before it was picked up and someone barked, "Grotto."

Susan asked for Tiffany, then waited several minutes before she came on. No sooner had she given her name than Tiffany exploded. "Dr. Susan, I never want to hear a word about that stupid ring again. Matt's mother phoned and told me to stop talking about him; she said that he's getting married. So I threw that dumb ring away! No disrespect to you, but now I wish I hadn't been listening to your show that day. And I wish Matt and I had never even gone in that stupid souvenir shop. And I wish especially that we hadn't been listening when the man who ran that dumb place told us that the guy who'd just been in had bought these rings for several of his girlfriends."

Susan sat straight up in bed. "Tiffany, this is important. Did you *see* that man?"

"Sure I did. He was a doll. A class act. Not like Matt."

"Tiffany, I *have* to talk to you. Come into the city tomorrow. We'll have lunch together, and please tell me, is it possible to get your ring back?"

"Dr. Susan, by now it's under tons of chicken bones and pizza, and that's where it's gonna stay. I don't want to talk about it anymore. I feel like such an idiot, telling the whole world how great Matt is. What a jerk! Listen, I gotta go. My boss is giving me the evil eye."

"Tiffany, have you remembered where you bought that ring?" Susan begged.

"I told you, in the Village. The West Village. I know it wasn't too far from a subway stop. The only thing I remember for certain about where it was is that there was a porn shop opposite. I gotta go. Bye, Dr. Susan."

Completely awake now, Susan replaced the receiver slowly. Tiffany had thrown away her turquoise ring, which was too bad, but she seemed to remember a man who apparently had bought several others. I was going to call Chris Ryan to run a check on Douglas Layton, she thought. I'll give him Tiffany's home phone number as well. He'll be able to get her address for me. And if he can't, then tomorrow evening I'll be sitting in The Grotto, having the best Italian food in Yonkers.

56

Tiffany had managed to get through the night, and during most of it she had kept up her usual wisecracking and her sassy veneer. It helped that The Grotto had been busy, and that she hadn't had much time to think. There had been only a couple of times, like when she had gone to the ladies' room and been forced to look at her own reflection, that the hurt and anger came flooding back.

Around eleven o'clock some guy had come in and sat at the bar. She could feel him undressing her with his eyes every time she passed him on the way to her tables.

Jerk, she thought.

At twenty of twelve he had grabbed her hand and asked her to come have a drink at his place when she got off.

"Get lost, creep!" she had told him.

Then he had squeezed her hand so hard that she couldn't help yelping in pain. "You don't have to get nasty," he had snapped.

"Let go of her!" Joey, the bartender, had been around the bar in a shot. "You've had enough, mister," he said. "Pay your bill and get out of here."

The guy stood up. He was big, but Joey was bigger. Then the jerk threw some money on the bar and left.

Right after that, Dr. Susan phoned, and once again Tiffany was made aware of just how rotten she was feeling. All I want to do is go home and pull the covers over my head, she thought after that.

At five of twelve, Joey called Tiffany over. "Listen, kid, when you're ready to go, I'll walk you to your car. That guy could be hanging around outside."

But then, just as Tiffany was buttoning her coat to leave, a bowling team came in and the bar got busy. Tiffany could see that Joey wouldn't be free for at least ten minutes.

"I'll be okay, Joey. See you tomorrow," she called to him, and darted out.

It wasn't until she was outside that she remembered leaving her car in the far corner of the parking lot. What a pain, Tiffany thought. If that guy *is* hanging around, he could be a problem. Carefully she scanned every inch of the lot. There was one person out there, a guy who looked like he had just gotten out of his car and was probably headed to the bar. Even in the shadowy light, though, she could tell he wasn't the jerk who had tried to come on to her. This guy was tall and thinner.

Still, something made her feel funny, made her want to get out of there as quickly as possible. As she walked rapidly toward her car, she fumbled in her bag for her keys. Her fingers closed over them. She was almost there.

Then suddenly the guy she had seen across the lot

was standing in front of her. There was something shiny in his hand.

A knife! she thought, the realization making her freeze almost in midstep.

No! she thought, disbelieving, as she saw him move toward her.

Why? she wondered, incredulous that this was happening.

"Please," she begged. *"Please!"*

Tiffany lived long enough to see her attacker's face, long enough for her excellent memory to help her recognize her killer as the classy guy she had glimpsed in that Village souvenir shop—the one who had bought those rings inscribed "You belong to me."

57

As he drove back to the city, traveling along the Cross Bronx Expressway, he could feel the perspiration pouring from him. It had been a close call. He had just stepped over the low wall that separated The Grotto's property from the locked gas station where he had parked his car, when he heard some guy yelling "Tiffany."

He had left his car on the other side of the station, and fortunately there was an incline and he didn't have to start the engine until he reached the road. Once there he turned right and merged with the traffic, so chances were no one had seen him.

Next week it would be all over, he reminded himself. He would choose someone to "See the jungle when it's wet with rain," and his mission would be completed.

Veronica, so trusting—she had been the first—now buried in Egypt: "See the pyramids along the Nile."

Regina. He had won her trust in Bali: "Watch the sunrise on a tropic isle."

Constance, who had replaced Carolyn in Algiers: "See the marketplace in old Algiers."

"Fly the ocean in a silver plane." He thought of Monica, the timid heiress he had met on the flight to London. He remembered how he had talked to her about the sun gleaming on the wing of the plane.

The rings had been a mistake, of course. He knew that now. They had been his private joke, like the connection between the names that he used on the special trips. He should have just kept his jokes to himself.

But Parki, who made the rings, was out of the way. Now Tiffany, who had seen him buying one of them, was gone. He was certain that, like Carolyn, she had recognized him at the end. Granted, Tiffany had seen him clearly and in his normal appearance in the souvenir shop, but even so it was unsettling that despite the shadowy light of the parking lot, she still had recognized him.

Well, these were feathers in the wind, and he could never recover them now, but surely they would blow away unnoticed. No matter how much he had tried to stay out of camera range, it was inevitable that he had been caught in the background of some photos taken on the cruise ships. Photos that people all over the world had no doubt framed, to remind themselves of their fabulous vacation . . . Photos that now went unnoticed on countless bedroom bureaus or study walls. He found the prospect both amusing and alarming.

After all, Carolyn Wells had been about to send a photo with him in the background to Susan Chandler. The thought of that narrow escape still unnerved him. He could imagine Susan opening that package, her eyes widening in surprise and horror when she recognized him.

At last he was at his garage. He drove down the ramp, stopped, got out and nodded to the attendant, who greeted him with the warmth reserved for long-time customers. It was almost one o'clock now, and he walked the short distance home, glad to feel the cool, bracing wind on his face.

A week from tonight, all this will be over, he promised himself. *By then I will have begun the last leg of my journey. Susan Chandler will have been eliminated, and I'll be starting my final cruise.*

He knew that once that was accomplished, the terrible burning inside him would go away, and finally he would be free—free to become the person his mother had always believed he was capable of being

58

Early Thursday morning, Pamela Hastings stopped at the hospital to visit Carolyn Wells, hoping to find her greatly improved. Instead she learned that her condition remained unchanged.

"She called for 'Win' again," Gladys, the head nurse on the morning shift, told her. "Only it sounded to me more like, 'Oh, Win,' as though she were trying to talk to him."

"Did her husband hear her when she spoke, Gladys?"

"No. He hasn't been here since yesterday afternoon."

"He *hasn't?*" Pamela was shocked. "Do you know if he has phoned? Is he ill?"

"We haven't heard from him."

"But that's crazy," Pam said, almost to herself. "I'll call him. May I look in on Carolyn?"

"Of course."

It had been only two and a half days since the accident, but Pamela felt such familiarity with the intensive care unit that it seemed as though she must have made this journey many times. Yesterday there had been curtains drawn around the bed of an elderly man who had come in with a massive heart attack. Today that bed was empty. Pamela decided not to ask; she felt sure the man had died during the night.

The part of Carolyn's face that was visible seemed even more swollen and bruised this morning than it had yesterday. It still seemed impossible to Pam that this woman, swathed in bandages and clips, and linked to IVs and tubes, was her pretty, vibrant friend.

Carolyn's hands were lying on top of the coverlet. Pam entwined her own fingers with her friend's, noting the absence of Carolyn's simple gold wedding band. It made her think of Carolyn's aversion to a lot of items of jewelry. A few good costume pins and earrings and her grandmother's single strand of pearls were as much as she had ever seen her wear.

"Carolyn," she said softly. "It's Pam. Just wanted to

see how you were doing. Everyone's asking about you. As soon as you're feeling better you'll have lots of company. Vickie and Lynn and I are planning your recovery party. Champagne, caviar, smoked salmon. You name it. The 'gang of four' knows how to party. Right?"

Pam knew she was prattling, but they had told her that it was possible Carolyn could hear her. She didn't want to talk about Justin. The thought occurred to Pam that if he had been the one who pushed Carolyn in front of that van, and she was aware of it, she might be terrified if in fact she was able to hear his voice, or even to sense his presence.

But I don't know what I can do about it, Pam thought. If only she would recover consciousness, even for a minute. "I've got to go, Car," she said, "but I'll be back later. Love you." She brushed Carolyn's cheek with her lips; she could detect no response.

Wiping tears away with the back of her hand, she left the ICU. As she passed the waiting room she was taken aback to see Justin there, slouched in a chair. He was unshaven and wearing the same clothes he had had on yesterday afternoon. Their eyes met, and he came out into the corridor. "Did Carolyn talk to you?" he asked eagerly.

"No, she didn't. Justin, what in God's name is going on? Why didn't you come back last night?"

He hesitated before answering. "Because although I'm not yet formally charged with anything, the police seem to think that *I* pushed Carolyn in front of that van."

He returned Pamela's stare. "You're shocked, aren't you, Pam? Shocked, but not surprised. That possibility *has* been running through your head, hasn't it?" His face crumbled and he began to sob. "Doesn't anyone understand how I feel about her?" Then he quickly shook his head and pointed to the ICU. "I'm not going back in there. If Carolyn *was* pushed and realized it, but didn't see the person, even she might think I did it. But I've got just one question for all of you: If she *is* involved with this guy, this 'Win' she keeps calling for, then why the hell isn't he here with her now?"

59

Chris Ryan had been an FBI agent for thirty years before he retired and set up his own small security firm on East Fifty-second Street. Now sixty-nine years old, with a full head of iron gray hair, a somewhat overweight frame, an affable expression, and merry blue eyes, he looked the perfect choice to play Santa Claus at his grandchildren's grammar school.

His easygoing personality and sardonic humor made him universally popular, but those who had dealt with him professionally had considerable respect for his investigating skills.

He and Susan had become friends when the family of a murder victim hired him to try to solve the crime independently of the police. As an assistant district attorney, she was directly involved with the case, and information Chris uncovered and shared with her helped her obtain a confession.

Ryan had been flabbergasted when she told him of her decision to quit her job in the prosecutor's office and go back to school. "You're a natural," he had told her. "A great trial lawyer. Why do you want to waste your time listening to a bunch of pampered whiners moan about their troubles?"

"Trust me. It's a little more than that, Chris," Susan had laughed.

They still saw each other for dinner every few months, so when Susan called him on Thursday morning, Chris was delighted. "Need a free meal?" he asked her genially. "There's a new steak house down the block. Corner of Forty-ninth and Third. Prime beef. Makes you glad to be raising your cholesterol count. When can you do it?"

"New steak house on Forty-ninth and Third, you say? Seems to me that's where Smith & Wollensky is located," Susan said. "And I happen to know that it's been there about seventy years and that some people think you own it." She laughed. "Sure I'll go, but first I have to ask a favor, Chris. I need a fast check on someone."

"Who?"

"A lawyer, Douglas Layton. He's with Hubert March and Associates. It's a legal and investment advice kind of firm. Layton is also a director of the Clausen Family Trust."

"Sounds successful. Are you thinking of marrying him?"

"No, I'm not."

Ryan leaned back in his swivel chair as Susan filled him in on the background, and explained that Jane Clausen had expressed concern to her about Layton. Then he listened intently as Susan told him about the events since the radio program on Monday on which Regina Clausen's disappearance was first discussed.

"And you say this guy did a disappearing act when you expected that woman who called herself Karen to show up in your office?"

"Yes. And something Layton said to Mrs. Clausen on Tuesday suggested he *knew* her daughter—a fact he's always denied."

"I'll get busy," Ryan promised. "There hasn't been anything interesting around lately. Just checking out guys for nervous brides-to-be. Nobody trusts anybody these days." He reached for a pad and pen. "As of now the clock is ticking. Where do I bill Mrs. Clausen?"

He caught the hesitation in Susan's voice. "It's not that simple, I'm afraid. I found a message from Mrs. Clausen on my machine this morning, saying she had had to go into the hospital for more chemotherapy but felt she had been unfair when she mentioned her suspicions about Layton to me. Clearly the implication was that I should forget about it, but I can't. I don't think she was unfair at all, and I'm worried for her. So bill it to me," Susan said.

Chris Ryan groaned. "Thank God for my pension. I kiss J. Edgar Hoover's picture on the first of every month. Okay. Consider it done. I'll get back to you, Susie."

60

Doug Layton's secretary, Leah, a no-nonsense woman in her early fifties, studied her boss with disapproving eyes. He looks as if he was out all night, she thought as Layton passed her and mumbled a perfunctory good morning greeting.

Without asking, she went to the coffeemaker, poured him a cup, tapped on his door, then opened it without waiting for a response. "I don't mean to spoil you, Doug," she said, "but you look like you could use this."

Clearly he was not up to lighthearted banter today. There was a note of irritability in his tone as he said, "I know, Leah. You're the only assistant who ever makes coffee for the boss."

She was about to tell him that he looked exhausted but decided she already had said enough. He also looks as though he's had a few too many drinks, she thought. He'd better watch his step they won't put up with that around here.

"Let me know when you want a refill," she said tersely as she placed the cup in front of him.

"Leah, Mrs. Clausen is back in the hospital," Doug said quietly. "I saw her last night. I don't think she has very much time left."

"Oh, I'm so sorry." Leah suddenly felt guilty. She knew that to Doug, Jane Clausen was a lot more than just another client. "Will you still go to Guatemala next week?"

"Oh, absolutely. But I'm not going to wait to show

her the surprise I was planning for her when I came back with my report."

"The orphanage?"

"Yes. She doesn't realize how rapidly they've been working to renovate the old facility and build the new wing. Mr. March and I agreed that it would give her so much pleasure to see it actually completed. She still doesn't know that the people running the orphanage begged us to name it after Regina."

"I bet that was your suggestion, wasn't it, Doug?"

He smiled. "Maybe. It was certainly my suggestion that we not only accept renaming the orphanage, but surprise Mrs. Clausen with the news. Even though the dedication isn't till next week, I don't think we should wait any longer to show the pictures to her. Get me the file, please."

Together they studied the eight-by-ten photos that depicted the ongoing construction of the new section of the orphanage. The most recent picture showed the completed building, a handsome, L-shaped, white-washed structure with a green tile roof. "Room for two hundred more children," Doug said. "Equipped with a state-of-the-art clinic. You don't know how many of those infants arrive there malnourished. Now I'm proposing to add a residence on the grounds so that prospective parents can get to spend time with the babies they'll be adopting."

He opened his desk drawer. "Here's the sign we're going to unveil at the dedication. It will be placed here." He put his finger on a spot on the lawn in front of the building and drew a circle. "It will be clearly visible from the road and as you come up the driveway."

His voice lowered. "I was going to have a local

artist there do a rendering after the unveiling, but I think we should have one painted immediately. Get Peter Crown at the agency to take care of it."

Leah studied the handsome sign, carved in the shape of a cradle. The engraved and gilded lettering read THE REGINA CLAUSEN HOME.

"Oh, Doug, that will make Mrs. Clausen so happy!" Leah said, her eyes misting over. "It means that at least *something* good is coming out of her tragedy."

"Indeed it is," Douglas Layton agreed fervently.

61

It was ten after nine when Susan's secretary buzzed her on the intercom: "Dr. Pamela Hastings to see you, Doctor."

She had begun to worry that Hastings might not show up, so it was with relief that Susan asked Janet to show her in.

That the woman was distressed, showed clearly in her face—her forehead creased with worry lines, her lips firmly clamped together. But when she spoke, Susan instinctively liked her, sensing that she possessed both warmth and intelligence.

"Dr. Chandler, I feel that I must have sounded very rude to you the other night when you called the hospital. It was just that I was so surprised when you introduced yourself."

"And undoubtedly even more so when you heard why I was calling, Dr. Hastings." Susan reached out her hand. "Please, let's make it Susan and Pamela, if that's all right."

"Absolutely." Hastings shook Susan's hand, then glanced behind her as she sat down. Once seated, she pulled the chair a little closer to Susan's desk, as though afraid other ears might pick up what she was going to say.

"I'm sorry to be late, and I can't stay long. I've been at the hospital so much in the last two days that I'm really not prepared for my eleven-fifteen class."

"And I go on the air in less than fifty minutes," Susan said, "so I guess we'd better get to the heart of it. Have you heard the tape of the phone call Carolyn Wells made to my program on Monday?"

"The tape Justin denied requesting? No."

"I left the copy I had with the police yesterday," Susan told her. "I will have another one made for you, because, while I am confident that it was Carolyn Wells who called, I would like you to verify that it is indeed her voice on the tape. But let me tell you what she said."

As she described talking about Regina Clausen's disappearance from a cruise and the call she had received from a listener who called herself "Karen," Susan watched the concern deepen on Pamela Hastings's face.

When she was finished, the other woman said, "I don't need to hear the tape. I saw a turquoise ring with that inscription last Friday night. Carolyn showed it to me." Briefly she told Susan about the fortieth birthday party.

Susan opened the side drawer of her desk and pulled out her purse. "Regina Clausen's mother was listening to the program and heard Carolyn's call. Afterwards she phoned me and came here with a souvenir ring that she said had been found among her daughter's possessions. Will you look at it, please?"

She opened her purse, reached in for her wallet, and extracted the turquoise ring. She held it out.

Pamela Hastings paled. She did not attempt to take the ring from Susan's hand, but sat staring at it. Finally she said, "It looks exactly like the one Carolyn showed me. Is the inside of this band engraved with the sentiment 'You belong to me'?"

"Yes. Here, look at it closely."

Hastings shook her head. "No, I don't want to touch it. As a psychologist you'll probably think I'm crazy, but I am gifted—or cursed, as the case may be—with very keen intuition, or second sight, or whatever you want to call it. When I touched the ring Carolyn had the other night, I warned her that it might be the cause of her death."

Susan smiled reassuringly. "I don't think you're crazy. I absolutely respect the kind of gift you're talking about. And while I don't understand it, I am convinced that it exists. Please tell me. What do you sense about this ring?" She held it out again.

Pamela Hastings shrunk back and looked away. "I can't touch it. I'm sorry."

Susan knew she had the answer she was expecting: This ring was also a harbinger of death.

There was an awkward pause, then Susan said, "There was very real fear in Carolyn Wells's voice when she called me on Monday. I'm going to be frank. She sounded as though she was afraid of her husband. The police captain who heard the tape had the same reaction."

Pamela was silent for a while. "Justin is very possessive of Carolyn," she said quietly.

It was obvious to Susan that Pamela Hastings was choosing her words carefully. "Possessive, and perhaps *jealous* enough to hurt her?"

"I don't know." The words were anguished, as though they had been wrung from her. Then she raised her hands in an almost pleading gesture. "Carolyn is unconscious. When she wakes up—if she wakes up—we may get an entirely different picture of what happened, but I think I should tell you that she seems to be calling for someone."

"You mean someone you don't know."

"A number of times she's very clearly said 'Win.' Then early this morning, according to the nurse, she said, 'Oh, Win.'"

"You feel sure it was a name?"

"I asked her that yesterday, as I stood next to her, holding her hand, and she pressed my palm. In fact, for a moment there I really thought she was about to regain consciousness."

"Pamela, I know we both have to go, but there's one other question I have to ask you now," Susan said. "Do you think that Justin Wells is capable of hurting his wife in a jealous rage?"

She thought for a moment. "I think he *was* capable of that," she said. "Maybe he still is, I don't know. He's been absolutely distraught since Monday night, and now the police have been talking to him."

Susan thought of Hilda Johnson, the elderly woman who had claimed she saw someone push Carolyn Wells in front of the van—and who was murdered a scant few hours later. "Were you at the hospital Monday night with Justin Wells?"

Pamela Hastings nodded. "I was there from five-thirty Monday evening to six o'clock Tuesday morning."

"Was he there that entire time?"

"Of course," she said, then hesitated. "No, actually not quite the whole time. I remember that after Carolyn came down from surgery—it was about ten-thirty that night—Justin went out for a walk. He was afraid of getting one of his migraine headaches and wanted fresh air. But I remember that he was gone for less than an hour."

Hilda Johnson lived only blocks from Lenox Hill Hospital, Susan thought. "How did Justin seem when he came back to the hospital?" she asked.

"Much calmer," she said, then paused. "Almost too calm, if you know what I mean. I would say he was almost in shock."

62

On Thursday morning at nine-thirty, Captain Tom Shea was once again interviewing the witness Oliver Baker at his office in the 19th Precinct headquarters. This time Baker was visibly nervous. His first words were, "Captain, Betty—that's my wife—has been a wreck ever since you phoned last night. She's beginning to wonder if you think that I pushed that poor woman, and that this is your way of getting me to talk about the accident and trip myself up."

Shea looked into Baker's face, noting that the man's

lumpy cheeks, narrow mouth, and thin nose seemed all squished together this morning, as though he feared a blow. "Mr. Baker," he said with weary patience, "you have been requested to come here only to see if there are any other details, however minor, that you may have remembered."

"I'm not under suspicion?"

"Absolutely not."

Baker heaved a dramatic sigh of relief. "Would it be all right if I called Betty right now? She was having an anxiety attack when I left."

Shea picked up the phone. "What's your number?" He dialed, and when there was an answer, said, "Mrs. Baker? Good, I'm glad to reach you. This is Captain Shea of the 19th Precinct. I wanted to personally assure you that I asked your husband to come in to see me again today only because he is a valuable witness who has been extremely helpful to us. Sometimes witnesses will remember little details days after an incident, and that's what we're hoping we may learn from Oliver. Now I'll put him on for a minute, and you have yourself a good day."

A beaming Oliver Baker took the phone Shea handed him. "Did you hear that, honey? I'm a valuable witness. Sure. If the girls phone from school you can tell them that their father isn't going to end up in the clink. Ha-ha. You bet I'll be home straight from work. Bye-bye."

I should have let him worry, Shea thought as he replaced the receiver. "Now, Mr. Baker, let's go over a few facts. You said you saw someone take the manila envelope from Mrs. Wells?"

Baker shook his head. "Not 'take.' As I told you, I

thought he was trying to steady her and catch the envelope for her."

"And you can't remember anything about this man's appearance? You never even glanced at his face?"

"No. The woman, Mrs. Wells, half turned. I was looking right at her because I could sense something was wrong, that she was off balance. And then that man, whoever he was, had the envelope."

"You're *sure* it was a man?" Shea asked quickly. "Why are you sure?"

"I saw his arm—you know, the sleeve of his coat, his hand."

Now we're getting somewhere, Shea thought hopefully. "What kind of coat was he wearing?"

"An all-weather coat. But a good one, I could tell that much. Good clothes speak for themselves, don't you think? I can't be sure, but I bet his was a Burberry."

"A Burberry?"

"Right."

"I've got that in my notes. You said that last time. Did you notice if he was wearing a ring?"

Baker shook his head. "Positively no ring. You have to understand, Captain, this whole thing took place in a split second, and then my eyes were riveted on that poor woman. I just knew the van was going to hit her."

An all-weather coat like a Burberry, Shea thought. We'll check on what Wells wore to work that day. He got up. "Sorry to inconvenience you, Mr. Baker, but thanks for coming in again this morning."

Baker, assured he was a nonsuspect, now seemed reluctant to leave. "I don't know if this is helpful, Captain, but . . ." He hesitated.

"*Anything* may be helpful," Shea said quickly. "What is it?"

"Well, I may be wrong, but I did get the impression that the man who took the envelope was wearing a watch with a dark leather band."

An hour later, Detective Marty Power was in Justin Wells's office. Wells himself was not there, but the detective, sent there by Shea, had an informative chat with the friendly receptionist, Barbara Gingras. In less than three minutes he had learned all about how Barbara heard Carolyn Wells on the *Ask Dr. Susan* program on Monday, and how she had told Mr. Wells about it when he came back from lunch.

"I think it made him mad or upset or something," she confided, "because later he went out without telling me when he'd be back."

"Do you remember if he was wearing a coat when he left?" Power asked.

Barbara bit her lip and frowned thoughtfully. "Let's see. In the morning he had on his tweed topcoat. He's a sharp dresser, and I always notice what he's wearing. You see, my boyfriend, Jake, is about Mr. Wells's size and has dark hair too, so when I want to buy him clothing of some kind as a present, I try to find something like what I've seen Mr. Wells wear."

Barbara smiled at the detective. "In fact, Jake's birthday was just last week, and I got him a blue-and-white striped shirt with a white collar and cuffs, and Mr. Wells has one just like it. Cost a fortune but he loved it. And the tie . . ."

Not being interested in the tie Jake had received for

his birthday, Marty Power interrupted, "You're positive Justin Wells was wearing a tweed topcoat on Monday?"

"Absolutely. But wait a minute. You know something? When Mr. Wells went out Monday afternoon, he was wearing the tweed topcoat, but when he came back, he had on his Burberry. I hadn't thought of it before, but I guess he must have gone home."

Her final piece of information that the detective found pertinent was that Mr. Wells always wore a watch with a dark leather strap.

63

Alex Wright had appointments scheduled for most of Thursday, so he had Jim Curley, his chauffeur, pick him up at quarter of nine in the morning. Jim always extended cheerful greetings to his boss, but then let him take the lead, speaking only when he sensed it was either desired or appropriate.

Sometimes Alex Wright obviously felt like talking, and they would bat the breeze about anything from the weather or politics, to scheduled events, to Jim's grandchildren. On other days, Mr. Alex would greet him pleasántly, and then open his briefcase or *The New York Times* and sit silently for most of the trip.

Whichever way the day went was fine with Jim. His devotion to Alex Wright was unquestioning, ever since that day two years ago when he had made it possible for Jim's granddaughter to go to Princeton. She had been accepted on her own, but even with a scholarship and the financial aid that was offered her, it was just too big a financial commitment for the family.

Mr. Alex, himself a Princeton graduate, had been adamant that she attend school there. "Are you kidding, Jim?" he had asked incredulously. "Sheila can't turn down Princeton. Whatever the scholarship doesn't cover, I'll take care of. Tell her to wave to me at the football games."

It certainly hadn't been like that when Jim Jr. was going to college twenty-five years ago, Curley remembered. I asked Mr. Alex's father for a raise, and he told me I was lucky to have a job.

Right away, Jim could tell that this morning was going to be one of the quiet ones. After he said, "Good morning, Jim," Alex Wright opened his briefcase and pulled out a file. He studied it in silence as the car threaded through the East Side Drive traffic on its way down to Wall Street. But then around the Manhattan Bridge, he put the file back in the briefcase and began to talk. "I could really do without that trip next week, Jim," Alex Wright said.

"Where in Russia are you going, Mr. Alex?"

"St. Petersburg. Beautiful city. The Hermitage is magnificent. Trouble is I won't have time to see any of it. I'll be lucky to have time to finalize the plans for the hospital we're building. I'm a little troubled about the site they've chosen."

Their exit was coming up, so Jim concentrated on the driving and waited until he had switched lanes before he asked, "Surely you can take a few days extra for yourself, can't you?" Glancing in the rearview mirror, he was surprised to see the sudden smile that warmed Alex Wright's face, making it seem almost boyish.

"I could, but the truth is, I don't want to."

It's Susan Chandler, Jim thought. By God, I think he's really interested in her. Couldn't make a better choice, he said to himself, and I've only met her once.

Jim believed wholeheartedly in that moment when you meet someone, and lightning strikes. It had happened to him forty years ago when he had a blind date and she turned out to be Moira. The minute he had looked into her face, and saw those blue eyes, he had given up his heart to her.

The car phone rang. When his boss was in the car, Jim never answered the phone unless he was asked—just about all the calls were personal and for Mr. Alex. He listened as Alex Wright's voice changed from its initial warm greeting to a more reserved tone. "Oh, Dee, how are you? I'm in the car. Call Forwarding from the house. . . . You took the red-eye? Then you must be dead. . . . Sure, but do you think you'll be up to it? . . . Okay, if you say so I'll meet you at the St. Regis at five. The real estate guy I spoke to called you, I gather. . . . Good. I'm trying to reach Susan to see if she'll join us this evening. . . . All right. See you."

He hung up, then picked up the phone again and dialed.

Jim heard him ask for Dr. Chandler, then heard him say, with an edge in his voice: "I had hoped to reach her before she left for the studio. Please see that she gets this message as soon as she returns to the office."

Jim watched in the rearview mirror as Alex Wright

hung up the phone, a frown on his face. Who the heck is Dee, he wondered, and what's worrying him?

If he had been able to read Alex Wright's mind, Jim would have understood that his boss was annoyed that Susan's secretary had not given her his earlier message, before Susan left for the studio, and that he was equally annoyed that having left Call Forwarding on his home phone, he had been reached by the very person he had been anxious to avoid.

64

Susan reached the studio with ten minutes to spare. As usual, she poked her head into Jed Geany's office, already prepared for his reminder that one of these days she wasn't going to get there by broadcast time, followed by "Don't say I didn't warn you."

But today when he looked up at her his face was grim. "I'm beginning to think we jinx our callers, Susan."

"What's that supposed to mean?" she asked.

"You haven't heard? Tiffany, the waitress at that restaurant in Yonkers, was stabbed to death last night when she was leaving work."

"She was *what!*" Susan felt as if she had been punched, as if someone had slammed into her with his full weight. She clutched the side of Jed's desk to steady herself.

"Easy, take it easy," he cautioned, standing. "You've got a program to do in a couple of minutes. You also have to be prepared for the fact that a lot of listeners probably will phone in about her."

Tiffany, Susan thought, remembering their phone conversation late last night, so anxious to get back with her boyfriend, so hurt when his mother phoned her to tell her to stop talking about him. Don Richards and I talked about how lonely she sounded. Oh, God, Susan thought. The poor girl.

"Remember how you tried to stop her from giving the name of the place she worked?" Jed said. "Well, apparently some guy went in looking for her. Made a pass at her. Got sore when she told him off. He's a bad apple. Has a record a mile long."

"Are they sure he did it?" Susan asked numbly.

"From what I hear, the cops have him dead to rights," Jed told her. "Although I don't think he has confessed or anything yet. Come on, we've got to get into the studio. I'll get you a cup of coffee."

Somehow Susan managed to get through the program. As Jed had predicted, the lines were flooded with calls about Tiffany. At Susan's suggestion, during a commercial break Jed phoned The Grotto, and she spoke to the owner, Tony Sepeddi.

"Joey, our bartender, told Tiffany to wait, that he'd walk her out to her car," Sepeddi explained, his voice choked with emotion. "But he got busy, and she took off. When he saw she was gone, he ran out to make sure she was okay. That's when he saw a guy hurrying off in the direction of the gas station next door. By the time they found Tiffany's body, the guy was gone, but Joey is pretty sure it was the one who was bothering her earlier in the bar."

Have they got the right man? This just doesn't

seem like an isolated incident, Susan thought. Carolyn Wells phoned me, and a few hours later was run over; she's alive, but just barely. Hilda Johnson swore for all the world to hear that she saw someone push Carolyn Wells; a few hours later she was murdered. Tiffany saw a man buying a turquoise "You belong to me" ring and called in to talk about it. Now she's been stabbed to death. Coincidence? I don't think so. But did the man in police custody kill Tiffany? And Hilda Johnson? And did he push Carolyn Wells?

As she was winding up the program for the day, Susan told her listeners, "I'm grateful for all your calls. I think in those few times Tiffany spoke to me, we all felt we'd come to know her. Now I know many of you feel the same terrible regret I do at her death. If only Tiffany had waited those few moments to let the bartender walk her to her car. There are a lot of 'if only's' in our lives, and perhaps there's a lesson here too. We don't know if Tiffany's assailant went to that bar because she told us on air yesterday where she worked, but if he did, this is one more tragedy that proves we should never casually reveal our home addresses or workplaces to just anyone."

Susan felt her voice breaking as she concluded, "Please, all of you remember Tiffany and her family in your prayers. Our time is up. I'll be back with you tomorrow."

Immediately after signing off, she left the studio for her office. She had to review the file of her one o'clock patient, but she also hoped to make some phone calls.

A contrite Janet told her about Alex Wright's two calls. "You had said to take messages when you were talking to Dr. Hastings, and then you ran out of here so fast I didn't remember to ask you to call him. Then he left a second message."

"I see." The first message was to please call Alex before the program. The second one Susan read and reread. Big sister, she thought, I love you, but there are limits. You not only got invited to the dinner Saturday night, but you've managed to set up a meeting with him this evening as well.

As Janet watched, Susan tore up both notes and threw them in the wastebasket.

"Dr. Chandler, please, when you talk to Mr. Wright, tell him how sorry I am that I didn't tell you about his first call. He sounded really angry at me."

Susan realized that knowing he had gotten angry made her feel better, although she also knew she had no intention of joining Alex and Dee tonight for a drink or anything else. "If he calls again, I'll tell him," she said, careful to make her tone sound indifferent.

She checked her watch; it was twelve-thirty. That gave her half an hour before her appointment. Which means I can take ten minutes to make some calls, she told herself.

The first one was to the Yonkers police. From her days in the Westchester County District Attorney's office, she knew several detectives there. She reached one of them, Pete Sanchez, and explained her interest in the murder of Tiffany Smith.

"Pete, I'm heartsick at the thought that she is dead because she talked to me on air."

From Sanchez she learned that the cops there were convinced they had their killer, and that they expected it was just a matter of hours before the suspect, Sharkey Dion, confessed.

"Sure he denies it, Susan," Pete told her. "They all

do. You know that. Listen, a guy who was coming into The Grotto when this bum was thrown out heard him muttering how he'd be back to take care of her."

"That still doesn't mean he killed her," Susan said. "Do you have the weapon?"

Pete Sanchez sighed. "Not yet."

Then she told him about the turquoise rings, but he showed little interest. "Uh-huh. Give me your number; I'll let you know when Dion signs on the dotted line. Don't trash yourself over this. The real culprit in this tragedy is the parole system that lets a guy with a record as long as my arm out of prison. He only served eight years of a twenty-five-year term. Guess what the crime was? Manslaughter!"

Unconvinced, Susan put down the receiver and sat for a moment, deep in thought. The element connecting everything here is the turquoise ring, she thought. Regina Clausen had one and is dead. Carolyn Wells had one and may die. Tiffany had one and is dead. Pamela Hastings, an intelligent woman who says she has powers of precognition, wouldn't touch Regina's ring, and only a few days before had warned Carolyn Wells that hers could be the cause of her death.

Tiffany told me last night that her ring was buried under tons of chicken bones and pizza, Susan thought. That sounds like a garbage pail. But *tons*?

Did she mean in a Dumpster? she wondered. And if she did, what more likely Dumpster than one on the site of The Grotto restaurant? Susan's mind was racing. How often would The Grotto's Dumpster normally be emptied? Would the police have impounded it, looking for the weapon?

She looked up the number for The Grotto and in a

moment was speaking to Tony Sepeddi. "Look, Dr. Chandler, I've been answering questions since midnight," he said. "The Dumpster is in the parking lot and is emptied every morning. Only *this* morning the police impounded it. Guess they're looking for the weapon. Any other questions? I'm almost dead here myself."

Susan made one more call before she reviewed her patient's file. It was to Pete Sanchez again, begging him to have the Dumpster sifted not only for the murder weapon, but also for a turquoise ring with the inscription "You belong to me" inside the band.

65

Thursday was always a busy day for Dr. Donald Richards, and as usual, he had gotten an early start. His first patient was a man who ran an international corporation; he came to him each Thursday at eight o'clock, and was followed at nine, ten, and eleven by other regular patients. Several of them expressed dismay when they learned that Richards would be out of town Thursday of next week, on a publicity tour for his book.

When Donald Richards sat down at noon for a quick lunch, he was already weary, and, of course, he had a busy afternoon ahead of him as usual. At one o'clock he had an appointment with Captain Shea at the 19th Precinct to talk with him about Justin Wells.

While Rena placed a cup of soup in front of him, he turned on the television to catch the local news. The lead story was the murder of the young waitress in Yonkers, and on screen was a tape of the crime scene.

"This is the parking lot of The Grotto trattoria in Yonkers where twenty-five-year-old Tiffany Smith was stabbed to death shortly after midnight," the anchorman said. "Sharkey Dion, a paroled killer who had been asked to leave the bar when he reportedly harassed Ms. Smith earlier in the evening, is in custody and is expected to be charged with the crime."

"Doctor, isn't that the woman who called in the other day when you were on that *Ask Dr. Susan* show?" Rena asked, shock clear in her voice.

"Yes, it is," Richards said quietly. He looked at his watch. Susan would be on her way back to the office by now. She certainly must have heard about Tiffany and would no doubt expect to hear from him as well.

I'll call her when I get back from the police station, he decided as he pushed his chair back. "Rena, the soup looks delicious, but I'm afraid I'm not very hungry right now." His eyes lingered on the television screen as the camera panned to show a bright red pump with a stiletto heel on the ground next to the cloth that covered the mortal remains of Tiffany Smith.

That pathetic girl, he thought as he turned off the set. I know Susan will be upset. First Carolyn Wells and now Tiffany. I bet she's somehow blaming herself for both women's misfortunes.

It was five minutes of four that afternoon before he spoke to Susan. "I'm so sorry," he said.

"I'm heartsick," Susan told him. "I pray to God that

if Sharkey Dion is the murderer, he didn't go into that bar looking for Tiffany because he heard her talking to me on air."

"From what I heard on the news earlier, the police don't seem to have much doubt about him being the killer," Richards said. "Susan, I doubt very much that the kind of man Sharkey Dion seems to be would be listening to an advice program. I think it much more likely that he just happened into that bar."

"*If* he is the killer," Susan repeated tonelessly. "Don, I have a question you must answer. Do you think Justin Wells pushed his wife in front of that van?"

"No, I do not," Richards told her. "I think it much more likely that it was an accident. I went to see Captain Shea today and told him as much. In fact, I warned him that any psychiatrist who examined Wells would probably reach the same conclusion. True, he is obsessed about his wife, but part of that obsession is an extreme fear of losing her. In my opinion, he would never hurt her deliberately."

"Then you think that Hilda Johnson, the witness who said she saw someone push Carolyn Wells, was wrong?" Susan asked.

"Not necessarily. You can't rule out the possibility that if Justin Wells followed Carolyn and wanted to see what she had in that envelope, he might inadvertently have caused her to lose her balance. I understand that he was extremely upset when the receptionist told him what his wife had said when she called in to the program. Don't forget that when Karen—or Carolyn—phoned you, she promised to give you a picture of the man she had met on that cruise. Doesn't it seem likely it might have been in that envelope?"

"Does Captain Shea agree with your theory?"

"That's hard to say, but I did warn him that if someone else pushed Carolyn Wells, whether by accident or by design, and Justin Wells learns who he is, his anger will be such that Wells may be capable of anything, including murder."

As they talked further, Richards could tell from Susan's almost emotionless voice just how deeply disturbed she was by the recent events. "Look," he said, "this has been rotten for you. Believe me, I understand how you feel. I enjoyed dinner very much last night. The call I had hoped to make to you today was simply to tell you that. Why don't we grab a bite this evening? We'll find a restaurant somewhere around your place. I'll even pick you up this time."

"I'm afraid I can't," Susan told him. "I've set up a project for myself, and I don't know how long it will take."

It was four o'clock. Richards knew his last patient would be waiting in the reception room by now. "I'm good at projects," he said hurriedly. "Let me know if I can help."

He frowned when he put down the phone. Susan had politely but firmly refused his assistance. What was she up to? he wondered.

It was a question he needed to have answered.

66

Jane Clausen, clearly exhausted from the effects of chemotherapy, managed a faint smile. "Just a little played out, Vera," she said.

She could see that her housekeeper of twenty years was reluctant to go. "Don't worry. I'll be fine. I'm just going to rest," she assured her.

"I almost forgot, Mrs. Clausen," Vera said anxiously. "I think you may get a call from Dr. Chandler. She phoned just before I left the apartment, and I told her you were here in the hospital. She sounds nice."

"She is very nice."

"I don't like to leave you alone." Vera sighed. "I wish you'd let me just sit here and keep you company."

I do have company, Jane Clausen thought as she glanced toward the nightstand, at the framed photograph of Regina that Vera had brought to the hospital at her request. In the photo, Regina was captured posing with the captain of the *Gabrielle*.

"I'll be asleep in five minutes, Vera. You go on now."

"Then good night, Mrs. Clausen," Vera said, adding with a catch in her throat, "and be sure to call me if you need anything."

After the housekeeper left, Jane Clausen reached over and picked up the photograph. *It's not been a good day, Regina,* she thought. *I'm winding down and I know it. Yet I feel like something is making me hang on. I don't quite understand it, but we'll see what happens.*

The phone rang. Jane Clausen put the picture down and answered, anticipating that the call might be from Douglas Layton.

Instead it was Susan Chandler, and once again the warmth in her voice reminded Jane Clausen of Regina. She found herself admitting to Susan that it had been a difficult day. "But tomorrow should be much easier," she added, "and Doug Layton is hinting that he has quite a surprise for me. I'm looking forward to it."

Susan heard the momentary lifting of Mrs. Clausen's tone and knew there was no way she could possibly tell her that without clearing it with her, she had requested a check on Layton.

Instead she said, "I'd really like to stop by and see you sometime in the next few days—that is, of course, if you think you'd enjoy a visit."

"Let's talk tomorrow," Clausen suggested. "We'll see how the day is going. Right now I'm taking it day by day." Then she surprised herself by saying, "My housekeeper just brought over a photograph of Regina. Sometimes it makes me very sad to look at Regina's pictures. Tonight it's quite comforting. Isn't that odd?" Then she added apologetically, "Dr. Chandler, I can tell you're a fine psychologist. It really isn't my custom to discuss my personal feelings, but I find it very easy to confide in you."

"Having a picture of someone you love can be very comforting," Susan said. "Are you together in it?"

"No, it's one of those photos they're forever taking on the cruise ships, the kind they put on display for people to order. From the date on the back I can tell it was taken on the *Gabrielle* just two days before Regina disappeared."

The conversation ended with Susan promising to phone the next day. Then, just after they said goodbye, and as the phone was being returned to its cradle, Susan heard Jane Clausen murmur with obvious pleasure, "Oh, Doug, how kind of you to come by."

Susan sighed as she replaced the receiver, then, leaning forward slightly, she kneaded her temples with the tips of her fingers. It was six o'clock, and she was still at her desk. The unopened container of soup that was supposed to have been lunch was a reminder of the reason she was feeling the beginnings of a headache.

The office was quiet. Janet was long gone. Susan sometimes had a mental image of a fire alarm going off in her secretary's head at the stroke of five, given her rush to be out of there each day.

"Sufficient unto the day is the evil thereof," she thought, then wondered why the biblical quotation had occurred to her at this moment. That's an easy one, she decided. This day began with an evil deed—Tiffany's murder.

I'd stake my life that Tiffany would still be alive if she hadn't phoned me about the turquoise ring! Susan thought. She stood and stretched wearily. I'm hungry. Maybe I should have met Alex and Dee, she thought wryly. I'm sure Dee won't let him get away with just buying her a drink.

Alex had phoned again. "You did get my messages, didn't you?" he asked. "I know your secretary forgot to give you the first one this morning."

She had felt somewhat penitent about not returning

his calls. "Alex, forgive me. It's been one of those days," she had said, then begged off from meeting him. "I wouldn't be good company for anyone tonight," she told him, knowing it was only too true.

As she was leaving, she noticed that Nedda's light was on. She hadn't planned to visit, but impulsively she stopped and tried the law offices' door, pleased to find that this time it was locked.

Why not visit for a minute? she thought, then rapped on the glass. Five minutes later, she was nibbling on cheese and crackers and sipping a glass of chardonnay with Nedda.

She filled her in on what had been happening, then added, "Something just dawned on me. It's odd, but both Mrs. Clausen and Dr. Richards mentioned photographs taken on cruise ships to me today. Mrs. Clausen has one of her daughter that was taken on the *Gabrielle*, and Don Richards reminded me that when Carolyn Wells phoned in to the show on Monday, she promised to give me a picture that showed the man she met on a cruise, the man who wanted her to get off the ship in Algiers."

"What are you getting at, Susan?" Nedda asked.

"What I'm getting at is this—I wonder if the outfit, or outfits, that take those cruise pictures keep a file of the negatives. Don Richards used to spend a lot of time on cruise ships. Maybe I'll ask him."

67

Pamela Hastings spent Thursday in her office at Columbia, catching up on the work she had been neglecting. She called the hospital twice and spoke to a nurse with whom she had become friendly. From her she received the cautiously optimistic news that Carolyn Wells was again showing signs of coming out of the coma.

"At least we'll find out what really happened to her," Pamela said.

"Not necessarily," the nurse cautioned her. "Many people who have received a head injury such as the one she suffered have no memory of the actual incident, even if they experience no other significant memory lapses."

In the afternoon the nurse reported that Carolyn once again had tried to speak. "Only that one word, 'Win,' or 'Oh, Win,'" the nurse said. "But remember, the mind does funny things. She could be referring to someone she knew as a child."

The second conversation with the nurse had left Pamela feeling uneasy and somewhat guilty. Justin is convinced that Carolyn is calling for someone important to her, and I'm beginning to believe he is right, she thought. But when I talked with Dr. Chandler earlier, I indicated that I think he *could* have done this to her. So what do I *really* believe? she wondered dismally.

When she was finally ready to leave her office and go to the hospital, she realized why she was so reluctant to make the visit tonight—she was ashamed to face Justin.

He was sitting at the far end of the waiting room for the intensive care unit, his back to her. There were other people there today, the parents of a teenager who had been rushed in the day before after having been injured in football practice. When Pamela stopped to inquire about him, the boy's mother happily reported that he was out of danger.

Out of danger, Pamela thought. The words chilled her. Is Carolyn out of danger? she wondered. If she comes out of the coma and is put in a regular room, that means she won't be watched every instant. Then Justin would have practically unlimited access to her. Suppose she has no memory of the incident, and Justin was the one who tried to kill her.

As she walked across the room to Justin she felt a dizzying mix of emotions wash over her. She felt compassion for this man who loved Carolyn, perhaps too intensely; guilt for suspecting him of causing her injuries, a lingering fear that he still might want to harm her.

When she tapped him on the shoulder, he looked up at her. "Ahh, first friend," he said, "have the police gotten to you yet?"

Pamela sank into the chair next to him. "I don't know what you mean, Justin. Why would the police want to talk to me?"

"I thought you might have something to add to the

gathering evidence. They called me back to the police station this afternoon to have me explain why I changed from a tweed coat to a Burberry Monday afternoon. They think I tried to kill Carolyn. Anything you want to contribute to help tighten the noose, old pal?"

She decided not to take the bait. "Justin, this isn't getting us anywhere. How do you think Carolyn is doing today?"

"I looked in on her, but only when the nurse was with me. Next thing you know they'll accuse me of trying to pull the plug." He put his face in his hands and shook his head. "Oh, Christ, I don't *believe* this."

A nurse came to the door of the waiting room. "Dr. Susan Chandler is on the phone," she said. "She'd like to speak to you, Mr. Wells. You can take it over there." She indicated an extension phone in the waiting room.

"Well, I don't want to speak to her," he snapped. "All this started with Carolyn making that call to her."

"Justin, please," Pamela said, standing and crossing to the phone, "she's only trying to help." She picked up the receiver and held it out to him.

He stared at her for a moment, then took it. "Dr. Chandler," he said, "why are you hounding me? From what I understand, my wife wouldn't be in the hospital in the first place if she hadn't been on her way to the post office to mail something to you. Haven't you done enough harm? Please stay out of our lives."

He started to hang up, but stopped with the receiver in midair.

"*I don't think for one minute that you pushed your wife in front of that van!*" Susan's voice was so loud that Pamela could hear it from across the room.

Justin Wells pressed the receiver against his ear. "And why do you say that?" he asked.

"Because I think someone else tried to kill her, and I think that person *did* kill Hilda Johnson, who was a witness to your wife's injury, and Tiffany Smith, another woman who called in to my show," Susan said. "I've got to meet with you. Please. You may have something I need."

When he hung up, Justin Wells looked at Pamela. Now she saw only exhaustion in his face. "It may be just a trap to search the apartment without a warrant, but I'm going to meet her there at eight. Pam, she tells me that she thinks that Carolyn is still in danger—but from the guy she met on that ship, not from me."

68

As they entered the cocktail lounge of the St. Regis Hotel, Alex Wright did not need the appreciative glances of the people at the tables around them to be aware of the fact that Dee Chandler Harriman was a very beautiful woman. She was wearing a black velvet jacket and silk pants; a single strand of pearls and pearl-and-diamond earrings were her only jewelry. Her hair was caught up in a seemingly casual French twist, so that wisps and tendrils brushed the porcelain skin of her face. Skillfully applied mascara and liner brought out the vivid blue of her eyes.

Once seated, Alex found himself relaxing. When he had spoken to Susan earlier, she had sounded genuinely tired and had explained that she had some projects to complete that evening, so she couldn't join them.

When he pressed her to reconsider, she had added, "Alex, in addition to the radio show, which I do every weekday morning, I have a full private practice schedule every afternoon, and while the show is great fun, seeing these patients is really what I'm all about. Together with the show, they pretty much take up all my time." Then she had assured him that she wasn't going to back out on Saturday evening and that she was looking forward to it.

At least she doesn't seem to be annoyed that I'm meeting Dee, Alex thought as he glanced about the room, and I'm sure she realized I didn't instigate this little get-together. As he forced himself to focus on Dee, he acknowledged how important this last point was to him.

Dee had been talking about California. "I've really *loved* it out there," she said, her voice warm, throaty, and very seductive. "But a New Yorker is a New Yorker is a New Yorker—at some point most of us want to come home. And by the way, the real estate broker you recommended is great."

"Did you see any places you'd be interested in?" Alex asked.

"Just one. The nice part of it is that the people would be willing to rent for a year, with an option to buy. They're moving to London and still aren't sure if they'll want to relocate permanently."

"Where is it?"

"East Seventy-eighth just off Fifth."

Alex raised an eyebrow. "You'll be able to borrow a cup of sugar from me. I'm on Seventy-eighth between Madison and Park." He smiled. "Or did you know that already?"

Dee laughed, showing perfect teeth. "Don't flatter yourself," she told him. "Ask the broker how many places we looked at this afternoon. But I do have a favor to ask, and please don't say no. Would you mind swinging by the place and taking a look at it with me when we're ready to go? I'd *love* to get your opinion." She stared at him, her eyes wide open.

"I don't know what it's worth," Alex said evenly. "But sure."

A very persuasive lady, he thought an hour later, as, having genuinely admired the potential rental, he found himself showing Dee around his own home.

In the drawing room, she paid special attention to the portraits of his mother and father. "Hmmm, they didn't *smile* very much, did they?" she said.

Alex considered the question. "Let's see . . . I think I remember my father cracking a smile when I was ten. My mother wasn't quite that lighthearted."

"Well, from what I understand, they certainly were very charitable people," Dee said. "And looking at the two of them, I can see where you get your good looks."

"I think the proper response to that is that flattery will get you everywhere. It's getting late. Do you have dinner plans?"

"If *you* do."

"I don't. I'm just sorry that Susan is too busy to join us." Deliberately he added, "But I'll be seeing her on

Saturday, and on a lot of other evenings I'm sure. Now let me see about getting us a reservation. I'll be right back."

Dee smiled to herself as she pulled out a compact and touched up her lip rouge. She had not missed the sidelong glance Alex had given her as he left the room.

He's getting interested in me, she thought, *very* interested. She glanced around the drawing room. A bit drab; I could do a lot with this place, she told herself.

69

Yonkers Detective Pete Sanchez was beginning to worry that they might not be able to pin the Tiffany Smith murder on Sharkey Dion. It had seemed like an open-and-shut case, but now it was becoming apparent that if they didn't find the knife used to kill Tiffany and trace it to Dion, or if he didn't break down and confess, their case was actually very weak.

A big problem was that Joey, the bartender from The Grotto, could not be one hundred percent sure it was Sharkey he had seen disappearing in back of the gas station. As it stood, if the case ever came to trial, the defense would annihilate his testimony. Pete could imagine the scenario:

"Isn't it a fact that Mr. Dion simply asked Miss Smith for a date? Is that a criminal offense?"

Joey had described how Dion had made a pass at

Tiffany, then had grabbed her hand and tightened his grip when she tried to shake him off. "He made her yell, and he wouldn't let go when she tried to pull away," he said.

Sanchez shook his head. It makes a good case for a harassment charge maybe, but not for murder, he thought. A squad was presently sifting through the mounds of garbage in the Dumpster they had hauled from The Grotto parking lot. He was keeping his fingers crossed that they would find the murder weapon there.

His other great hope was that someone would call in on the hotline with something more concrete than suspicions. The owner of The Grotto had put up a ten-thousand-dollar reward for information leading to the conviction of Tiffany Smith's killer. He knew that, to the kind of scum who hung around with Sharkey, ten thousand bucks was big money. Half of them were crackheads. Most of those bums would sell out their own mothers for a fix, Pete thought, let alone for ten grand.

At six-thirty P.M. he received two calls within moments of each other. The first one was from an informant known as Billy. Speaking in a hoarse whisper, he told Pete that after being thrown out of The Grotto, Sharkey had gone to a place called The Lamps. There he reportedly had downed a couple of quick ones and told the bartender and another guy that he was going back to take care of the bimbo who dissed him.

The Lamps, Pete thought. A rough joint. And only five minutes from The Grotto. "What time did he leave there?" he snapped.

"Five of twelve. He said the bimbo got off work at midnight."

"You're my boy, Billy," Pete said happily.

A moment later the head of the squad assigned to sift through the contents of the Dumpster called. "Pete, remember that turquoise ring you told us to look out for? We have it. It landed right in the middle of a hunk of lasagna."

So what? Pete thought. It's for sure Sharkey didn't give it to Tiffany. But at least I can let Susan know we have it.

70

After reaching Justin Wells at the hospital and arranging to meet him at his apartment, Susan stopped to grab a hamburger, french fries, and coffee at the counter of a luncheonette near her office. My least favorite way to eat, she thought, wryly thinking of the wonderful dinners she had enjoyed recently with Alex Wright and Don Richards. And I'll bet dollars to donuts that Dee manages to get Alex to take her out to dinner tonight.

She picked up a french fry, dabbed it in ketchup, and nibbled slowly. Satisfactory, she thought, and it also takes away some of the sting of knowing that my big sister once again is making a play for a guy who showed interest in me.

It isn't about having any strong feelings for Alex, she thought as she took a bite of hamburger. It's much too soon for that. No, it's about fairness and loyalty and all those old-fashioned virtues that seem to have gone out of fashion in our family, she thought in assessing the hurt she felt at her sister's behavior.

Sensing a growing lump in her throat, and knowing that in another moment she would have tears in her eyes, she shook her head and scornfully said to herself, Okay, crybaby, knock it off.

She took a big gulp of coffee, then quickly grabbed the water glass. Nothing like a second-degree burn to get your mind off self-pity, she thought.

It really isn't the Dee scene that's bothering me, she told herself as she ate. It's Tiffany, that poor, sad kid. She was hungry to be loved, and now she'll never get the chance. And unless Pete Sanchez can show me a signed confession from the guy they have arrested, I will swear that her death had to do with the turquoise ring, and not with some guy being thrown out of the restaurant because he made a pass.

You belong to me. Tiffany said her ring had that inscription. So did the one Jane Clausen found in Regina's effects. So did the one Carolyn Wells promised to give me, Susan thought. Neither Captain Shea nor Pete Sanchez had shown much interest in the rings, but these murders and probable murders and attempted murders were all tied somehow to those rings, and to those cruises Regina and Carolyn took. Of that she was sure.

Susan checked her watch, then accepted a refill of coffee and asked for the check. Justin Wells had agreed to meet her at his Fifth Avenue apartment at eight o'clock. She had just enough time to get there.

* * *

Susan didn't know what she had expected Wells to look like. Pamela Hastings, Captain Shea, and Don Richards had all portrayed him as being excessively jealous. I guess I thought he would look sinister somehow, she realized as he opened the door to his apartment and she found herself looking into the troubled eyes of an attractive man in his early forties. Dark hair, broad shoulders, athletic build—he was downright good-looking, she decided as she studied him. If looks were any criterion, certainly he was the last person whose appearance would indicate a man given to bouts of jealous rage.

But then I, of all people, should know appearances deceive, she thought as she extended her hand to him and introduced herself.

"Come in, Dr. Chandler. Pam is here as well. But before we say another word, I'd like to apologize for the way I spoke to you earlier."

"It's Susan, not Dr. Chandler," she said. "And no apologies necessary. As I indicated, I think you're absolutely right that your wife's call to my program is the reason she's in the hospital tonight."

The living room clearly reflected the fact that an architect and an interior designer lived there. Narrow, fluted columns separated the room from the foyer, and the room itself had crown moldings, an intricately carved marble fireplace, satiny parquet floors, a delicately beautiful Persian carpet, comfortable-looking couches and chairs, and antique tables and lamps.

Pamela Hastings greeted Susan warmly. "This is very kind of you, Susan," she said. "I can't tell you what your coming here means to me personally."

She feels as though she's betrayed Justin Wells, Susan thought as she listened to Pamela's words. She gave the other woman a reassuring smile, then said, "Look, I know how spent you both have to be, so I'll get to the point. When Carolyn phoned me on Monday, she said she would come to my office and bring with her a turquoise ring and a picture of the man who gave it to her. We know now that she may have changed her mind and decided to mail those things to me instead. What I hope is that there are perhaps other things—souvenirs or whatever—that she kept from her cruise that would give us some indication of the mystery man she mentioned, the one who tried to convince her to leave the ship to go to Algiers. Remember she said that when she tried to phone him at the hotel where he was supposed to be staying, they said they'd never heard of him."

"You can understand that Carolyn and I didn't dwell on that trip," Justin Wells said flatly. "It was a terrible time, and we were both anxious to put that separation behind us."

"Justin, that's exactly the point," Pamela said. "Carolyn hadn't shown you the turquoise ring. She certainly hadn't shown you the picture of that man. What Dr. Chandler hopes is that there might have been other souvenirs that she kept from you as well."

Wells's face flushed. "Doctor," he said, "as I told you on the phone, you are welcome to look for anything here that will help us to find the person who did this to Carolyn."

Susan noted an ominous quality in the tone of his voice. Don Richards is right, Susan thought. Justin

Wells might be capable of killing anyone who harmed his wife.

"Let's get started," she suggested.

Carolyn Wells kept an office in the apartment, a large room complete with a spacious desk, a couch, a drafting board, and files. "She has a business office in the Design building also," Wells explained to Susan. "But, in fact, she does most of her creative work here, and certainly this is where she takes care of all of her personal mail."

Susan caught the strain in his voice. "Is the desk locked?" she asked.

"I don't know. I never touch it." Justin Wells turned away as though overwhelmed by emotion at the sight of the desk where his wife usually sat.

Pamela Hastings put her hand on his arm. "Justin, why don't you wait for us in the living room?" she suggested. "You don't need this."

"You're right; I don't." He got as far as the door before he turned. "But I insist on this; I want to know anything and everything you find, good or bad, that may be useful," he said, his tone almost accusatory. "Do I have your word?"

Both women nodded. When he turned to go down the hall, Susan turned to Pamela Hastings. "Let's get started," she said.

Susan went through the desk, while Pamela rifled through file drawers. How would I like this to happen to me? Susan wondered. Other than my patients' files, which would be protected by confidentiality, what would I be embarrassed for someone else to find, and perhaps to discuss?

She came up with a ready answer: the note Jack had written after he told her that he and Dee were in love. Some of it she still remembered: "The great sadness I have is that I have hurt you, something I would never willingly do."

It's time to burn that letter, Susan decided.

She realized she felt very much a voyeur, going through the personal papers of a woman she never had met. Carolyn Wells had a touch of the sentimentalist in her makeup, she decided. In the bottom drawer of the desk she found files with names written on them: "Mom"; "Justin"; "Pam."

Susan glanced in them just enough to see that they contained things like birthday cards, personal notes, and snapshots. In the file marked "Mom" she saw a death notice that was three years old. Skimming it, she saw that Carolyn had been an only child and her father had predeceased her mother by ten years.

Her mother had been dead only a year when she separated from her husband and went on that cruise, Susan thought. Chances are she would have been emotionally fragile and extremely vulnerable to an apparently caring person.

Susan tried to recall exactly what her own mother had said about meeting Regina Clausen once at a stockholders meeting. She remembered it was something like how excited Regina was at the prospect of going on a cruise and how Regina's father had died while he was only in his forties, and before that, he had talked about regretting the vacations he'd never taken.

Two vulnerable women, Susan thought as she closed the last of the files. That much is clear. But there's nothing helpful here. She looked up and saw that Pamela Hastings had almost finished examining the three-drawer file. "How is it going?" she asked.

Pamela shrugged. "It isn't. From what I can see, Carolyn kept a mini-file here of her most recent jobs: personal notes from the clients, pictures of completed rooms, that kind of thing." Then she paused: "Wait a minute," she said. "This may be it." She was holding a file marked *"Seagodiva."* "That's the cruise ship Carolyn sailed on."

She carried the file to the desk and pulled up a chair. "Let's hope," Susan murmured as they both began to go through it.

But the file seemed useless. It contained only the sort of information people save as mementos of a trip, things like the itinerary, the *Seagodiva*'s daily bulletins listing the activities of the day, and information about the approaching ports of call.

"Mumbai, that's the new, or at least the old and restored name of Bombay," Pamela said. "Carolyn boarded the ship there. Oman, Haifa, Alexandria, Athens, Tangier, Lisbon—those were her ports of call."

"Algiers is where Carolyn almost went sightseeing with the mystery man," Susan said. "Look at the date. The ship was scheduled to stop in Tangier on October 15th. That's exactly two years ago next week."

"She arrived home on the 20th," Pamela Hastings observed. "I remember because it was my husband's birthday."

Susan glanced through the bulletins. The last one

described possible excursions from the ship. The headline was, SEE THE MARKETPLACE IN OLD ALGIERS.

That's a line in the song—"You Belong to Me," she thought. Then she noticed that there was something written lightly in pencil on the last page. She bent down to examine it closely. It read, "Win, Palace Hotel, 555-0634."

She showed it to Pamela. "I think we can be sure that Win is the man she was meeting," she said quietly.

"Dear God, do you think that means she is calling for him now?" Pamela asked.

"I don't know. If only the picture she promised to give me was still here," Susan said. "I'll bet anything she kept it in this file." Her eyes swept the desk as though expecting the photograph to materialize. Then she noticed a sliver of bright blue cardboard next to a small pair of scissors.

"Does Carolyn have a housekeeper?" she asked.

"Yes, she comes in on Monday and Friday mornings from about eight until eleven. Why?"

"Because Carolyn phoned me shortly before twelve. Say a prayer that . . ." Susan did not finish the sentence as she reached under the desk for the wastebasket. Retrieving it, she dumped its contents on the rug. Bits of blue cardboard scattered, and a photograph with an uneven border fell out.

Susan picked it up and studied it. "This is Carolyn, with the ship's captain, isn't it?"

"Yes, it is," Pamela said, "but why did she cut it like that?"

"My guess is Carolyn wanted to send only the part of the photograph that pictured the man who gave her the turquoise ring. She didn't want to be involved or identified herself."

"And now it's gone," Pamela said.

"It may be gone," Susan told her as she put together the scraps of cardboard, "but look at this. The name of the outfit in London that takes those pictures is printed on the folder, and there are instructions for ordering additional copies."

She pushed back the chair and stood up. "I'm going to call that outfit, and if they still have the negative of this photograph I'm going to get it. Pamela," she said, her voice rising with excitement, "do you realize that if that's possible we may be on our way to learning the identity of a serial killer?"

71

Nat Small was a little surprised at how much he actually missed his friend and fellow shop owner Abdul Parki. Only three days ago, on Monday morning, when he had seen Parki outside, sweeping the sidewalk in front of his shop, he'd yelled across to him, jokingly suggesting that he bring his broom over and spruce up the Dark Delights sidewalk too.

Parki had smiled his mild, shy little grin, and called back, "Nat, you know I'd be glad to do what I could for you, but I think it might take more than me and my broom to clean up your place." They both had had a good laugh. Then Tuesday he had seen Parki outside his shop again, this time sweeping up after some dumb kid dropped popcorn all over the place. After that, there had been nothing; he had never seen Parki again. It bothered Nat that both the police and media had paid so little attention to Parki's death. Sure, there had been a mention of the murder on the local TV news, including a seconds-long glimpse of the store, but a big-time Mafia guy had been arrested the same day, so that got all the play. No, they didn't bother much about Parki: "a suspected drug-related crime," was how they phrased it, and everybody seemed to be content to let it go at that.

In the two days since then, the Khyem Specialty Shop had taken on a deserted look. You'd think it had been closed for years, Nat said to himself. There was even a FOR RENT sign on the door. I hope I don't get any competition moving in there, he thought. It's tough enough as it is.

On Thursday night Nat closed his shop at nine o'clock. Before leaving, however, he made a few changes in the window display. As he looked out through the window to the street, it reminded him of how on Tuesday, just around one o'clock, that sharp-looking guy had been looking in this same window, and then he had crossed the street and gone into Parki's shop. Maybe he should have mentioned him to the cops, after all, Nat thought. Then he immediately changed his mind. It would just be a bad waste of good time, he reasoned. The guy was probably in and out of Parki's shop like a yo-yo. His type was more likely to browse through the wares on sale at Dark Delights than to buy anything at Khyem Specialty. Parki's stuff was strictly for tourists, and the man he had seen didn't look like a tourist.

Nat grinned when he thought about the dopey-looking gift Parki had given him last year—a fat little guy with the head of an elephant, sitting on a throne.

"You are a good friend, Nat," Parki had said in that singsong accent of his. "I made this for you. This is Ganesh, the elephant-headed god. There is a legend. By accident, Shiva, his father, cut off Ganesh's head when he was five years old, and when his mother demanded that the father put it back, by mistake he gave the child instead the head of an elephant. When the mother protested that her son was so ugly that he would be shunned, the father said, 'I will make him the god of wisdom, prosperity, and happiness. You will see, he will be loved.'"

Nat knew that Parki had put a lot of effort into making the little figure. And like most of the stuff Parki made by hand, it was inlaid with turquoise.

Nat Small rarely yielded to a sentimental impulse, but in honor of his murdered friend, he went back into the storage room, dug out the elephant god, and put it in the window, positioning it so that the elephant's trunk was pointed at Parki's store. I'll leave it there until somebody rents the place, he decided. It'll be a kind of memorial to a nice little guy.

Feeling both sad and somewhat virtuous, Nat Small locked up and went home, cheered by the thought that maybe a bagel shop would take over Parki's space. That would be not only handy for him, but real good for business.

72

Donald Richards had told Rena, his housekeeper, that he had dinner plans, then, not wanting to dine alone, had on impulse phoned Mark Greenberg, a good friend and fellow psychiatrist whom he had seen professionally for a while after his wife's death. By lucky chance, Greenberg was free for dinner. "Betsy is going with her mother to the opera," he said. "I begged off."

They met at Kennedy's, on West Fifty-seventh Street. Greenberg, a scholarly-looking man in his late forties, waited until their drinks arrived, then said, "Don, we haven't talked doctor to patient in a long time. How's it going?"

Richards smiled. "I'm restless. I guess that's a good sign."

"I read your book. I liked it. Tell me why you wrote it."

"That's the second time I've been asked that in as many nights," Richards said. "Obviously the subject interested me. I had a patient whose wife vanished. He was a basket case. Two years ago, when her car was found with her body in it, he was finally able to put his life back together again. She'd driven off the road and into a lake. That death happened to have been the result of an accident. Most of the women in the book met with foul play. My point in writing it was to make other women aware of the dangers out there, and to show them how to avoid the circumstances that ensnared those victims."

"Personal redemption? Still blame yourself for Kathy's death?" Greenberg asked quietly.

"I'd like to believe I'm starting to get over that, but sometimes it still hits me hard. Mark, you've heard it from me enough times. Kathy didn't want to do that shoot. She was feeling queasy. Then she told me, 'I know what you're going to say, Don. It isn't fair to the others to pull out at the last minute.' I was always on her case about her habit of canceling plans at the last minute, especially when it came to work commitments. Well, listening to me cost her her life."

Don Richards took a long sip of his drink.

"But Kathy didn't tell you that she suspected she was pregnant," Greenberg reminded him. "If anything, you'd have urged her to stay home when she told you she felt queasy."

"No, she didn't tell me. Afterwards I started thinking back and realized she hadn't had a period in six weeks." Don Richards shrugged. "There're still rough times, but it's getting better. Maybe turning forty soon is making me realize that it's time to let go of the past."

"Have you considered taking a cruise, even a short one? I think that's an important step for you to take."

"Actually I am hoping to take one soon. I wrap up the publicity for the book next week in Miami, and I'm looking to see if I can find a cruise that I can fit in."

"That's good news," Greenberg said. "Last question: Are you dating anyone?"

"I had a date last night. Susan Chandler, a psychologist. She has a daily radio program as well as a private practice. Very attractive and interesting lady."

"Then I gather you plan to see her again?"

Don Richards smiled. "I'd say I have big plans for her, Mark."

When Don Richards got home at ten o'clock, he debated calling Susan, then decided it wasn't too late to try.

She answered on the first ring.

"Susan, you sounded pretty down this afternoon. How do you feel now?"

"Oh, better, I guess," Susan said. "I'm glad you called, Don. I wanted to ask you something."

"Go ahead."

"You used to take a lot of cruises, right?"

Richards realized he was clenching the phone. "Both before I was married, and after. My wife and I both loved the sea."

"And you were on the *Gabrielle* a number of times?"

"Yes."

"I've never been on a cruise, so please bear with me. I gather that there's a photography service on ships, and that they take a lot of pictures."

"Oh, sure. It's a big moneymaking operation."

"Do you know if they keep the negatives from past cruises on file?"

"I have no idea."

"Well, by any chance do you have any pictures that might have been taken on the *Gabrielle?* What I'm hoping to learn is the name of the photography outfit that works—or worked—the *Gabrielle.*"

"I'm sure I have some pictures from when Kathy and I were on cruises."

"Would you mind checking? I'd really appreciate it. I could ask Mrs. Clausen, but I don't like to disturb her about this."

"Hold on."

Donald Richards laid down the phone and went to the closet where he had stored pictures and mementos of his marriage. He pulled down a box from the top shelf that was marked "Vacations," and brought it back to the phone.

"Bear with me a minute," he told Susan. "If I have it, it'll be in the box I'm going through right now. I'm glad you're on the other end of the phone. Poring over old memories can be depressing."

"That's just what I've been doing in Justin Wells's apartment," Susan told him.

"You were with Justin Wells?" Don Richards did not attempt to conceal the surprise he felt.

"Yes. I thought I might be helpful to him."

That's all she's going to say about it, Richards realized. He had come across what he was looking for, a pile of bright blue cardboard folders.

He opened the one on top and looked at a picture of Kathy and himself at their table on the *Gabrielle*. Behind them he could see the large picture window that framed the sun setting over the ocean.

He removed the picture from the folder and turned it over. On the back was information about reorders. His voice was steady as he read it to Susan.

"That's a real break," Susan said. "The same company handled the pictures on both the *Gabrielle* and the ship Carolyn sailed on. I might be able to get a copy of the picture we think Carolyn Wells was going to mail to me."

"You mean of the man who gave her the turquoise ring?"

Susan didn't answer directly. "I suppose I shouldn't be optimistic. They probably don't even have the negative any longer."

"Look, I'm going out of town next week, on the final leg of the publicity tour for my book," Don Richards said. "I leave on Monday, but I'd really like to see you before I go. How's brunch, lunch, or dinner on Sunday?"

Susan laughed. "Let's make it dinner. I have plans for Sunday afternoon."

When he hung up the phone a few minutes later, Donald Richards sat there for a while, going through the pictures of the trips he and Kathy had taken together. It suddenly seemed a remote part of his life.

Clearly a change was due. He knew that in another week he might very well have put to rest all the torment of the past four years.

73

Susan looked at her watch. It was after ten. It had been a long day—unfortunately it wasn't going to be a long night. In less than six hours she had to be up and on the phone.

Four A.M. in New York would be 9 A.M. in London. That's when she intended to call Ocean Cruise Pictures Ltd. and inquire about ordering photographs taken on the *Gabrielle* and the *Seagodiva* during those cruises when Regina Clausen and Carolyn Wells had been passengers.

Even though it was late, however, she wanted to take a shower, and maybe in the process slough off some of the day's wearying effects. For long minutes she stood enveloped in steam, glad for the comfort of the hot water pelting her body. Then she toweled vigorously, wrapped a terry-cloth band around her still-damp hair, put on a nightshirt and a robe, and feeling considerably less uptight, went into the kitchen to fix a cup of hot cocoa to be sipped in bed. This is positively the last thing on the agenda for the day, she decided fervently, as she set the alarm clock for four.

When the alarm went off, Susan gave a protesting groan, then struggled awake. As she was wont to do, before going to bed she had opened the windows and turned off the heat, so the room felt like what Gran Susie used to call an icebox.

She sat up in bed, keeping the covers wrapped tightly around her, then reached for the phone and the pad and pen beside it. With mounting anticipation, she pushed the long series of numbers that would connect her to the studio in London.

"Ocean Cruise Pictures Ltd. Good morning."

For an instant Susan waited for the onset of the inevitable instructions on which number to press if you wanted to talk to a live human being. Instead she heard, "How may I help you?"

A moment later she was talking to the reorder department. "We may indeed have the pictures from those cruises, madam. We tend to keep the round-the-world photos a bit longer than the others."

But when Susan realized how many pictures had been taken between Mumbai and Athens on the *Seagodiva*, and between Perth and Hong Kong on the *Gabrielle*, she was shocked.

"You see, both ships were obviously quite full," the clerk explained. "So if you have seven hundred people on board, the odds are that while perhaps five hundred of them are couples, there still are many single passengers, and we try to take a number of photos of each person. We have photographers there while passengers are embarking on the ship, and many want snaps taken at the various ports of call, and with the captain at the receptions, and at their tables and at all the major social events, such as the black-and-white costume ball. So you see there really are many opportunities for photographic keepsakes."

Hundreds of pictures at twelve-fifty each, Susan thought; this could cost a fortune. "Wait a minute," she said. "The picture I want on the *Seagodiva* shows a single woman with the captain. Could you possibly go through those negatives and make a copy of all the pictures taken of a single woman posing with the captain?"

"On the leg from Mumbai to Athens in October two years ago?"

"That's right."

"We would, of course, need to be paid in advance."

"Of course." Dad could wire the money for me, from his office, Susan thought. I can pay him back later.

"Look," she said, "I need this picture as soon as possible. If the money is wired today, can you send the pictures by courier by tonight?"

"Certainly by tomorrow. You do realize we may be talking about as many as four hundred prints?"

"Yes, I do."

"I'm sure we'd be happy to offer a discount. Unfortunately you'd need to discuss it with Mr. Mayhew, and he won't be in until late this afternoon."

Susan interrupted the clerk. "I can't worry about that right now. Give me the information on the bank to which the money should be wired. It will be there by three o'clock your time today, at the latest."

"Oh, then I really am afraid that we can't complete the job until tomorrow. But you'd still have the pictures on Monday."

With that, Susan had to be satisfied.

She did manage to get back to sleep after the phone call, but not for long. By eight o'clock she was dressed and ready to leave for work. She had debated whether to wait until nine and try to reach her father at the office, but she was afraid he might not go directly there this morning. Keeping her fingers crossed that she would get him and not Binky, she phoned the house in Bedford Hills.

The new housekeeper answered. Mr. and Mrs. Chandler were weekending at the New York apartment, she told Susan. "They went down last evening."

That must be a relief for you, Susan thought. Binky had a reputation for not being able to keep household help.

She called the apartment and groaned inwardly when her stepmother answered. There was no trilling note in her voice this morning. "Good Lord, Susan, couldn't it have waited?" she asked petulantly. "Your father's in the shower. I'll have him call you back."

"Please do that," Susan said shortly.

Fifteen minutes later, her father returned the call. "Susan, Binky is positively contrite. She was so sleepy when she answered the phone, she didn't even think to ask how you were."

Oh, *please*, Susan thought. Dad, are you so dense you don't realize that what she's letting me know, in case I missed it, is that I woke her up. "Tell her I was never better," she said, "but Dad—I mean Charles—I need a favor."

"Anything for my girl."

"Great. I need you to wire fifty-three hundred dollars to London as fast as possible. I can phone your office and give the information to your secretary if you want, but it needs to be done immediately. I'll pay you back, of course. I'll just need to transfer some funds from my investment account, and that will take a few days."

"Don't worry about that. I'm glad to do it, honey. But is something wrong? This sounds like an emergency. You're not sick or having trouble, are you?"

Very nice, Susan thought. You're sounding like a father. "No, nothing like that. I'm doing a little pro bono police work for a friend of mine. We need to try to identify someone from cruise ship pictures."

"That's a relief. Give me the information; I'll take care of it right away. You know, Susan, I wish you would call me for help more often. It makes me feel mighty good. I don't see enough of you and I miss you."

Susan felt a momentary wave of nostalgia wash over her, but it quickly abated when she heard Binky's voice in the background.

Her father chuckled indulgently. "I'd better get off now, honey. Binky wants to get all her beauty rest, so I have to let her get back to sleep."

74

On Friday morning, Chris Ryan settled back in his ancient swivel chair and began to study the preliminary feedback he had gotten from his sources about Douglas Layton.

The initial piece of information checked out: Layton's educational background was exactly what he claimed it to be, so he wasn't one of those guys who say they graduated from a college they had seen only in pictures. The next item, however, was a clear indication to Chris that there was something funny about Layton: He'd had four different jobs since graduating from law school, and even though he seemed to have all the attributes that would guarantee he would make partner, it never had happened.

Chris arched his eyebrows as he read the details of Layton's present situation. He's definitely in the catbird seat now, he thought. A trusteeship with the Clausen Family Trust offered great potential, as well as the prospect of leading to a very cushy job, especially when old Hubert March, who appeared to be treating him as heir apparent, retired. From what Susan tells me, he's really buttering up Mrs. Clausen too, Ryan mused.

As he studied the report, he highlighted some

points for further investigation. One significant point
stood out: For someone who was paid to both preserve
and spend impressive sums of money, Layton seemed
to have precious little of his own. "What gives?" Chris
muttered to himself. Here's a guy in his mid-thirties,
single, with no apparent financial responsibilities, he
thought. He has worked with good companies for
good bucks, yet it looks like he's worth nothing. His
car is leased; his apartment's a rental. Checking
account deposits just about cover monthly expenses.
There's no record of a savings account.

So what does Layton do with his money? he wondered. He could have a drug habit, of course. And if he
does, chances are, like most addicts, he's finding a way to
support it, and he's probably not relying just on his salary.

Chris smiled grimly. There was definitely enough
here to justify a more probing investigation. He liked
the moment when he picked up the scent and began
the chase. I'll give Susan a call, he decided. She always
wants to be in on everything from the beginning. And
she'll probably derive a certain satisfaction from
knowing she was right—as far as Doug Layton is concerned, there's something rotten in Denmark.

75

When Susan arrived at her office, there was a call from
Pete Sanchez waiting on the answering machine. She
listened with a sense of triumph to the news that they

had found the ring. This could be important, she thought.

She sat at her desk for a minute, mentally putting together some of the pieces of the puzzle. The rings might not prove to be the key to solving these crimes, but clearly they connected all the victims. And if she was right, Tiffany's death had been caused not by the fact she *owned* the ring, but out of fear that she might have been able to identify the man who purchased several others like it at a souvenir shop in the Village.

I'll try out my theory on Pete and see what happens, she thought as she reached for the phone.

She could tell by Sanchez's voice that he was in excellent spirits. "The D.A.'s office is grilling the suspect," he told her happily. "One of my sources led us to a couple of witnesses who heard him threaten what he'd do to Tiffany, and he even said that he was on his way back to The Grotto to take care of her. He'll break. Anyhow, what's with that crummy ring?"

Susan chose her words carefully. "Pete, I may be dead wrong, but I think that these turquoise rings have everything to do with this case. One was found in the personal effects of a woman who vanished three years ago. Monday, a woman called in to my program and promised to show another one of them to me. We think she changed her mind and was going to mail it; she was hit by a van on the way to the post office. The police are still investigating, but it appears she was pushed. Tiffany promised to send her ring to me, then changed her mind and decided to keep it for sentimental reasons, then threw it away, but whoever murdered her didn't know that, and besides, I'm not sure—"

Sanchez interrupted: "Susan, the guy who hit on Tiffany is in custody. I don't see where a turquoise ring has anything to do with this case. We learned she was talking to you about the ex-boyfriend, a guy named Matt Bauer, and we've checked him out. Wednesday night he and his parents were in Babylon, visiting his girlfriend's home. They were going over wedding plans. He drove out with his folks and came back with them well after midnight. So he's clear."

"Pete, trust me. That ring may be significant. Have you got it there?"

"Right here."

"Wait a minute." Susan reached for her shoulder bag and from her wallet extracted the ring Jane Clausen had given her. "Pete, will you describe the ring you have?"

"Sure. Chips of turquoise set in a cheap band. Susan, these things are a dime a dozen."

"Any inscription on the inside?"

"Oh, yeah. Hard to read, though. Okay, it says, 'You belong to me.' "

Susan yanked open the top desk drawer and rummaged inside until she found her magnifying glass. She placed Regina Clausen's ring under the light to examine it closely. "Pete, have you got a magnifying glass?"

"Around here somewhere, I guess."

"Bear with me, please. I want to compare the writing on the inside of the bands. The one I'm holding has a broad capital *Y*, the *t* is narrow and uncrossed, and there's a big loop on the letter *m*."

"The *Y* and *t* sound alike. There's no loop on the *m*, though," Pete reported. "Susan, what is this about?"

"Pete, let's do it this way," Susan begged. "Please treat

the ring as evidence and have your lab make enlarged photographs of it from every angle and fax them to me. And one more thing—I want to talk to Matt Bauer myself. Will you give me his phone number?"

"Susan, the guy's clean." Pete's tone was indulgent.

"I'm sure he is. Come on, Pete. I did some favors for you when I was in the D.A.'s office."

There was a moment of silence, then Sanchez said, "Got a pencil? Here's the number." After Susan read the number back to him, he said in a voice that was totally professional, "Susan, I'm sure we've got Tiffany Smith's killer, but if you're onto something else, I want to know about it."

"It's a deal," Susan promised.

She had barely replaced the receiver before Janet announced a call from Chris Ryan, who filled her in on what he had learned so far about Douglas Layton.

He concluded his observations by saying, "Susie, we're hot on the scent."

Yes, we are, Susan thought, and in more ways than you know. She asked Chris to keep her posted, then alerted Janet to be on the lookout for a fax from Yonkers.

76

For a brief moment on Friday morning, it appeared that Carolyn Wells came close to regaining consciousness. Her mind didn't clear so much as it focused on the moment. Carolyn was aware of a floating sensation, as though she were immersed in a dark and murky sea. Nothing was clear. Even the pain—and there was a lot of it—was unfocused, as though it was just *there*, throughout her body.

Where was Justin, she wondered. She needed him. What had happened to her? Why was there all this pain? It was so hard to remember. He had phoned her . . . He was angry at her . . . She had talked about a man she met on the ship . . . Justin had phoned her about it . . . Justin, don't be angry. I love you . . . there's never been anyone else, she cried, but of course no one heard her. She was still under water.

Why did she feel so sick? Where was she? Carolyn felt herself rise to the surface. "Justin," she whispered.

She was not aware that a nurse was leaning over her bed. She just wanted to tell Justin not to feel hurt, not to be angry at her. "Justin, please *don't!*" she begged, then she slipped under again, away from the pain and into the welcoming waves of darkness.

Having been told to report anything that Carolyn Wells said, the duty nurse phoned Captain Tom Shea at the 19th Precinct. Her call was put through to the room in which the captain was once again going over Justin Wells's account of his actions on Monday afternoon—how he had phoned his wife, expressed his anger over her call to the radio program, then had gone home to talk to her in person, and not finding her there, had changed topcoats and returned to the office. At no point had he actually seen her.

Shea listened to the nurse's report, then said, "Mr. Wells, why don't you listen to this yourself?"

Justin Wells's lips tightened and his face flushed as the nurse hesitantly repeated Carolyn's words.

"Thank you," he said quietly; then he replaced the receiver and stood up. "Are you detaining me?" he demanded of Shea.

"Not yet."

"Well, you'll find me at the hospital. When my wife regains full consciousness, she's going to need me there. Whether she remembers what happened to her or not, one thing I can promise you: no matter how hard you try to build a case against me, Carolyn knows that I'd kill myself before I'd harm her in any way."

Shea waited until Wells left, then called the desk sergeant. "Send a female officer over to Lenox Hill Hospital," he ordered. "Tell her to make damn sure that Justin Wells is never left alone with his wife in her hospital room."

For long minutes afterward he sat, mentally reviewing the case and wincing at the prospect of another session with Oliver Baker, who had phoned requesting an appointment. But Baker *was* turning out to be an important witness, he reflected. He had seen the envelope pulled from under Carolyn Wells's arm; he was positive it had been stamped and was addressed to "Dr. Something"; he had been sure that the man who grabbed it was wearing a Burberry coat.

Maybe Baker's memory got jogged a little more, Shea thought, hence the request for another meeting. As one of the handful of mourners at Hilda Johnson's funeral service a few hours earlier, he was itching to see that Justin Wells was brought to justice. What stranger, he reasoned, would Hilda have admitted to her apartment at night, unless it were someone who identified himself as the husband of the woman she had seen pushed in front of the van?

Wells was guilty—Shea was sure of it. And it infuriated him to think that Hilda's murderer had just walked out of this room, still a free man.

77

It would have been too difficult and caused too much comment to break the morning's appointments, especially when he was going away in a few days' time, so he was able to catch only a little of Susan's radio program. As he had expected, the listeners were still anxious to talk about Tiffany's death:

"Dr. Susan, my friend and I were saying how we hoped she'd get back together with Matt. You could tell she really liked him . . ."

"Dr. Susan, do you think Matt might have done this to her? I mean maybe he met her and they had a fight or something? . . ."

"Dr. Susan, I live in Yonkers and the guy they're questioning about Tiffany's murder is really bad. He served time for manslaughter. We all think he killed her . . ."

"Dr. Susan, was Tiffany wearing the turquoise ring when she was murdered?"

This last was an interesting question, and one that disturbed him. *Had* she been wearing the ring? He didn't think so, but he wished now that he had thought to look for it.

Susan had responded to the questions very much as he had expected: that from what she understood, Matt was absolutely not a suspect; that she hadn't heard any mention of the ring in the media; that one always must remember there is a presumption of innocence, even in cases where a suspect has been convicted of a previous crime.

He knew what *that* meant. Susan wasn't buying the police theory as to Tiffany's murderer. She was too smart not to connect Tiffany's death to the others. The mind of a prosecutor is never at rest, he thought grimly.

And neither is mine, he mused with smug satisfaction. He wasn't worried. He had worked out the time frame for eliminating Susan. All that remained was to plan the details.

In the hidden compartment in his briefcase, he was carrying the turquoise rings he had taken from Parki's shop—three of them, plus the one Carolyn Wells had intended to mail to Susan. He only needed one, of course. The others he would toss in the ocean after he was finished with the final lonely lady. He would love to put one on Susan Chandler's finger once he had killed her, but then that would raise too many questions. No, he couldn't risk leaving it on her hand, but maybe for just a minute he would slip it on her finger, to give himself the satisfaction of knowing that she, like the others, belonged to him.

78

"Until Monday, this is Dr. Susan Chandler saying good-bye."

The red on-air signal over the studio door flashed off as Susan looked up at the control room where Jed was taking off his headset. "How did it go?" she asked anxiously.

"Fine. A lot of listener participation. You're always good—you know that—but I thought you were especially good today. Did anybody say anything in particular that worried you?"

Susan collected her notes. "No. I guess I just feel terribly distracted."

Jed's voice softened. "It's been a tough couple of days. I know that. But things are looking up. Hey! You got to the studio today with twenty minutes to spare, and now it's the weekend!"

Susan made a face at him. "Cute," she said as she pushed back her chair and stood up. "See you Monday."

Janet handed Susan the faxes from Yonkers as soon as she walked through the door. "Detective Sanchez phoned to see if they came through clearly," she said. "He's funny. He said to keep him posted on anything you learn, or else next time he won't clean the lasagna off the evidence before photographing it."

"I'll do that. Thanks, Janet. Oh, and order the usual

gourmet delight for me, please, and tell them to rush it. Mrs. Price will be here in twenty minutes."

"I already ordered your lunch, Doctor," she said, an implied reproach in her voice.

I seem to be stepping on everyone's toes today, Susan thought as she walked into her office. First Binky, now Janet. Who's next? she wondered. She sat at her desk and laid out the faxes of the enlarged photos and compared them with the ring Jane Clausen had given her.

The photographer had clearly made an extra effort, even managing to get some excellent shots of the inscription on the inside of the band. As Susan had expected, there were remarkable similarities between the ring in the photographs and the ring that had been Regina's.

I'm right, she thought. This *is* all about the rings. The one Mrs. Clausen gave me simply has to have been made by the same guy who made Tiffany's, which means it almost certainly was bought at the souvenir shop in the Village that Tiffany told me about. I'd stake my life that Tiffany was murdered because someone heard her when she talked to me on air about a man she had seen buying one of these rings, and he was afraid she could identify him.

Janet came into Susan's office, the bag from the luncheonette in hand. She placed it on Susan's desk; then when Susan put down the turquoise ring, Janet picked it up and examined it. "What a nice sentiment," she said, squinting as she read the inscription. "My mother loves the old songs, and 'You Belong to Me' is one of her favorites."

In a voice that was low and only slightly off key, she

began to sing: "'See the pyramids along the Nile / Watch the sunrise on a tropic isle.'" She paused and hummed a few bars . . . "Then there's something about a 'marketplace in old Algiers,' and then something else about 'photographs and souvenirs.' I don't remember how that part goes, but it's really a nice song."

"Yes, it is," Susan agreed absentmindedly. Almost like an alarm she couldn't shut off, the words of the song were sounding in her head. What is it about them? she wondered. She took the ring back and tucked it in her wallet.

It was ten minutes of one. She should be preparing for her next session, but she didn't want to wait until two to try to reach Matt Bauer, Tiffany's former boyfriend and the one other person who might be able to tell her the location of the souvenir shop in the Village at which he had bought the ring.

Bauer's mother answered the phone. "Dr. Chandler, my son is at work. We have already spoken to the police. I am very, very sorry about Tiffany's death, but it has nothing to do with my son, who dated her only a few times. She simply wasn't his type. My friends told me about Tiffany's calls to you, and I have to tell you they were very embarrassing for Matthew. I phoned Tiffany yesterday and informed her of his impending marriage. Wednesday night we had dinner with his fiancée's family—lovely, refined people. I can't imagine what they would think if Matthew's name is brought up publicly in this case. Why, I—"

Susan interrupted the flow of words. "Mrs. Bauer, the best way to be sure Matthew's name stays out of this is to have him speak to me off the record. Now where can I reach him?"

Reluctantly Matt's mother told her that he worked for the Metropolitan Life Insurance Company in midtown Manhattan and gave her his office number. Susan called, but learned that Bauer was out and not expected back in his office until three. She left a message that it was urgent for him to call her.

While she was spooning soup from the cardboard container, Pete Sanchez phoned. "Susan, just to keep you abreast of what's going on, you should know that things are breaking. This guy not only announced that he was going back to The Grotto to take care of Tiffany, but now he admits that he did go to the restaurant's parking lot. He claims he got scared off, though, because some guy was hanging out there."

"Maybe he was telling the truth," Susan suggested.

"Come on, Susan. You were in the D.A.'s office. The bad guys always have the same line: 'I swear, your honor. The guy who did it went that-a-way!' Susan, what else is new when you're dealing with these creeps?"

79

By late Friday afternoon, Chris Ryan had managed to find both concrete facts and abundant rumors about Douglas Layton.

The facts were that he was a compulsive gambler who was seminotorious in Atlantic City, and it was widely known that on at least half a dozen occasions he had lost a great deal of money. And that explains why he doesn't have a nickel to his name, Chris thought.

One rumor was that Layton had been barred from ever traveling on several of the cruise lines because of his suspected cheating at their gaming tables. Another rumor was that he had been asked to resign from jobs at two investment firms because of complaints that he frequently displayed a condescending attitude toward female employees.

At ten of five on Friday afternoon Chris Ryan was digesting the information he had gathered when he received a phone call from Susan. "I'm getting some interesting stuff on Layton," he told her. "Nothing necessarily incriminating, but interesting."

"I'm anxious to hear it," Susan told him, "but first I have a question for you. Is there any way to get a list of all the porn shops in Greenwich Village?"

"You've got to be kidding me," Chris said. "Nobody in that business takes out an ad in the Yellow Pages."

"That's what I'm starting to realize," Susan replied. "How about souvenir shops?"

"Look at every listing from 'Antiques' to 'Junk.' "

Susan laughed. "Some help you are. Now tell me what you've found out about Douglas Layton."

80

It had been an exciting week for Oliver Baker. His brief appearance on television on Monday afternoon had changed his life. Suddenly he had become a kind of celebrity. His produce customers all wanted to talk to him about the accident. The woman who worked at the neighborhood dry cleaners made a fuss over him like he was a star. He even got a nod from the stone-faced Wall Street executive who never before had given him the time of day.

At home, Oliver was a hero to Betty and the girls. Even Betty's sister, who always groaned and grimaced when he gave an opinion on anything, called to get his personal account of what it was like to give testimony at the police station. Of course, she wasn't content to leave it at that. Instead, she went on about the coincidence of how another witness, the old woman who claimed it wasn't an accident, had been murdered. And she ended by cautioning him, "You just be careful that something like that doesn't happen to you." He wasn't worried, of course, but it did spook him a little.

Oliver was, in fact, enjoying his contact with the police, and he especially liked Captain Shea. He was the kind of authority figure who made Oliver feel comfortable and secure. He had had a particularly good feeling, sitting in the captain's office, just the two of them, with Shea hanging on his every word.

On Friday, page six of the *Post* reported that architect Justin Wells was being questioned about his wife's accident, and the article included a picture of him leaving the hospital.

All morning Oliver kept the *Post* on his desk at work, with the paper open to the article. Then shortly before noon, he had phoned Captain Shea to say that he would like to see him after work.

That was why at five-thirty Friday afternoon, Oliver Baker was back in Captain Shea's office, the picture from the newspaper in hand. Savoring his return to this seat of power, he related why he had requested another interview. "Captain, the more I look at this man's picture, the more positive I am that he was the one I saw take that envelope as—or so I thought at the time—he tried to steady the woman who fell in front of the van."

Oliver smiled into Shea's understanding eyes. "Captain, maybe I was more in shock than I realized," he said. "Do you think that's why I just blotted out his face at first?"

81

Matt Bauer liked his job with Met Life. He intended to sit in one of the executive offices someday, and with that goal in mind he worked diligently to sell insurance programs to small businesses—his area of expertise. At twenty-five his game plan was already beginning to show results. He had been tapped for the management training course, and now he was engaged to his boss's niece, Debbie, who was the sort of woman who would be the perfect partner to accompany him on his path to the top. What made it even better was the fact that he genuinely loved her.

That was why he was visibly distressed when he met Susan Chandler at five-thirty in a coffee shop at Grand Central Station.

Susan immediately liked the earnest-faced, clean-cut young man, and she understood his concern. She believed him when he said he was very, very sorry about Tiffany, and she was sympathetic when he explained why he did not want to get involved in a murder investigation.

"Dr. Chandler," he said, "I only went out with Tiffany a couple of times. Literally three times, I believe. The first time came about when I was having dinner one night at The Grotto; I asked her to go out, and she invited me to be her date at a friend's wedding."

"You didn't want to go?" Susan guessed.

"Not really. Tiffany was fun, but I could tell right away there wasn't any spark between us, if you know what I mean, and I could tell right away that what she wanted was a serious relationship, not an occasional date."

Remembering Tiffany's eager, hopeful voice, Susan nodded in comprehension.

The waitress poured their coffee, and Matt Bauer took a sip before continuing. "At her friend's wedding, I did happen to mention a film I wanted to see. It had won a big award at the Cannes Film Festival and had been written up in the papers. Tiffany said she was dying to see it too."

"So, of course, you invited her?"

Matt nodded. "Yes. It was playing at a little theater down in the Village. I could tell Tiffany hated it, although she pretended she thought it was good. We went to lunch before the show. I asked her if she liked sushi, and she told me she loved it. Dr. Chandler, she almost turned green when the food arrived. She had asked me to order for her, and I assumed she knew that sushi was raw fish. Afterwards we just kind of walked around a little, looking in shop windows. I don't know one end of the Village from the other, and neither did she."

"That was when you went into the souvenir shop?" Susan asked. Let him remember where it was, she prayed.

"Yes. Actually, Tiffany was the one who stopped when something in the window caught her eye. She said she was having so much fun that she wanted a souvenir of our date, so we went inside."

"Was that what you wanted to do?" Susan asked.

He shrugged. "Not really."

"What do you remember about the shop, Matt?" Susan paused. "Or do you prefer Matthew?"

He smiled. "To my mother, it's Matthew. To the rest of the world, it's Matt."

"All right, Matt, what do you remember about the shop?"

He thought for a minute. "It was stuffed with cheap souvenirs, but it was still neat, if you know what I mean. The owner—or clerk, whichever he was—was from India, and the fun thing was that in addition to the usual Statues of Liberty, and tee shirts and I Love New York buttons, he had an array of brass monkeys and elephants and Taj Mahals and Hindu gods—that sort of thing."

Susan opened her purse and took out the turquoise ring Regina Clausen's mother had given her. Holding it in the palm of her hand, she showed it to Matt Bauer. "Do you recognize this?"

He studied the ring carefully but did not take it. "Does it say 'You belong to me' on the inside of the band?"

"Yes, it does."

"Then I'd say from what I remember that it's the ring I gave Tiffany, or one just like it."

And just like Carolyn's I'll bet, Susan thought. She

said, "From what Tiffany told me, the reason you bought the ring was that some man came in and purchased one, and the clerk told you that the same man already had bought several others. Do you remember that?"

"I remember it, but I never actually saw that guy," Matt said. "As I remember the shop, it was small to begin with, and there was a painted wooden screen that blocked my view of the counter. Also, as I recall, I was reading about one of the figurines—it had the head of an elephant and the body of a man and it was supposed to be the god of wisdom, prosperity, and happiness, according to the legend on the card. I thought it would make a nice souvenir, but when I turned to show it to Tiffany, she was talking to the clerk at the counter. She was holding the turquoise ring, and he was telling her about how the customer who just left had bought several of them.

"I showed her the elephant god, but Tiffany wasn't interested—the ring was the souvenir she wanted."

Bauer smiled. "She was funny. When I showed her the elephant god and read her the legend, she said that it looked like too many of her customers at The Grotto to convince her it was going to bring her prosperity, so I put it back and bought the ring."

Matt's smile vanished, and he shook his head. "It was only ten bucks, but you'd have thought I'd bought her an engagement ring. Later, all the way to the subway, she kept holding my hand and singing, 'You belong to me.'"

"How often did you see her after that?"

"Only once. She kept calling my house, and if she got the message tape, she'd sing a few bars of that song. Finally I took her out for a drink and told her that she was making too much of the ring, and that while our couple of dates had been fun, I thought we should leave it at that."

He finished his coffee and looked at his watch. "Dr. Chandler, I'm sorry, but I honestly have to leave in just a few minutes. I'm meeting my fiancée, Debbie, at six-thirty." He signaled for the check.

"This is on me," Susan said. She purposely had not asked about the location of the shop. She still held a faint hope that Matt might have caught a glimpse of the customer who had bought the ring, and that as he talked about what happened in the shop, something about the location would emerge from his subconscious.

When she did ask, the only thing he could tell her about the location was that the film they had seen was shown in a theater not far from Washington Square, that the sushi place was about four blocks away from the theater, and that they were not far from the subway stop at West Fourth and Sixth Avenue when they saw the souvenir shop.

Susan had one final question she hoped might be helpful. "Matt, Tiffany mentioned something about a porn shop across the street from where you bought the ring. Do you remember that?"

As he got up to go, he shook his head. "No, I don't. Look, Dr. Chandler, I wish I could be more helpful." He paused. "You know, underneath that tough exterior, Tiffany was a sweet kid. I know that whenever I think of her remark about how the customers at The Grotto look like the elephant god, I want to laugh. I hope they find who did this to her. Good-bye."

Susan paid the check, picked up her shoulder bag, and took a cab downtown to West Fourth Street and

Sixth Avenue. On the way she consulted her map of Greenwich Village. Even though she had lived there for several years, the area was still a little confusing to her. Her plan was to move out from the subway station along the haphazard streets of the Village until she found a souvenir store featuring Indian goods that was located across the street from a porn shop. It sounded simple enough; how many could there be?

I could ask Chris Ryan to help, she thought, but the Village isn't *that* big, and I'd rather at least *try* to do it alone. She had decided that if she found the shop, she would go in and try to get friendly with the Indian clerk. Then, once she had the cruise picture of Carolyn Wells that showed the man who had given her the turquoise ring, she would ask the clerk if he recognized him.

She wasn't there yet, but she was narrowing the circle around the killer. She could *feel* it.

82

Carolyn could feel the pain again, and she was very afraid. She didn't know where she was, and when she tried to talk, her lips wouldn't move. She tried to lift her hand, but something was holding it down.

She wanted to tell Justin how sorry she was. But where was he? Why didn't he come to her?

She sensed something rushing at her in the darkness. It was going to hurt her! Where was Justin? He would help her. At last she could move her lips; finally she could hear the words rising from her throat: "No . . . please . . . no! Justin!" And then it was upon her, and she felt herself sinking again, her mind retreating from the terrible pain.

Had her conscious mind still been aware, she would have heard Justin's anguished cry as the monitors emitted a frantic warning and Code 9 was activated, but she didn't.

Nor did she see the condemnation in the face of the police officer who looked accusingly across the bed at Justin.

83

On Friday evening, Alex Wright did not get home until nearly seven o'clock. To clear the schedule for his trip next week, he had spent the entire day at the office, even to the point of having lunch at his desk, something he detested.

After such an intense day, he was looking forward to a quiet evening, and went straight to his dressing room, where he changed into chinos and a sweater. As he often did, he congratulated himself mentally on finally tackling the problem of inadequate closet space.

A few years ago, his dressing room had been carved from an adjoining bedroom and was spacious enough to comfortably house his considerable wardrobe. A convenience he particularly liked was the tabletop shelf that always held an open suitcase ready for packing. Framed on the wall above it was a reminder list of items he would need to take with him for various climates and events.

The suitcase was already half filled with articles of clothing that were laundered or cleaned and immediately replaced in it after a trip: underwear, socks, handkerchiefs, pajamas, a robe, dress shirts.

For longer trips, like the one he was about to undertake to Russia, Alex preferred to do the packing himself. If for any reason he was too busy, then Jim Curley would attend to it. It was a long-standing private joke between them that on the one occasion when Alex trusted his housekeeper, Marguerite, to do his packing, she had forgotten to include a formal shirt, a fact he had not discovered until he was in the process of dressing for a black-tie dinner in London.

As Alex pushed his bare feet into comfortable old moccasins, he smiled, remembering what Jim had said of that occurrence: "Your father, God rest him, would have booted her out of the house without a second thought."

Before he left the dressing room, Alex glanced at the checklist, reminding himself that October was usually very cold in Russia, and that it probably would be wise to have his heavier coat with him.

He went downstairs, poured himself a scotch on the rocks, and as he began to rattle the ice as he sipped his drink, realized he was thoroughly out of sorts. It had been gnawing at him that Susan had been very cool on the phone yesterday when she had refused his invitation to join him and Dee for a drink.

What would it be like tomorrow night at the library event, with Dee on one side of him and Susan on the other? he wondered. Chances are, it was going to be uncomfortable.

Then he smiled. I've got an idea, he thought. I'll invite Binky and Charles to join us as well. There are going to be four tables of ten. I'll put Dee with Binky and Charles at another table, he decided. That should make a definite statement to Susan. "And to Dee," he said aloud.

84

The names of the streets she had walked echoed like a litany in her mind: Christopher, Grove, Barrow, Commerce, Morton. Unlike the grid in which the streets of uptown Manhattan had been laid out, the streets of the Village followed an irregular pattern all their own. Finally Susan gave up, bought the *Post*, and dropped in to Tutta Pasta on Carmine for a late dinner.

She nibbled on warm bread dipped in olive oil and sipped a Chianti as she read the paper. On page three she saw a picture of Tiffany taken from her senior yearbook, with a follow-up story on the progress of the investigation into her murder. An indictment was expected shortly, it said.

Then on page six she was startled to see the photograph of Justin Wells and the report that he was being questioned about circumstances surrounding his wife's accident.

I'm not going to be able to convince anyone there's a connection between these two cases until I locate that souvenir shop and talk to the clerk, she thought. And, pray God, show him that cruise picture that's supposed to arrive Monday. I didn't find the place tonight, she told herself, but I'll be back looking first thing in the morning.

She arrived home at ten o'clock and wearily dropped her shoulder bag onto the foyer table. Why do I carry so much stuff in that thing all the time? she wondered as she flexed her shoulders. It's heavy enough to have a dead body in it.

"And isn't that a happy thought," she said to herself as Tiffany's picture flashed through her mind. She looked exactly as I had pictured her, Susan thought sadly. Too much eyeliner, hair teased within an inch of its life, but still cute and saucy.

Reluctantly she went to the answering machine; the message light was blinking. Alex Wright had phoned at nine: "Just calling to say hello. Looking forward to tomorrow evening. In case we don't touch base during the day, I'll pick you up at six-thirty."

He's letting me know that he's home tonight, Susan thought. That's good.

The next call was from her mother. "It's nine-thirty. I'll try you later, dear."

Probably just as I get into the shower, Susan thought, deciding to return the call at once.

It was clear from the tone of her voice that her mother was not happy. "Susan, did you know that Dee is not only planning to move back to New York but has already leased an apartment?"

"No," Susan said, adding after a pause, "Isn't that a bit sudden?"

"Yes, it is. She's always been restless, but I must tell you it really offends me that she took the Trophy with her today when she went to sign the lease."

"She took Binky? How come?"

" 'To get another woman's take on it,' she said. So I reminded her that I'm not blind, and that I'd have liked to see it, but Dee said someone else was interested in the place and she had to move quickly."

"Maybe she did," Susan suggested. "Mom, please don't let that sort of thing get under your skin. It isn't worth it. You know you'll enjoy having Dee back in New York."

"Yes, I will," her mother admitted, her tone somewhat mollified. "But I worry about . . . Well, you know what we were discussing the other night."

God give me strength, Susan thought. "Mom, if you mean Alex Wright, I've had exactly one date with him. I wouldn't say that we're in a committed relationship."

"I know. Still, I think this precipitous rush to New York is a bit unusual, even for Dee. And something else, Susan: If you need money, you don't have to go to your father. I know how much he's hurt you. I have cash in the bank too, you know."

"What's that about?" Susan asked.

"Didn't you ask Charley-Charles to wire money to London for you?"

"How did you find that out?"

"Not from your father, certainly. Dee told me."

And she heard it from Binky, no doubt, Susan thought. Not that it matters, but what a pain! "Mom, I don't need money. It's just that there was something I wanted to order today for immediate delivery, and I didn't have time to arrange for a transfer of funds to my checking account, so I asked Dad. I'm going to pay him back next week."

"Why should you? He has plenty, and he's sending Dee off on a cruise. Don't be so proud, Susan. Take the money as due you."

A minute ago you were telling me *not* to take money from him, Susan thought. "Mom, I just got in and I'm really kind of tired. I'll call you tomorrow or Sunday. Any plans for the weekend?"

"A blind date, God help us. Helen Evans set it up. I never thought at my age I'd be looking forward to anything like that."

Susan smiled, hearing the pleasure in her mother's voice. "Good news," she said heartily. "Have fun."

It's not going to be a shower tonight, she thought as she hung up. After this day, I need a long, hot soak in the tub. There isn't a physical or mental piece of me that isn't worried, sad, irritated, or aching.

Forty minutes later, she opened the bedroom windows, her final task before getting into bed. When she glanced down into the street, she noticed that it was deserted except for a solitary stroller, whose silhouette she could barely make out.

He could never make it in the marathon, she thought. If he were walking any slower, he'd be going backwards.

85

Despite—or perhaps because of—the exhaustion she had felt earlier, Susan was unable to sleep well. Three different times during the night she woke up and found herself listening intently for any sound that might suggest someone was in the apartment. The first time she woke, she thought she had heard the outer door opening. The sensation was so vivid that she got up and ran to the door, only to find that it was bolted. Then, despite feeling slightly foolish, she tested the locks on the windows in the living room, den, and kitchen.

She returned to her bedroom, still haunted by the sensation that something was amiss, but determined not to close the bedroom windows. I am two flights up, she told herself sternly. Unless Spiderman is in the neighborhood, it's highly unlikely that anyone is going to scale the wall.

The temperature had dropped sharply since she went to bed, and the room was almost icy cold. She pulled the blankets around her neck, recalling the dream that had made her so uneasy and finally awakened her. In it she had seen Tiffany running out of a door and into a dimly lighted space. She had the turquoise ring and was tossing it in the air. Then a hand appeared out of the shadows and grabbed the ring, and Tiffany cried out, "No! Don't take it! I want to keep it. Maybe Matt will call me." Then her eyes widened in terror and she screamed.

Susan shivered. And now Tiffany is dead because she called me, she thought. Oh God, I'm so sorry.

Suddenly the window shade rattled, blown by a sharp breeze. That's what startled me, she realized, and for a moment she considered getting up and locking that window as well. Instead she pulled the covers still tighter against her chin and was asleep in just a few minutes.

The second time Susan awoke, she bolted up in bed, sure there had been someone at the window. Get a grip on yourself, she thought, as she once again rearranged the bedding and pulled the blankets almost over her head.

She awoke for the third time at six o'clock. Although she had been sleeping, her mind had been active, and she realized that sometime in between the interruptions in her sleep her subconscious had been dwelling on the passenger list from the *Seagodiva*. She had found it in Carolyn Wells's file, and Justin Wells had allowed her to take it.

When she awoke, her mind had focused on the fact that Carolyn had written the name "Win" on one of the daily shipboard news bulletins from the ship. Win was almost certainly the man she had been planning to go to Algiers with, Susan thought. I should have studied the passenger list right away. We know the guy she met was a passenger on the ship, so that means his name has to be on the list.

Awake now, with no hope of going back to sleep, she decided that coffee would help to clear her brain. After it was made, she brought a cup back to bed, propped herself up with pillows, and began to study the ship's manifest. "Win" must be short for something else, she decided. Running down the list of passenger names, she looked for a Winston or Winthrop, but no one with either of those names was listed as being on board.

It could be a nickname, she thought. There were passengers with last names that were possibilities, including Winne and Winfrey. But Winne and Winfrey were both listed as being with wives.

The middle initials of very few passengers were listed on the manifest, so if the man Carolyn met was known as Win because of his middle name, the list would be of little help.

She noted that in the case of married couples, the names were listed in alphabetical order, so that Mrs. Alice Jones was followed by Mr. Robert Jones, and so on. Eliminating all those who were clearly married couples, Susan went down the manifest, checking off the names of men who were listed without a woman's name preceding or following. The first name on the manifest that appeared to be that of a single man was Mr. Owen Adams.

Interesting, she thought when she had finished running down the entire list of passengers; of six hundred people on the ship, there were one hundred and twenty-five women listed singly, but only sixteen men who apparently were traveling alone. That narrowed it down a lot.

Then another thought struck her: Would the manifest of the *Gabrielle* be among Regina Clausen's effects? she wondered. And if so, was it possible that one of those sixteen men from the *Seagodiva* had been a passenger on that ship too?

Susan tossed back the covers and headed to the shower. Even if Mrs. Clausen isn't up to seeing me, I'm going to ask her about the *Gabrielle* passenger list, she decided, and if it *was* returned with Regina's things, I'll beg her to let her housekeeper give it to me.

86

Feathers in the wind. Feathers in the wind. He could feel them scattering, dancing, mocking him. But now he knew for sure he could never retrieve them all. Ask Dr. Susan if you don't believe that, he thought angrily. He wished there were some way he could accelerate his plan, but it was too late. The steps had been laid out, and it couldn't be changed now. He would leave on schedule, but then he would double back, and that's when he would eliminate her.

Last night, when he had been walking past Susan's brownstone, she had happened to come to the window. He knew she couldn't have been able to see him clearly, but it did make him realize that he must not take a risk like that again.

When he returned to New York, he would find a way to take care of her. He would not follow her and try to force her into traffic as he had with Carolyn Wells. That had proved to be less than successful, for while Carolyn remained in a coma, with little apparent chance of recovery, she was still alive; and as long as she was alive, she was still a threat. No, he would have to corner Susan alone, as he had Tiffany—that would be best.

Although there *might* be another way, he thought suddenly.

This afternoon, in the guise of a messenger, he would check out her office building, studying the security in the lobby and the layout of the floor on which her office was located. It was Saturday, so it wouldn't be crowded. There would be fewer curious eyes to observe him.

The thought of killing Susan in her office was eminently satisfying. He had decided that he would honor her with the same form of death that he had accorded Veronica, Regina, Constance, and Monica—the same death that was awaiting his final victim, someone on a voyage to see "the jungle wet with rain."

He would overpower her, tie her up, and gag her, and then, as she watched, tortured with fear, he would slowly unwrap the long plastic bag and, inch by agonizing inch, he would cover her with it. Once she was covered head-to-toe, he would seal the bag. Inevitably there would be a little air still inside—just enough so that she would have a few minutes to struggle. Then as he saw the plastic begin to stick to her face and seal her mouth and nostrils, he would leave.

However, he would not be able to dispose of Susan's body as he had the others. The others he had either buried in sand, or weighted down with stones and watched disappear into murky waters. So Susan Chandler he would have to leave, but he could take comfort in the fact that after she was out of the way, the next—and final—victim would share the burial arrangement of her sisters in death.

87

Susan left her apartment at nine o'clock and walked directly to Seventh Avenue. From there she explored the blocks that slanted west toward the Hudson River, starting with West Houston and St. Luke's Place, then Clarkson and Morton Street. She made the decision to go only as far west as Greenwich Street, which ran parallel to the avenues, before turning north to the next block and then heading back east until she reached Sixth Avenue. Once there, she would reverse and head west on the next street.

Most of these streets were largely residential, although she did find several souvenir shops. In none of them, however, did she see a sign of Indian-style objects. She considered asking at some of these places if they were aware of the kind of shop she was looking for, but she decided against it. If she *did* succeed in finding the shop, she did not want the Indian clerk forewarned that she was coming.

At noon, she used her cell phone to call Jane Clausen at Memorial Sloan-Kettering Hospital. To her surprise, Mrs. Clausen readily agreed to her request to visit her. In fact, she seemed almost anxious to have her come by. "If you're free later this afternoon, it would be very nice to see you, Susan," she said.

"I'll be there by four," Susan promised.

She had planned to stop somewhere for lunch, but decided instead to buy a pretzel and a cola from a street vendor, and to eat in Washington Square Park.

Although she had removed some of the contents of her shoulder bag, as time passed she became more and more aware of its weight, and of the fact that her feet were getting tired.

The day had started out overcast and chilly, but by early afternoon the sun had broken through, and the streets, almost deserted earlier, were now teeming with people. Seeing all those people—from Village regulars to gawking tourists—made the walking much more pleasant. Susan loved Greenwich Village. There's no other place like it, she thought. Gran Susie was lucky to grow up here.

Was it this kind of day when Tiffany and Matt walked around here a year ago? she wondered. She decided to continue her search by exploring the area just east of Sixth Avenue and turned onto MacDougal Street. As she walked downtown from Washington Square, she thought of her conversation with Matt Bauer. She smiled at the memory of the elephant god who he said Tiffany had likened to some of her customers at The Grotto.

The elephant god.

Susan stopped so suddenly that the teenager behind her bumped into her. "Sorry," he muttered.

Susan did not answer him. She was staring into the window of a shop she had just come upon. She glanced quickly at the entrance to the shop, over which there hung an oval-shaped sign that read DARK DELIGHTS.

Dark delights, indeed, she thought as she looked again at the display window. Inside, a red satin garter belt was draped over a pile of videotapes with crudely suggestive titles emblazoned on the boxes. A variety of other supposedly "erotic" paraphernalia was scattered around, but Susan ignored it. Her attention was riveted on an object in the center of the window: a turquoise-inlaid elephant god, its trunk facing outward.

She spun around. Across the street she saw a FOR RENT sign in the window of the Khyem Specialty Shop.

Oh no! she thought. Threading her way through the traffic, she crossed the narrow street to the shop, stood at the door and peered inside. Even though the shop seemed to be fully stocked, the interior had a deserted look. A counter with a cash register was visible directly in front of the entrance. To the left, she could see a large painted screen that acted as a room divider. That must be the screen Matt described, she thought, the one behind which he and Tiffany had been standing when the man came into the shop to purchase a turquoise ring.

But where was the proprietor or clerk who had been there that day? she wondered.

Then she realized suddenly that there was one person who might know. She rushed back across the street to the porn shop. The door was open, and the place seemed to be doing a brisk business. One man was paying at the cash register, and two untidy-looking adolescents with long, lank hair were on line behind him.

His purchase completed, the man eyed her as he came out, but turned his head when Susan stared him down. A few minutes later the two boys emerged, guiltily averting their eyes as they passed her. They're definitely underage to be buying that garbage, she thought, the ex-prosecutor in her coming to the fore.

Now that she saw no other customers, she went inside. There appeared to be only one clerk, a thin, unattractive man who, like his surroundings, seemed a little seedy.

He looked at her nervously as she approached the counter. She realized instantly that he thought she might be a plainclothes policewoman who was going to give him grief for an illegal sale to minors.

I've got him on the defensive, she thought. Too bad I can't keep him there. She pointed to the Khyem Specialty Shop across the street. "When did that store close?" she asked.

She detected an immediate change in his attitude. The clerk's nervous demeanor vanished, and a brief, condescending smile twitched at the corners of his lips.

"Lady, you haven't heard what happened? Abdul Parki, the guy who owned that place, was murdered Tuesday afternoon."

"*Murdered!*" Susan made no effort to hide the dismay in her voice. Another one, she thought—another one. Tiffany talked about the shop's owner on my program.

"Did you know Parki?" the man asked. "He was a sweet little guy."

She shook her head, while struggling to compose herself. "A friend of mine recommended his shop," she said carefully. "Someone gave her one of the turquoise rings he made. Look," she said, and opened her bag and pulled out the ring Jane Clausen had given her.

The man glanced at the ring and then at her. "Yeah, that's one of Parki's rings, all right. He was nuts about turquoise. Oh, by the way, I'm Nat Small. I own this place."

"I'm Susan Chandler." Susan held out her hand. "I can tell he was a good friend of yours. How did it happen?"

"Stabbed. The cops think it was druggies, although they didn't take nothing so far as anyone can tell. He was really a nice little guy, too. And do you know, he was lying there almost a day before they found him. I was the one who called the cops, when he didn't open up on Wednesday."

Susan could see the genuine sadness in Nat Small's face. "My friend said he was a very nice man," she said. "Were there any witnesses?"

"Nobody seen nothing." Small shook his head and looked away as he spoke.

He's not telling me something, Susan thought. I have to get him to level with me. "Actually, the young woman who told me about Parki was stabbed to death on Wednesday night," she said quietly. "I think the person who killed both her and Parki is a customer who bought several of these turquoise rings from him over the past three or four years."

Nat Small's sallow complexion turned a deeper gray as he met Susan's gaze. "Parki told me about that guy. Said he was a real gentleman."

"Did he describe him?"

Small shook his head. "Nothin' more than that."

Susan took a chance. "I think you know something you haven't told me, Nat."

"You're wrong." His eyes shifted toward the door. "Look, I don't mind talkin' with you, but you're scaring away my customers. There's a guy hanging around outside, and I know he won't come in while you're here."

Susan looked the little man directly in the eyes. "Nat, Tiffany Smith was twenty-five years old. She was stabbed as she left work on Wednesday night. I have a radio program that she called in to earlier and talked about a souvenir shop in the Village where her boyfriend bought her a turquoise ring that had the sentiment 'You belong to me' engraved inside the band. She described the shop, and she mentioned a man who she said was a native of India. She said that while she and her boyfriend were in the shop, a man—another customer—bought a turquoise ring, just like hers. And I'm convinced that's why she's dead—because of what she said she had seen. And I swear to you that Parki is dead as well because he could identify that same man. Nat, I sense that you know something you're not telling me. You've *got* to tell me before someone else dies."

Again Nat Small looked nervously toward the door as though he were afraid of something. "I don't want to get involved," he said, his voice low.

"Nat, if you know anything, you're *already* involved. Please tell me. What is it?"

His voice was almost a whisper now. "Just before one o'clock Tuesday afternoon, a guy was kind of hanging around, looking in my window—the way that guy out there is doing right now. I figured he was trying to pick out something he wanted, or maybe even that he was nervous about coming in here—he looked like a real uptown kind of guy—but then he went across the street and into Parki's shop. After that, a customer came in here, and I didn't pay attention anymore."

"Did you report what you saw to the police?"

"That's just what I didn't do. The police'd have me going through mug books or describing him for a sketch artist, but it would just be a waste. He was not the kind to be in mug books, and I'm no good telling people how to draw. I saw the guy in profile. He was classy looking, in his late thirties. He had a cap on, and a raincoat and sunglasses, but I still got a real good look at his profile."

"You think you'd recognize him if you saw him again?"

"Lady, in this business, I gotta recognize people. If I don't remember what the undercover cops look like, I might get busted, and if I can't spot a druggie, I might get murdered. Listen, you gotta get out of here. You're bad for business. The guys don't want to come in and shop with a classy-looking dame hanging around."

"Okay, I'll go. But Nat, tell me—would you recognize this man if I could show you his picture?"

"Yeah, I would. Now will you get out of here?"

"Right away. Oh, and one more thing, Nat. Don't talk about this—not to anybody. For your own safety, don't talk about it."

"Are you kidding? Of course I won't. I promise. Now get out of here and let me make a buck, okay?"

88

When Douglas Layton went into Jane Clausen's hospital room at three-thirty, he found her sitting in a chair. She was dressed in a soft blue cashmere robe, and a blanket was tucked around her.

"Douglas," she said, weariness showing in her voice, "have you brought me my surprise? I've been trying to imagine what it could possibly be."

"Close your eyes, Mrs. Clausen."

Her irritation was apparent in her tight smile, but she obeyed nonetheless. "I'm not a child, you know," she murmured.

He had been about to kiss her on the forehead, but drew back. A bad mistake, he thought. Don't be a fool and go over the line.

"I hope you'll be pleased," he said as he turned the framed sketch so that she could see the rendering of the orphanage that showed Regina's name on the carved sign.

Jane Clausen opened her eyes, and for long moments she studied the picture. Only a tear in the corner of her left eye hinted at the emotion she was feeling. "How very lovely," she said. "I can't think of a nicer tribute to Regina. Now when did you people put this over on me, naming the orphanage after her?"

"The administrators of the orphanage begged us to let it be named for Regina. It will be announced at the dedication of the new wing that I'll be attending next week. We were going to wait and show you this and the pictures from the ceremony at the same time, but my hunch was that it would give you a lift to see this one now."

"You mean you wanted me to see it before I die?" Jane Clausen said matter-of-factly.

"No, I don't mean that, Mrs. Clausen."

"Doug, don't look so guilt stricken. I *am* going to die. We both know that. And seeing this does give me great happiness." She smiled sadly. "You know what else is a comfort to me?"

He knew it was a rhetorical question. He held his breath, hoping that she would talk about his sensitivity, and his devotion to the trust.

"It's that the money Regina would have inherited is going to be used to help other people. In a way, it's as though she'll be living through the people whose lives are touched and bettered because of her."

"I can promise you, Mrs. Clausen, that every cent we spend in Regina's name will be carefully committed."

"I'm sure of that." She paused, then looked at Douglas Layton, standing tensely next to her. "Douglas, I'm afraid Hubert is getting quite absentminded. I think that I want to see a different situation in place," she said.

Layton waited. This is what he had come to hear.

There was a soft tap at the door. Susan Chandler looked in. "Oh, Mrs. Clausen, I didn't know you had company. I'll stay in the waiting area while you two visit."

"Absolutely not. Come in, Susan. You remember Douglas Layton, don't you? You met last Monday in your office."

Susan thought of what Chris Ryan had told her about Layton. "Yes, I do remember," she said coolly. "How are you, Mr. Layton?"

"Very well, Doctor Chandler." She knows something, Layton thought. I'd better stick around. She wouldn't dare say anything about me while I'm here.

He smiled at Susan. "I owe you an apology," he said. "I bolted out of your office the other day as though I'd heard a fire alarm, but I had an elderly client coming in from Connecticut, and I'd confused the times on my calendar."

He's very smooth, Susan thought, as she took the chair he held out for her. She had hoped he would leave, but he pulled up another chair, signaling his intention to continue his visit.

"Douglas, I won't keep you," Jane Clausen told him. "I need to have a few words with Susan, then I'm afraid I'll have to rest."

"Oh, of course." He sprang up, his expression and manner solicitous.

A classy-looking guy in his late thirties, Susan thought, reflecting on the description Nat Small had given of the man he saw standing outside his shop on the day Abdul Parki was murdered. But then, it fits many dozens of other men. And just because he changed his story about a conversation with Regina Clausen doesn't mean that he murdered her, she thought, reproaching herself for jumping to conclusions.

There was another tap on the door, and a nurse put her head in the room. "Mrs. Clausen, the doctor will be here to see you in just a minute."

"Oh, dear. Susan, I'm afraid I've dragged you up here for nothing. Will you call me in the morning?"

"Of course."

"Before you go, you must see the surprise I told you Doug had for me." She pointed to the framed sketch. "This is an orphanage in Guatemala that is being dedicated next week to Regina."

Susan examined it closely. "How lovely," she said sincerely. "I understand there's a desperate need for facilities like this in many countries, and especially in Central America."

"That's exactly right," Layton assured her. "And the Clausen Family Trust is helping to build them."

As she got up to leave, Susan noticed a bright blue folder on the nightstand next to the bed. It appeared to be identical to the one she had found pieces of in the wastebasket in Carolyn Wells's home office. She walked over and picked it up. As she had expected, the front of the folder displayed the logo of Ocean Cruise Pictures. She looked at Mrs. Clausen. "May I?"

"Absolutely. That was probably the last picture ever taken of Regina."

There was no mistaking that the woman in the picture was Jane Clausen's daughter. The eyes were the same, and they both had the same straight nose; even the widow's peak on the hairline was similar. Regina was pictured standing next to the *Gabrielle*'s captain. The obligatory cruise photo, Susan thought, but it's a very good one. When she had done the research on Regina Clausen for her radio program, she had seen pictures of her in newspaper clippings, but none had been as flattering as this one.

"Regina was very attractive, Mrs. Clausen," she said sincerely.

"Yes, she was. From the date on the folder, I know that photograph was made two days before she disappeared," Jane Clausen said. "She looks very happy in it. Knowing that has been a comfort in some ways, a torment in others. I wonder if her happiness has to do with trusting the person responsible for her disappearance."

"Try not to think about it that way," Doug Layton suggested.

"I'm sorry I have to interrupt." The doctor was standing in the doorway. Clearly he expected them to leave.

Susan could not wait any longer for Layton to depart. "Mrs. Clausen," she said hurriedly, "do you remember if a passenger list from the cruise ship was among the things found in Regina's stateroom?"

"I'm sure I saw one in the envelope with other information about the cruise. Why, Susan?"

"Because if I may, I would very much like to borrow it for a few days. Could I pick it up tomorrow?"

"No, if it's important, you'd better get it now. I insisted that Vera take a few days off and visit her daughter, and she's planning to leave very early in the morning."

"I'd be happy to get it now, if you're sure you don't mind," Susan said.

"Not at all. Doctor Markey, I'm sorry to delay you," Jane Clausen said, her voice suddenly brisk. "Douglas, hand me my purse, please. It's in the drawer of the night table."

She took out her wallet and pulled a card from inside. After jotting a note on it, she handed it to Susan.

"I know Vera is there still, and I'll phone her to let her know you're coming, but you can take this note just in case; it has my address. We'll talk tomorrow," she said.

Douglas Layton left with Susan. Together they went down in the elevator and out to the street. "I'd be happy to go with you," he suggested. "Vera knows me very well."

"No, that's fine. Here's a cab. I'll grab it."

The traffic was typically heavy, and it was five o'clock before she reached the Beekman Place address. Knowing that she was going to have to rush back to her apartment to get ready for the evening, she tried unsuccessfully to persuade the cabbie to wait for her while she ran upstairs.

She was grateful that Jane Clausen had phoned the housekeeper. "These are all Regina's things," she explained, as she took Susan into the guest room. "The furniture is from her apartment. Mrs. Clausen sits in here by herself sometimes. It would make your heart break to see her."

It is a beautiful room, Susan thought. Elegant, but still comfortable and inviting. Rooms tell a lot about the people who furnish them.

Vera opened the top drawer of an antique desk and took out a legal-size manila envelope. "All the papers found in Regina's stateroom are here."

Inside were the kinds of memorabilia that Carolyn Wells had brought back from her cruise as well. In addition to the passenger list, there were a half-dozen copies of the daily shipboard news bulletins, with information about the upcoming ports of call, and a variety of postcards that seemed to be from those ports. Regina probably bought them as mementos of the places she had seen, Susan thought. Chances are she would have mailed them before reaching Hong Kong if she had intended to send them.

She put the passenger list in her shoulder bag, then decided to take a quick look at the postcards and bulletins. She flipped through the postcards, stopping when she noticed one from Bali that featured an outdoor restaurant. A table overlooking the ocean had been neatly circled in pen.

Did she dine there? Susan wondered. And if she

did, why was it special? She skimmed through the newsletters until she found the one about Bali.

"I'm going to take this card and this bulletin," she told Vera. "I'm sure it will be all right with Mrs. Clausen. I'm seeing her tomorrow, and I'll tell her I have them."

It was twenty after five when she finally managed to hail a cab, and it was ten of six before she opened the door of her apartment. Forty minutes to get ready for the big date, she thought, and I haven't even decided what to wear.

89

Pamela Hastings sat in the waiting room of the intensive care unit at Lenox Hill Hospital, trying to comfort a sobbing Justin Wells. "I thought I'd lost her," he said, his voice breaking with emotion. "I thought I'd lost her."

"Carolyn's a fighter—she'll pull through," Pamela said reassuringly. "Justin, a Dr. Donald Richards phoned the hospital to inquire about Carolyn and about you. He left his number. Isn't he the psychiatrist you consulted for quite a while when you and Carolyn had problems earlier?"

"The psychiatrist I was *supposed* to consult," Wells said. "I only saw him once."

"His message was that he'd be glad to help in any

way possible." She paused, worried how he would react to what she was going to say next. "Justin, may I call him? I think you need to talk to someone." She felt his body stiffen.

"Pam, you still think I did that to Carolyn, don't you?"

"No, I don't," she said firmly. "I'll say it to you as straight as I can. I believe that Carolyn is going to make it, but I also know we are not out of the woods yet. If— God forbid—she doesn't make it, you're going to need an awful lot of help. Please let me call him."

Justin nodded slowly. "Okay."

When she returned to the waiting room a few minutes later, Pamela was smiling. "He's on his way over, Justin," she said. "He sounds like a nice man. Please let him help you if he can."

90

"I think I have solved a perplexing problem, Jim," Alex Wright said cheerfully.

It was clear to Jim Curley that his boss was in good spirits. He looks terrific, he thought as he glanced in the rearview mirror, and better than that, he looks happy.

They were on the way to Downing Street to pick up Susan Chandler for the dinner at the main library, on Fifth Avenue. Alex had insisted on leaving early, just in case they got caught in heavy traffic. Instead, there were fewer cars than usual on Seventh Avenue, so they made excellent time. Must be Murphy's Law or something, Jim thought. "What kind of problem did you solve, Mr. Alex?"

"By inviting Dr. Chandler's father and stepmother to the dinner tonight, I was able to ask them to stop by the St. Regis and collect Dr. Chandler's sister. It would have been quite awkward for me to arrive with a lady on each arm."

"Oh, you could handle it, Mr. Alex."

"The question is not *if* I could handle it, Jim. The question is do I *want* to handle it? And the answer is no."

Meaning, Jim thought, that he wants to zero in on Susan, and not Dee. From what he had seen of the two women, he agreed with his boss. There was no question that Dee was a spectacular-looking lady, of course. He had seen that the other night when he had driven them. She seemed nice also. But there was something about her sister, Susan, that grabbed Jim. She seemed more natural, more like the kind of person you could invite into your home without apologizing because the place wasn't so fancy, he thought.

At five after six they were in front of the brownstone where Susan lived. "Jim, how do you always manage to get a parking place?" Alex Wright asked.

"Clean living, Mr. Alex. You want me to turn on the radio?"

"No, I'm going upstairs."

"You're early."

"That's all right. I'll sit in the parlor and twiddle my thumbs."

* * *

Y ou're early," Susan said when she answered the lobby intercom, dismay apparent in her voice.

"I won't get in your way, I promise," Alex said. "I hate to wait in cars. Makes me feel like a taxi driver."

Susan laughed. "All right, come on up. You can watch the rest of the six o'clock news."

Of all the luck, she thought. Her hair was still wrapped in a towel. Her gown, a black tuxedo jacket with a long, narrow skirt, was hanging over the tub in the bathroom, an effort to steam out the last of the wrinkles. She was wearing the fuzzy white bathrobe that made her feel like an Easter bunny.

Alex laughed when she opened the door. "You look about ten years old," he told her. "Want to play doctor?"

She made a face at him. "Behave yourself and turn on the news."

She closed the bedroom door, sat at the vanity, and pulled out the hair dryer. I'd be out of luck if I couldn't do my own hair, she thought. Although it never looks as good as Dee's. "Dear God, I *am* late," she murmured as she turned the dryer onto the highest setting.

Fifteen minutes later, at exactly 6:28, she looked in the mirror. Her hair was fine, the extra makeup obscured the strain from lack of sleep she had seen earlier in her face, the wrinkles were just about all out of the skirt, so everything seemed to be in order. Yet somehow she didn't feel right. Had she been too worried, too rushed, or what? she asked herself as she picked up her evening bag.

She found Alex sitting in the den, watching the television as instructed. He looked at her and smiled. "You're lovely," he said.

"Thank you."

"I watched the news, so I'll tell you all about what went on in New York today once we're in the car."

"I can't wait."

S he looks great, Jim Curley thought as he held open the car door. Really great. During the drive uptown to the library, he kept his eyes on the traffic, but he focused his attention on the conversation in the back-seat.

"Susan, there's one thing I'd like to clear up," Alex Wright said. "I had not planned to ask your sister to the dinner tonight."

"Please don't worry about that. Dee is my sister and I love her."

"I'm sure you do. But I suspect you don't love Binky, and maybe I made a mistake inviting her and your father as well."

Oh boy, Jim thought.

"I didn't know they were coming," Susan said, an edge of irritation apparent in her voice.

"Susan, please understand that I only wanted you with me tonight. Inviting Dee was not my intention, and when it happened, I thought that if I included your father and Binky, and asked them to bring Dee, I'd be making a statement."

Good explanation, Jim thought. Now come on, Susan. Give the guy a break.

He heard her laugh. "Alex, please, I think I'm sending the wrong signals. I didn't mean to sound so irritable. You've got to forgive me. This has been a dreadful week."

"Tell me about it, then."

"Not now, but thanks for asking."

It's going to go okay, Jim thought, with a sigh of relief.

"Susan, this is something I don't discuss much, but I do understand how you feel about Binky. I had a stepmother too, although in my case it was a little different. My father remarried after my mother died. Her name was Gerie."

He usually never talks about her, Jim thought. He really is opening up to Susan.

"What was your relationship with Gerie?" Susan inquired.

Don't ask, Jim thought.

91

Although she had been inside the huge Fifth Avenue branch of the New York Public Library many times, Susan Chandler didn't remember ever seeing the McGraw Rotunda, where the party was taking place—it was a magnificent space. With its soaring stone walls and life-size murals, it made her feel as though she had been transported back in time, to another century.

Despite the elegant setting, and despite the fact that she really was enjoying Alex Wright's company, an hour later Susan found herself distracted and unable to relax. I should be enjoying a very pleasant evening, she thought, and here I am, preoccupied with thoughts of a very questionable man who runs a porn shop, and who may be able to identify the murderer of Regina Clausen, Hilda Johnson, Tiffany Smith, and Abdul Parki, the man who attempted to murder Carolyn Wells.

Four of those names had been added to the list during the last week.

Were there others?

Would there be others?

Why was she so sure that the answer was yes?

Maybe I should have stayed in the district attorney's office, she thought as she sipped from a glass of wine and half listened to Gordon Mayberry, an elderly gentleman intent on telling her of the generosity of the Wright Family Foundation toward the New York Public Library.

As soon as they had arrived, Alex had pointedly introduced her to a number of what she gathered were key people. She wasn't sure whether to be amused or flattered, since it was clearly his way of proclaiming that she was his date for the evening.

Dee and her father and Binky came in minutes after she and Alex arrived. Dee, exquisite in a white sheath, had hugged her warmly. "Susie, have you heard I'm moving back, lock, stock, and barrel? We'll have fun. I've missed not having you around."

I actually believe she *means* it, Susan thought. That's why what she's been trying to pull with Alex is so unfair.

"Have you seen the book that is being presented to Alex tonight?" Gordon Mayberry asked.

"No, I haven't," Susan replied, forcing herself to focus her attention.

"A limited edition, of course. A copy will be given to all the guests, but you may enjoy taking a look at it before dinner. It will give you some idea of the enormous amount of good work the Wright Family Foundation has accomplished in the sixteen years of its existence." He pointed to a lighted stand near the entrance to the rotunda. "It's over there."

The book was open to the center pages, but Susan turned it back to the beginning. On the dust jacket there were pictures of Alex's father and mother, Alexander and Virginia Wright. Not a very cheerful looking couple, she thought as she studied their unsmiling faces. A quick study of the book's table of contents showed that the first few pages contained a short history of the Alexander and Virginia Wright Family Foundation; the rest of the book was divided into sections according to the various charities: hospitals, libraries, orphanages, research facilities

She leafed through it at random, then, thinking of Jane Clausen, she turned to the section that dealt with orphanages. Midway through those pages she stopped and studied a photograph of an orphanage. That must be a typical structure for that use, she thought. Typical kind of landscaping too.

"Really fascinating, isn't it?"

Alex was at her side.

"Pretty impressive, I'd say," she told him.

"Well, if you can tear yourself away, they're about to serve dinner."

Despite the elegance of the dinner, Susan once again found herself distracted so that she didn't notice what she was eating. Her sense of foreboding was so strong as to seem like a physical presence. Nat Small, the porn shop proprietor—she couldn't stop thinking about him. Suppose it occurred to the killer that Nat might have noticed him hanging around the display window? He surely would get rid of Nat, too, Susan thought. Carolyn Wells may not recover, or if she does, she may not even remember what happened to her. That means that Nat is perhaps the only one who can identify the man who murdered Parki and the others, and pushed Carolyn.

Suddenly aware that Alex was asking her something, she focused enough to respond. "Oh no, everything is fine. And I absolutely *love* the food," she said. "I'm just not very hungry."

I should have the pictures from Carolyn's cruise Monday, she thought. But what will I find? When Carolyn had phoned the program and mentioned the photograph, she had said the man who invited her to see Algiers was just in the background of that shot. What about Regina's cruise? Maybe there are other, clearer pictures from that trip that caught him. I should have ordered them as well, she thought, mentally chastising herself for not having done that earlier. I've got to get them before it's too late—before someone else gets killed.

The presentation of the book was made after the main course had been cleared. The director of the library spoke about the generosity of the Wright Family Foundation, and about the grant to purchase and maintain rare books. She spoke also of the "modesty and dedication of Alexander Carter Wright, who so unselfishly devotes his life to running the foundation and who shuns personal recognition."

"See what a nice guy I am," Alex whispered to

Susan as he stood to accept the book the director was presenting.

Alex was a good speaker, his manner easy, gracious, and laced with a touch of humor. When he was seated again, Susan murmured, "Alex, do you mind if I switch places with Dee for dessert?"

"Susan, is anything wrong?"

"No, not at all. Peace in the family and all that. I can see that Dee is unhappy, having her ear bent by Gordon Mayberry. Maybe if I rescue her we'll bond a little." She laughed. "And I also need to have a word with Dad."

Alex's amused chuckle followed her as she walked to the nearby table and asked Dee to trade places. *There's another reason to do this*, she acknowledged to herself—*if I'm going to start dating Alex, I want to be very sure that Dee won't be in the picture. If there is going to be a competition, then I want to head it off before it can get started. I don't want to go through another situation like we had with Jack.*

She waited until Mayberry had Binky's car before she turned to her father. "Dad, I mean Charles, this may sound crazy, but I need to have you send fifteen thousand dollars more to that photo studio in London first thing Monday morning."

He looked at her, his expression changing from surprise to concern. "Sure I will, honey, but are you in some kind of trouble? No matter what it is, I can help."

Sure I will. I can help.

The bottom line is that despite Binky and her obvious dislike of me, Dad's always willing to be there for me, Susan thought. I've got to remember that. "I promise I'm not in any trouble, but I do ask that we keep this between us," she told him. "I'm helping someone else."

I know Nat Small may be at risk, she thought. And he may not be the only one. There could be another person marked to receive one of those turquoise rings with "You belong to me" engraved inside the band.

Why did the lyrics of that song keep running through her head? she wondered. Now she was hearing *"Watch the sunrise on a tropic isle."*

Of course! Those words had been on the bulletin from the *Gabrielle* that she had found among Regina Clausen's effects earlier in the day.

I'll have the pictures from the *Seagodiva* on Monday, Susan thought. I'll ask Nedda if I can use the long conference table in her office to lay them out. That means by Monday night I should have found Carolyn's picture. If the studio can make copies of the photographs from the *Gabrielle* by Tuesday afternoon, I'll have them Wednesday. I'll spend as much time as necessary going through them even if I have to stay up all night.

Binky finally had managed to deflect Gordon Mayberry onto someone else. "What are you two talking about?" she demanded as she turned her attention to Susan and Charles.

Susan caught her father's conspiratorial wink as he said, "Susan was just telling me that she's interested in collecting art, dear."

92

Pamela Hastings arrived at Lenox Hill Hospital at noon on Sunday, and made her way through the now-familiar corridors to the ICU waiting room. As expected, she found Justin Wells was there already, looking disheveled, unshaven, and half-asleep.

"You didn't go home last night," she said accusingly.

He peered up at her with bloodshot eyes. "I couldn't. They tell me she has stabilized somewhat, but still I'm afraid to leave her for any length of time. I'm not going inside her room again, though. The impression around here is that on Friday Carolyn started to come out of the coma, then must have remembered what happened to her, and the panic and fear drove her back under. She was conscious long enough, however, to say, 'No . . . please . . . no! Justin.'"

"You know that doesn't necessarily mean, 'Please, don't push me under a car, Justin,'" she said as she sat next to him.

"Tell that to the cops. And to the doctors and nurses here. I swear, if I try to go near Carolyn, they all act like they expect to see me pull the plug."

Pam noticed the convulsive opening and closing of his hands. He's on the verge of a breakdown, she thought. "Did you at least have dinner with Dr. Richards last night?" she asked.

"Yes. We went to the cafeteria."

"How did it go?"

"It helped. And, of course, *now* I realize I should have stayed with him two years ago. Ever hear that old poem, Pam?"

"What's that?"

" 'For want of a nail the shoe is lost, for want of a shoe the horse is lost, for want of a horse the rider is lost.' Or something like that."

"Justin, you're not making sense."

"Yes I am. If I'd gotten my head straightened out, I wouldn't have overreacted so strongly when I heard that Carolyn had phoned the radio program about that guy she met on the trip. If I hadn't upset her with my phone call, she might have kept her appointment with Dr. Chandler. That means she would have gotten into a cab in front of the apartment and wouldn't have been walking to the post office."

"Justin, *stop* it! You'll drive yourself crazy with this kind of 'what if' thinking." She took his hand. "Justin, you didn't cause this terrible thing, and you've got to stop blaming yourself."

"That's exactly what Don Richards said I need to do: 'Stop it!' " Tears welled in his eyes, and a sob rose in his throat.

Pamela put one arm around him and smoothed back his hair. "You need to get out of here. If we stay here like this, people are going to start talking about us," she said gently.

"Don't tell me George is going to beat up on me too. When is he coming home?"

"Tonight. And now I want you to go home. Fall into bed, sleep for at least five hours, then shower, shave, put on fresh clothes, and come back. When Carolyn wakes up, she's going to need you, and if she sees you looking the way you do now, she'll sign up for another cruise."

Pamela held her breath, praying that she had not gone too far, but finally she was rewarded by a faint chuckle. "Best friend, you're a doll," Justin said.

She walked with him to the elevator. On the way, she made him look in on Carolyn. The police officer followed them into the cubicle.

Justin picked up his wife's hand, kissed the palm, and closed her fingers around the kiss. He did not speak to her.

When the elevator doors shut behind him, Pamela started back to the waiting room, but was stopped by the nurse at the desk. "She spoke again, just a moment ago, right after you left."

"What did she say?" Pamela asked, almost afraid of the answer.

"The same. She said, 'Win, oh, Win.' "

"Do me a favor and don't tell that to her husband."

"I won't. If he asks, I'll just say she's trying to talk, and that's a good sign."

Pamela passed the waiting room and went to the public phones. Before she had left for the hospital, Susan Chandler had called her and explained that she was trying to trace the name Win through the *Seagodiva's* passenger list. "Tell them to listen carefully if Carolyn tries to say the name again," she said. "Maybe she'll give more of it. Win must be a nickname or a shortened version of something like Winston or Winthrop."

Susan was not at home, so Pamela Hastings left a message on the answering machine: "Carolyn's trying to talk again. But all she said was the usual—'Win, oh, Win.' "

93

"On Sunday mornings, Regina and I often attended services at St. Thomas's and then, afterwards, went out for brunch," Jane Clausen told Susan. "The music there is simply wonderful. I couldn't bring myself to go back there for over a year after I lost her."

"I just came from the ten-fifteen at St. Pat's," Susan told her. "The music is magnificent there as well." She had walked to the hospital from the cathedral. It was another beautiful fall day, and she found herself wondering what Tiffany Smith had been doing last Sunday. Had she had any sense that it was to be her last Sunday, that her life was going to end in just a few days? Of course she didn't, Susan decided, then chided herself for being so morbid.

Jane Clausen clearly realized that she had very little time left. It seemed to Susan that everything she said reflected that inevitability. Today she was propped up in bed, a shawl around her shoulders. Her complexion had lost its pallor, but Susan was sure that was because she had developed a fever.

"It's very kind of you to stop by again today," Mrs. Clausen said. "Sundays in a hospital have a way of passing very slowly. Also, yesterday I didn't have the opportunity to speak with you privately, and I do need to do that. Douglas Layton has been very thoughtful, very kind. I told you that I felt I had misjudged him earlier, and that my doubts about him were unfounded. On the other hand, if I make the move I'm contemplating—that is, asking the current director of the family trust to step aside and let Douglas take over—I will be giving him a great deal of authority over a substantial amount of money."

Don't do that! Susan thought.

Jane Clausen continued, "I do realize that at this time I am particularly susceptible to expressions of concern or to displays of affection or thoughtfulness—whatever label you want to put on it."

She paused and reached for the glass of water beside the bed, took a few sips, and continued. "That's why I want to ask you to have Douglas Layton thoroughly investigated before I take this major step. I realize it's an imposition, and that I've only known you a week. Still, in that time I've come to think of you as a trusted friend. It's a gift you have, you know. And it's probably why you are so good at what you do, and so successful."

"Please, I'm happy to do anything I can. And thank you for your kind words." Susan knew that it was not the moment to tell Jane Clausen that Layton already was being checked out, and that based on just the earliest information had been found wanting. She chose her words carefully. "I think it's always wise to be very cautious before making major changes, Mrs. Clausen. I promise you I'll take care of it."

"Thank you. That relieves me greatly."

It seemed to Susan that Jane Clausen's eyes were becoming larger from one day to the next. This morning they had a luminous quality, yet the expression remained tranquil. Even a few days ago, they were so sad, Susan thought, but now they're different, as if she knows what's ahead and has accepted it. Susan searched for a moment to find an appropriate way to explain her next request, but realized she had best save explanations for later. "Mrs. Clausen, I have my camera with me. Would you mind if I took a few Polaroids of the sketch of the orphanage?"

Jane Clausen had been drawing the shawl closer around her shoulders. She waited until she had adjusted it to her satisfaction before she responded, "You have a reason for wanting that, Susan. What is it?"

"Will you let me tell you tomorrow?"

"I'd rather know now, of course, but I can wait; and it will be nice to know that I have another visit to look forward to. But Susan, before you go, tell me, did you ever hear from the young woman who phoned your program Monday morning, the one who said she had a turquoise ring like the one that had belonged to Regina?"

Susan answered carefully. "You mean 'Karen'? Yes and no. Her real name is Carolyn Wells. She was seriously injured a few hours after she made the call, and I haven't been able to speak to her because she's in a coma."

"How terrible."

"She keeps calling for someone named Win. I think it might be the name of the man she met on the cruise ship, but I haven't been able to confirm it. Mrs. Clausen, did Regina ever phone you from the *Gabrielle?*"

"Several times."

"Did she ever mention anyone named Win?"

"No, she never discussed any of her fellow passengers by name."

Susan could hear the fatigue in Mrs. Clausen's

voice. "I'm going to take those pictures and be on my way," she said. "I'll be out of here in just a few minutes. I can tell you need to rest."

Jane Clausen closed her eyes. "The medication makes me terribly sleepy."

The sketch was propped on the bureau opposite the bed. Using her flash, Susan shot four pictures, watching them develop one by one. Satisfied that she had enough, she replaced the camera in her purse and quietly started for the door.

"Good-bye, Susan," Jane Clausen said, her voice heavy with sleep. "You know, you've just reminded me of something very pleasant. At my debut, one of my escorts was a handsome young man named Owen. I hadn't thought of him in years, but at the time I had quite a crush on him. Of course, that was very long ago."

Owen, Susan thought. Oh my God, that's what Carolyn is saying. Not "Oh, Win," but *Owen*.

She remembered there was an Owen Adams on the passenger list of the *Seagodiva*. He was the first man she had checked off as traveling without a wife.

Twenty minutes later, Susan rushed into her apartment, ran to her desk and grabbed the passenger list from the *Gabrielle*. Be here, she thought, be here.

There was no "Owen Adams" listed, something she was able to determine almost immediately, but realizing the man she was looking for might very well travel under a false name, she continued searching through the passenger list.

She was almost at the end when she found it. One of the very few passengers whose middle name appeared on that list was Henry Owen Young. There must be a connection, she thought.

94

Alex Wright called Susan at her apartment at ten, eleven, and twelve, before finally reaching her at one. "Tried you earlier, but you were out," he said.

"You could have left a message."

"I don't like talking to machines. I wanted to see if you would let me buy you brunch."

"Thanks, but I couldn't have made it," Susan told him. "I went to see a friend in the hospital. Which reminds me, Alex, is there any such thing as a standard orphanage in Central America?"

"Standard? I'm not sure what you mean, but I don't think so. If you're referring to what they look like, though, then as with hospitals or schools, there are certain characteristics that are indigenous to the type of institution. Why?"

"Because I have some pictures I need to show you. When do you leave tomorrow?"

"Early, I'm afraid. That's why I wanted to see you today. How about dinner tonight?"

"I'm sorry, I have plans."

"All right, for you I'll make the arduous trip downtown. Are you going to be home for a while?"

"All afternoon."

"I'm on my way."

I know I'm right, Susan thought as she replaced the receiver. These two buildings aren't just similar—they're the same. But this way, I'll be absolutely sure. The book about the Wright Family Foundation was lying on her desk, its pages open to the picture of the orphanage in Guatemala that had caught her eye. Line for line, it appeared to be exactly like the sketch Jane Clausen had in her hospital room. But it *is* a sketch, not a photograph, she reminded herself. Maybe Alex will see some distinguishing features I've missed.

When he studied the photographs, Alex did see something she had overlooked, but rather than distinguishing one building from the other, it confirmed the fact that they were the same. In the sketch Mrs. Clausen had, the artist had painted a small animal over the front door of the orphanage. "Look at this," Alex said. "That's an antelope. Now look at the photograph in the book. It's there as well. The antelope is taken from our family crest; we always have one over the door of any building we fund."

They were sitting side by side at the desk in Susan's den.

"Then certainly there wouldn't be a carved sign with Regina Clausen's name on it in front of your building," Susan exclaimed.

"The sketch of the sign is definitely a phony, Susan. My guess is that someone is pocketing the money that was supposedly used to fund this building."

"I had to be sure." Susan thought of Jane Clausen, and of how disappointed and sad she would be when she realized that Douglas Layton was cheating her.

"Susan, you look really upset," Alex said.

"I am, but not for myself." She attempted a smile. "How about a cup of fresh coffee? I don't know about you, but I need one."

"Yes, thank you. In fact, I want to see how good your coffee is. That could be very important."

Susan closed the Wright Family Foundation book. "I'll show this photograph to Mrs. Clausen tomorrow. She's got to know as soon as possible." She looked at her desk, suddenly realizing how untidy it must seem in Alex's eyes.

"I'm not usually this messy," she explained. "I've had a couple of projects I've been working on, and the papers have piled up."

Alex picked up the booklet with the passenger list from the *Seagodiva* and opened it. "Was this a cruise you were on?"

"No. I've never been on a cruise." Susan hoped Alex wouldn't ask any more questions about it. She didn't want to talk about what she was doing to anyone, not even him.

"Neither have I," he said as he dropped the booklet back on the desk. "I get seasick."

Over coffee he told her that Binky had phoned to invite him to brunch. "I asked her if you were coming, and when she said you weren't, I turned her down."

"I'm afraid Binky doesn't like me very much," Susan said. "And I suppose I can't blame her. I practically begged Dad on bended knee not to marry her."

"Which knee?" Alex asked.

"What?" Susan stared at him, then caught the amused twinkle in his eyes.

"I ask because I went down on bended knee to beg my father not to marry Gerie. In the end it didn't do any good either, and for the same reason Binky can't stand you, Gerie hated my guts."

He stood up. "I should go. I've got a messy desk that should be cleared as well." He turned to her at the door. "Susan, I'll be gone a week or ten days," he said. "Stay as busy as you want during that time, but after that, don't get too booked up. Okay?"

Just as she closed the door behind him, the phone rang. It was Dee calling to say good-bye. "I'm leaving for Costa Rica tomorrow. I pick up the ship there," she said. "I'm going to stay on it till Callao. Wasn't last night fun?"

"It was great."

"I called Alex to thank him, but he's out."

Susan heard the question in her sister's voice, but she had no intention of explaining that Alex had been with her, or of giving her the reason for his visit. "Maybe you'll catch him later. Have a marvelous time, Dee."

She hung up, painfully aware that the reason she could not take greater pleasure in being with Alex was that she still felt something could develop between him and Dee, especially if Dee kept pursuing him. And Susan had no intention of going through the distress of losing another man to her sister.

95

Don Richards had felt restless all day. Early Sunday morning he had run in Central Park. Afterwards he came home and made a cheese omelet, reflecting that during his marriage he had been the regular Sunday-morning chef, but he had gotten out of the habit and almost never bothered to fix anything for himself now. He read the *Times* while he ate, but finally, after pouring a second cup of coffee, he found he was unable to concentrate, so he laid down the paper and walked to the window.

It was eleven o'clock. His apartment overlooked the park, and he could see that the crisp, sunny day had already brought out a host of New Yorkers. Below he could see dozens of joggers. Daredevils on in-line skates were whizzing past people out for a stroll. There were many couples and family groups. Richards watched one elderly woman settle on a bench and turn her face so that the sun shone directly on it.

He turned away from the window and went into the bedroom. He had to pack for his trip tomorrow, and the prospect irritated him. It was almost over though. There was only one week more of publicity for the book, and then he was taking a week off to himself. The travel agent had faxed a list of cruise ships with empty first-class space that would accommodate his schedule.

He went back to his desk to look at it.

By two o'clock he was in Tuxedo Park. His mother arrived home from having lunch at the club with friends to find him sitting on her porch steps. "Don, dear, why didn't you tell me you were coming?" she asked, feigning irritation.

"When I got in the car, I still wasn't sure that I was. You look very nice, Mother."

"So do you. I like you in a sweater. It makes you look younger." She saw the suitcase beside him. "Are you moving in, dear?"

He smiled. "No, I just wanted to ask you to put this away in the attic somewhere."

It's all those pictures of Kathy, she thought. "Lots of room in the attic for a suitcase—or anything else for that matter," Elizabeth Richards said.

"You're not going to ask me what's in it?"

"If you want me to know, you'll tell me. I suspect it has something to do with Kathy."

"I've taken every single thing that I still had of Kathy's out of the apartment, Mother. Does that shock you?"

"Don, I suspect you needed those reminders until now. I sense now, though, that you're trying to go forward with your personal life—and you know Kathy can't be part of it. Turning forty has a way of making most people take a long, sober look at both the past and the future. By the way, I know you have a key to the house. Why didn't you just go in?"

"I saw your car was gone, and I suddenly realized I didn't want to go into an empty house." He got up and stretched. "I'll have a cup of tea with you, then I'm off. I have a date tonight. That's two in a week with the same person. How about that?"

He called Susan from the vestibule of her building promptly at seven. "I seem to be making a habit of apologizing for not being on time," she told him when she let him into the apartment. "My producer has been yelling at me all week about arriving just as we're ready to go on the air. A couple of times this week I barely got back to the office before a patient arrived—and you know as well as I that you don't keep people in therapy waiting. And tonight—well, I'll be perfectly honest: a couple of hours ago I closed my eyes for a few minutes and just now woke up. I was dead asleep."

"Then you probably needed it," he said.

"I'll give you a glass of wine if you'll give me fifteen minutes to get myself ready," Susan offered.

"It's a deal."

She could see that he was openly studying the apartment. "You have very nice digs, Dr. Chandler," he said. "One of my patients is a real estate broker. She tells me that the minute she walks into a home, she gets vibrations about the people who live there."

"I believe that," Susan said. "Well, I don't know what kind of vibrations this place sends out, but I'm mighty comfortable in it. Now let me get you that glass of wine, and you can look around while I get changed."

Don went into the kitchen with her. "Please don't get dressed up," he said. "As you can see, I didn't. I dropped in on my mother this afternoon, and she told me I looked good in a sweater, so I just put a jacket over it."

There is something strange about Don Richards, Susan thought as she adjusted the collar of a tailored blue blouse and reached for her herringbone jacket. I don't know what it is, but there's something about him that I just don't *get*.

She crossed from her bedroom into the foyer and was about to say, "I'm ready," when she saw Donald

Richards standing at her desk in the den, examining the two passenger lists from the cruise ships.

He had obviously heard her, because he looked up. "Any reason for collecting these, Susan?" he asked quietly.

She did not answer immediately, and he put them down. "Sorry if I overstepped your invitation to look around. This is a beautiful nineteenth-century desk, and I wanted a closer look at it. The passenger lists didn't seem to be confidential material."

"You said you've often been a passenger on the *Gabrielle*, didn't you?" Susan asked. She didn't like the idea of his going through papers on her desk, but decided to let it drop.

"Yes, many times. She's a beautiful ship." He walked over to where she stood. "You look very nice, and I'm very hungry. Let's go."

They ate at an intimate seafood restaurant on Thompson Street. "The father of one of my patients owns it," he explained. "He gives me a discount."

"Even without the discount, you got your money's worth," Susan told him later, as the waiter removed their plates. "That pompano was marvelous."

"So was the salmon." He paused and took a sip of his wine. "Susan, there's something I have to ask you. I stopped by the hospital both yesterday and late this afternoon to see Justin Wells. He tells me you've met with him also."

"That's right."

"That's all you're going to say about it?"

"I think that's all I *should* say, except that I absolutely believe his wife's injury was no accident and that he is innocent of harming her."

"I know hearing that has been a great boost for him at a time when he needs it desperately."

"I'm glad. I like him."

"So do I, but as I told you the other evening I hope he resumes therapy with me—or with anyone, for that matter—once his wife is out of the woods. And, by the way, they told me at the hospital that she's showing signs of improvement. Right now, though, Justin's carrying too much self-imposed guilt about the accident for *anyone* to handle. You know how the guilt scenario goes. He's decided that if he hadn't phoned and upset his wife, she would have kept the appointment with you and taken a cab instead of walking to the post office and therefore ending up under the wheels of that van."

Richards shrugged. "Of course, I'd probably be out of a practice if so many people weren't guilt ridden. It's something I can certainly empathize with. Oh, here's the coffee."

The waiter placed the cups before them.

Susan took a sip, then asked bluntly, "Are *you* guilt ridden, Don?"

"I have been. I think I'm getting over it at last. But you said something the other night that touched me. You said that after your parents' divorce, you felt as though you'd all gotten into different lifeboats. Why is that?"

"Hey, don't analyze *me*," Susan protested.

"I'm asking as a friend."

"Then I'll answer. It's the usual thing that happens

when there's a divorce: divided loyalties. My mother was heartbroken and my father was running around saying he'd never been happier. Kind of made me question all the years when I was obviously under the mistaken impression that we were a very happy family."

"How about your sister? Are you close to her? You don't even have to answer. You should see the look on your face."

Susan heard herself saying, "Seven years ago I was about to get engaged, then Dee came into the picture. Guess who got the guy and became a bride?"

"Your sister."

"That's right. Then Jack was killed in a skiing accident, and now she's in the process of trying to move in on someone I'm dating. Nice, huh?"

"Do you still love Jack?"

"I don't think you ever stop loving someone you cared that deeply about. I also don't think you should try to erase any part of your past, because, in fact, you can't anyhow. The difference, as I preach to my mother, is to let go of the pain and get on with life."

"Have you done that?"

"Yes, I think I have."

"Are you interested in this new guy?"

"It's much too soon to say. And now can we please talk about the weather, or even better, will you tell me why you were so interested in those passenger lists?"

The understanding warmth in Don Richards's eyes disappeared. "If you'll tell me why you checked off some names and circled two: Owen Adams and Henry Owen Young."

"Owen is one of my favorite names," Susan said. "It's getting late, Don. You're leaving early in the morning, and I have a very long day ahead of me."

She thought of the 8 A.M. phone call she was going to make to Chris Ryan, and the package of pictures she should be receiving from London in the afternoon.

"In fact, I could be there as late as nine o'clock."

96

On Monday mornings, Chris Ryan liked to get into the office early. Sundays were for family, and typically at least two of his six children and their families would drift in to visit him and his wife, and would stay for dinner.

Both he and his wife loved the fact that the grand-kids wanted to be around them, but sometimes, when they finally had collapsed into bed, Chris would happily remember that the people he would be investigating tomorrow wouldn't be fighting about whose turn it was on the big bike, or who said the bad word first.

Yesterday had been a particularly strenuous Sunday of togetherness, and as a result, Chris was unlocking his office door at 8:20 A.M. He checked his messages and found several that warranted immediate attention. The first had been left on Saturday by a source in Atlantic City, and it contained interesting information about Douglas Layton. The second, from Susan Chandler, had come in earlier this morning. "Chris, it's Susan; call me right away," was all it said.

She answered on the first ring. "Chris, I'm onto something and I need you to check out two people for me. One was a passenger on a cruise ship, the *Gabrielle*, three years ago; the second was on another cruise ship, the *Seagodiva*, two years ago. The thing is, I don't think they're different people at all. I think they may be one and the same person, and if I am right, we're talking about a serial killer."

Chris fumbled in his breast pocket for his pen and grabbed a sheet of paper. "Give me the names and dates." When he heard them he commented, "Both mid-October. Cruise ships give a discount then?"

"The dates have been in the back of my mind, Chris," Susan told him. "If mid-October is part of a pattern, then some woman could be in terrible danger right now."

"Let me get on it with Quantico. My guys at the FBI can do a fast trace. Oh, Susan, it turns out your pal, Doug Layton, may be in big trouble. He lost big time at the tables in Atlantic City last week."

"You know he's not my pal, and what do you mean by 'big time'?"

"Try four hundred thousand dollars. I hope he's got a rich aunt."

"The trouble is that he thinks he does." The sum of four hundred thousand dollars startled her. A man who can run up gambling losses that great is in *serious* trouble. He could also be desperate and dangerous. "Thanks, Chris," Susan said. "We'll be talking."

She hung up the phone and looked at her watch. She would have enough time to visit briefly with Mrs. Clausen before she went to the studio.

She's got to know about Layton immediately, Susan thought. If he owes that much money to gamblers, he'll need to cover it right away, and the Clausen Family Trust is where he'll go for it.

97

Jane Clausen knew something was seriously wrong when Susan phoned and requested such an early morning visit. She had also heard the tension in Douglas Layton's voice when he called a few minutes later to say he needed to stop by on his way to the airport. He said that another requisition concerning the orphanage required her signature.

"You'll have to wait at least till nine o'clock," she told him firmly.

"Mrs. Clausen, I'm afraid that might make me late for my plane."

"And I'm afraid you should have thought of that sooner, Douglas. Susan Chandler is coming to see me in a few minutes." She paused, then added in a cool tone, "Yesterday, Susan was by to take some Polaroids of the sketch of the orphanage. She wouldn't tell me why she needed them, but I have a feeling that's what she wants to discuss with me now. I hope there's no problem about the building, Douglas."

"Of course not, Mrs. Clausen. Perhaps I can do without that signature for the present."

"Well, I'll be able to see you at nine, Douglas, and I'll be expecting you."

"Yes, yes, thank you, Mrs. Clausen."

When Susan arrived, Jane Clausen said, "You don't have to worry about my reaction to anything you might tell me, Susan. I've come to believe that Douglas Layton is cheating or is trying to cheat me. But I would be interested in seeing the proof."

As Susan opened the book about the Wright Family Foundation, Jane Clausen made a call to Hubert March, who was still at home. "Hubert, get down to the office, call in your auditors and make sure that Douglas Layton can't get his hands on any of our bank accounts or liquidate any of our assets. And do it *now!*"

She put down the phone and studied the picture of the orphanage in the book on her lap. "Everything is the same except the name on the sign," she commented.

"I'm sorry," Susan said quietly.

"Don't be. Even when Douglas was being so solicitous, that uneasy feeling about him just wouldn't go away."

She closed the book and looked at the jacket; then she chuckled. "Gerie must be spinning in her grave," she said. "She wanted the foundation named after *her* and Alexander. Her real name was Virginia Marie, hence 'Gerie,' as she was called by everyone. The stupid woman forgot that Alexander's first wife was also Virginia. And I see young Alex had them put his mother's image on all the Wright Foundation literature."

"Good for him!" Susan said. They laughed together.

98

Douglas Layton now knew what it felt like to be a trapped animal. He had called Jane Clausen from a phone in a hotel near the hospital, anticipating that he could go right to her room and get the necessary signature.

You fool, he told himself. You've tipped her off. She may be dying, but she's still smart. Now she'll get Hubert on the phone and tell him to contact the banks. If that happens, you're done for—the people you're dealing with won't listen to excuses.

He absolutely had to have the money. He shivered at the thought of what would happen to him if he didn't honor his debt to the casino. If only he hadn't felt lucky the other night. He had intended to put the money he had gotten on Jane Clausen's signature into a separate account for his trip. But then he went to the casino because he really had felt lucky. And for a while, things had gone his way. He had been up nearly eight hundred thousand dollars at one point, but then he lost all that and several hundred thousand dollars more.

They told him he had until tomorrow to come up with the money, but he knew that if he waited until tomorrow, it might all be over. By then, Susan Chandler would no doubt know more about him. Then she would definitely go to Mrs. Clausen. They might even call the police. Susan Chandler was the problem. She was the one who had started everything.

He stood at the phone, trying to decide what to do

next. His palms were clammy. He saw the woman at the next phone staring at him, curiosity in her eyes.

There was one thing he could try that might work. But "might" wasn't good enough. It *had* to work. What was Hubert March's home phone number?

He caught Hubert just as he was leaving for the office. Hubert's salutatory question, "Douglas, what is this all about?" confirmed his suspicion that Mrs. Clausen had phoned him.

"I'm with Mrs. Clausen," Doug said. "I'm afraid she's in and out of reality. She thinks she may have just phoned you and apologizes for anything she said."

Hubert March's relieved laugh was balm to Douglas Layton's soul. "No apologies necessary to me, but I hope she apologized to you, my boy."

99

Jim Curley drove Alex Wright to Kennedy Airport and placed his bags on the curbside check-in line. "Awfully busy at this hour, Mr. Alex," he said as he glanced nervously at the policewoman hovering about, threatening to ticket cars left too long at curbside. "What do you expect at nine o'clock on Monday morning, Jim?" Alex Wright asked. "Get back in the car and take off before I'm stuck with paying a fine. And do you remember what I told you?"

"Of course, Mr. Alex. I phone Dr. Chandler and tell her that I'm at her disposal."

"Right," Alex said encouragingly. "And . . . ?"

"And she'll probably give me—what did you call it, sir?—the 'appropriate disclaimers' about how she doesn't need a car, that sort of thing. That's my cue to say, 'Mr. Alex begs you to allow me to serve you, but with one proviso: Dr. Chandler may not bring a date in his car.'"

Alex Wright laughed and clapped his chauffeur on the shoulder. "I know I can count on you, Jim. Now get out of here. That cop has a book to fill, and she's heading for my car."

100

For a change, Susan finished her radio program and got back to the office knowing that she had a full hour and a half until her first appointment, at two o'clock. The extra time was a luxury she wasn't used to.

She spent it studying the file she had compiled as a result of the events of the past week. It included Regina Clausen's memorabilia from her cruise on the *Gabrielle*, Carolyn Wells's similar memorabilia from the *Seagodiva*, and the photographs of Tiffany's turquoise ring that Pete Sanchez had sent her.

Study as she might, however, they revealed nothing new to her. Finally she listened to segments of three of last week's programs: the one with Carolyn Wells calling on Monday, and the ones with calls from Tiffany Smith on Tuesday and Wednesday. She listened carefully to Carolyn, so upset and fearful of becoming involved; Tiffany, so apologetic on Wednesday because when she called in on Tuesday she had belittled the gift of the turquoise ring.

Susan's careful attention to the tapes proved fruitless too, however—they revealed nothing new.

She had asked Janet to hold off ordering lunch until after one o'clock. At one-thirty, Janet came in with the usual lunch bag. She was humming "You Belong to Me."

"Dr. Chandler," she said as she placed the lunch bag on Susan's desk, "that song has been going through my head all weekend. I just can't shake it. It was also driving me crazy, because I couldn't remember all the lyrics, so I phoned my mother and she sang them to me. It really is a pretty song."

"Yes, it is," Susan agreed absentmindedly as she opened the paper bag and took out the soup of the day. It was split pea, which she detested, and which Janet knew she detested.

She's getting married next month and moving to Michigan, Susan reminded herself. Don't say anything. This too will pass.

"'*See the pyramids along the Nile . . . /Watch the sunrise on a tropic isle . . .*'"

Unasked, Janet was singing the lyrics of "You Belong to Me."

"'*See the marketplace in old Algiers . . .*'"

Susan suddenly forgot her annoyance about the soup. "Stop for a minute, Janet," she said.

Janet looked embarrassed. "I'm sorry if my singing is bothering you, Doctor."

"No, no, you're not bothering me at all," Susan

said. "It's just that while listening to you, something occurred to me about that song."

Susan thought of the news bulletin from the *Gabrielle* that had referred to Bali as a tropic isle, and the postcard of a restaurant in Bali, with a circle drawn around a table on the dining verandah.

With a sinking feeling in the pit of her stomach, Susan could sense that the pieces of the puzzle were falling into place. Yes, the pieces were there, but she still hadn't figured out who had been manipulating them.

"Win"—or Owen—wanted to show Carolyn Wells around Algiers, she thought. *"See the marketplace in old Algiers."*

"Janet, could you sing the rest of the lyrics, please? Now," Susan requested.

"If you want, Doctor. I'm not much of a singer. Let's see. Oh, I have them. *'Fly the ocean in a silver plane . . .'"*

Three years ago, Regina disappeared after being in Bali, Susan thought. Two years ago, it could have been Carolyn—and there may have been someone else chosen in her stead—in Algiers. Last year he may have met a woman on a plane rather than a cruise ship. What would have been before that? she asked herself. Let's go back: Did he meet a woman four years ago in Egypt? That would fit the pattern, she decided.

"'See the jungle when it's wet with rain . . .'" Janet was singing.

That could be the lyric for this year's victim, Susan thought. Somebody new. Somebody who has no idea she's being staked out for death.

"'Just remember 'til you're home again . . .'" Janet obvi-

ously liked to sing the song. She softened her voice, giving it a plaintive touch as she concluded, "'. . .*You belong to me.*'"

Susan called Chris Ryan as soon as Janet left her office. "Chris, will you see if you can track something else down? I need to know if there are any reports of a woman—probably a tourist—who vanished in Egypt in mid-October, four years ago."

"That shouldn't be too hard," Ryan assured her. "I was just about to call you anyhow. You remember those names you gave me this morning? Of those passengers on the two cruise ships?"

"What about them?" Susan asked.

"Those guys don't exist. The passports they used were fakes."

I *knew* it! Susan thought. I *knew* it!

A t ten of five that afternoon, Susan took an urgent phone call from Chris Ryan. Susan broke one of her own cardinal rules and left her patient alone while she took the call. "You're pushing the right buttons, Susan," Ryan said. "Four years ago a thirty-nine-year-old widow from Birmingham, Alabama, disappeared while in Egypt. She was on a cruise to the Middle East. She apparently had skipped the regular land tour and gone off by herself. Her body was never found, and it was assumed that, given Egypt's ongoing political unrest, she had met with foul play from one of the various terrorist groups trying to overthrow the government."

"I'm fairly certain that had nothing to do with why she died, Chris," Susan said.

A few minutes later, as she was walking her patient to the door, a bulky package was delivered. The sender was Ocean Cruise Pictures Ltd. of London.

"I'll open it, Doctor," Janet volunteered.

"Not necessary," Susan told her. "Just leave it. I'll get to it later."

Her day was filled with late appointments, and she wouldn't be finished with her last patient until seven. Then she finally would be able to go through the photographs that might just reveal the face of the man who had killed Regina Clausen and so many others.

Her fingers itched to go through the photographs right away. The identity of this killer *had* to be discovered before someone else died.

Another reason to find him immediately was especially significant to Susan: She wanted to be able to tell the dying Jane Clausen that the man who had deprived her of her daughter would never again break another parent's heart.

101

Donald Richards had arrived on schedule at West Palm Beach Airport at nine Monday morning. He was met there by an escort from his publisher, and was driven to Liberty's, in Boca Raton, where he was scheduled to autograph his book at ten-thirty. When he arrived, he was pleasantly surprised to find people lined up and waiting for him.

"We've had forty phone orders as well," the clerk assured him. "I hope you're writing a sequel to *Vanishing Women.*"

More Vanishing Women? I don't think so, Richards said to himself as he settled at the table set up for him, picked up his pen, and began to sign. He knew what lay ahead that day, and he knew as well what he had to do; a wild restlessness was making him desperate to bolt from the seat.

One hour and eighty signed books later, he was on his way to Miami, where he was scheduled for another autographing at two o'clock.

"I'm sorry, but signatures only, no personal messages," he told the bookshop proprietor. "Something has come up, and I have to leave here promptly at three."

A few minutes after three he was back in the car.

"Next stop, the Fontainebleau," the driver said cheerfully.

"Wrong. Next stop, the airport," Don told him. There was a plane leaving for New York at four. He intended to be on it.

102

Dee had arrived in Costa Rica on Monday morning and had gone directly from the airport to the harbor, where her cruise ship, the *Valerie*, had just docked.

Monday afternoon she halfheartedly joined the

sightseeing tour she had signed up for. When she had impulsively decided to take this cruise, it had seemed a great idea. "The big escape," her father had called it. Now she wasn't so sure. Besides, now that she was here, she couldn't decide what she had been escaping from.

She returned to the *Valerie*, bedraggled from a cloudburst in the rain forest and regretting that she hadn't canceled the trip. Yes, her stateroom on the sun deck was beautiful and even had its own private verandah, and it was clear already that her fellow passengers were congenial enough. Still she felt restless, even anxious—she sensed that this just wasn't the time to be away from New York.

The next stop on the cruise was scheduled for tomorrow, at Panama's San Blas Islands. The ship would dock at noon. Maybe it would be possible to catch a plane there and fly back to New York, she decided. She could always say that she wasn't feeling well.

By the time she had reached the sun deck, Dee had definitely decided to try to head back home tomorrow. There was a lot to be taken care of in New York.

As she left the elevator and headed for her stateroom, the room stewardess stopped her. "The most beautiful bouquet just arrived for you," she said. "I put it on your dresser."

Forgetting that she felt wet and clammy, Dee rushed to her room. There she found a vase holding two dozen pale gold roses. She quickly read the card. It was signed, "Guess Who."

Dee cupped the card in her hand. She didn't have to guess. She *knew* who had sent them.

At the dinner Saturday night, when she had changed places with Susan, Alex Wright had said to her, "I'm glad Susan suggested you sit next to me. I can't abide seeing a beautiful woman be lonely. I guess I'm more like my father than I realized. My step-mother was beautiful like you, and also a lonely widow when my father met her on a cruise ship. He solved her loneliness by marrying her."

Dee remembered that she had joked that it seemed a little radical to marry someone just to cure her lone-liness, and Alex had taken her hand and said, "Perhaps, but not as radical as some solutions."

It's Jack all over again, she thought as she inhaled the scent of the roses. I didn't want to hurt Susan then, and I certainly don't want to hurt her now. But I don't think she's really that interested in Alex yet. She hardly *knows* him. I'm sure she'll understand.

Dee showered, washed her hair, and dressed for dinner, imagining what fun it would be if instead of his going to Russia, Alex were a passenger on the ship with her.

103

"Thank you, Dr. Chandler. I'll see you next week."

At ten of seven, Susan escorted Anne Ketler, her last patient of the day, to the door. As she passed Janet's desk, Susan saw that the package of pho-tographs had been opened, and the photographs were stacked on the desk. *Thou hast ears, but hear not*, she thought.

She opened the office's outer door for Mrs. Ketler, and from its easy click realized that it had been left unlocked. Janet's a really nice person, she thought, and in many ways a good secretary, but she's careless. And irritating. It's a good thing she's leaving next month; I would hate to have to fire her.

"It's very dark out there," Mrs. Ketler said as she stepped into the hallway.

Susan looked over the woman's shoulder. Only a couple of lights illuminated the hallway, which was filled with shadows. "You're absolutely right," she told Mrs. Ketler. "Here, take my arm. I'll walk with you to the elevator." Though not frail, Mrs. Ketler, a woman in her seventies, was prone to skittishness. She had come to Susan a year ago, looking to overcome the depression that had settled over her after she sold her home and moved into an assisted-living facility.

Susan waited until the elevator came, and she pushed the lobby button for Anna Ketler before hurrying back down the corridor. She paused for a minute at Nedda's office and tried the door. It was locked.

Things are improving here, at least, she thought. She had decided against the idea of asking Nedda for the use of her conference room tonight. With only four hundred or so pictures to go through, she wouldn't really need it.

It would be a different matter tomorrow evening, when she had the thousands of pictures from the *Gabrielle* to sort through. Nedda's long, wide table would be the perfect place to spread them out and group them. I'll have Chris Ryan help me, she decided. He has a good, quick eye.

Maybe this "Owen" person will be in the background of more than one picture, Susan thought. That would make the job much easier.

Entering the reception area, she picked up the stacks of photographs from Janet's desk, not noticing the note that Janet had left under the phone for her. She crossed to her office, aware of both the silence in the building and the accelerated heartbeat she felt at the thought of finally seeing a picture of the man responsible for this series of murders. What am I so nervous about? she wondered as she passed the supply closet. The door was open a fraction, but with her arms full she didn't pause to close it.

As she set the photos on her desk, she accidentally hit the beautiful Waterford vase Alex Wright had given her, sending it crashing to the floor. What a shame, she thought, as she swept up the shards of glass and loaded them into the wastebasket.

It's the effect of everything that's been going on, she decided as she put Anna Ketler's file in the bottom drawer of her desk. This past week has been a nightmare. She locked the drawer and put the key in the pocket of her jacket. I'll put it on the key ring later, she decided: Right now I just want to get at those pictures.

What will he look like? she wondered, aware that there was very little likelihood she would recognize him. I just pray the photo is clear enough to give the police something to go on, she thought.

An hour later she was still going through the photographs, still searching for the one with Carolyn Wells. It *has* to be here, Susan thought. They said they were going to send every print they had of a woman posing with the captain.

She had the crumpled piece of a picture that Carolyn had thrown in her wastebasket, and she kept referring to it, searching for its match in the stacks of photographs she had spread out before her. But no matter how many times she went through them, she couldn't find it. That photograph simply wasn't there.

"Where in God's name is it?" she asked out loud, exasperation and disappointment threatening to overwhelm her. "Why, of all of them, is *that one* missing?"

"Because *I* have it, Susan," a familiar voice said in response.

Susan spun around in time to receive the blow of a paperweight smashing against the side of her head.

104

Just as he had planned, he would follow the same procedure with Susan Chandler that he had used for all the others. He would bind her arms and hands to her sides; bind her legs together; truss her so that as she woke up and realized what was happening, she would be able to squirm a little—just enough to give her hope, but not enough to save her.

While he twisted the rope around her limp body, he would explain to her why it was happening. He had explained it to the others, and while Susan's death was not a part of his original plan, but more a matter of expedience, she nonetheless deserved to know that she too had become a part of the ritual he had undertaken to expiate the sins of his stepmother.

Had he wanted, he could have killed her with the paperweight, but he hadn't hit her that hard. The blow had only stunned her, and already she was beginning to stir. Surely she was alert enough now to absorb what he had to tell her.

"You must understand, Susan," he began, in a reasoning tone of voice, "I never would have harmed you if only you hadn't butted in. In fact, I quite *like* you. I do sincerely. You're an interesting woman, and very smart too. But then that's been your undoing, hasn't it? Perhaps you're too smart for your own good."

He began to wind the rope around her arms, lifting her body gently. She was lying on the floor beside her desk; he had found a pillow and placed it under her head. He had dimmed the overhead lights. He liked soft light, and whenever possible used candlelight. Of course, that would be impossible here.

"Why did you have to talk about Regina Clausen on your radio program, Susan? You should have left it alone. She's been dead three years. Her body's at the bottom of Kowloon Bay, you know. Have you ever seen Kowloon Bay? She liked it there. It's very picturesque. All those hundreds of small houseboats filled with families, all living there, never knowing that a lonely lady lies beneath them."

He crossed and crisscrossed the rope over her upper body. "Hong Kong is Regina's final resting place, but it was in Bali that she fell in love with me. For such a smart woman, it was remarkably easy to convince her to leave the ship. But that's what happens when you're lonely. You want to fall in love, so you're anxious to believe someone who pays attention to you."

He began to tie Susan's legs. Lovely legs, he thought. Even though she was wearing a trouser suit, he could feel their shapeliness as he lifted them and wrapped the cord around them. "My father was easily duped as well, Susan. Isn't that funny? He and my mother were a grim, humorless pair, but he missed her when she died. My father was wealthy, but my mother had a lot of money of her own. In her will she left it all to him, but she thought he'd eventually pass it on to me. She wasn't a warm, or tender, or generous person, but in her own way she did care about me. She told me that I was to be like my father—make a lot of money, be diligent, develop a good head for business."

He yanked the cord more tightly than he had intended as he recalled the endless lectures. "This is what my mother would tell me, Susan. She would say, 'Alex, someday you will be a man with a great fortune. You must learn to preserve it. You will have children someday. Teach them properly. You must not spoil them.'"

He was on his knees beside Susan now, leaning over her. Despite the anger apparent in his words, his voice remained calm and steady, his tone conversational. "I had less spending money than anyone else at school, and because of it I never could go out with the crowd. As a result, I became a loner; I learned to amuse myself. The theater was part of it. I took any role I could get in school productions. There was even a fully equipped miniature theater on the third floor of our house, the one big present I ever received, although it wasn't from my parents but from a friend of the family who had made a fortune because my father gave him a stock tip. He told me I could have anything I wanted, and that's what I chose. I used to act out whole plays all by myself. I'd play all the parts. I became very good at it, maybe even good enough to be a professional. I learned how to become anyone I wanted to, and I taught myself to look and sound like the characters I made up."

Susan was aware of a familiar voice just above her, but her head was splitting with pain, and she didn't dare open her eyes. What is happening to me? she wondered. Alex Wright *was* here, but who hit me? She had gotten just a glimpse of him before she blacked out. He had untidy, longish hair and was wearing a cap and a shabby sweat suit.

Wait, she thought, making herself focus. The voice is Alex's; that means he's still here. So why wasn't Alex helping her instead of just talking to her, she wondered, as some of the disorienting effect of the blow to her head began to abate.

Then what she had been hearing sank in, and she opened her eyes. His face was only inches away from hers. His eyes were glittering, shining with the kind of madness she had seen in the eyes of patients in locked wards. He's mad! she thought. She could see now—it was Alex in that straggly wig! Alex in those shabby clothes! Alex, whose eyes were like sharp chips of turquoise slicing deeply into her.

"I have your shroud, Susan," he whispered. "Even though you were not one of the lonely ladies, I wanted you to have it. It's exactly the same as the ones the others wore."

He stood, and she could see that he was holding up a long plastic bag, much like the kind used to protect expensive gowns. Oh God! she thought. He's going to suffocate me!

"I do this slowly, Susan," he said. "It's my favorite part. I want to watch your face. I want you to anticipate that moment when the air is cut off and the final struggle begins. So I'll do it slowly, and I won't wrap it too tightly. That way it will take longer for you to die, a few minutes, at least."

He knelt in front of her and lifted her feet, sliding the plastic bag underneath her so that her feet and legs were inside. She tried to kick it away, but he leaned across her, staring into her eyes as he pulled it over her hips and then her waist. Her struggles had no effect, not even slowing him as he continued to slide the plastic bag up her body. Finally, when he reached her neck, he paused.

"You see, soon after my mother died, my father took a cruise," he explained. "On it, he met Virginia Marie Owen, a lonely widow, or so she claimed. She was very girlish, not at all like my mother. She called herself 'Gerie.' She was thirty-five years my father's junior and attractive. He told me she liked to sing in his ear while they danced. Her favorite song was 'You Belong to Me.' You know how they spent their honeymoon? They followed the lyrics of that song, starting out in Egypt."

Susan watched Alex's face. He was clearly engrossed in his story now. But all the while his hands kept playing with the plastic, and Susan knew that at any moment he was going to pull it over her head. She thought of screaming, but who would hear? Her chance of escape was nil, and she was alone with him in what seemed an otherwise empty building. Even Nedda had gone home uncharacteristically early this evening.

"My father was smart enough to have Gerie sign a prenuptial agreement, but she hated me so much that she dedicated herself to persuading him to establish the foundation rather than leave his money to me. It would then be my role in life to administer it. She pointed out to my father that I would have a generous salary while I gave away his money. *My money*. She told him that in that way their names would be immortalized. He resisted for a while but eventually gave in. The final piece of persuasion had come as the result of my own carelessness—Gerie found and gave to my father a rather infantile list I had made of 'things' that I wanted to buy as soon as I had control over the money. I hated her for that and swore to myself I would get even. But then she died, right after my father, and I never had the chance. Can you imagine how frustrating that was? To hate her with such a passion, and then for her to deprive me of the satisfaction of killing her?"

Susan studied his face as he knelt above her, a distant look in his eyes. He's *definitely* mad, she thought. He's mad, and he's going to kill me. Just the way he killed all the others!

105

By eight o'clock that night, Doug Layton was at a blackjack table in one of Atlantic City's slightly less fashionable casinos. Through some rapid manipulation of funds, he had been able to come up with the money he needed to cover the debts he had racked up during his last visit, but still his favorite casino had turned him away. To many of the people who knew him in Atlantic City, Layton was getting the reputation of a deadbeat.

The guys he paid back, however, celebrated by taking him out to lunch. In a way, Doug had felt a little relieved with how things were working out. Sooner or later the auditors would have caught up with him for stealing from the Clausen Family Trust, and there was still a good chance that Jane Clausen would get to Hubert March again; she might even convince him to call the police. Forewarned, he planned now to get out with the half-million-dollar stake he had gotten hold of today, before it was too late. He already had made a reservation for a flight to St. Thomas. From there he would manage to get to one of the islands where there was no extradition policy with the U.S. It was what his father had done—and he never had been caught.

Half a million would buy a good start on a new life. Layton knew that, and was determined to leave the country with that amount.

"You can't leave this place without trying your luck at least one more time," one of his new friends told him.

Doug Layton considered the challenge; he acknowledged that he felt lucky. "Well, maybe a hand of blackjack," he said in agreement.

It was only nine o'clock when he left the casino. Barely aware of his surroundings, he walked onto the beach. There was no way to get the money he needed now, the money he owed to the guys who had staked him again today, when his luck turned sour for the last time. It was all over for him. He knew what would follow: conviction for embezzlement. Prison. Or worse.

He took off his suit jacket and laid his watch and his wallet on it. It was something he'd read about, and it seemed to make sense.

He could hear the surf pounding. A stiff, cold wind blew off the ocean, and the surf was high. He shivered in his shirtsleeves. He wondered how long it would take to drown—and decided it was better not to know, that it was just one of those things that you wouldn't know about until you did it, like so much else in his life. He stepped into the water gingerly, then took another, bigger step.

It's all Susan Chandler's fault, he thought, as the icy water lapped at his ankles. If only she had stayed out of it, no one would have known, and I'd have had years more at the trust . . . He held his breath against the cold and plunged on until his feet were no longer touching bottom. A big wave caught him, then another, then he was choking, lost in a world of cold and darkness, pummeled by the waves. He tried not to struggle.

Silently he cursed Susan Chandler. *I hope she dies.* It was Douglas Layton's last conscious thought.

106

Don Richards caught the plane to La Guardia with only minutes to spare. It was not a direct flight. He cursed the layover in Atlanta, but it couldn't be helped. As soon as they had cleared the airport and he was able to use the telephone, he called Susan Chandler's office.

"I'm sorry, Dr. Richards, but she's with a patient and can't be interrupted," her secretary informed him. "I'd be happy to take a message and leave it for her. I do know, though, that she has another patient right after this one, so she may not—"

"How long will Dr. Chandler be there?" Don asked impatiently.

"Sir, she has patients until seven o'clock; she mentioned earlier that after that she's planning to do some paperwork."

"Then please take down this message, exactly as I give it: 'Don Richards needs to see you about Owen. His plane gets in about eight o'clock. He'll pick you up at your office. Wait for him.'"

"I'll leave it right on my desk where she'll see it, sir," the secretary said, her tone a little icy.

And so Susan would have, if it weren't hidden under the telephone.

The flight attendant was offering a drink and snacks. "Just coffee, please," Don Richards said. He knew he needed a clear head. Later, Susan and I will have a drink and dinner, Don thought. I'll tell her what I think she's already guessed—that the person poor Carolyn is trying to talk about is named Owen, not Win. Ever since he had seen the name Owen circled on both passenger lists on the desk in Susan's apartment, he had been turning this over in his mind, and he thought that was the most likely explanation.

He would also tell Susan—and that was the reason he was desperate to get back to New York—that whoever "Owen" really was, he was very likely the killer. And if Don was right, Susan was in grave jeopardy.

I was on Susan's program both when Carolyn and Tiffany phoned in, Don thought, as he stared into the darkening sky. Carolyn was almost killed by that van. Tiffany was stabbed to death. The killer won't stop there to protect his secret, whatever it is.

I told Susan, when I was on her program, that my goal was to help women help themselves, to be aware of and sensitive to danger signs. I've spent four years angry with myself, thinking I could have saved Kathy. Now I realize I was wrong. Hindsight is a wonderful thing, but if we were to relive those same last few minutes together, I still wouldn't tell her to stay home.

The clouds were drifting past the plane like waves lapping at the side of a ship. Don thought of the two cruises he'd tried to take in the past two years—brief ones to the Caribbean. In both cases, he got off at the first port. He kept seeing Kathy's face in the water. He knew it wouldn't happen anymore.

Anxiety was gnawing at him. Susan can't go this route alone any longer, Don vowed to himself. It was too dangerous. Much more dangerous than she knew.

The plane landed at quarter of eight. "Bear with us, and relax," the captain announced. "They're having a busy evening, and all the gates are presently occupied."

It was eight-ten before Don got off the plane. He rushed to a phone and called Susan's office. There was no answer, and he hung up without leaving a message.

Maybe she finished early and went home, he thought. But he got no response at her apartment either, just the answering machine.

Maybe I should try again at the office, he thought. She may have just stepped out. But again he got no answer; this time, however, he decided to leave her a message. "Susan," he said. "I'm going to stop by your office. I hope you got the message I left earlier with your secretary, and you're still around. With luck I'll be there in half an hour."

107

"Susan, surely you can understand why I'm so angry. Gerie saw my having to run the family trust as a form of poetic justice. Every day I had to sign checks giving away money that belonged to *me*. Can you imagine? When the foundation was established sixteen years ago, it was worth one hundred million dollars. Now it's worth a billion, and I can take the credit for most of its growth. But no matter how much money there is in the coffers, I still get only my paltry salary."

I've got to keep him talking, Susan told herself. What time do the people in the cleaning staff come in? she wondered, then remembered with a sinking feeling that they had been emptying wastebaskets when Mrs. Ketler arrived at six. That meant they were long gone.

His fingers were caressing her throat now. "I really think I could have been happy with you, Susan," he went on. "If I had married you, I might have tried to put the past behind me. But, of course, that wouldn't have worked, would it? The other night you sent Dee to take your place next to me at the table. You did it because you didn't want to be with me, didn't you? You know that, don't you? That was the reason."

I know I wasn't comfortable Saturday night, Susan thought. But was *that* the reason? I thought it was because of what Nat Small told me earlier in the day about Abdul Parki's death.

Nat Small. He was a witness. Would Alex get to him too?

"Alex," she said, her voice coaxing. "It's not going to do any good to kill me. There are hundreds more pictures being delivered to my office tomorrow. You're not going to be able to destroy them. The police will study them one by one. They'll study the people in the background."

"Feathers in the wind," Alex murmured, his tone dismissive.

I may be getting to him, Susan thought. "Someone will recognize you, Alex. You don't go to big parties, yet that first night, when I agreed to have dinner with you, you said you met Regina at a Futures Industry dinner. That's a big one, Alex. Something started troubling me about you that night."

"Feathers in the wind," he said again. "But, Susan, you're the one who scattered mine. I know I can't go on much longer, but I *will* finish my mission before

I'm stopped. Remember the song? *'See the jungle when it's wet with rain.'* You know who was in the jungle today? Dee. She was on a tour in the rain forest in Costa Rica. That's close enough. Tomorrow people will be grieving for you when your body is discovered. But that won't happen until nine o'clock or so. By then, Dee and I will be having breakfast in Panama. Her ship docks at eight, and I will surprise her by joining her there. I have a turquoise ring for her. She'll read a great deal into it." He paused. "Actually, Susan, now that I think about it, you've been a great help to me. You've provided me with my last lonely lady. Dee will be perfect."

Slowly, very slowly, he was closing the bag. It was covering her chin. "Alex, you need help, a lot of help," Susan pleaded, trying to keep the desperation from showing in her voice. "Your luck is running out. You can save yourself if you stop now."

"But I don't *want* to stop, Susan," he said matter-of-factly. The ringing of the telephone made him jump to his feet. They both listened intently as Don Richards left a message, saying he was on his way to her office.

Please God, let him get here soon, Susan thought.

"It's time," Alex Wright said calmly. And with a sudden movement of his hand, he pulled the bag the rest of the way over her head and quickly sealed it. Then he pushed her under the desk.

He stood up and looked down at his handiwork. "You'll die long before Richards gets here," he said with the casual assurance of someone who had done this before. "It will take about ten minutes." He paused to let his words sink in. "That's how long Regina lasted."

108

"Look, mister, I didn't invent traffic jams," the cabby told Don Richards. "The Midtown Tunnel is tied up. What else is new?"

"You've been on the phone with the dispatcher. Shouldn't he be able to warn you about tie-ups? Couldn't you have avoided this?"

"Mister, some guy has a fender-bender. Thirty seconds later you got a tie-up and a traffic jam."

Arguing with him is not doing any good, Don cautioned himself, nor will it get me there any faster. But it is *so* frustrating being stuck like this with horns blaring all around me.

Susan, he thought, your secretary must have left that message for you. When you heard that I was calling about Owen, you would have waited for me. So why aren't you answering? "Please, Susan," he half-whispered. "Be there, and be safe."

109

The little air that had been trapped in the bag was almost gone. Susan felt herself getting lightheaded. Take short, shallow breaths, she told herself. Don't use up the oxygen.

Air. Air, her lungs screamed.

The memory suddenly flashed through her head of one of the first cases she worked on as an assistant district attorney. It had involved a woman found with a plastic bag over her head. I was the one who said her death couldn't be suicide, and I was right. The woman had loved her children too much to leave them willingly.

I can't breathe. I can't breathe. The pain was starting to gather in her chest.

Don't pass out, she warned herself fiercely.

The murdered woman with the plastic bag over her head had been rosy faced when she was found. Carbon monoxide does that when it kills you, the medical examiner had explained.

I can't breathe. I want to go to sleep. She could feel her mind relaxing, as though ready to give up the fight.

Dee. Alex was going to meet her tomorrow. She was going to be his final victim.

I'm going to sleep, Susan thought. I can't stop myself from going to sleep.

I don't want to die. And I don't want Dee to die. Her mind struggled to continue, struggled to survive with no air.

She was wedged under the desk. With a sudden thrust, she kicked her feet against the front panel and managed to push her body out a few inches. She felt the wastebasket against her right side.

The wastebasket! The glass from the broken vase was in it!

Gasping now, Susan heaved her body to the side, felt the basket topple over, heard the broken glass scatter on the floor. As she twisted her head toward the sound, she felt the basket move away, felt blackness overwhelming her.

With one last effort, she moved her head from side to side. A sudden, terrible pain hit her as the jagged glass, caught between the floor and her body, cut through the heavy plastic under her. Blood soaked her shoulder, but she could feel the plastic start to separate. She continued to gasp as she moved her body back and forth, back and forth, feeling the blood gush from her wounds, but feeling also the first faint hint of air.

It was there, on the floor of her office, that Don Richards found her half an hour later. She was barely conscious; her temple was bruised, her hair matted with blood; her back was bleeding profusely; her arms and legs were bruised and swollen from her struggles with the cord that bound her. Jagged glass lay all around her.

But she was alive! Alive!

110

Alex Wright was waiting at the dock when the *Valerie* sailed into San Blas on Tuesday morning. It was eight o'clock. He had left New York last night, going directly to the airport from Susan Chandler's office. He wondered if Don Richards, who had phoned her, asking that she wait for him, had finally given up. Alex had turned off all the lights when he left, so Richards must have assumed she simply *hadn't* waited for him. In all likelihood, her secretary would find her body in another hour or so.

A good number of the passengers on the *Valerie* were standing on the deck. There was something magical about being aboard a ship as it steamed into harbor, he thought. Although perhaps it was symbolic, because each new harbor signified an end of the journey for someone.

This would be Dee's final journey. She was his last lonely lady. And then he'd be on his way to Russia. That's where he'd be when he was notified of the tragic death of the two sisters who had been his guests on Saturday evening. Susan had said that he might be spotted in some of the pictures from Regina's cruise. Maybe, he thought. But he had looked very different on that cruise. Could anyone positively identify him? I don't think so, he decided confidently.

He spotted Dee standing on deck. She was smiling and waving at him. Or was she *pointing* to him?

He was suddenly aware that men had moved up to stand on either side of him. Then he heard a low, deep voice say, "You're under arrest, Mr. Wright. Please come with us quietly."

Alex Wright stifled his surprise and shrugged. Then he turned to go. He realized, with a touch of bitter irony that this was the end of the journey for him.

Don Richards waited in the hospital lobby while Susan visited Jane Clausen. This morning she was lying in bed, a single pillow beneath her head. Her hands were folded on the coverlet. The shades were drawn.

Despite the room's darkness, she was quick to notice the bruise on Susan's temple. "What happened, Susan?" she asked.

"Oh, nothing. A bad bump, that's all." Susan felt tears come to her eyes as she bent to kiss Jane Clausen's cheek.

"How very dear you've become to me," Jane Clausen said. "Susan, I don't think I'll be here tomorrow, but at least yesterday I managed to take care of the trust. Some good, reliable people will watch over it for me. You've heard about Douglas?"

"Yes. I didn't know if you knew."

"I'm so sorry for him. He could have amounted to so much. And I worry for his mother; he's an only son."

"Mrs. Clausen, there's no easy way to tell you this, but I think it's something you will want to know. The man who killed Regina, and at least five other people, has been arrested. There's overwhelming proof of his guilt. And your coming forward to talk to me when you did played a vital role in solving the crimes."

She saw the long shudder that went through the dying woman's body. "I'm glad. Did he talk about Regina? I mean, I wonder if she was very frightened."

Regina must have been terrified, Susan thought. I know I was. "I hope not," she said.

Jane Clausen looked up at her. "Susan, all that matters now is that I'll be with her soon. Good-bye, my dear, and thank you for all your kindness."

As Susan rode down in the elevator, she thought back on the events of the preceding week. Could it really have been so short a time? she wondered. Was it really only nine days ago that I first met Jane Clausen? Yes, the mystery of Regina Clausen's disappearance had been solved, but in the process three other people had died, and a fourth was seriously injured.

She thought of Carolyn Wells and her husband Justin. She had talked to him this morning—Carolyn was out of her coma, and the doctors now were predicting a full, though protracted, recovery. Susan had started to apologize to him; after all, had it not been for her raising the whole subject of Regina Clausen's disappearance, none of these terrible things would have happened to either Carolyn or himself. Justin had insisted, however, that despite the agony of the past week, all things had happened for a reason. He was planning to go back in therapy with Dr. Richards, and hopeful that once his extreme jealousy was in check, the kind of fear that had driven Carolyn to be so secretive would no longer be a part of their lives. "Besides," Justin had said with a chuckle, "I wouldn't have missed the great pleasure of watching Captain Shea stumble through an embarrassed apology. He really thought I was a killer."

At least he and Carolyn will be okay, Susan thought. But not poor Tiffany Smith, nor the other two people whose deaths are tied to the case—Hilda Johnson and Abdul Parki. She made a mental note to visit Nat Small's shop on MacDougal Street later in the week to let him know that his friend's killer had been caught.

It had all started so innocently. Susan had intended only to raise the issue of how lonely, unsuspecting women, despite their intelligence and apparent sophistication, can be lured into dubious and sometimes fatal relationships by men who prey on them. It was a great topic and had produced a few lively shows. And three murders, she thought. Then she asked herself: Will I be afraid to do that kind of investigative show in the future? I hope not, she decided. After all, a serial killer has been apprehended; who knows who else he might have killed—besides me and Dee—had he not been caught?

And a couple of good things had come out of it. She had gotten to know Jane Clausen and been of some comfort to her. And she had met Don Richards. He was a strange bird, she thought—a psychiatrist who denied himself the kind of help he offered on a daily basis, yet who finally summoned the strength to face his own demons.

I might have bled to death if I'd been lying there all night, she thought, wincing from the pain of the stitches in her shoulders and back. When Don got to her office and found it locked, some instinct had made him demand the security guard open the door and check the office with him. I was never so glad to see anyone in my life, she thought. As he ripped the bag open and lifted her up, there was tenderness and relief on his face.

As Susan emerged from the elevator, Don Richards stood up and crossed to meet her. They looked at each other for a moment, then Susan smiled at him, and he put his arm around her. It seemed to both of them that it was the natural thing for him to do.

**POCKET
BOOKS**

Also by

MARY HIGGINS CLARK
Second Time Around

A gripping tale of deception and tantalizing suspense.

Nicholas Spencer, charismatic head of the medical
research company Gen-Stone, involved in the
development of an anticancer vaccine, suddenly
disappears. His private plane crashes en route to
Puerto Rico, but his body is not found.

Rocking the financial and medical world even more,
comes the shocking revelation that Spencer had looted
Gen-Stone of huge sums of money – and that his wife,
Lynn, is accused of having participated in the scam.

Lynn Spencer, narrowly escaping death when her
mansion is set on fire, turns to her stepsister, Carley,
a columnist for the *Wall Street Weekly*, to help prove
that she was not her husband's accomplice.

As Carley proceeds with her investigation, she is
confronted by seemingly impenetrable questions: Is
Nicholas Spencer dead or in hiding? Was he guilty or
set up? And as the facts begin to unfold, she becomes
the focus of a dangerous group involved in a sinister
and fraudulent scheme.

'Plays out her story like the pro that she is . . .
flawless' DAILY MIRROR

PRICE £6.99
ISBN 0 7434 6773 6

**POCKET
BOOKS**

MARY HIGGINS CLARK
Daddy's Little Girl

Ellie Cavanaugh was only seven years old
when her teenage sister, Andrea, was
murdered. It was Ellie who led her parents to
the secret hideout in which Andrea's body was
found. And it was Ellie's testimony that led to
the conviction of the man she firmly believed
to be the killer.

Now, twenty-two years later, the convicted
killer is set free from prison. He returns to
Ellie's hometown intent on white-washing his
reputation. Ellie, now an investigative reporter,
also returns home determined to thwart his
attempts and conclusively prove his guilt.
As she delves deeper into her research, she
uncovers horrifying facts that shed new light
on her sister's murder. With each discovery,
she comes closer to a confrontation with a
desperate killer.

PRICE £6.99
ISBN 0 7434 4937 1

**POCKET
BOOKS**

These books and other **Mary Higgins Clark** titles are available from your bookshop or can be ordered direct from the publisher.

☐ 0 7434 6773 6	**Second Time Around**	£6.99
☐ 0 7434 4937 1	**Daddy's Little Girl**	£6.99
☐ 0 7434 1499 3	**On the Street Where You Live**	£6.99
☐ 0 671 01039 5	**Before I Say Goodbye**	£6.99
☐ 0 7434 8427 4	**The Cradle Will Fall**	£6.99
☐ 0 7434 8430 4	**Moonlight Becomes You**	£6.99
☐ 0 7434 8428 2	**Stillwatch**	£6.99
☐ 0 7434 8429 0	**Let Me Call You Sweetheart**	£6.99
☐ 0 7434 8431 2	**We'll Meet Again**	£6.99
☐ 0 7434 8432 0	**You Belong To Me**	£6.99
☐ 0 7434 8433 9	**Pretend You Don't See Her**	£6.99
☐ 0 7434 4099 4	**He Sees You When You're Sleeping**	£4.99
☐ 0 7434 1501 9	**Deck the Halls**	£4.99
☐ 0 671 02284 9	**All Through The Night**	£4.99

Please send cheque or postal order for the value of the book, free postage and packing within the UK; OVERSEAS including Republic of Ireland £1 per book. OR: Please debit this amount from my:

VISA/ACCESS/MASTERCARD ....

CARD NO ....

EXPIRY DATE ....

AMOUNT £ ....

NAME ....

ADDRESS ....

....

SIGNATURE ....

Send orders to: SIMON & SCHUSTER CASH SALES
PO Box 29, Douglas, Isle of Man, IM99 1BQ
Tel: 01624 675137, Fax 01624 670923
www.bookpost.co.uk
Please allow 14 days for delivery.
Prices and availability subject to change without notice.